A CLERGYMAN'S DAUGHTER

GEORGE ORWELL

A CLERGYMAN'S DAUGHTER

W. Books

This is a W. Books publication, a division of Grupo Ciranda Cultural.

Text: George Orwell
First Publication: 1935
Graphic Design: Linea Editora
Cover Design and Illustrations: © Sweet Cherry Publishing Limited, 2024

Dados Internacionais de Catalogação na Publicação (CIP) de acordo com ISBD

O79c Orwell, George.

A Clergyman's Daughter / George Orwell. - Jandira, SP : W. Books, 2025.
288 p. : 12,80cm x 19,70cm. - (Classics).

ISBN: 978-65-5294-060-5

1. Literatura inglesa. 2. Clássicos. 3. Séries. 4. Filmes. 5. Inglês. I. Título. II. Série.

2024-2430 CDD 823.91
CDU 821.111-3

Elaborada por Lucio Feitosa - CRB-8/8803

Índice para catálogo sistemático:
1. Literatura inglesa 823.91
Literatura inglesa 821.111-3

www.cirandacultural.com.br

CONTENTS

CHAPTER 1

1

As the alarm clock on the chest of drawers exploded like a horrid little bomb of bell metal, Dorothy, wrenched from the depths of some complex, troubling dream, awoke with a start and lay on her back looking into the darkness in extreme exhaustion.

The alarm clock continued its nagging, feminine clamour, which would go on for five minutes or thereabouts if you did not stop it. Dorothy was aching from head to foot, and an insidious and contemptible self-pity, which usually seized upon her when it was time to get up in the morning, caused her to bury her head under the bedclothes and try to shut the hateful noise out of her ears. She struggled against her fatigue, however, and, according to her custom, exhorted herself sharply in the second person plural. Come on, Dorothy, up you get! No snoozing, please! Proverbs vi, 9. Then she remembered that if the noise went on any longer it would wake her father, and with a hurried movement she bounded out of bed, seized the clock from the chest of drawers, and turned off the alarm. It was kept on the chest of drawers precisely in order that she should have to get out of bed to silence it. Still in darkness, she knelt down at her bedside and repeated the Lord's Prayer, but rather distractedly, her feet being troubled by the cold.

It was just half past five, and coldish for an August morning. Dorothy (her name was Dorothy Hare, and she was the only child of the Reverend Charles Hare, Rector of St Athelstan's, Knype Hill, Suffolk) put on her aged flannelette dressing-gown and felt her way downstairs. There was a chill morning smell of dust, damp plaster, and the fried dabs from yesterday's supper, and from either side of the passage on the second floor she could hear the antiphonal snoring of her father and of Ellen, the maid of all work. With care—for the kitchen table had a nasty trick of reaching out of the darkness and banging you on the hip-bone—Dorothy felt her way into the kitchen, lighted the candle on the mantelpiece, and, still aching with fatigue, knelt down and raked the ashes out of the range.

The kitchen fire was a 'beast' to light. The chimney was crooked and therefore perpetually half choked, and the fire, before it would light, expected to be dosed with a cupful of kerosene, like a drunkard's morning nip of gin. Having set the kettle to boil for her father's shaving-water, Dorothy went upstairs and turned on her bath. Ellen was still snoring, with heavy youthful snores. She was a good hard-working servant once she was awake, but she was one of those girls whom the Devil and all his angels cannot get out of bed before seven in the morning.

Dorothy filled the bath as slowly as possible—the splashing always woke her father if she turned on the tap too fast—and stood for a moment regarding the pale, unappetizing pool of water. Her body had gone goose-flesh all over. She detested cold baths; it was for that very reason that she made it a rule to take all her baths cold from April to November. Putting a tentative hand into the water— and it was horribly cold—she drove herself forward with her usual exhortations. Come on, Dorothy! In you go! No funking, please! Then she stepped resolutely into the bath, sat down and let the icy girdle of water slide up her body and immerse her all except her hair, which she had twisted up behind her head. The next moment she came to the surface gasping and wriggling, and had no sooner got her breath back than she remembered her 'memo list', which she had brought down in her dressing-gown pocket and intended to read. She reached out for it, and, leaning over the side of the bath, waist deep in icy water, read through the 'memo list' by the light of the candle on the chair.

It ran:

7 oc. H.C.

Mrs T baby? Must visit.

BREAKFAST. Bacon. MUST ask father money. (P)

Ask Ellen what stuff kitchen father's tonic NB. to ask about stuff for curtains at Solepipe's.

Visiting call on Mrs P cutting from Daily M angelica tea good for rheumatism Mrs L's cornplaster.

12 oc. Rehearsal Charles I. NB. to order 1/2 lb glue 1 pot aluminium paint.

DINNER (crossed out) LUNCHEON... ?

Take round Parish Mag NB. Mrs F owes 3/6d.

4.30 pm Mothers' U tea don't forget 2 1/2 yards casement cloth.

Flowers for church NB. 1 tin Brasso.

SUPPER. Scrambled eggs.

Type Father's sermon what about new ribbon typewriter?

NB. to fork between peas bindweed awful.

Dorothy got out of her bath, and as she dried herself with a towel hardly bigger than a table napkin—they could never afford decent- sized towels at the Rectory—her hair came unpinned and fell down over her collar-bones in two heavy strands. It was thick, fine, exceedingly pale hair, and it was perhaps as well that her father had forbidden her to bob it, for it was her only positive beauty. For the rest, she was a girl of middle height, rather thin, but strong and shapely, and her face was her weak point. It was a thin, blonde, unremarkable kind of face, with pale eyes and a nose just a shade too long; if you looked closely you could see crow's feet round the eyes, and the mouth, when it was in repose, looked tired. Not definitely a spinsterish face as yet, but it certainly would be so in a few years' time. Nevertheless, strangers commonly took her to be several years younger than her real age (she was not quite twenty-eight) because of the expression of almost childish earnestness in her eyes. Her left forearm was spotted with tiny red marks like insect bites.

Dorothy put on her nightdress again and cleaned her teeth—plain water, of course; better not to use toothpaste before H.C. After all, either you are fasting or you aren't. The R.C.s are quite right there—and, even as she did so, suddenly faltered and stopped. She put her toothbrush down. A deadly pang, an actual physical pang, had gone through her viscera.

She had remembered, with the ugly shock with which one remembers something disagreeable for the first time in the morning, the bill at Cargill's, the butcher's, which had been owing for seven months. That dreadful bill—it might be nineteen pounds or even twenty, and there was hardly the remotest hope of paying it—was one of the chief torments of her life. At all hours of the night or day it was waiting just round the corner of her consciousness, ready to spring upon her and agonize her; and with it came the memory of a score of lesser bills, mounting up to a figure of which she dared not even think. Almost involuntarily she began to pray, 'Please God, let not Cargill send in his bill again today!' but the next moment she decided that this prayer was worldly and blasphemous, and she asked forgiveness for it. Then she put on her dressing- gown and ran down to the kitchen in hopes of putting the bill out of mind.

The fire had gone out, as usual. Dorothy relaid it, dirtying her hands with coal-dust, dosed it afresh with kerosene and hung about anxiously until the kettle boiled. Father expected his shaving- water to be ready at a quarter past six. Just seven minutes late, Dorothy took the can upstairs and knocked at her father's door.

'Come in, come in!' said a muffled, irritable voice.

The room, heavily curtained, was stuffy, with a masculine smell. The Rector had lighted the candle on his bed-table, and was lying on his side, looking at his gold watch, which he had just drawn from beneath his pillow. His hair was as white and thick as thistledown. One dark bright eye glanced irritably over his shoulder at Dorothy.

'Good morning, father.'

'I do wish, Dorothy,' said the Rector indistinctly—his voice always sounded muffled and senile until he put his false teeth in— 'you would make some effort to get Ellen out of bed in the mornings. Or else be a little more punctual yourself.'

'I'm so sorry, Father. The kitchen fire kept going out.'

'Very well! Put it down on the dressing-table. Put it down and draw those curtains.'

It was daylight now, but a dull, clouded morning. Dorothy hastened up to her room and dressed herself with the lightning speed which she found necessary six mornings out of seven. There was only a tiny square of mirror in the room, and even that she did not use. She simply hung her gold cross about her neck—plain gold cross; no crucifixes, please!—twisted her hair into a knot behind, stuck a number of hairpins rather sketchily into it, and threw her clothes (grey jersey, threadbare Irish tweed coat and skirt, stockings not quite matching the coat and skirt, and much-worn brown shoes) on to herself in the space of about three minutes. She had got to 'do out' the dining-room and her father's study before church, besides saying her prayers in preparation for Holy Communion, which took her not less than twenty minutes.

When she wheeled her bicycle out of the front gate the morning was still overcast, and the grass sodden with heavy dew. Through the mist that wreathed the hillside St Athelstan's Church loomed dimly, like a leaden sphinx, its single bell tolling funereally boom! boom! boom! Only one of the bells was now in active use; the other seven had been unswung from their cage and had lain silent these three years past, slowly splintering the floor of the belfry beneath their weight. In the distance, from the mists below, you could hear the offensive clatter of the bell in the R.C. church—a nasty, cheap, tinny little thing which the Rector of St Athelstan's used to compare with a muffin-bell.

Dorothy mounted her bicycle and rode swiftly up the hill, leaning over her handlebars. The bridge of her thin nose was pink in the morning cold. A redshank whistled overhead, invisible against the clouded sky. Early in the morning my song shall rise to Thee! Dorothy propped her bicycle against the lychgate, and, finding her hands still grey with coal-dust, knelt down and scrubbed them clean in the long wet grass between the graves. Then the bell stopped ringing, and she jumped up and hastened into church, just as Proggett, the sexton, in ragged cassock and vast labourer's boots, was clumping up the aisle to take his place at the side altar.

The church was very cold, with a scent of candle-wax and ancient dust. It was a large church, much too large for its congregation, and ruinous and more than half empty. The three narrow islands of pews stretched barely half-way down the nave, and beyond them were great wastes of bare stone floor in which a few worn inscriptions marked the sites of ancient graves. The roof over the chancel was sagging visibly; beside the Church Expenses box two fragments of riddled beam explained mutely that this was due to that mortal foe of Christendom, the death-watch beetle. The light filtered, pale- coloured, through windows of anaemic glass. Through the open south door you could see a ragged cypress and the boughs of a lime-tree, greyish in the sunless air and swaying faintly.

As usual, there was only one other communicant—old Miss Mayfill, of The Grange. The attendance at Holy Communion was so bad that the Rector could not even get any boys to serve him, except on Sunday mornings, when the boys liked showing off in front of the congregation in their cassocks and surplices. Dorothy went into the pew behind Miss Mayfill, and, in penance for some sin of yesterday, pushed away the hassock and knelt on the bare stones. The service was beginning. The Rector, in cassock and short linen surplice, was reciting the prayers in a swift practised voice, clear enough now that his teeth were in, and curiously ungenial. In his fastidious, aged face, pale as a silver coin, there was an expression of aloofness, almost of contempt. 'This is a valid sacrament,' he seemed to be saying, 'and it is my duty to administer it to you. But remember that I am only your priest, not your friend. As a human being I dislike you and despise you.' Proggett, the sexton, a man of forty with curly grey hair and a red, harassed face, stood patiently by, uncomprehending but reverent, fiddling with the little communion bell which was lost in his huge red hands.

Dorothy pressed her fingers against her eyes. She had not yet succeeded in concentrating her thoughts—indeed, the memory of Cargill's bill was still worrying her intermittently. The prayers, which she knew by heart, were flowing through her head unheeded. She raised her eyes for a moment, and they began immediately to stray. First upwards, to the headless roof-angels on whose necks you could still see the sawcuts of the Puritan soldiers, then back again, to Miss Mayfill's black, quasi-pork-pie hat and tremulous jet ear-rings. Miss Mayfill wore a long musty black overcoat, with a little collar of greasy-looking astrakhan, which had been the same ever since Dorothy could remember. It was of some very peculiar stuff, like watered silk but coarser, with rivulets of black piping wandering all over it in no discoverable pattern. It might even have been that legendary and proverbial substance, black bombazine. Miss Mayfill was very old, so old that no one remembered her as anything but an old woman. A faint scent radiated from her—an ethereal scent, analysable as eau-de-Cologne, mothballs, and a sub-flavour of gin.

Dorothy drew a long glass-headed pin from the lapel of her coat, and furtively, under cover of Miss Mayfill's back, pressed the point against her forearm. Her flesh tingled apprehensively. She made it a rule, whenever she caught herself not attending to her prayers, to prick her arm hard enough to make blood come. It was her chosen form of self-discipline, her guard against irreverence and sacrilegious thoughts.

With the pin poised in readiness she managed for several moments to pray more collectedly. Her father had turned one dark eye disapprovingly upon Miss Mayfill, who was crossing herself at intervals, a practice he disliked. A starling chattered outside. With a shock Dorothy discovered that she was looking vaingloriously at the pleats of her father's surplice, which she herself had sewn two years ago. She set her teeth and drove the pin an eighth of an inch into her arm.

They were kneeling again. It was the General Confession. Dorothy recalled her eyes—wandering, alas! yet again, this time to the stained-glass window on her right, designed by Sir Warde Tooke, A.R.A., in 1851 and representing St Athelstan's welcome at the gate of heaven by Gabriel and a legion of angels all remarkably like one another and the Prince Consort—and pressed the pinpoint against a different part of her arm. She began to meditate conscientiously upon the meaning of each phrase of the prayer, and so brought her mind back to a more attentive state. But even so she was all but obliged to use the pin again when Proggett tinkled the bell in the middle of 'Therefore with Angels and Archangels'—being visited, as always, by a dreadful temptation to begin laughing at that passage. It was because of a story her father had told her once, of how when he was a little boy, and serving the priest at the altar, the communion bell had a screw-on clapper, which had come loose; and so the priest had said: 'Therefore with Angels and Archangels, and with all the company of Heaven, we laud and magnify Thy glorious name; evermore praising Thee, and saying, Screw it up, you little fat-head, screw it up!'

As the Rector finished the consecration Miss Mayfill began to struggle to her feet with extreme difficulty and slowness, like some disjointed wooden creature picking itself up by sections, and disengaging at each movement a powerful whiff of mothballs. There was an extraordinary creaking sound—from her stays, presumably, but it was a noise as of bones grating against one another. You could have imagined that there was only a dry skeleton inside that black overcoat.

Dorothy remained on her feet a moment longer. Miss Mayfill was creeping towards the altar with slow, tottering steps. She could barely walk, but she took bitter offence if you offered to help her. In her ancient, bloodless face her mouth was surprisingly large, loose, and wet. The underlip, pendulous with age, slobbered forward, exposing a strip of gum and a row of false teeth as yellow as the keys of an old piano. On the upper lip was a fringe of dark, dewy moustache. It was not an appetizing mouth; not the kind of mouth that you would like to see drinking out of your cup. Suddenly, spontaneously, as though the Devil himself had put it there, the prayer slipped from Dorothy's lips: O God, let me not have to take the chalice after Miss Mayfill!

The next moment, in self-horror, she grasped the meaning of what she had said, and wished that she had bitten her tongue in two rather than utter that deadly blasphemy upon the altar steps. She drew the pin again from her lapel and drove it into her arm so hard that it was all she could do to suppress a cry of pain. Then she stepped to the altar and knelt down meekly on Miss Mayfill's left, so as to make quite sure of taking the chalice after her.

Kneeling, with head bent and hands clasped against her knees, she set herself swiftly to pray for forgiveness before her father should reach her with the wafer. But the current of her thoughts had been broken. Suddenly it was quite useless attempting to pray; her lips moved, but there was neither heart nor meaning in her prayers. She could hear Proggett's boots shuffling and her father's clear low voice murmuring 'Take and eat', she could see the worn strip of red carpet beneath her knees, she could smell dust and eau-de-Cologne and mothballs; but of the Body and Blood of Christ, of the purpose for which she had come here, she was as though deprived of the power to think. A deadly blankness had descended upon her mind. It seemed to her that actually she COULD not pray. She struggled, collected her thoughts, uttered mechanically the opening phrases of a prayer; but they were useless, meaningless—nothing but the dead shells of words. Her father was holding the wafer before her in his shapely, aged hand. He held it between finger and thumb, fastidiously, somehow distastefully, as though it had been a spoon of medicine. His eye was upon Miss Mayfill, who was doubling herself up like a geometrid caterpillar, with many creakings and crossing herself so elaborately that one might have imagined that she was sketching a series of braid frogs on the front of her coat. For several seconds Dorothy hesitated and did not take the wafer. She dared not take it. Better, far better to step down from the altar than to accept the sacrament with such chaos in her heart!

Then it happened that she glanced sidelong, through the open south door. A momentary spear of sunlight had pierced the clouds. It struck downwards through the leaves of the limes, and a spray of leaves in the doorway gleamed with a transient, matchless green, greener than jade or emerald or Atlantic waters. It was as though some jewel of unimaginable splendour had flashed for an instant, filling the doorway with green light, and then faded. A flood of joy ran through Dorothy's heart. The flash of living colour had brought back to her, by a process deeper than reason, her peace of mind, her love of God, her power to worship. Somehow, because of the greenness of the leaves, it was again possible to pray. O all ye green things upon the earth, praise ye the Lord! She began to pray, ardently, joyfully, thankfully. The wafer melted upon her tongue. She took the chalice from her father, and tasted with repulsion, even with an added joy in this small act of self- abasement, the wet imprint of Miss Mayfill's lips on its silver rim.

2

St Athelstan's Church stood at the highest point of Knype Hill, and if you chose to climb the tower you could see ten miles or so across the surrounding country. Not that there was anything worth looking at—only the low, barely undulating East Anglian landscape, intolerably dull in summer, but redeemed in winter by the recurring patterns of the elms, naked and fanshaped against leaden skies.

Immediately below you lay the town, with the High Street running east and west and dividing unequally. The southern section of the town was the ancient, agricultural, and respectable section. On the northern side were the buildings of the Blifil-Gordon sugar- beet refinery, and all round and leading up to them were higgledy- piggledly rows of vile yellow brick cottages, mostly inhabited by the employees of the factory. The factory employees, who made up more than half of the town's two thousand inhabitants, were newcomers, townfolk, and godless almost to a man.

The two pivots, or foci, about which the social life of the town moved were Knype Hill Conservative Club (fully licensed), from whose bow window, any time after the bar was open, the large, rosy- gilled faces of the town's elite were to be seen gazing like chubby goldfish from an aquarium pane; and Ye Olde Tea Shoppe, a little farther down the High Street, the principal rendezvous of the Knype Hill ladies. Not to be present at Ye Olde Tea Shoppe between ten and eleven every morning, to drink your 'morning coffee' and spend your half-hour or so in that agreeable twitter of upper-middle- class voices ('My dear, he had NINE spades to the ace-queen and he went one no trump, if you please. What, my dear, you don't mean to say you're paying for my coffee AGAIN? Oh, but my dear, it is simply TOO sweet of you! Now tomorrow I shall SIMPLY INSIST upon paying for yours. And just LOOK at dear little Toto sitting up and looking such a CLEVER little man with his little black nose wiggling, and he would, would he, the darling duck, he would, he would, and his mother would give him a lump of sugar, she would, she would. THERE, Toto!'), was to be definitely out of Knype Hill society. The Rector in his acid way nicknamed these ladies 'the coffee brigade'. Close to the colony of sham-picturesque villas inhabited by the coffee brigade, but cut off from them by its larger grounds, was The Grange, Miss Mayfill's house. It was a curious, machicolated, imitation castle of dark red brick— somebody's Folly, built about 1870—and fortunately almost hidden among dense shrubberies.

The Rectory stood half way up the hill, with its face to the church and its back to the High Street. It was a house of the wrong age, inconveniently large, and faced with chronically peeling yellow plaster. Some earlier Rector had added, at one side, a large greenhouse which Dorothy used as a workroom, but which was constantly out of repair. The front garden was choked with ragged fir-trees and a great spreading ash which shadowed the front rooms and made it impossible to grow any flowers. There was a large vegetable garden at the back. Proggett did the heavy digging of the garden in the spring and autumn, and Dorothy did the sowing, planting, and weeding in such spare time as she could command; in spite of which the vegetable garden was usually an impenetrable jungle of weeds.

Dorothy jumped off her bicycle at the front gate, upon which some officious person had stuck a poster inscribed 'Vote for Blifil- Gordon and Higher Wages!' (There was a by-election going on, and Mr Blifil-Gordon was standing in the Conservative interest.) As Dorothy opened the front door she saw two letters lying on the worn coconut mat. One was from the Rural Dean, and the other was a nasty, thin-looking letter from Catkin & Palm, her father's clerical tailors. It was a bill undoubtedly. The Rector had followed his usual practice of collecting the letters that interested him and leaving the others. Dorothy was just bending down to pick up the letters, when she saw, with a horrid shock of dismay, an unstamped envelope sticking to the letter flap.

It was a bill—for certain it was a bill! Moreover, as soon as she set eyes on it she 'knew' that it was that horrible bill from Cargill's, the butcher's. A sinking feeling passed through her entrails. For a moment she actually began to pray that it might not be Cargill's bill—that it might only be the bill for three and nine from Solepipe's, the draper's, or the bill from the International or the baker's or the dairy—anything except Cargill's bill! Then, mastering her panic, she took the envelope from the letter-flap and tore it open with a convulsive movement.

'To account rendered: L21 7S. 9d.'

This was written in the innocuous handwriting of Mr Cargill's accountant. But underneath, in thick, accusing-looking letters, was added and heavily underlined: 'Shd. like to bring to your notice that this bill has been owing a VERY LONG TIME. The EARLIEST POSSIBLE settlement will oblige, S. Cargill.'

Dorothy had turned a shade paler, and was conscious of not wanting any breakfast. She thrust the bill into her pocket and went into the dining-room. It was a smallish, dark room, badly in need of repapering, and, like every other room in the Rectory, it had the air of having been furnished from the sweepings of an antique shop. The furniture was 'good', but battered beyond repair, and the chairs were so worm-eaten that you could only sit on them in safety if you knew their individual foibles. There were old, dark, defaced steel engravings hanging on the walls, one of them—an engraving of Van Dyck's portrait of Charles I—probably of some value if it had not been ruined by damp.

The Rector was standing before the empty grate, warming himself at an imaginary fire and reading a letter that came from a long blue envelope. He was still wearing his cassock of black watered silk, which set off to perfection his thick white hair and his pale, fine, none too amiable face. As Dorothy came in he laid the letter aside, drew out his gold watch and scrutinized it significantly.

'I'm afraid I'm a bit late, Father.'

'Yes, Dorothy, you are A BIT LATE,' said the Rector, repeating her words with delicate but marked emphasis. 'You are twelve minutes late, to be exact. Don't you think, Dorothy, that when I have to get up at a quarter past six to celebrate Holy Communion, and come home exceedingly tired and hungry, it would be better if you could manage to come to breakfast without being A BIT LATE?'

It was clear that the Rector was in what Dorothy called, euphemistically, his 'uncomfortable mood'. He had one of those weary, cultivated voices which are never definitely angry and never anywhere near good humour—one of those voices which seem all the while to be saying, 'I really CANNOT see what you are making all this fuss about!' The impression he gave was of suffering perpetually from other people's stupidity and tiresomeness.

'I'm so sorry, Father! I simply had to go and ask after Mrs Tawney.' (Mrs Tawney was the 'Mrs T' of the 'memo list'.) 'Her baby was born last night, and you know she promised me she'd come and be churched after it was born. But of course she won't if she thinks we aren't taking any interest in her. You know what these women are—they seem so to hate being churched. They'll never come unless I coax them into it.'

The Rector did not actually grunt, but he uttered a small dissatisfied sound as he moved towards the breakfast table. It was intended to mean, first, that it was Mrs Tawney's duty to come and be churched without Dorothy's coaxing; secondly, that Dorothy had no business to waste her time visiting all the riffraff of the town, especially before breakfast. Mrs Tawney was a labourer's wife and lived in partibus infidelium, north of the High Street. The Rector laid his hand on the back of his chair, and, without speaking, cast Dorothy a glance which meant: 'Are we ready NOW? Or are there to be any MORE delays?'

'I think everything's here, Father,' said Dorothy. 'Perhaps if you'd just say grace—'

'Benedictus benedicat,' said the Rector, lifting the worn silver coverlet off the breakfast dish. The silver coverlet, like the silver-gilt marmalade spoon, was a family heirloom; the knives and forks, and most of the crockery, came from Woolworths. 'Bacon again, I see,' the Rector added, eyeing the three minute rashers that lay curled up on squares of fried bread.

'It's all we've got in the house, I'm afraid,' Dorothy said.

The Rector picked up his fork between finger and thumb, and with a very delicate movement, as though playing at spillikins, turned one of the rashers over.

'I know, of course,' he said, 'that bacon for breakfast is an English institution almost as old as parliamentary government. But still, don't you think we might OCCASIONALLY have a change, Dorothy?'

'Bacon's so cheap now,' said Dorothy regretfully. 'It seems a sin not to buy it. This was only fivepence a pound, and I saw some quite decent-looking bacon as low as threepence.'

'Ah, Danish, I suppose? What a variety of Danish invasions we have had in this country! First with fire and sword, and now with their abominable cheap bacon. Which has been responsible for the more deaths, I wonder?'

Feeling a little better after this witticism, the Rector settled himself in his chair and made a fairly good breakfast off the despised bacon, while Dorothy (she was not having any bacon this morning—a penance she had set herself yesterday for saying 'Damn' and idling for half an hour after lunch) meditated upon a good conversational opening.

There was an unspeakably hateful job in front of her—a demand for money. At the very best of times getting money out of her father was next door to impossible, and it was obvious that this morning he was going to be even more 'difficult' than usual. 'Difficult' was another of her euphemisms. He's had bad news, I suppose, she thought despondently, looking at the blue envelope.

Probably no one who had ever spoken to the Rector for as long as ten minutes would have denied that he was a 'difficult' kind of man. The secret of his almost unfailing ill humour really lay in the fact that he was an anachronism. He ought never to have been born into the modern world; its whole atmosphere disgusted and infuriated him. A couple of centuries earlier, a happy pluralist writing poems or collecting fossils while curates at 40 pounds a year administered his parishes, he would have been perfectly at home. Even now, if he had been a richer man, he might have consoled himself by shutting the twentieth century out of his consciousness. But to live in past ages is very expensive; you can't do it on less than two thousand a year. The Rector, tethered by his poverty to the age of Lenin and the Daily Mail, was kept in a state of chronic exasperation which it was only natural that he should work off on the person nearest to him—usually, that is, on Dorothy.

He had been born in 1871, the younger son of the younger son of a baronet, and had gone into the Church for the outmoded reason that the Church is the traditional profession for younger sons. His first cure had been in a large, slummy parish in East London—a nasty, hooliganish place it had been, and he looked back on it with loathing. Even in those days the lower class (as he made a point of calling them) were getting decidedly out of hand. It was a little better when he was curate-in-charge at some remote place in Kent (Dorothy had been born in Kent), where the decently down- trodden villagers still touched their hats to 'parson'. But by that time he had married, and his marriage had been diabolically unhappy; moreover, because clergymen must not quarrel with their wives, its unhappiness had been secret and therefore ten times worse. He had come to Knype Hill in 1908, aged thirty-seven and with a temper incurably soured—a temper which had ended by alienating every man, woman, and child in the parish.

It was not that he was a bad priest, merely AS a priest. In his purely clerical duties he was scrupulously correct—perhaps a little too correct for a Low Church East Anglian parish. He conducted his services with perfect taste, preached admirable sermons, and got up at uncomfortable hours of the morning to celebrate Holy Communion every Wednesday and Friday. But that a clergyman has any duties outside the four walls of the church was a thing that had never seriously occurred to him. Unable to afford a curate, he left the dirty work of the parish entirely to his wife, and after her death (she died in 1921) to Dorothy. People used to say, spitefully and untruly, that he would have let Dorothy preach his sermons for him if it had been possible. The 'lower classes' had grasped from the first what was his attitude towards them, and if he had been a rich man they would probably have licked his boots, according to their custom; as it was, they merely hated him. Not that he cared whether they hated him or not, for he was largely unaware of their existence. But even with the upper classes he had got on no better. With the County he had quarrelled one by one, and as for the petty gentry of the town, as the grandson of a baronet he despised them, and was at no pains to hide it. In twenty-three years he had succeeded in reducing the congregation of St Athelstan's from six hundred to something under two hundred.

This was not solely due to personal reasons. It was also because the old-fashioned High Anglicanism to which the Rector obstinately clung was of a kind to annoy all parties in the parish about equally. Nowadays, a clergyman who wants to keep his congregation has only two courses open to him. Either it must be Anglo- Catholicism pure and simple—or rather, pure and not simple; or he must be daringly modern and broad-minded and preach comforting sermons proving that there is no Hell and all good religions are the same. The Rector did neither. On the one hand, he had the deepest contempt for the Anglo-Catholic movement. It had passed over his head, leaving him absolutely untouched; 'Roman Fever' was his name for it. On the other hand, he was too 'high' for the older members of his congregation. From time to time he scared them almost out of their wits by the use of the fatal word 'Catholic', not only in its sanctified place in the Creeds, but also from the pulpit. Naturally the congregation dwindled year by year, and it was the Best People who were the first to go. Lord Pockthorne of Pockthorne Court, who owned a fifth of the county, Mr Leavis, the retired leather merchant, Sir Edward Huson of Crabtree Hall, and such of the petty gentry as owned motor-cars, had all deserted St Athelstan's. Most of them drove over on Sunday mornings to Millborough, five miles away. Millborough was a town of five thousand inhabitants, and you had your choice of two churches, St Edmund's and

St Wedekind's. St Edmund's was Modernist—text from Blake's 'Jerusalem' blazoned over the altar, and communion wine out of liqueur glasses—and St Wedekind's was Anglo-Catholic and in a state of perpetual guerrilla warfare with the Bishop. But Mr Cameron, the secretary of the Knype Hill Conservative Club, was a Roman Catholic convert, and his children were in the thick of the Roman Catholic literary movement. They were said to have a parrot which they were teaching to say 'Extra ecclesiam nulla salus'. In effect, no one of any standing remained true to St Athelstan's, except Miss Mayfill, of The Grange. Most of Miss Mayfill's money was bequeathed to the Church—so she said; meanwhile, she had never been known to put more than sixpence in the collection bag, and she seemed likely to go on living for ever.

The first ten minutes of breakfast passed in complete silence. Dorothy was trying to summon up courage to speak—obviously she had got to start SOME kind of conversation before raising the money- question—but her father was not an easy man with whom to make small talk. At times he would fall into such deep fits of abstraction that you could hardly get him to listen to you; at other times he was all too attentive, listened carefully to what you said and then pointed out, rather wearily, that it was not worth saying. Polite platitudes—the weather, and so forth— generally moved him to sarcasm. Nevertheless, Dorothy decided to try the weather first.

'It's a funny kind of day, isn't it?' she said—aware, even as she made it, of the inanity of this remark.

'WHAT is funny?' inquired the Rector.

'Well, I mean, it was so cold and misty this morning, and now the sun's come out and it's turned quite fine.'

'IS there anything particularly funny about that?'

That was no good, obviously. He MUST have had bad news, she thought. She tried again.

'I do wish you'd come out and have a look at the things in the back garden some time, Father. The runner beans are doing so splendidly! The pods are going to be over a foot long. I'm going to keep all the best of them for the Harvest Festival, of course. I thought it would look so nice if we decorated the pulpit with festoons of runner beans and a few tomatoes hanging in among them.'

This was a faux pas. The Rector looked up from his plate with an expression of profound distaste.

'My dear Dorothy,' he said sharply, 'IS it necessary to begin worrying me about the Harvest Festival already?'

'I'm sorry, Father!' said Dorothy, disconcerted. 'I didn't mean to worry you. I just thought—'

'Do you suppose', proceeded the Rector, 'it is any pleasure to me to have to preach my sermon among festoons of runner beans? I am not a greengrocer. It quite puts me off my breakfast to think of it. When is the wretched thing due to happen?'

'It's September the sixteenth, Father.'

'That's nearly a month hence. For Heaven's sake let me forget it a little longer! I suppose we must have this ridiculous business once a year to tickle the vanity of every amateur gardener in the parish. But don't let's think of it more than is absolutely necessary.'

The Rector had, as Dorothy ought to have remembered, a perfect abhorrence of Harvest Festivals. He had even lost a valuable parishioner—a Mr Toagis, a surly retired market gardener—through his dislike, as he said, of seeing his church dressed up to imitate a coster's stall. Mr Toagis, anima naturaliter Nonconformistica, had been kept 'Church' solely by the privilege, at Harvest Festival time, of decorating the side altar with a sort of Stonehenge composed of gigantic vegetable marrows. The previous summer he had succeeded in growing a perfect leviathan of a pumpkin, a fiery red thing so enormous that it took two men to lift it. This monstrous object had been placed in the chancel, where it dwarfed the altar and took all the colour out of the east window. In no matter what part of the church you were standing, the pumpkin, as the saying goes, hit you in the eye. Mr Toagis was in raptures. He hung about the church at all hours, unable to tear himself away from his adored pumpkin, and even bringing relays of friends in to admire it. From the expression of his face you would have thought that he was quoting Wordsworth on Westminster Bridge:

Earth has not any thing to show more fair: Dull would he be of soul who could pass by A sight so touching in its majesty!

Dorothy even had hopes, after this, of getting him to come to Holy Communion. But when the Rector saw the pumpkin he was seriously angry, and ordered 'that revolting thing' to be removed at once. Mr Toagis had instantly 'gone chapel', and he and his heirs were lost to the Church for ever.

Dorothy decided to make one final attempt at conversation.

'We're getting on with the costumes for Charles I,' she said. (The Church School children were rehearsing a play entitled Charles I in aid of the organ fund.) 'But I do wish we'd chosen something a bit easier. The armour is a dreadful job to make, and I'm afraid the jackboots are going to be worse. I think next time we must really have a Roman or Greek play. Something where they only have to wear togas.'

This elicited only another muted grunt from the Rector. School plays, pageants, bazaars, jumble sales, and concerts in aid of were not quite so bad in his eyes as Harvest Festivals, but he did not pretend to be interested in them. They were necessary evils, he used to say. At this moment Ellen, the maidservant, pushed open the door and came gauchely into the room with one large, scaly hand holding her sacking apron against her belly. She was a tall, round-shouldered girl with mouse-coloured hair, a plaintive voice, and a bad complexion, and she suffered chronically from eczema. Her eyes flitted apprehensively towards the Rector, but she addressed herself to Dorothy, for she was too much afraid of the Rector to speak to him directly.

'Please, Miss—' she began.

'Yes, Ellen?'

'Please, Miss,' went on Ellen plaintively, 'Mr Porter's in the kitchen, and he says, please could the Rector come round and baptize Mrs Porter's baby? Because they don't think as it's going to live the day out, and it ain't been baptized yet, Miss.'

Dorothy stood up. 'Sit down,' said the Rector promptly, with his mouth full.

'What do they think is the matter with the baby?' said Dorothy.

'Well, Miss, it's turning quite black. And it's had diarrhoea something cruel.'

The Rector emptied his mouth with an effort. 'Must I have these disgusting details while I am eating my breakfast?' he exclaimed. He turned on Ellen: 'Send Porter about his business and tell him I'll be round at his house at twelve o'clock. I really cannot think why it is that the lower classes always seem to choose mealtimes to come pestering one,' he added, casting another irritated glance at Dorothy as she sat down.

Mr Porter was a labouring man—a bricklayer, to be exact. The Rector's views on baptism were entirely sound. If it had been urgently necessary he would have walked twenty miles through snow to baptize a dying baby. But he did not like to see Dorothy proposing to leave the breakfast table at the call of a common bricklayer.

There was no further conversation during breakfast. Dorothy's heart was sinking lower and lower. The demand for money had got to be made, and yet it was perfectly obvious that it was foredoomed to failure. His breakfast finished, the Rector got up from the table and began to fill his pipe from the tobacco-jar on the mantelpiece. Dorothy uttered a short prayer for courage, and then pinched herself. Go on, Dorothy! Out with it! No funking, please! With an effort she mastered her voice and said:

'Father—'

'What is it?' said the Rector, pausing with the match in his hand.

'Father, I've something I want to ask you. Something important.'

The expression of the Rector's face changed. He had divined instantly what she was going to say; and, curiously enough, he now looked less irritable than before. A stony calm had settled upon his face. He looked like a rather exceptionally aloof and unhelpful sphinx.

'Now, my dear Dorothy, I know very well what you are going to say. I suppose you are going to ask me for money again. Is that it?'

'Yes, Father. Because—'

'Well, I may as well save you the trouble. I have no money at all— absolutely no money at all until next quarter. You have had your allowance, and I can't give you a halfpenny more. It's quite useless to come worrying me now.'

'But, Father—'

Dorothy's heart sank yet lower. What was worst of all when she came to him for money was the terrible, unhelpful calmness of his attitude. He was never so unmoved as when you were reminding him that he was up to his eyes in debt. Apparently he could not understand that tradesmen occasionally want to be paid, and that no house can be kept going without an adequate supply of money. He allowed Dorothy eighteen pounds a month for all the household expenses, including Ellen's wages, and at the same time he was 'dainty' about his food and instantly detected any falling off in its quality. The result was, of course, that the household was perennially in debt. But the Rector paid not the smallest attention to his debts—indeed, he was hardly even aware of them. When he lost money over an investment, he was deeply agitated; but as for a debt to a mere tradesman—well, it was the kind of thing that he simply could not bother his head about.

A peaceful plume of smoke floated upwards from the Rector's pipe. He was gazing with a meditative eye at the steel engraving of Charles I and had probably forgotten already about Dorothy's demand for money. Seeing him so unconcerned, a pang of desperation went through Dorothy, and her courage came back to her. She said more sharply than before:

'Father, please listen to me! I MUST have some money soon! I simply MUST! We can't go on as we're doing. We owe money to nearly every tradesman in the town. It's got so that some mornings I can hardly bear to go down the street and think of all the bills that are owing. Do you know that we owe Cargill nearly twenty-two pounds?'

'What of it?' said the Rector between puffs of smoke.

'But the bill's been mounting up for over seven months! He's sent it in over and over again. We MUST pay it! It's so unfair to him to keep him waiting for his money like that!'

'Nonsense, my dear child! These people expect to be kept waiting for their money. They like it. It brings them more in the end. Goodness knows how much I owe to Catkin & Palm—I should hardly care to inquire. They are dunning me by every post. But you don't hear ME complaining, do you?'

'But, Father, I can't look at it as you do, I can't! It's so dreadful to be always in debt! Even if it isn't actually wrong, it's so HATEFUL. It makes me so ashamed! When I go into Cargill's shop to order the joint, he speaks to me so shortly and makes me wait after the other customers, all because our bill's mounting up the whole time. And yet I daren't stop ordering from him. I believe he'd run us in if I did.'

The Rector frowned. 'What! Do you mean to say the fellow has been impertinent to you?'

'I didn't say he'd been impertinent, Father. But you can't blame him if he's angry when his bill's not paid.'

'I most certainly can blame him! It is simply abominable how these people take it upon themselves to behave nowadays—abominable! But there you are, you see. That is the kind of thing that we are exposed to in this delightful century. That is democracy— PROGRESS, as they are pleased to call it. Don't order from the fellow again. Tell him at once that you are taking your account elsewhere. That's the only way to treat these people.'

'But, Father, that doesn't settle anything. Really and truly, don't you think we ought to pay him? Surely we can get hold of the money somehow? Couldn't you sell out some shares, or something?'

'My dear child, don't talk to me about selling out shares! I have just had the most disagreeable news from my broker. He tells me that my Sumatra Tin shares have dropped from seven and fourpence to six and a penny. It means a loss of nearly sixty pounds. I am telling him to sell out at once before they drop any further.'

'Then if you sell out you'll have some ready money, won't you? Don't you think it would be better to get out of debt once and for all?'

'Nonsense, nonsense,' said the Rector more calmly, putting his pipe back in his mouth. 'You know nothing whatever about these matters. I shall have to reinvest at once in something more hopeful—it's the only way of getting my money back.'

With one thumb in the belt of his cassock he frowned abstractedly at the steel engraving. His broker had advised United Celanese. Here—in Sumatra Tin, United Celanese, and numberless other remote and dimly imagined companies—was the central cause of the Rector's money troubles. He was an inveterate gambler. Not, of course, that he thought of it as gambling; it was merely a lifelong search for a 'good investment'. On coming of age he had inherited four thousand pounds, which had gradually dwindled, thanks to his 'investments', to about twelve hundred. What was worse, every year he managed to scrape together, out of his miserable income, another fifty pounds which vanished by the same road. It is a curious fact that the lure of a 'good investment' seems to haunt clergymen more persistently than any other class of man. Perhaps it is the modern equivalent of the demons in female shape who used to haunt the anchorites of the Dark Ages.

'I shall buy five hundred United Celanese,' said the Rector finally.

Dorothy began to give up hope. Her father was now thinking of his 'investments' (she new nothing whatever about these 'investments', except that they went wrong with phenomenal regularity), and in another moment the question of the shop-debts would have slipped entirely out of his mind. She made a final effort.

'Father, let's get this settled, please. Do you think you'll be able to let me have some extra money fairly soon? Not this moment, perhaps—but in the next month or two?'

'No, my dear, I don't. About Christmas time, possibly—it's very unlikely even then. But for the present, certainly not. I haven't a halfpenny I can spare.'

'But, Father, it's so horrible to feel we can't pay our debts! It disgraces us so! Last time Mr Welwyn-Foster was here' (Mr Welwyn- Foster was the Rural Dean) 'Mrs Welwyn-Foster was going all round the town asking everyone the most personal questions about us— asking how we spent our time, and how much money we had, and how many tons of coal we used in a year, and everything. She's always trying to pry into our affairs. Suppose she found out that we were badly in debt!'

'Surely it is our own business? I fail entirely to see what it has to do with Mrs Welwyn-Foster or anyone else.'

'But she'd repeat it all over the place—and she'd exaggerate it too! You know what Mrs Welwyn-Foster is. In every parish she goes to she tries to find out something disgraceful about the clergyman, and then she repeats every word of it to the Bishop. I don't want to be uncharitable about her, but really she—'

Realizing that she DID want to be uncharitable, Dorothy was silent.

'She is a detestable woman,' said the Rector evenly. 'What of it? Who ever heard of a Rural Dean's wife who wasn't detestable?'

'But, Father, I don't seem to be able to get you to see how serious things are! We've simply nothing to live on for the next month. I don't even know where the meat's coming from for today's dinner.'

'Luncheon, Dorothy, luncheon!' said the Rector with a touch of irritation. 'I do wish you would drop that abominable lower-class habit of calling the midday meal DINNER!'

'For luncheon, then. Where are we to get the meat from? I daren't ask Cargill for another joint.'

'Go to the other butcher—what's his name? Salter—and take no notice of Cargill. He knows he'll be paid sooner or later. Good gracious, I don't know what all this fuss is about! Doesn't everyone owe money to his tradesmen? I distinctly remember'—the Rector straightened his shoulders a little, and, putting his pipe back into his mouth, looked into the distance; his voice became reminiscent and perceptibly more agreeable—'I distinctly remember that when I was up at Oxford, my father had still not paid some of his own Oxford bills of thirty years earlier. Tom' (Tom was the Rector's cousin, the Baronet) 'owed seven thousand before he came into his money. He told me so himself.'

At that, Dorothy's last hope vanished. When her father began to talk about his cousin Tom, and about things that had happened 'when I was up at Oxford', there was nothing more to be done with him. It meant that he had slipped into an imaginary golden past in which such vulgar things as butchers' bills simply did not exist. There were long periods together when he seemed actually to forget that he was only a poverty-stricken country Rector—that he was not a young man of family with estates and reversions at his back. The aristocratic, the expensive attitude was the one that in all circumstances came the most naturally to him. And of course while he lived, not uncomfortably, in the world of his imagination, it was Dorothy who had to fight the tradesmen and make a leg of mutton last from Sunday to Wednesday. But she knew the complete uselessness of arguing with him any longer. It would only end in making him angry. She got up from the table and began to pile the breakfast things on to the tray.

'You're absolutely certain you can't let me have any money, Father?' she said for the last time, at the door; with the tray in her arms.

The Rector, gazing into the middle distance, amid comfortable wreaths of smoke, did not hear her. He was thinking, perhaps, of his golden Oxford days. Dorothy went out of the room distressed almost to the point of tears. The miserable question of the debts was once more shelved, as it had been shelved a thousand times before, with no prospect of final solution.

3

On her elderly bicycle with the basketwork carrier on the handle- bars, Dorothy free-wheeled down the hill, doing mental arithmetic with three pounds nineteen and fourpence—her entire stock of money until next quarter-day.

She had been through the list of things that were needed in the kitchen. But indeed, was there anything that was NOT needed in the kitchen? Tea, coffee, soap, matches, candles, sugar, lentils, firewood, soda, lamp oil, boot polish, margarine, baking powder— there seemed to be practically nothing that they were not running short of. And at every moment some fresh item that she had forgotten popped up and dismayed her. The laundry bill, for example, and the fact that the coal was running short, and the question of the fish for Friday. The Rector was 'difficult' about fish. Roughly speaking, he would only eat the more expensive kinds; cod, whiting, sprats, skate, herrings, and kippers he refused.

Meanwhile, she had got to settle about the meat for today's dinner— luncheon. (Dorothy was careful to obey her father and call it LUNCHEON, when she remembered it. On the other hand, you could not in honesty call the evening meal anything but 'supper'; so there was no such meal as 'dinner' at the Rectory.) Better make an omelette for luncheon today, Dorothy decided. She dared not go to Cargill again. Though, of course, if they had an omelette for luncheon and then scrambled eggs for supper, her father would probably be sarcastic about it. Last time they had eggs twice in one day, he had inquired coldly, 'Have you started a chicken farm, Dorothy?' And perhaps tomorrow she would get two pounds of sausages at the International, and that staved off the meat- question for one day more.

Thirty-nine further days, with only three pounds nineteen and fourpence to provide for them, loomed up in Dorothy's imagination, sending through her a wave of self-pity which she checked almost instantly. Now then, Dorothy! No snivelling, please! It all comes right somehow if you trust in God. Matthew vi, 25. The Lord will provide. Will He? Dorothy removed her right hand from the handle-bars and felt for the glass-headed pin, but the blasphemous thought faded. At this moment she became aware of the gloomy red face of Proggett, who was hailing her respectfully but urgently from the side of the road.

Dorothy stopped and got off her bicycle.

'Beg pardon, Miss,' said Proggett. 'I been wanting to speak to you, Miss—PARTIC'LAR.'

Dorothy sighed inwardly. When Proggett wanted to speak to you PARTIC'LAR, you could be perfectly certain what was coming; it was some piece of alarming news about the condition of the church. Proggett was a pessimistic, conscientious man, and very loyal churchman, after his fashion. Too dim of intellect to have any definite religious beliefs, he showed his piety by an intense solicitude about the state of the church buildings. He had decided long ago that the Church of Christ meant the actual walls, roof, and tower of St Athelstan's, Knype Hill, and he would poke round the church at all hours of the day, gloomily noting a cracked stone here, a worm-eaten beam there—and afterwards, of course, coming to harass Dorothy with demands for repairs which would cost impossible sums of money.

'What is it, Proggett?' said Dorothy.

'Well, Miss, it's they —'—here a peculiar, imperfect sound, not a word exactly, but the ghost of a word, all but formed itself on Proggett's lips. It seemed to begin with a B. Proggett was one of those men who are for ever on the verge of swearing, but who always recapture the oath as it is escaping between their teeth. 'It's they BELLS, Miss,' he said, getting rid of the B sound with an effort. 'They bells up in the church tower. They're a-splintering through that there belfry floor in a way as it makes you fair shudder to look at 'em. We'll have 'em down atop of us before we know where we are. I was up the belfry 'smorning, and I tell you I come down faster'n I went up, when I saw how that there floor's a- busting underneath 'em.'

Proggett came to complain about the condition of the bells not less than once a fortnight. It was now three years that they had been lying on the floor of the belfry, because the cost of either reswinging or removing them was estimated at twenty-five pounds, which might as well have been twenty-five thousand for all the chance there was of paying for it. They were really almost as dangerous as Proggett made out. It was quite certain that, if not this year or next year, at any rate at some time in the near future, they would fall through the belfry floor into the church porch. And, as Proggett was fond of pointing out, it would probably happen on a Sunday morning just as the congregation were coming into church.

Dorothy sighed again. Those wretched bells were never out of mind for long; there were times when the thought of their falling even got into her dreams. There was always some trouble or other at the church. If it was not the belfry, then it was the roof or the walls; or it was a broken pew which the carpenter wanted ten shillings to mend; or it was seven hymn-books needed at one and sixpence each, or the flue of the stove choked up—and the sweep's fee was half a crown—or a smashed window-pane or the choir-boys' cassocks in rags. There was never enough money for anything. The new organ which the rector had insisted on buying five years earlier—the old one, he said, reminded him of a cow with the asthma—was a burden under which the Church Expenses fund had been staggering ever since.

'I don't know WHAT we can do,' said Dorothy finally; 'I really don't. We've simply no money at all. And even if we do make anything out of the school-children's play, it's all got to go to the organ fund. The organ people are really getting quite nasty about their bill. Have you spoken to my father?'

'Yes, Miss. He don't make nothing of it. "Belfry's held up five hundred years," he says; "we can trust it to hold up a few years longer."'

This was quite according to precedent. The fact that the church was visibly collapsing over his head made no impression on the Rector; he simply ignored it, as he ignored anything else that he did not wish to be worried about.

'Well, I don't know WHAT we can do,' Dorothy repeated. 'Of course there's the jumble sale coming off the week after next. I'm counting on Miss Mayfill to give us something really NICE for the jumble sale. I know she could afford to. She's got such lots of furniture and things that she never uses. I was in her house the other day, and I saw a most beautiful Lowestoft china tea service which was put away in a cupboard, and she told me it hadn't been used for over twenty years. Just suppose she gave us that tea service! It would fetch pounds and pounds. We must just pray that the jumble sale will be a success, Proggett. Pray that it'll bring us five pounds at least. I'm sure we shall get the money somehow if we really and truly pray for it.'

'Yes, Miss,' said Proggett respectfully, and shifted his gaze to the far distance.

At this moment a horn hooted and a vast, gleaming blue car came very slowly down the road, making for the High Street. Out of one window Mr Blifil-Gordon, the Proprietor of the sugar-beet refinery, was thrusting a sleek black head which went remarkably ill with his suit of sandy-coloured Harris tweed. As he passed, instead of ignoring Dorothy as usual, he flashed upon her a smile so warm that it was almost amorous. With him were his eldest son Ralph—or, as he and the rest of the family pronounced it, Walph—an epicene youth of twenty, given to the writing of sub-Eliot vers libre poems, and Lord Pockthorne's two daughters. They were all smiling, even Lord Pockthorne's daughters. Dorothy was astonished, for it was several years since any of these people had deigned to recognize her in the street.

'Mr Blifil-Gordon is very friendly this morning,' she said.

'Aye, Miss. I'll be bound he is. It's the election coming on next week, that's what 'tis. All honey and butter they are till they've made sure as you'll vote for them; and then they've forgot your very face the day afterwards.'

'Oh, the election!' said Dorothy vaguely. So remote were such things as parliamentary elections from the daily round of parish work that she was virtually unaware of them—hardly, indeed, even knowing the difference between Liberal and Conservative or Socialist and Communist. 'Well, Proggett,' she said, immediately forgetting the election in favour of something more important, 'I'll speak to Father and tell him how serious it is about the bells. I think perhaps the best thing we can do will be to get up a special subscription, just for the bells alone. There's no knowing, we might make five pounds. We might even make ten pounds! Don't you think if I went to Miss Mayfill and asked her to start the subscription with five pounds, she might give it to us?'

'You take my word, Miss, and don't you let Miss Mayfill hear nothing about it. It'd scare the life out of her. If she thought as that tower wasn't safe, we'd never get her inside that church again.'

'Oh dear! I suppose not.'

'No, Miss. We shan't get nothing out of HER; the old—'

A ghostly B floated once more across Proggett's lips. His mind a little more at rest now that he had delivered his fortnightly report upon the bells, he touched his cap and departed, while Dorothy rode on into the High Street, with the twin problems of the shop-debts and the Church Expenses pursuing one another through her mind like the twin refrains of a villanelle.

The still watery sun, now playing hide-and-seek, April-wise, among woolly islets of cloud, sent an oblique beam down the High Street, gilding the house-fronts of the northern side. It was one of those sleepy, old-fashioned streets that look so ideally peaceful on a casual visit and so very different when you live in them and have an enemy or a creditor behind every window. The only definitely offensive buildings were Ye Olde Tea Shoppe (plaster front with sham beams nailed on to it, bottle-glass windows and revolting curly roof like that of a Chinese joss-house), and the new, Doric- pillared post office. After about two hundred yards the High Street forked, forming a tiny market-place, adorned with a pump, now defunct, and a worm-eaten pair of stocks. On either side of the pump stood the Dog and Bottle, the principal inn of the town, and the Knype Hill Conservative Club. At the end, commanding the street, stood Cargill's dreaded shop.

Dorothy came round the corner to a terrific din of cheering, mingled with the strains of 'Rule Britannia' played on the trombone. The normally sleepy street was black with people, and more people were hurrying from all the sidestreets. Evidently a sort of triumphal procession was taking place. Right across the street, from the roof of the Dog and Bottle to the roof of the Conservative Club, hung a line with innumerable blue streamers, and in the middle a vast banner inscribed 'Blifil-Gordon and the Empire!' Towards this, between the lanes of people, the Blifil-Gordon car was moving at a foot-pace, with Mr Blifil-Gordon smiling richly, first to one side, then to the other. In front of the car marched a detachment of the Buffaloes, headed by an earnest-looking little man playing the trombone, and carrying among them another banner inscribed:

Who'll save Britain from the Reds?
BLIFIL-GORDON
Who'll put the Beer back into your Pot?
BLIFIL-GORDON
Blifil-Gordon for ever!

From the window of the Conservative Club floated an enormous Union Jack, above which six scarlet faces were beaming enthusiastically.

Dorothy wheeled her bicycle slowly down the street, too much agitated by the prospect of passing Cargill's shop (she had got to pass, it, to get to Solepipe's) to take much notice of the procession. The Blifil-Gordon car had halted for a moment outside Ye Olde Tea Shoppe. Forward, the coffee brigade! Half the ladies of the town seemed to be hurrying forth, with lap-dogs or shopping baskets on their arms, to cluster about the car like Bacchantes about the car of the vine-god. After all, an election is practically the only time when you get a chance of exchanging smiles with the County. There were eager feminine cries of 'Good luck, Mr Blifil-Gordon! DEAR Mr Blifil-Gordon! We DO hope you'll get in, Mr Blifil-Gordon!' Mr Blifil-Gordon's largesse of smiles was unceasing, but carefully graded. To the populace he gave a diffused, general smile, not resting on individuals; to the coffee ladies and the six scarlet patriots of the Conservative Club he gave one smile each; to the most favoured of all, young Walph gave an occasional wave of the hand and a squeaky 'Cheewio!'

Dorothy's heart tightened. She had seen that Mr Cargill, like the rest of the shopkeepers, was standing on his doorstep. He was a tall, evil-looking man, in blue-striped apron, with a lean, scraped face as purple as one of his own joints of meat that had lain a little too long in the window. So fascinated were Dorothy's eyes by that ominous figure that she did not look where she was going, and bumped into a very large, stout man who was stepping off the pavement backwards.

The stout man turned round. 'Good Heavens! It's Dorothy!' he exclaimed.

'Why, Mr Warburton! How extraordinary! Do you know, I had a feeling I was going to meet you today.'

'By the pricking of your thumbs, I presume?' said Mr Warburton, beaming all over a large, pink, Micawberish face. 'And how are you? But by Jove!' he added, 'What need is there to ask? You look more bewitching than ever.'

He pinched Dorothy's bare elbow—she had changed, after breakfast, into a sleeveless gingham frock. Dorothy stepped hurriedly backwards to get out of his reach—she hated being pinched or otherwise 'mauled about'—and said rather severely:

'PLEASE don't pinch my elbow. I don't like it.'

'My dear Dorothy, who could resist an elbow like yours? It's the sort of elbow one pinches automatically. A reflex action, if you understand me.'

'When did you get back to Knype Hill?' said Dorothy, who had put her bicycle between Mr Warburton and herself. It's over two months since I've seen you.'

'I got back the day before yesterday. But this is only a flying visit. I'm off again tomorrow. I'm taking the kids to Brittany. The BASTARDS, you know.'

Mr Warburton pronounced the word BASTARDS, at which Dorothy looked away in discomfort, with a touch of naive pride. He and his 'bastards' (he had three of them) were one of the chief scandals of Knype Hill. He was a man of independent income, calling himself a painter—he produced about half a dozen mediocre landscapes every year—and he had come to Knype Hill two years earlier and bought one of the new villas behind the Rectory. There he lived, or rather stayed periodically, in open concubinage with a woman whom he called his housekeeper. Four months ago this woman—she was a foreigner, a Spaniard it was said—had created a fresh and worse scandal by abruptly deserting him, and his three children were now parked with some long-suffering relative in London. In appearance he was a fine, imposing-looking man, though entirely bald (he was at great pains to conceal this), and he carried himself with such a rakish air as to give the impression that his fairly sizeable belly was merely a kind of annexe to his chest. His age was forty-eight, and he owned to forty-four. People in the town said that he was a 'proper old rascal'; young girls were afraid of him, not without reason.

Mr Warburton had laid his hand pseudo-paternally on Dorothy's shoulder and was shepherding her through the crowd, talking all the while almost without a pause. The Blifil-Gordon car, having rounded the pump, was now wending its way back, still accompanied by its troupe of middle-aged Bacchantes. Mr Warburton, his attention caught, paused to scrutinize it.

'What is the meaning of these disgusting antics?' he asked.

'Oh, they're—what is it they call it?—electioneering. Trying to get us to vote for them, I suppose.'

'Trying to get us to vote for them! Good God!' murmured Mr Warburton, as he eyed the triumphal cortege. He raised the large, silver-headed cane that he always carried, and pointed, rather expressively, first at one figure in the procession and then at another. 'Look at it! Just look at it! Look at those fawning hags, and that half-witted oaf grinning at us like a monkey that sees a bag of nuts. Did you ever see such a disgusting spectacle?'

'Do be careful!' Dorothy murmured. 'Somebody's sure to hear you.'

'Good!' said Mr Warburton, immediately raising his voice. 'And to think that low-born hound actually has the impertinence to think that he's pleasing us with the sight of his false teeth! And that suit he's wearing is an offence in itself. Is there a Socialist candidate? If so, I shall certainly vote for him.'

Several people on the pavement turned and stared. Dorothy saw little Mr Twiss, the ironmonger, a weazened, leather-coloured old man, peering with veiled malevolence round the corner of the rush baskets that hung in his doorway. He had caught the word Socialist, and was mentally registering Mr Warburton as a Socialist and Dorothy as the friend of Socialists.

'I really MUST be getting on,' said Dorothy hastily, feeling that she had better escape before Mr Warburton said something even more tactless. 'I've got ever such a lot of shopping to do. I'll say good-bye for the present, then.'

'Oh, no, you won't!' said Mr Warburton cheerfully. 'Not a bit of it! I'll come with you.'

As she wheeled her bicycle down the street he marched at her side, still talking, with his large chest well forward and his stick tucked under his arm. He was a difficult man to shake off, and though Dorothy counted him as a friend, she did sometimes wish, he being the town scandal and she the Rector's daughter, that he would not always choose the most public places to talk to her in. At this moment, however, she was rather grateful for his company, which made it appreciably easier to pass Cargill's shop—for Cargill was still on his doorstep and was regarding her with a sidelong, meaning gaze.

'It was a bit of luck my meeting you this morning,' Mr Warburton went on. 'In fact, I was looking for you. Who do you think I've got coming to dinner with me tonight? Bewley—Ronald Bewley. You've heard of him, of course?'

'Ronald Bewley? No, I don't think so. Who is he?'

'Why, dash it! Ronald Bewley, the novelist. Author of Fishpools and Concubines. Surely you've read Fishpools and Concubines?'

'No, I'm afraid I haven't. In fact, I'd never even heard of it.'

'My dear Dorothy! You HAVE been neglecting yourself. You certainly ought to read Fishpools and Concubines. It's hot stuff, I assure you—real high-class pornography. Just the kind of thing you need to take the taste of the Girl Guides out of your mouth.'

'I do wish you wouldn't say such things!' said Dorothy, looking away uncomfortably, and then immediately looking back again because she had all but caught Cargill's eye. 'Where does this Mr Bewley live?' she added. 'Not here, surely, does he?'

'No. He's coming over from Ipswich for dinner, and perhaps to stay the night. That's why I was looking for you. I thought you might like to meet him. How about your coming to dinner tonight?'

'I can't possibly come to dinner,' said Dorothy. 'I've got Father's supper to see to, and thousands of other things. I shan't be free till eight o'clock or after.'

'Well, come along after dinner, then. I'd like you to know Bewley. He's an interesting fellow—very au fait with all the

Bloomsbury scandal, and all that. You'll enjoy meeting him. It'll do you good to escape from the church hen-coop for a few hours.'

Dorothy hesitated. She was tempted. To tell the truth, she enjoyed her occasional visits to Mr Warburton's house extremely. But of course they were VERY occasional—once in three or four months at the oftenest; it so obviously DIDN'T DO to associate too freely with such a man. And even when she did go to his house she was careful to make sure beforehand that there was going to be at least one other visitor.

Two years earlier, when Mr Warburton had first come to Knype Hill (at that time he was posing as a widower with two children; a little later, however, the housekeeper suddenly gave birth to a third child in the middle of the night), Dorothy had met him at a tea-party and afterwards called on him. Mr Warburton had given her a delightful tea, talked amusingly about books, and then, immediately after tea, sat down beside her on the sofa and begun making love to her, violently, outrageously, even brutally. It was practically an assault. Dorothy was horrified almost out of her wits, though not too horrified to resist. She escaped from him and took refuge on the other side of the sofa, white, shaking, and almost in tears. Mr Warburton, on the other hand, was quite unashamed and even seemed rather amused.

'Oh, how could you, how could you?' she sobbed.

'But it appears that I couldn't,' said Mr Warburton.

'Oh, but how could you be such a brute?'

'Oh, THAT? Easily, my child, easily. You will understand that when you get to my age.'

In spite of this bad beginning, a sort of friendship had grown up between the two, even to the extent of Dorothy being 'talked about' in connexion with Mr Warburton. It did not take much to get you 'talked about' in Knype Hill. She only saw him at long intervals and took the greatest care never to be alone with him, but even so he found opportunities of making casual love to her. But it was done in a gentlemanly fashion; the previous disagreeable incident was not repeated. Afterwards, when he was forgiven, Mr Warburton had explained that he 'always tried it on' with every presentable woman he met.

'Don't you get rather a lot of snubs?' Dorothy could not help asking him.

'Oh, certainly. But I get quite a number of successes as well, you know.'

People wondered sometimes how such a girl as Dorothy could consort, even occasionally, with such a man as Mr Warburton; but the hold that he had over her was the hold that the blasphemer and evil- liver always has over the pious. It is a fact—you have only to look about you to verify it—that the pious and the immoral drift naturally together. The best brothel-scenes in literature have been written, without exception, by pious believers or pious unbelievers. And of course Dorothy, born into the twentieth century, made a point of listening to Mr Warburton's blasphemies as calmly as possible; it is fatal to flatter the wicked by letting them see that you are shocked by them. Besides, she was genuinely fond of him. He teased her and distressed her, and yet she got from him, without being fully aware of it, a species of sympathy and understanding which she could not get elsewhere. For all his vices he was distinctly likeable, and the shoddy brilliance of his conversation—Oscar Wilde seven times watered—which she was too inexperienced to see through, fascinated while it shocked her. Perhaps, too, in this instance, the prospect of meeting the celebrated Mr Bewley had its effect upon her; though certainly Fishponds and Concubines sounded like the kind of book that she either didn't read or else set herself heavy penances for reading. In London, no doubt, one would hardly cross the road to see fifty novelists; but these things appeared differently in places like Knype Hill.

'Are you SURE Mr Bewley is coming?' she said.

'Quite sure. And his wife's coming as well, I believe. Full chaperonage. No Tarquin and Lucrece business this evening.'

'All right,' said Dorothy finally; 'thanks very much. I'll come round—about half past eight, I expect.'

'Good. If you can manage to come while it is still daylight, so much the better. Remember that Mrs Semprill is my next-door neighbour. We can count on her to be on the qui vive any time after sundown.'

Mrs Semprill was the town scandalmonger—the most eminent, that is, of the town's many scandalmongers. Having got what he wanted (he was constantly pestering Dorothy to come to his house more often), Mr Warburton said au revoir and left Dorothy to do the remainder of her shopping.

In the semi-gloom of Solepipe's shop, she was just moving away from the counter with her two and a half yards of casement cloth, when she was aware of a low, mournful voice at her ear. It was Mrs Semprill. She was a slender woman of forty, with a lank, sallow, distinguished face, which, with her glossy dark hair and air of settled melancholy, gave her something the appearance of a Van Dyck portrait. Entrenched behind a pile of cretonnes near the window, she had been watching Dorothy's conversation with Mr Warburton. Whenever you were doing something that you did not particularly want Mrs Semprill to see you doing, you could trust her to be somewhere in the neighbourhood. She seemed to have the power of materializing like an Arabian jinneeyeh at any place where she was not wanted. No indiscretion, however small, escaped her vigilance. Mr Warburton used to say that she was like the four beasts of the Apocalypse—'They are full of eyes, you remember, and they rest not night nor day.'

'Dorothy DEAREST,' murmured Mrs Semprill in the sorrowful, affectionate voice of someone breaking a piece of bad news as gently as possible. 'I've been so WANTING to speak to you.

I've something simply DREADFUL to tell you—something that will really HORRIFY you!'

'What is it?' said Dorothy resignedly, well knowing what was coming—for Mrs Semprill had only one subject of conversation.

They moved out of the shop and began to walk down the street, Dorothy wheeling her bicycle, Mrs Semprill mincing at her side with a delicate birdlike step and bringing her mouth closer and closer to Dorothy's ear as her remarks grew more and more intimate.

'Do you happen to have noticed,' she began, 'that girl who sits at the end of the pew nearest the organ in church? A rather PRETTY girl, with red hair. I've no idea what her name is,' added Mrs Semprill, who knew the surname and all the Christian names of every man, woman, and child in Knype Hill.

'Molly Freeman,' said Dorothy. 'She's the niece of Freeman the greengrocer.'

'Oh, Molly Freeman? Is THAT her name? I'd often wondered. Well—'

The delicate red mouth came closer, the mournful voice sank to a shocked whisper. Mrs Semprill began to pour forth a stream of purulent libel involving Molly Freeman and six young men who worked at the sugar-beet refinery. After a few moments the story became so outrageous that Dorothy, who had turned very pink, hurriedly withdrew her ear from Mrs Semprill's whispering lips. She stopped her bicycle.

'I won't listen to such things!' she said abruptly. 'I KNOW that isn't true about Molly Freeman. It CAN'T be true! She's such a nice quiet girl—she was one of my very best Girl Guides, and she's always been so good about helping with the church bazaars and everything. I'm perfectly certain she wouldn't do such things as you're saying.'

'But, Dorothy DEAREST! When, as I told you, I actually saw with my own eyes…'

'I don't care! It's not fair to say such things about people. Even if they were true it wouldn't be right to repeat them. There's quite enough evil in the world without going about looking for it.'

'LOOKING for it!' sighed Mrs Semprill. 'But, my dear Dorothy, as though one ever wanted or NEEDED to look! The trouble is that one can't HELP seeing all the dreadful wickedness that goes on in this town.'

Mrs Semprill was always genuinely astonished if you accused her of LOOKING for subjects for scandal. Nothing, she would protest, pained her more than the spectacle of human wickedness; but it was constantly forced upon her unwilling eyes, and only a stern sense of duty impelled her to make it public. Dorothy's remarks, so far from silencing her, merely set her talking about the general corruption of Knype Hill, of which Molly Freeman's misbehaviour was only one example. And so from Molly Freeman and her six young men she proceeded to Dr Gaythorne, the town medical officer, who had got two of the nurses at the Cottage Hospital with child, and then to Mrs Corn, the Town Clerk's wife, found lying in a field dead drunk on eau-de-Cologne, and then to the curate at St Wedekind's in Millborough, who had involved himself in a grave scandal with a choirboy; and so it went on, one thing leading to another. For there was hardly a soul in the town or the surrounding country about whom Mrs Semprill could not disclose some festering secret if you listened to her long enough.

It was noticeable that her stories were not only dirty and libellous, but they had nearly always some monstrous tinge of perversion about them. Compared with the ordinary scandalmongers of a country town, she was Freud to Boccaccio. From hearing her talk you would have gathered the impression that Knype Hill with its thousand inhabitants held more of the refinements of evil than Sodom, Gomorrah, and Buenos Aires put together. Indeed, when you reflected upon the lives led by the inhabitants of this latter-day City of the Plain—from the manager of the local bank squandering his clients' money on the children of his second and bigamous marriage, to the barmaid of the Dog and Bottle serving drinks in the taproom dressed only in high-heeled satin slippers, and from old Miss Channon, the music-teacher, with her secret gin bottle and her anonymous letters, to Maggie White, the baker's daughter, who had borne three children to her own brother—when you considered these people, all, young and old, rich and poor, sunken in monstrous and Babylonian vices, you wondered that fire did not come down from Heaven and consume the town forthwith. But if you listened just a little longer, the catalogue of obscenities became first monstrous and then unbearably dull. For in a town in which EVERYONE is either a bigamist, a pederast, or a drug-taker, the worst scandal loses its sting. In fact, Mrs Semprill was something worse than a slanderer; she was a bore.

As to the extent to which her stories were believed, it varied. At times the word would go round that she was a foul-mouthed old cat and everything she said was a pack of lies; at other times one of her accusations would take effect on some unfortunate person, who would need months or even years to live it down. She had certainly been instrumental in breaking off not less than half a dozen engagements and starting innumerable quarrels between husbands and wives.

All this while Dorothy had been making abortive efforts to shake Mrs Semprill off. She had edged her way gradually across the street until she was wheeling her bicycle along the right-hand kerb; but Mrs Semprill had followed, whispering without cease. It was not until they reached the end of the High Street that Dorothy summoned up enough firmness to escape. She halted and put her right foot on the pedal of her bicycle.

'I really can't stop a moment longer,' she said. 'I've got a thousand things to do, and I'm late already.'

'Oh, but, Dorothy dear! I've something else I simply MUST tell you—something most IMPORTANT!'

'I'm sorry—I'm in such a terrible hurry. Another time, perhaps.'

'It's about that DREADFUL Mr Warburton,' said Mrs Semprill hastily, lest Dorothy should escape without hearing it. 'He's just come back from London, and do you know—I most PARTICULARLY wanted to tell you this—do you know, he actually—'

But here Dorothy saw that she must make off instantly, at no matter what cost. She could imagine nothing more uncomfortable than to have to discuss Mr Warburton with Mrs Semprill. She mounted her bicycle, and with only a very brief 'Sorry—I really CAN'T stop!' began to ride hurriedly away.

'I wanted to tell you—he's taken up with a new woman!' Mrs Semprill cried after her, even forgetting to whisper in her eagerness to pass on this juicy titbit.

But Dorothy rode swiftly round the corner, not looking back, and pretending not to have heard. An unwise thing to do, for it did not pay to cut Mrs Semprill too short. Any unwillingness to listen to her scandals was taken as a sign of depravity, and led to fresh and worse scandals being published about yourself the moment you had left her.

As Dorothy rode homewards she had uncharitable thoughts about Mrs Semprill, for which she duly pinched herself. Also, there was another, rather disturbing idea which had not occurred to her till this moment—that Mrs Semprill would certainly learn of her visit to Mr Warburton's house this evening, and would probably have magnified it into something scandalous by tomorrow. The thought sent a vague premonition of evil through Dorothy's mind as she jumped off her bicycle at the Rectory gate, where Silly Jack, the town idiot, a third-grade moron with a triangular scarlet face like a strawberry, was loitering, vacantly flogging the gatepost with a hazel switch.

4

It was a little after eleven. The day, which, like some overripe but hopeful widow playing at seventeen, had been putting on unseasonable April airs, had now remembered that it was August and settled down to be boiling hot.

Dorothy rode into the hamlet of Fennelwick, a mile out of Knype Hill. She had delivered Mrs Lewin's corn-plaster, and was dropping in to give old Mrs Pither that cutting from the Daily Mail about angelica tea for rheumatism. The sun, burning in the cloudless sky, scorched her back through her gingham frock, and the dusty road quivered in the heat, and the hot, flat meadows, over which even at this time of year numberless larks chirruped tiresomely, were so green that it hurt your eyes to look at them. It was the kind of day that is called 'glorious' by people who don't have to work.

Dorothy leaned her bicycle against the gate of the Pithers' cottage, and took her handkerchief out of her bag and wiped her hands, which were sweating from the handle-bars. In the harsh sunlight her face looked pinched and colourless. She looked her age, and something over, at that hour of the morning. Throughout her day—and in general it was a seventeen-hour day—she had regular, alternating periods of tiredness and energy; the middle of the morning, when she was doing the first instalment of the day's 'visiting', was one of the tired periods.

'Visiting', because of the distances she had to bicycle from house to house, took up nearly half of Dorothy's day. Every day of her life, except on Sundays, she made from half a dozen to a dozen visits at parishioners' cottages. She penetrated into cramped interiors and sat on lumpy, dust-diffusing chairs gossiping with overworked, blowsy housewives; she spent hurried half-hours giving a hand with the mending and the ironing, and read chapters from the Gospels, and readjusted bandages on 'bad legs', and condoled with sufferers from morning-sickness; she played ride-a-cock-horse with sour-smelling children who grimed the bosom of her dress with their sticky little fingers; she gave advice about ailing aspidistras, and suggested names for babies, and drank 'nice cups of tea' innumerable—for the working women always wanted her to have a 'nice cup of tea', out of the teapot endlessly stewing.

Much of it was profoundly discouraging work. Few, very few, of the women seemed to have even a conception of the Christian life that she was trying to help them to lead. Some of them were shy and suspicious, stood on the defensive, and made excuses when urged to come to Holy Communion; some shammed piety for the sake of the tiny sums they could wheedle out of the church alms box; those who welcomed her coming were for the most part the talkative ones, who wanted an audience for complaints about the 'goings on' of their husbands, or for endless mortuary tales ('And he had to have glass chubes let into his veins,' etc., etc.) about the revolting diseases their relatives had died of. Quite half the women on her list, Dorothy knew, were at heart atheistical in a vague unreasoning way. She came up against it all day long—that vague, blank disbelief so common in illiterate people, against which all argument is powerless. Do what she would, she could never raise the number of regular communicants to more than a dozen or thereabouts. Women would promise to communicate, keep their promise for a month or two, and then fall away. With the younger women it was especially hopeless. They would not even join the local branches of the church leagues that were run for their benefit—Dorothy was honorary secretary of three such leagues, besides being captain of the Girl Guides. The Band of Hope and the Companionship of Marriage languished almost memberless, and the Mothers' Union only kept going because gossip and unlimited strong tea made the weekly sewing-parties acceptable. Yes, it was discouraging work; so discouraging that at times it would have seemed altogether futile if she had not known the sense of futility for what it is—the subtlest weapon of the Devil.

Dorothy knocked at the Pithers' badly fitting door, from beneath which a melancholy smell of boiled cabbage and dish-water was oozing. From long experience she knew and could taste in advance the individual smell of every cottage on her rounds. Some of their smells were peculiar in the extreme. For instance, there was the salty, feral smell that haunted the cottage of old Mr Tombs, an aged retired bookseller who lay in bed all day in a darkened room, with his long, dusty nose and pebble spectacles protruding from what appeared to be a fur rug of vast size and richness.

But if you put your hand on the fur rug it disintegrated, burst and fled in all directions. It was composed entirely of cats—twenty- four cats, to be exact. Mr Tombs 'found they kept him warm', he used to explain. In nearly all the cottages there was a basic smell of old overcoats and dish-water upon which the other, individual smells were superimposed; the cesspool smell, the cabbage smell, the smell of children, the strong, bacon-like reek of corduroys impregnated with the sweat of a decade.

Mrs Pither opened the door, which invariably stuck to the jamb, and then, when you wrenched it open, shook the whole cottage. She was a large, stooping, grey woman with wispy grey hair, a sacking apron, and shuffling carpet slippers.

'Why, if it isn't Miss Dorothy!' she exclaimed in a dreary, lifeless but not unaffectionate voice.

She took Dorothy between her large, gnarled hands, whose knuckles were as shiny as skinned onions from age and ceaseless washing up, and gave her a wet kiss. Then she drew her into the unclean interior of the cottage.

'Pither's away at work, Miss,' she announced as they got inside. 'Up to Dr Gaythorne's he is, a-digging over the doctor's flower- beds for him.'

Mr Pither was a jobbing gardener. He and his wife, both of them over seventy, were one of the few genuinely pious couples on Dorothy's visiting list. Mrs Pither led a dreary, wormlike life of shuffling to and fro, with a perpetual crick in her neck because the door lintels were too low for her, between the well, the sink, the fireplace, and the tiny plot of kitchen garden. The kitchen was decently tidy, but oppressively hot, evil-smelling and saturated with ancient dust. At the end opposite the fireplace Mrs Pither had made a kind of prie-dieu out of a greasy rag mat laid in front of a tiny, defunct harmonium, on top of which were an oleographed crucifixion, 'Watch and Pray' done in beadwork, and a photograph of Mr and Mrs Pither on their wedding day in 1882.

'Poor Pither!' went on Mrs Pither in her depressing voice, 'him a- digging at his age, with his rheumatism THAT bad! Ain't it cruel hard, Miss? And he's had a kind of a pain between his legs, Miss, as he can't seem to account for—terrible bad he's been with it, these last few mornings. Ain't it bitter hard, Miss, the lives us poor working folks has to lead?'

'It's a shame,' said Dorothy. 'But I hope you've been keeping a little better yourself, Mrs Pither?'

'Ah, Miss, there's nothing don't make ME better. I ain't a case for curing, not in THIS world, I ain't. I shan't never get no better, not in this wicked world down here.'

'Oh, you mustn't say that, Mrs Pither! I hope we shall have you with us for a long time yet.'

'Ah, Miss, you don't know how poorly I've been this last week! I've had the rheumatism a-coming and a-going all down the backs of my poor old legs, till there's some mornings when I don't feel as I can't walk so far as to pull a handful of onions in the garden. Ah, Miss, it's a weary world we lives in, ain't it, Miss? A weary, sinful world.'

'But of course we must never forget, Mrs Pither, that there's a better world coming. This life is only a time of trial—just to strengthen us and teach us to be patient, so that we'll be ready for Heaven when the time comes.'

At this a sudden and remarkable change came over Mrs Pither. It was produced by the word 'Heaven'. Mrs Pither had only two subjects of conversation; one of them was the joys of Heaven, and the other the miseries of her present state. Dorothy's remark seemed to act upon her like a charm. Her dull grey eye was not capable of brightening, but her voice quickened with an almost joyful enthusiasm.

'Ah, Miss, there you said it! That's a true word, Miss! That's what Pither and me keeps a-saying to ourselves. And that's just the one thing as keeps us a-going—just the thought of Heaven and the long, long rest we'll have there. Whatever we've suffered, we gets it all back in Heaven, don't we, Miss? Every little bit of suffering, you gets it back a hundredfold and a thousandfold. That IS true, ain't it, Miss? There's rest for us all in Heaven—rest and peace and no more rheumatism nor digging nor cooking nor laundering nor nothing. You DO believe that, don't you, Miss Dorothy?'

'Of course,' said Dorothy.

'Ah, Miss, if you knew how it comforts us—just the thoughts of Heaven! Pither he says to me, when he comes home tired of a night and our rheumatism's bad, "Never you mind, my dear," he says, "we ain't far off Heaven now," he says. "Heaven was made for the likes of us," he says; "just for poor working folks like us, that have been sober and godly and kept our Communions regular." That's the best way, ain't it, Miss Dorothy—poor in this life and rich in the next? Not like some of them rich folks as all their motorcars and their beautiful houses won't save from the worm that dieth not and the fire that's not quenched. Such a beautiful text, that is. Do you think you could say a little prayer with me, Miss Dorothy? I been looking forward all the morning to a little prayer.

Mrs Pither was always ready for a 'little prayer' at any hour of the night or day. It was her equivalent to a 'nice cup of tea'. They knelt down on the rag mat and said the Lord's Prayer and the Collect for the week; and then Dorothy, at Mrs Pither's request, read the parable of Dives and Lazarus, Mrs Pither coming in from time to time with 'Amen! That's a true word, ain't it, Miss Dorothy? "And he was carried by angels into Abraham's bosom." Beautiful! Oh, I do call that just too beautiful! Amen, Miss Dorothy—Amen!'

Dorothy gave Mrs Pither the cutting from the Daily Mail about angelica tea for rheumatism, and then, finding that Mrs Pither had been too 'poorly' to draw the day's supply of water, she drew three bucketfuls for her from the well. It was a very deep well, with such a low parapet that Mrs Pither's final doom would almost certainly be to fall into it and get drowned, and it had not even a winch—you had to haul the bucket up hand over hand. And then they sat down for a few minutes, and Mrs Pither talked some more about Heaven. It was extraordinary how constantly Heaven reigned in her thoughts; and more extraordinary yet was the actuality, the vividness with which she could see it. The golden streets and the gates of orient pearl were as real to her as though they had been actually before her eyes. And her vision extended to the most concrete, the most earthly details. The softness of the beds up there! The deliciousness of the food! The lovely silk clothes that you would put on clean every morning! The surcease from everlasting to everlasting from work of any description! In almost every moment of her life the vision of Heaven supported and consoled her, and her abject complaints about the lives of 'poor working folks' were curiously tempered by a satisfaction in the thought that, after all, it is 'poor working folks' who are the principal inhabitants of Heaven. It was a sort of bargain that she had struck, setting her lifetime of dreary labour against an eternity of bliss. Her faith was almost TOO great, if that is possible.

For it was a curious fact, but the certitude with which Mrs Pither looked forward to Heaven—as to some kind of glorified home for incurables—affected Dorothy with strange uneasiness.

Dorothy prepared to depart, while Mrs Pither thanked her, rather too effusively, for her visit, winding up, as usual, with fresh complaints about her rheumatism.

'I'll be sure and take the angelica tea,' she concluded, 'and thank you kindly for telling me of it, Miss. Not as I don't expect as it'll do me much good. Ah, Miss, if you knew how cruel bad my rheumatism's been this last week! All down the backs of my legs, it is, like a regular shooting red-hot poker, and I don't seem to be able to get at them to rub them properly. Would it be asking too much of you, Miss, to give me a bit of a rub-down before you go? I got a bottle of Elliman's under the sink.'

Unseen by Mrs Pither, Dorothy gave herself a severe pinch. She had been expecting this, and—she had done it so many times before—she really did NOT enjoy rubbing Mrs Pither down. She exhorted herself angrily. Come on, Dorothy! No sniff-ishness, please! John xiii, 14. 'Of course I will, Mrs Pither!' she said instantly.

They went up the narrow, rickety staircase, in which you had to bend almost double at one place to avoid the overhanging ceiling. The bedroom was lighted by a tiny square of window that was jammed in its socket by the creeper outside, and had not been opened in twenty years. There was an enormous double bed that almost filled the room, with sheets perennially damp and a flock mattress as full of hills and valleys as a contour map of Switzerland. With many groans the old woman crept on to the bed and laid herself face down. The room reeked of urine and paregoric. Dorothy took the bottle of Elliman's embrocation and carefully anointed Mrs Pither's large, grey-veined, flaccid legs.

Outside, in the swimming heat, she mounted her bicycle and began to ride swiftly homewards. The sun burned in her face, but the air now seemed sweet and fresh. She was happy, happy! She was always extravagantly happy when her morning's 'visiting' was over; and, curiously enough, she was not aware of the reason for this. In Borlase the dairy-farmer's meadow the red cows were grazing, knee- deep in shining seas of grass. The scent of cows, like a distillation of vanilla and fresh hay, floated into Dorothy's nostrils. Though she had still a morning's work in front of her she could not resist the temptation to loiter for a moment, steadying her bicycle with one hand against the gate of Borlase's meadow, while a cow, with moist shell-pink nose, scratched its chin upon the gatepost and dreamily regarded her.

Dorothy caught sight of a wild rose, flowerless of course, growing beyond the hedge, and climbed over the gate with the intention of discovering whether it were not sweetbriar. She knelt down among the tall weeds beneath the hedge. It was very hot down there, close to the ground. The humming of many unseen insects sounded in her ears, and the hot summery fume from the tangled swathes of vegetation flowed up and enveloped her. Near by, tall stalks of fennel were growing, with trailing fronds of foliage like the tails of sea-green horses. Dorothy pulled a frond of the fennel against her face and breathed in the strong sweet scent. Its richness overwhelmed her, almost dizzied her for a moment. She drank it in, filling her lungs with it. Lovely, lovely scent—scent of summer days, scent of childhood joys, scent of spice-drenched islands in the warm foam of Oriental seas!

Her heart swelled with sudden joy. It was that mystical joy in the beauty of the earth and the very nature of things that she recognized, perhaps mistakenly, as the love of God. As she knelt there in the heat, the sweet odour and the drowsy hum of insects, it seemed to her that she could momentarily hear the mighty anthem of praise that the earth and all created things send up everlastingly to their maker. All vegetation, leaves, flowers, grass, shining, vibrating, crying out in their joy. Larks also chanting, choirs of larks invisible, dripping music from the sky. All the riches of summer, the warmth of the earth, the song of birds, the fume of cows, the droning of countless bees, mingling and ascending like the smoke of ever-burning altars. Therefore with Angels and Archangels! She began to pray, and for a moment she prayed ardently, blissfully, forgetting herself in the joy of her worship. Then, less than a minute later, she discovered that she was kissing the frond of the fennel that was still against her face.

She checked herself instantly, and drew back. What was she doing? Was it God that she was worshipping, or was it only the earth? The joy ebbed out of her heart, to be succeeded by the cold, uncomfortable feeling that she had been betrayed into a half-pagan ecstasy. She admonished herself. None of THAT, Dorothy! No Nature-worship, please! Her father had warned her against Nature- worship. She had heard him preach more than one sermon against it; it was, he said, mere pantheism, and, what seemed to offend him even more, a disgusting modern fad. Dorothy took a thorn of the wild rose, and pricked her arm three times, to remind herself of the Three Persons of the Trinity, before climbing over the gate and remounting her bicycle.

A black, very dusty shovel hat was approaching round the corner of the hedge. It was Father McGuire, the Roman Catholic priest, also bicycling his rounds. He was a very large, rotund man, so large that he dwarfed the bicycle beneath him and seemed to be balanced on top of it like a golf-ball on a tee. His face was rosy, humorous, and a little sly.

Dorothy looked suddenly unhappy. She turned pink, and her hand moved instinctively to the neighbourhood of the gold cross beneath her dress. Father McGuire was riding towards her with an untroubled, faintly amused air. She made an endeavour to smile, and murmured unhappily, 'Good morning.' But he rode on without a sign; his eyes swept easily over her face and then beyond her into vacancy, with an admirable pretence of not having noticed her existence. It was the Cut Direct. Dorothy—by nature, alas! unequal to delivering the Cut Direct—got on to her bicycle and rode away, struggling with the uncharitable thoughts which a meeting with Father McGuire never failed to arouse in her.

Five or six years earlier, when Father McGuire was holding a funeral in St Athelstan's churchyard (there was no Roman Catholic cemetery at Knype Hill), there had been some dispute with the Rector about the propriety of Father McGuire robing in the church, or not robing in the church, and the two priests had wrangled disgracefully over the open grave. Since then they had not been on speaking terms. It was better so, the Rector said.

As to the other ministers of religion in Knype Hill—Mr Ward the Congregationalist minister, Mr Foley the Wesleyan pastor, and the braying bald-headed elder who conducted the orgies at Ebenezer Chapel—the Rector called them a pack of vulgar Dissenters and had forbidden Dorothy on pain of his displeasure to have anything to do with them.

5

It was twelve o'clock. In the large, dilapidated conservatory, whose roof-panes, from the action of time and dirt, were dim, green, and iridescent like old Roman glass, they were having a hurried and noisy rehearsal of Charles I.

Dorothy was not actually taking part in the rehearsal, but was busy making costumes. She made the costumes, or most of them, for all the plays the schoolchildren acted. The production and stage management were in the hands of Victor Stone—Victor, Dorothy called him—the Church schoolmaster. He was a small-boned, excitable, black-haired youth of twenty-seven, dressed in dark sub- clerical clothes, and at this moment he was gesturing fiercely with a roll of manuscript at six dense-looking children. On a long bench against the wall four more children were alternately practising 'noises off' by clashing fire-irons together, and squabbling over a grimy little bag of Spearmint Bouncers, forty a penny.

It was horribly hot in the conservatory, and there was a powerful smell of glue and the sour sweat of children. Dorothy was kneeling on the floor, with her mouth full of pins and a pair of shears in her hand, rapidly slicing sheets of brown paper into long narrow strips. The glue-pot was bubbling on an oil-stove beside her; behind her, on the rickety, ink-stained work-table, were a tangle of half-finished costumes, more sheets of brown paper, her sewing- machine, bundles of tow, shards of dry glue, wooden swords, and open pots of paint. With half her mind Dorothy was meditating upon the two pairs of seventeenth-century jackboots that had got to be made for Charles I and Oliver Cromwell, and with the other half listening to the angry shouts of Victor, who was working himself up into a rage, as he invariably did at rehearsals. He was a natural actor, and withal thoroughly bored by the drudgery of rehearsing half-witted children. He strode up and down, haranguing the children in a vehement slangy style, and every now and then breaking off to lunge at one or other of them with a wooden sword that he had grabbed from the table.

'Put a bit of life into it, can't you?' he cried, prodding an ox- faced boy of eleven in the belly. 'Don't drone! Say it as if it meant something! You look like a corpse that's been buried and dug up again. What's the good of gurgling it down in your inside like that? Stand up and shout at him. Take off that second murderer expression!'

'Come here, Percy!' cried Dorothy through her pins. 'Quick!'

She was making the armour—the worst job of the lot, except those wretched jackboots—out of glue and brown paper. From long practice Dorothy could make very nearly anything out of glue and brown paper; she could even make a passably good periwig, with a brown paper skull-cap and dyed tow for the hair. Taking the year through, the amount of time she spent in struggling with glue, brown paper, butter muslin, and all the other paraphernalia of amateur theatricals was enormous. So chronic was the need of money for all the church funds that hardly a month ever passed when there was not a school play or a pageant or an exhibition of tableaux vivants on hand—not to mention the bazaars and jumble sales.

As Percy—Percy Jowett, the blacksmith's son, a small curly-headed boy—got down from the bench and stood wriggling unhappily before her, Dorothy seized a sheet of brown paper, measured it against him, snipped out the neckhole and armholes, draped it round his middle and rapidly pinned it into the shape of a rough breastplate. There was a confused din of voices.

VICTOR: Come on, now, come on! Enter Oliver Cromwell—that's you! NO, not like that! Do you think Oliver Cromwell would come slinking on like a dog that's just had a hiding? Stand up. Stick your chest out. Scowl. That's better. Now go on, CROMWELL: 'Halt! I hold a pistol in my hand!' Go on.

A GIRL: Please, Miss, Mother said as I was to tell you, Miss—

DOROTHY: Keep still, Percy! For goodness' SAKE keep still!

CROMWELL: 'Alt! I 'old a pistol in my 'and!

A SMALL GIRL ON THE BENCH: Mister! I've dropped my sweetie! [Snivelling] I've dropped by swee-e-e-etie!

VICTOR: No, no, NO, Tommie! No, no, NO!

THE GIRL: Please, Miss, Mother said as I was to tell you as she couldn't make my knickers like she promised, Miss, because—

DOROTHY: You'll make me swallow a pin if you do that again.

CROMWELL: Halt! I Hold a pistol—

THE SMALL GIRL [in tears]: My swee-e-e-e-eetie!

Dorothy seized the glue-brush, and with feverish speed pasted strips of brown paper all over Percy's thorax, up and down, backwards and forwards, one on top of another, pausing only when the paper stuck to her fingers. In five minutes she had made a cuirass of glue and brown paper stout enough, when it was dry, to have defied a real sword-blade. Percy, 'locked up in complete steel' and with the sharp paper edge cutting his chin, looked down at himself with the miserable resigned expression of a dog having its bath. Dorothy took the shears, slit the breastplate up one side, set it on end to dry and started immediately on another child. A fearful clatter broke out as the 'noises off' began practising the sound of pistol-shots and horses galloping. Dorothy's fingers were getting stickier and stickier, but from time to time she washed some of the glue off them in a bucket of hot water that was kept in readiness. In twenty minutes she had partially completed three breastplates. Later on they would have to be finished off, painted over with aluminium paint and laced up the sides; and after that there was the job of making the thigh-pieces, and, worst of all, the helmets to go with them. Victor, gesticulating with his sword and shouting to overcome the din of galloping horses, was personating in turn Oliver Cromwell, Charles I, Roundheads, Cavaliers, peasants, and Court ladies. The children were now growing restive and beginning to yawn, whine, and exchange furtive kicks and pinches. The breastplates finished for the moment, Dorothy swept some of the litter off the table, pulled her sewing-machine into position and set to work on a Cavalier's green velvet doublet—it was butter muslin Twinked green, but it looked all right at a distance.

There was another ten minutes of feverish work. Dorothy broke her thread, all but said 'Damn!' checked herself and hurriedly re- threaded the needle. She was working against time. The play was now a fortnight distant, and there was such a multitude of things yet to be made—helmets, doublets, swords, jackboots (those miserable jackboots had been haunting her like a nightmare for days past), scabbards, ruffles, wigs, spurs, scenery—that her heart sank when she thought of them. The children's parents never helped with the costumes for the school plays; more exactly, they always promised to help and then backed out afterwards. Dorothy's head was aching diabolically, partly from the heat of the conservatory, partly from the strain of simultaneously sewing and trying to visualize patterns for brown paper jackboots. For the moment she had even forgotten the bill for twenty-one pounds seven and ninepence at Cargill's. She could think of nothing save that fearful mountain of unmade clothes that lay ahead of her. It was so throughout the day. One thing loomed up after another—whether it was the costumes for the school play or the collapsing floor of the belfry, or the shop-debts or the bindweed in the peas—and each in its turn so urgent and so harassing that it blotted all the others out of existence.

Victor threw down his wooden sword, took out his watch and looked at it.

'That'll do!' he said in the abrupt, ruthless tone from which he never departed when he was dealing with children. 'We'll go on on Friday. Clear out, the lot of you! I'm sick of the sight of you.'

He watched the children out, and then, having forgotten their existence as soon as they were out of his sight, produced a page of music from his pocket and began to fidget up and down, cocking his eye at two forlorn plants in the corner which trailed their dead brown tendrils over the edges of their pots. Dorothy was still bending over her machine, stitching up the seams of the green velvet doublet.

Victor was a restless, intelligent little creature, and only happy when he was quarrelling with somebody or something. His pale, fine-featured face wore an expression that appeared to be discontent and was really boyish eagerness. People meeting him for the first time usually said that he was wasting his talents in his obscure job as a village schoolmaster; but the truth was that Victor had no very marketable talents except a slight gift for music and a much more pronounced gift for dealing with children. Ineffectual in other ways, he was excellent with children; he had the proper, ruthless attitude towards them. But of course, like everyone else, he despised his own especial talent. His interests were almost purely ecclesiastical. He was what people call a CHURCHY young man. It had always been his ambition to enter the Church, and he would actually have done so if he had possessed the kind of brain that is capable of learning Greek and Hebrew. Debarred from the priesthood, he had drifted quite naturally into his position as a Church schoolmaster and organist. It kept him, so to speak, within the Church precincts. Needless to say, he was an Anglo-Catholic of the most truculent Church Times breed—more clerical than the clerics, knowledgeable about Church history, expert on vestments, and ready at any moment with a furious tirade against Modernists, Protestants, scientists, Bolshevists, and atheists.

'I was thinking,' said Dorothy as she stopped her machine and snipped off the thread, 'we might make those helmets out of old bowler hats, if we can get hold of enough of them. Cut the brims off, put on paper brims of the right shape and silver them over.'

'Oh Lord, why worry your head about such things?' said Victor, who had lost interest in the play the moment the rehearsal was over.

'It's those wretched jackboots that are worrying me the most,' said Dorothy, taking the doublet on to her knee and looking at it.

'Oh, bother the jackboots! Let's stop thinking about the play for a moment. Look here,' said Victor, unrolling his page of music, 'I want you to speak to your father for me. I wish you'd ask him whether we can't have a procession some time next month.'

'Another procession? What for?'

'Oh, I don't know. You can always find an excuse for a procession. There's the Nativity of the B.V.M. coming off on the eighth—that's good enough for a procession, I should think. We'll do it in style. I've got hold of a splendid rousing hymn that they can all bellow, and perhaps we could borrow their blue banner with the Virgin Mary on it from St Wedekind's in Millborough. If he'll say the word I'll start practising the choir at once.'

'You know he'll only say no,' said Dorothy, threading a needle to sew buttons on the doublet. 'He doesn't really approve of processions. It's much better not to ask him and make him angry.'

'Oh, but dash it all!' protested Victor. 'It's simply months since we've had a procession. I never saw such dead-alive services as we have here. You'd think we were a Baptist chapel or something, from the way we go on.'

Victor chafed ceaselessly against the dull correctness of the Rector's services. His ideal was what he called 'the real Catholic worship'—meaning unlimited incense, gilded images, and more Roman vestments. In his capacity of organist he was for ever pressing for more processions, more voluptuous music, more elaborate chanting in the liturgy, so that it was a continuous pull devil, pull baker between him and the Rector. And on this point Dorothy sided with her father. Having been brought up in the peculiar, frigid via media of Anglicanism, she was by nature averse to and half-afraid of anything 'ritualistic'.

'But dash it all!' went on Victor, 'a procession is such fun! Down the aisle, out through the west door and back through the south door, with the choir carrying candles behind and the Boy Scouts in front with the banner. It would look fine.' He sang a stave in a thin but tuneful tenor:

'Hail thee, Festival Day, blest day that art hallowed for ever!'

'If I had MY way,' he added, 'I'd have a couple of boys swinging jolly good censers of incense at the same time.'

'Yes, but you know how much Father dislikes that kind of thing. Especially when it's anything to do with the Virgin Mary. He says it's all Roman Fever and leads to people crossing themselves and genuflecting at the wrong times and goodness knows what. You remember what happened at Advent.'

The previous year, on his own responsibility, Victor had chosen as one of the hymns for Advent, Number 642, with the refrain 'Hail Mary, hail Mary, hail Mary full of grace!' This piece of popishness had annoyed the Rector extremely. At the close of the first verse he had pointedly laid down his hymn book, turned round in his stall and stood regarding the congregation with an air so stony that some of the choirboys faltered and almost broke down. Afterwards he had said that to hear the rustics bawling "Ail Mary! 'Ail Mary!' made him think he was in the four-ale bar of the Dog and Bottle.

'But dash it!' said Victor in his aggrieved way, 'your father always puts his foot down when I try and get a bit of life into the service. He won't allow us incense, or decent music, or proper vestments, or anything. And what's the result? We can't get enough people to fill the church a quarter full, even on Easter Sunday. You look round the church on Sunday morning, and it's nothing but the Boy Scouts and the Girl Guides and a few old women.'

'I know. It's dreadful,' admitted Dorothy, sewing on her button. 'It doesn't seem to make any difference what we do—we simply CAN'T get the people to come to church. Still,' she added, 'they do come to us to be married and buried. And I don't think the congregation's actually gone down this year. There were nearly two hundred people at Easter Communion.'

'Two hundred! It ought to be two thousand. That's the population of this town. The fact is that three quarters of the people in this place never go near a church in their lives. The Church has absolutely lost its hold over them. They don't know that it exists. And why? That's what I'm getting at. Why?'

'I suppose it's all this Science and Free Thought and all that,' said Dorothy rather sententiously, quoting her father.

This remark deflected Victor from what he had been about to say. He had been on the very point of saying that St Athelstan's congregation had dwindled because of the dullness of the services; but the hated words of Science and Free Thought set him off in another and even more familiar channel.

'Of course it's this so-called Free Thought!' he exclaimed, immediately beginning to fidget up and down again. 'It's these swine of atheists like Bertrand Russell and Julian Huxley and all that crowd. And what's ruined the Church is that instead of jolly well answering them and showing them up for the fools and liars they are, we just sit tight and let them spread their beastly atheist propaganda wherever they choose. It's all the fault of the bishops, of course.' (Like every Anglo-Catholic, Victor had an abysmal contempt for bishops.) 'They're all Modernists and time- servers. By Jove!' he added more cheerfully, halting, 'did you see my letter in the Church Times last week?'

'No, I'm afraid I didn't,' said Dorothy, holding another button in position with her thumb. 'What was it about?'

'Oh, Modernist bishops and all that. I got in a good swipe at old Barnes.'

It was very rarely that a week passed when Victor did not write a letter to the Church Times. He was in the thick of every controversy and in the forefront of every assault upon Modernists and atheists. He had twice been in combat with Dr Major, had written letters of withering irony about Dean Inge and the Bishop of Birmingham, and had not hesitated to attack even the fiendish Russell himself—but Russell, of course, had not dared to reply. Dorothy, to tell the truth, very seldom read the Church Times, and the Rector grew angry if he so much as saw a copy of it in the house. The weekly paper they took in the Rectory was the High Churchman's Gazette—a fine old High Tory anachronism with a small and select circulation.

'That swine Russell!' said Victor reminiscently, with his hands deep in his pockets. 'How he does make my blood boil!'

'Isn't that the man who's such a clever mathematician, or something?' said Dorothy, biting off her thread.

'Oh, I dare say he's clever enough in his own line, of course,' admitted Victor grudgingly. 'But what's that got to do with it? Just because a man's clever at figures it doesn't mean to say that— well, anyway! Let's come back to what I was saying. Why is it that we can't get people to come to church in this place? It's because our services are so dreary and godless, that's what it is. People want worship that IS worship—they want the real Catholic worship of the real Catholic Church we belong to. And they don't get if from us. All they get is the old Protestant mumbo-jumbo, and Protestantism's as dead as a doornail, and everyone knows it.'

'That's not true!' said Dorothy rather sharply as she pressed the third button into place. 'You know we're not Protestants. Father's always saying that the Church of England is the Catholic Church—he's preached I don't know how many sermons about the Apostolic Succession. That's why Lord Pockthorne and the others won't come to church here. Only he won't join in the Anglo- Catholic movement because he thinks they're too fond of ritualism for its own sake. And so do I.'

'Oh, I don't say your father isn't absolutely sound on doctrine— absolutely sound. But if he thinks we're the Catholic Church, why doesn't he hold the service in a proper Catholic way? It's a shame we can't have incense OCCASIONALLY. And his ideas about vestments— if you don't mind my saying it—are simply awful. On Easter Sunday he was wearing a Gothic cope with a modern Italian lace alb. Dash it, it's like wearing a top hat with brown boots.'

'Well, I don't think vestments are so important as you do,' said Dorothy. 'I think it's the spirit of the priest that matters, not the clothes he wears.'

'That's the kind of thing a Primitive Methodist would say!' exclaimed Victor disgustedly. 'Of course vestments are important! Where's the sense of worshipping at all if we can't make a proper job of it? Now, if you want to see what real Catholic worship CAN be like, look at St Wedekind's in Millborough! By Jove, they do things in style there! Images of the Virgin, reservation of the Sacrament—everything. They've had the Kensitites on to them three times, and they simply defy the Bishop.'

'Oh, I hate the way they go on at St Wedekind's!' said Dorothy. 'They're absolutely spiky. You can hardly see what's happening at the altar, there are such clouds of incense. I think people like that ought to turn Roman Catholic and have done with it.'

'My dear Dorothy, you ought to have been a Nonconformist. You really ought. A Plymouth Brother—or a Plymouth Sister or whatever it's called. I think your favourite hymn must be Number 567, "O my God I fear Thee, Thou art very High!"'

'Yours is Number 231, "I nightly pitch my moving tent a day's march nearer Rome!"' retorted Dorothy, winding the thread round the last button.

The argument continued for several minutes while Dorothy adorned a Cavalier's beaver hat (it was an old black felt school hat of her own) with plume and ribbons. She and Victor were never long together without being involved in an argument upon the question of 'ritualism'. In Dorothy's opinion Victor was a kind to 'go over to Rome' if not prevented, and she was very likely right. But Victor was not yet aware of his probable destiny. At present the fevers of the Anglo-Catholic movement, with its ceaseless exciting warfare on three fronts at once—Protestants to right of you, Modernists to the left of you, and, unfortunately, Roman Catholics to rear of you and always ready for a sly kick in the pants—filled his mental horizon. Scoring off Dr Major in the Church Times meant more to him than any of the serious business of life. But for all his churchiness he had not an atom of real piety in his constitution. It was essentially as a game that religious controversy appealed to him—the most absorbing game ever invented, because it goes on for ever and because just a little cheating is allowed.

'Thank goodness, that's done!' said Dorothy, twiddling the Cavalier's beaver hat round on her hand and then putting it down. 'Oh dear, what piles of things there are still to do, though! I wish I could get those wretched jackboots off my mind. What's the time, Victor?'

'It's nearly five to one.'

'Oh, good gracious! I must run. I've got three omelettes to make. I daren't trust them to Ellen. And, oh, Victor! Have you got anything you can give us for the jumble sale? If you had an old pair of trousers you could give us, that would be best of all, because we can always sell trousers.'

'Trousers? No. But I tell you what I have got, though. I've got a copy of The Pilgrim's Progress and another of Foxe's Book of Martyrs that I've been wanting to get rid of for years. Beastly Protestant trash! An old Dissenting aunt of mine gave them to me.— Doesn't it make you sick, all this cadging for pennies? Now, if we only held our services in a proper Catholic way, so that we could get up a proper congregation, don't you see, we shouldn't need—'

'That'll be splendid,' said Dorothy. 'We always have a stall for books—we charge a penny for each book, and nearly all of them get sold. We simply MUST make that jumble sale a success, Victor! I'm counting on Miss Mayfill to give us something really NICE. What I'm specially hoping is that she might give us that beautiful old Lowestoft china tea service of hers, and we could sell it for five pounds at least. I've been making special prayers all the morning that she'll give it to us.'

'Oh?' said Victor, less enthusiastically than usual. Like Proggett earlier in the morning, he was embarrassed by the word 'prayer'. He was ready to talk all day long about a point of ritual; but the mention of private devotions struck him as slightly indecent. 'Don't forget to ask your father about the procession,' he said, getting back to a more congenial topic.

'All right, I'll ask him. But you know how it'll be. He'll only get annoyed and say it's Roman Fever.'

'Oh, damn Roman Fever!' said Victor, who, unlike Dorothy, did not set himself penances for swearing.

Dorothy hurried to the kitchen, discovered that there were only five eggs to make the omelettes for three people, and decided to make one large omelette and swell it out a bit with the cold boiled potatoes left over from yesterday. With a short prayer for the success of the omelette (for omelettes are so dreadfully apt to get broken when you take them out of the pan), she whipped up the eggs, while Victor made off down the drive, half wistfully and half sulkily humming 'Hail thee, Festival Day', and passing on his way a disgusted-looking manservant carrying the two handleless chamber- pots which were Miss Mayfill's contribution to the jumble sale.

6

It was a little after ten o'clock. Various things had happened—nothing, however, of any particular importance; only the usual round of parish jobs that filled up Dorothy's afternoon and evening. Now, as she had arranged earlier in the day, she was at Mr Warburton's house, and was trying to hold her own in one of those meandering arguments in which he delighted to entangle her.

They were talking—but indeed, Mr Warburton never failed to manoeuvre the conversation towards this subject—about the question of religious belief.

'My dear Dorothy,' he was saying argumentatively, as he walked up and down with one hand in his coat pocket and the other manipulating a Brazilian cigar. 'My dear Dorothy, you don't seriously mean to tell me that at your age—twenty-seven, I believe—and with your intelligence, you will retain your religious beliefs more or less in toto?'

'Of course I do. You know I do.'

'Oh, come, now! The whole bag of tricks? All that nonsense that you learned at your mother's knee—surely you're not going to pretend to me that you still believe in it? But of course you don't! You can't! You're afraid to own up, that's all it is. No need to worry about that here, you know. The Rural Dean's wife isn't listening, and _I_ won't give the show away.'

'I don't know what you mean by "all that NONSENSE",' began Dorothy, sitting up straighter in her chair, a little offended.

'Well, let's take an instance. Something particularly hard to swallow—Hell, for instance. Do you believe in Hell? When I say BELIEVE, mind you, I'm not asking whether you believe it in some milk and water metaphorical way like these Modernist bishops young Victor Stone gets so excited about. I mean do you believe in it literally? Do you believe in Hell as you believe in Australia?'

'Yes, of course I do,' said Dorothy, and she endeavoured to explain to him that the existence of Hell is much more real and permanent than the existence of Australia.

'Hm,' said Mr Warburton, unimpressed. 'Very sound in its way, of course. But what always makes me so suspicious of you religious people is that you're so deucedly cold-blooded about your beliefs. It shows a very poor imagination, to say the least of it. Here am I an infidel and blasphemer and neck deep in at least six out of the Seven Deadly, and obviously doomed to eternal torment. There's no knowing that in an hour's time I mayn't be roasting in the hottest part of Hell. And yet you can sit there talking to me as calmly as though I'd nothing the matter with me. Now, if I'd merely got cancer or leprosy or some other bodily ailment, you'd be quite distressed about it—at least, I like to flatter myself that you would. Whereas, when I'm going to sizzle on the grid throughout eternity, you seem positively unconcerned about it.'

'I never said YOU were going to Hell,' said Dorothy somewhat uncomfortably, and wishing that the conversation would take a different turn. For the truth was, though she was not going to tell him so, that the point Mr Warburton had raised was one with which she herself had had certain difficulties. She did indeed believe in Hell, but she had never been able to persuade herself that anyone actually WENT there. She believed that Hell existed, but that it was empty. Uncertain of the orthodoxy of this belief, she preferred to keep it to herself. 'It's never certain that ANYONE is going to Hell,' she said more firmly, feeling that here at least she was on sure ground.

'What!' said Mr Warburton, halting in mock surprise. 'Surely you don't mean to say that there's hope for me yet?'

'Of course there is. It's only those horrid Predestination people who pretend that you go to Hell whether you repent or not. You don't think the Church of England are Calvinists, do you?'

'I suppose there's always the chance of getting off on a plea of Invincible Ignorance,' said Mr Warburton reflectively; and then, more confidently: 'Do you know, Dorothy, I've a sort of feeling that even now, after knowing me two years, you've still half an idea you can make a convert of me. A lost sheep—brand plucked from the burning, and all that. I believe you still hope against hope that one of these days my eyes will be opened and you'll meet me at Holy Communion at seven o'clock on some damned cold winter morning. Don't you?'

'Well—' said Dorothy, again uncomfortably. She did, in fact, entertain some such hope about Mr Warburton, though he was not exactly a promising case for conversion. It was not in her nature to see a fellow being in a state of unbelief without making some effort to reclaim him. What hours she had spent, at different times, earnestly debating with vague village atheists who could not produce a single intelligible reason for their unbelief! 'Yes,' she admitted finally, not particularly wanting to make the admission, but not wanting to prevaricate.

Mr Warburton laughed delightedly.

'You've a hopeful nature,' he said. 'But you aren't afraid, by any chance, that I might convert YOU? "The dog it was that died", you may remember.'

At this Dorothy merely smiled. 'Don't let him see he's shocking you'—that was always her maxim when she was talking to Mr Warburton. They had been arguing in this manner, without coming to any kind of conclusion, for the past hour, and might have gone on for the rest of the night if Dorothy had been willing to stay; for Mr Warburton delighted in teasing her about her religious beliefs. He had that fatal cleverness that so often goes with unbelief, and in their arguments, though Dorothy was always RIGHT, she was not always victorious. They were sitting, or rather Dorothy was sitting and Mr Warburton was standing, in a large agreeable room, giving on a moonlit lawn, that Mr Warburton called his 'studio'— not that there was any sign of work ever having been done in it. To Dorothy's great disappointment, the celebrated Mr Bewley had not turned up. (As a matter of fact, neither Mr Bewley, nor his wife, nor his novel entitled Fishpools and Concubines, actually existed. Mr Warburton had invented all three of them on the spur of the moment, as a pretext for inviting Dorothy to his house, well knowing that she would never come unchaperoned.) Dorothy had felt rather uneasy on finding that Mr Warburton was alone. It had occurred to her, indeed she had felt perfectly certain, that it would be wiser to go home at once; but she had stayed, chiefly because she was horribly tired and the leather armchair into which Mr Warburton had thrust her the moment she entered the house was too comfortable to leave. Now, however, her conscience was pricking her. It DIDN'T DO to stay too late at his house—people would talk if they heard of it. Besides, there was a multitude of jobs that she ought to be doing and that she had neglected in order to come here. She was so little used to idleness that even an hour spent in mere talking seemed to her vaguely sinful.

She made an effort, and straightened herself in the too-comfortable chair. 'I think, if you don't mind, it's really time I was getting home,' she said.

'Talking of Invincible Ignorance,' went on Mr Warburton, taking no notice of Dorothy's remark, 'I forget whether I ever told you that once when I was standing outside the World's End pub in Chelsea, waiting for a taxi, a damned ugly little Salvation Army lassie came up to me and said—without any kind of introduction, you know— "What will you say at the Judgement Seat?" I said, "I am reserving my defence." Rather neat, I think, don't you?'

Dorothy did not answer. Her conscience had given her another and harder jab—she had remembered those wretched, unmade jackboots, and the fact that at least one of them had got to be made tonight. She was, however, unbearably tired. She had had an exhausting afternoon, starting off with ten miles or so bicycling to and fro in the sun, delivering the parish magazine, and continuing with the Mothers' Union tea in the hot little wooden-walled room behind the parish hall. The Mothers met every Wednesday afternoon to have tea and do some charitable sewing while Dorothy read aloud to them. (At present she was reading Gene Stratton Porter's A Girl of the Limberlost.) It was nearly always upon Dorothy that jobs of that kind devolved, because the phalanx of devoted women (the church fowls, they are called) who do the dirty work of most parishes had dwindled at Knype Hill to four or five at most. The only helper on whom Dorothy could count at all regularly was Miss Foote, a tall, rabbit-faced, dithering virgin of thirty-five, who meant well but made a mess of everything and was in a perpetual state of flurry. Mr Warburton used to say that she reminded him of a comet—'a ridiculous blunt-nosed creature rushing round on an eccentric orbit and always a little behind time'. You could trust Miss Foote with the church decorations, but not with the Mothers or the Sunday School, because, though a regular churchgoer, her orthodoxy was suspect. She had confided to Dorothy that she could worship God best under the blue dome of the sky. After tea Dorothy had dashed up to the church to put fresh flowers on the altar, and then she had typed out her father's sermon—her typewriter was a rickety pre-Boer War 'invisible', on which you couldn't average eight hundred words an hour—and after supper she had weeded the pea rows until the light failed and her back seemed to be breaking. With one thing and another, she was even more tired than usual.

'I really MUST be getting home,' she repeated more firmly. 'I'm sure it's getting fearfully late.'

'Home?' said Mr Warburton. 'Nonsense! The evening's hardly begun.'

He was walking up and down the room again, with his hands in his coat pockets, having thrown away his cigar. The spectre of the unmade jackboots stalked back into Dorothy's mind. She would, she suddenly decided, make two jackboots tonight instead of only one, as a penance for the hour she had wasted. She was just beginning to make a mental sketch of the way she would cut out the pieces of brown paper for the insteps, when she noticed that Mr Warburton had halted behind her chair.

'What time is it, do you know?' she said.

'I dare say it might be half past ten. But people like you and me don't talk of such vulgar subjects as the time.'

'If it's half past ten, then I really must be going,' said Dorothy. I've got a whole lot of work to do before I go to bed.'

'Work! At this time of night? Impossible!'

'Yes, I have. I've got to make a pair of jackboots.'

'You've got to make a pair of WHAT?' said Mr Warburton.

'Of jackboots. For the play the schoolchildren are acting. We make them out of glue and brown paper.'

'Glue and brown paper! Good God!' murmured Mr Warburton. He went on, chiefly to cover the fact that he was drawing nearer to Dorothy's chair: 'What a life you lead! Messing about with glue and brown paper in the middle of the night! I must say, there are times when I feel just a little glad that I'm not a clergyman's daughter.'

'I think—' began Dorothy.

But at the same moment Mr Warburton, invisible behind her chair, had lowered his hands and taken her gently by the shoulders. Dorothy immediately wriggled herself in an effort to get free of him; but Mr Warburton pressed her back into her place.

'Keep still,' he said peaceably.

'Let me go!' exclaimed Dorothy.

Mr Warburton ran his right hand caressingly down her upper arm. There was something very revealing, very characteristic in the way he did it; it was the lingering, appraising touch of a man to whom a woman's body is valuable precisely in the same way as though it were something to eat.

'You really have extraordinary nice arms,' he said. 'How on earth have you managed to remain unmarried all these years?'

'Let me go at once!' repeated Dorothy, beginning to struggle again.

'But I don't particularly want to let you go,' objected Mr Warburton.

'PLEASE don't stroke my arm like that! I don't like it!'

'What a curious child you are! Why don't you like it?'

'I tell you I don't like it!'

'Now don't go and turn round,' said Mr Warburton mildly. 'You don't seem to realize how tactful it was on my part to approach you from behind your back. If you turn round you'll see that I'm old enough to be your father, and hideously bald into the bargain. But if you'll only keep still and not look at me you can imagine I'm Ivor Novello.'

Dorothy caught sight of the hand that was caressing her—a large, pink, very masculine hand, with thick fingers and a fleece of gold hairs upon the back. She turned very pale; the expression of her face altered from mere annoyance to aversion and dread. She made a violent effort, wrenched herself free, and stood up, facing him.

'I DO wish you wouldn't do that!' she said, half in anger and half in distress.

'What is the matter with you?' said Mr Warburton.

He had stood upright, in his normal pose, entirely unconcerned, and he looked at her with a touch of curiosity. Her face had changed. It was not only that she had turned pale; there was a withdrawn, half-frightened look in her eyes—almost as though, for the moment, she were looking at him with the eyes of a stranger. He perceived that he had wounded her in some way which he did not understand, and which perhaps she did not want him to understand.

'What is the matter with you?' he repeated.

'WHY must you do that every time you meet me?'

'"Every time I meet you" is an exaggeration,' said Mr Warburton. 'It's really very seldom that I get the opportunity. But if you really and truly don't like it—'

'Of course I don't like it! You know I don't like it!'

'Well, well! Then let's say no more about it,' said Mr Warburton generously. 'Sit down, and we'll change the subject.'

He was totally devoid of shame. It was perhaps his most outstanding characteristic. Having attempted to seduce her, and failed, he was quite willing to go on with the conversation as though nothing whatever had happened.

'I'm going home at once,' said Dorothy. 'I can't stay here any longer.'

'Oh nonsense! Sit down and forget about it. We'll talk of moral theology, or cathedral architecture, or the Girl Guides' cooking classes, or anything you choose. Think how bored I shall be all alone if you go home at this hour.'

But Dorothy persisted, and there was an argument. Even if it had not been his intention to make love to her—and whatever he might promise he would certainly begin again in a few minutes if she did not go—Mr Warburton would have pressed her to stay, for, like all thoroughly idle people, he had a horror of going to bed and no conception of the value of time. He would, if you let him, keep you talking till three or four in the morning. Even when Dorothy finally escaped, he walked beside her down the moonlit drive, still talking voluminously and with such perfect good humour that she found it impossible to be angry with him any longer.

'I'm leaving first thing tomorrow,' he told her as they reached the gate. 'I'm going to take the car to town and pick up the kids—the BASTARDS, you know—and we're leaving for France the next day. I'm not certain where we shall go after that; eastern Europe, perhaps. Prague, Vienna, Bucharest.'

'How nice,' said Dorothy.

Mr Warburton, with an adroitness surprising in so large and stout a man, had manoeuvred himself between Dorothy and the gate.

'I shall be away six months or more,' he said. 'And of course I needn't ask, before so long a parting, whether you want to kiss me good-bye?'

Before she knew what he was doing he had put his arm about her and drawn her against him. She drew back—too late; he kissed her on the cheek—would have kissed her on the mouth if she had not turned her head away in time. She struggled in his arms, violently and for a moment helplessly.

'Oh, let me go!' she cried. 'DO let me go!'

'I believe I pointed out before,' said Mr Warburton, holding her easily against him, 'that I don't want to let you go.'

'But we're standing right in front of Mrs Semprill's window! She'll see us absolutely for certain!'

'Oh, good God! So she will!' said Mr Warburton. 'I was forgetting.'

Impressed by this argument, as he would not have been by any other, he let Dorothy go. She promptly put the gate between Mr Warburton and herself. He, meanwhile, was scrutinizing Mrs Semprill's windows.

'I can't see a light anywhere,' he said finally. 'With any luck the blasted hag hasn't seen us.'

'Good-bye,' said Dorothy briefly. 'This time I really MUST go. Remember me to the children.'

With this she made off as fast as she could go without actually running, to get out of his reach before he should attempt to kiss her again.

Even as she did so a sound checked her for an instant—the unmistakable bang of a window shutting, somewhere in Mrs Semprill's house. Could Mrs Semprill have been watching them after all? But (reflected Dorothy) of COURSE she had been watching them! What else could you expect? You could hardly imagine Mrs Semprill missing such a scene as that. And if she HAD been watching them, undoubtedly the story would be all over the town tomorrow morning, and it would lose nothing in the telling. But this thought, sinister though it was, did no more than flight momentarily through Dorothy's mind as she hurried down the road.

When she was well out of sight of Mr Warburton's house she stopped, took out her handkerchief and scrubbed the place on her cheek where he had kissed her. She scrubbed it vigorously enough to bring the blood into her cheek. It was not until she had quite rubbed out the imaginary stain which his lips had left there that she walked on again.

What he had done had upset her. Even now her heart was knocking and fluttering uncomfortably. I can't BEAR that kind of thing! she repeated to herself several times over. And unfortunately this was no more than the literal truth; she really could not bear it. To be kissed or fondled by a man—to feel heavy male arms about her and thick male lips bearing down upon her own—was terrifying and repulsive to her. Even in memory or imagination it made her wince. It was her especial secret, the especial, incurable disability that she carried through life.

If only they would leave you ALONE! she thought as she walked onwards a little more slowly. That was how she put it to herself habitually—'If only they would leave you ALONE!' For it was not that in other ways she disliked men. On the contrary, she liked them better than women. Part of Mr Warburton's hold over her was in the fact that he was a man and had the careless good humour and the intellectual largeness that women so seldom have. But why couldn't they leave you ALONE? Why did they always have to kiss you and maul you about? They were dreadful when they kissed you— dreadful and a little disgusting, like some large, furry beast that rubs itself against you, all too friendly and yet liable to turn dangerous at any moment. And beyond their kissing and mauling there lay always the suggestion of those other, monstrous things ('ALL THAT' was her name for them) of which she could hardly even bear to think.

Of course, she had had her share, and rather more than her share, of casual attention from men. She was just pretty enough, and just plain enough, to be the kind of girl that men habitually pester. For when a man wants a little casual amusement, he usually picks out a girl who is not TOO pretty. Pretty girls (so he reasons) are spoilt and therefore capricious; but plain girls are easy game. And even if you are a clergyman's daughter, even if you live in a town like Knype Hill and spend almost your entire life in parish work, you don't altogether escape pursuit. Dorothy was all too used to it—all too used to the fattish middle-aged men, with their fishily hopeful eyes, who slowed down their cars when you passed them on the road, or who manoeuvred an introduction and then began pinching your elbow about ten minutes afterwards. Men of all descriptions. Even a clergyman, on one occasion—a bishop's chaplain, he was....

But the trouble was that it was not better, but oh! infinitely worse when they were the right kind of man and the advances they made you were honourable. Her mind slipped backwards five years, to Francis Moon, curate in those days at St Wedekind's in Millborough. Dear Francis! How gladly would she have married him if only it had not been for ALL THAT! Over and over again he had asked her to marry him, and of course she had had to say No; and, equally of course, he had never known why. Impossible to tell him why. And then he had gone away, and only a year later had died so irrelevantly of pneumonia. She whispered a prayer for his soul, momentarily forgetting that her father did not really approve of prayers for the dead, and then, with an effort, pushed the memory aside. Ah, better not to think of it again! It hurt her in her breast to think of it.

She could never marry, she had decided long ago upon that. Even when she was a child she had known it. Nothing would ever overcome her horror of ALL THAT—at the very thought of it something within her seemed to shrink and freeze. And of course, in a sense she did not want to overcome it. For, like all abnormal people, she was not fully aware that she was abnormal.

And yet, though her sexual coldness seemed to her natural and inevitable, she knew well enough how it was that it had begun. She could remember, as clearly as though it were yesterday, certain dreadful scenes between her father and her mother—scenes that she had witnessed when she was no more than nine years old. They had left a deep, secret wound in her mind. And then a little later she had been frightened by some old steel engravings of nymphs pursued by satyrs. To her childish mind there was something inexplicably, horribly sinister in those horned, semi-human creatures that lurked in thickets and behind large trees, ready to come bounding forth in sudden swift pursuit. For a whole year of her childhood she had actually been afraid to walk through woods alone, for fear of satyrs. She had grown out of the fear, of course, but not out of the feeling that was associated with it. The satyr had remained with her as a symbol. Perhaps she would never grow out of it, that special feeling of dread, of hopeless flight from something more than rationally dreadful—the stamp of hooves in the lonely wood, the lean, furry thighs of the satyr. It was a thing not to be altered, not to be argued away. It is, moreover, a thing too common nowadays, among educated women, to occasion any kind of surprise.

Most of Dorothy's agitation had disappeared by the time she reached the rectory. The thoughts of satyrs and Mr Warburton, of Francis Moon and her foredoomed sterility, which had been going to and fro in her mind, faded out of it and were replaced by the accusing image of a jackboot. She remembered that she had the best part of two hours' work to do before going to bed tonight. The house was in darkness. She went round to the back and slipped in on tiptoe by the scullery door, for fear of waking her father, who was probably asleep already.

As she felt her way through the dark passage to the conservatory, she suddenly decided that she had gone wrong in going to Mr Warburton's house tonight. She would, she resolved, never go there again, even when she was certain that somebody else would be there as well. Moreover, she would do penance tomorrow for having gone there tonight. Having lighted the lamp, before doing anything else she found her 'memo list', which was already written out for tomorrow, and pencilled a capital P against 'breakfast',

P stood for penance—no bacon again for breakfast tomorrow. Then she lighted the oilstove under the glue-pot.

The light of the lamp fell yellow upon her sewing-machine and upon the pile of half-finished clothes on the table, reminding her of the yet greater pile of clothes that were not even begun; reminding her, also, that she was dreadfully, overwhelmingly tired. She had forgotten her tiredness at the moment when Mr Warburton laid his hands on her shoulders, but now it had come back upon her with double force. Moreover, there was a somehow exceptional quality about her tiredness tonight. She felt, in an almost literal sense of the words, washed out. As she stood beside the table she had a sudden, very strange feeling as though her mind had been entirely emptied, so that for several seconds she actually forgot what it was that she had come into the conservatory to do.

Then she remembered—the jackboots, of course! Some contemptible little demon whispered in her ear, 'Why not go straight to bed and leave the jackboots till tomorrow?' She uttered a prayer for strength, and pinched herself. Come on, Dorothy! No slacking please! Luke ix, 62. Then, clearing some of the litter off the table, she got out her scissors, a pencil, and four sheets of brown paper, and sat down to cut out those troublesome insteps for the jackboots while the glue was boiling.

When the grandfather clock in her father's study struck midnight she was still at work. She had shaped both jackboots by this time, and was reinforcing them by pasting narrow strips of paper all over them—a long, messy job. Every bone in her body was aching, and her eyes were sticky with sleep. Indeed, it was only rather dimly that she remembered what she was doing. But she worked on, mechanically pasting strip after strip of paper into place, and pinching herself every two minutes to counteract the hypnotic sound of the oilstove singing beneath the glue-pot.

CHAPTER 2

1

Out of a black, dreamless sleep, with the sense of being drawn upwards through enormous and gradually lightening abysses, Dorothy awoke to a species of consciousness.

Her eyes were still closed. By degrees, however, their lids became less opaque to the light, and then flickered open of their own accord. She was looking out upon a street—a shabby, lively street of small shops and narrow-faced houses, with streams of men, trams, and cars passing in either direction.

But as yet it could not properly be said that she was LOOKING. For the things she saw were not apprehended as men, trams, and cars, nor as anything in particular; they were not even apprehended as things moving; not even as THINGS. She merely SAW, as an animal sees, without speculation and almost without consciousness. The noises of the street—the confused din of voices, the hooting of horns and the scream of the trams grinding on their gritty rails— flowed through her head provoking purely physical responses. She had no words, nor any conception of the purpose of such things as words, nor any consciousness of time or place, or of her own body or even of her own existence.

Nevertheless, by degrees her perceptions became sharper. The stream of moving things began to penetrate beyond her eyes and sort themselves out into separate images in her brain. She began, still wordlessly, to observe the shapes of things. A long-shaped thing swam past, supported on four other, narrower long-shaped things, and drawing after it a square-shaped thing balanced on two circles. Dorothy watched it pass; and suddenly, as though spontaneously, a word flashed into her mind. The word was 'horse'. It faded, but returned presently in the more complex form: 'THAT IS A HORSE.' Other words followed—'house', 'street', 'tram', 'car', 'bicycle'— until in a few minutes she had found a name for almost everything within sight. She discovered the words 'man' and 'woman', and, speculating upon these words, discovered that she knew the difference between living and inanimate things, and between human beings and horses, and between men and women.

It was only now, after becoming aware of most of the things about her, that she became aware of HERSELF. Hitherto she had been as it were a pair of eyes with a receptive but purely impersonal brain behind them. But now, with a curious little shock, she discovered her separate and unique existence; she could FEEL herself existing; it was as though something within her were exclaiming 'I am I!' Also, in some way she knew that this 'I' had existed and been the same from remote periods in the past, though it was a past of which she had no remembrance.

But it was only for a moment that this discovery occupied her. From the first there was a sense of incompleteness in it, of something vaguely unsatisfactory. And it was this: the 'I am I' which had seemed an answer had itself become a question. It was no longer 'I am I', but 'WHO am I'?

WHO WAS SHE? She turned the question over in her mind, and found that she had not the dimmest notion of who she was; except that, watching the people and horses passing, she grasped that she was a human being and not a horse. And that the question altered itself and took this form: 'Am I a man or a woman?' Again neither feeling nor memory gave any clue to the answer. But at that moment, by accident possibly, her finger-tips brushed against her body. She realized more clearly than before that her body existed, and that it was her own—that it was, in fact, herself. She began to explore it with her hands, and her hands encountered breasts. She was a woman, therefore. Only women had breasts. In some way she knew, without knowing how she knew, that all those women who passed had breasts beneath their clothes, though she could not see them.

She now grasped that in order to identify herself she must examine her own body, beginning with her face; and for some moments she actually attempted to look at her own face, before realizing that this was impossible. She looked down, and saw a shabby black satin dress, rather long, a pair of flesh-coloured artificial silk stockings, laddered and dirty, and a pair of very shabby black satin shoes with high heels. None of them was in the least familiar to her. She examined her hands, and they were both strange and unstrange. They were smallish hands, with hard palms, and very dirty. After a moment she realized that it was their dirtiness that made them strange to her. The hands themselves seemed natural and appropriate, though she did not recognize them.

After hesitating a few moments longer, she turned to her left and began to walk slowly along the pavement. A fragment of knowledge had come to her, mysteriously, out of the blank past: the existence of mirrors, their purpose, and the fact that there are often mirrors in shop windows. After a moment she came to a cheap little jeweller's shop in which a strip of mirror, set at an angle, reflected the faces of people passing. Dorothy picked her reflection out from among a dozen others, immediately realizing it to be her own. Yet it could not be said that she had recognized it; she had no memory of ever having seen it till this moment. It showed her a woman's youngish face, thin, very blonde, with crow's- feet round the eyes, and faintly smudged with dirt. A vulgar black cloche hat was stuck carelessly on the head, concealing most of the hair. The face was quite unfamiliar to her, and yet not strange. She had not known till this moment what face to expect, but now that she had seen it she realized that it was the face she might have expected. It was appropriate. It corresponded to something within her.

As she turned away from the jeweller's mirror, she caught sight of the words 'Fry's Chocolate' on a shop window opposite, and discovered that she understood the purpose of writing, and also, after a momentary effort, that she was able to read. Her eyes flitted across the street, taking in and deciphering odd scraps of print; the names of shops, advertisements, newspaper posters. She spelled out the letters of two red and white posters outside a tobacconist's shop. One of them read, 'Fresh Rumours about Rector's Daughter', and the other, 'Rector's Daughter. Now believed in Paris'. Then she looked upwards, and saw in white lettering on the corner of a house: 'New Kent Road'. The words arrested her. She grasped that she was standing in the New Kent Road, and—another fragment of her mysterious knowledge—the New Kent Road was somewhere in London. So she was in London.

As she made this discovery a peculiar tremor ran through her. Her mind was now fully awakened; she grasped, as she had not grasped before, the strangeness of her situation, and it bewildered and frightened her. What could it all MEAN? What was she doing here? How had she got here? What had happened to her?

The answer was not long in coming. She thought—and it seemed to her that she understood perfectly well what the words meant: 'Of course! I've lost my memory!'

At this moment two youths and a girl who were trudging past, the youths with clumsy sacking bundles on their backs, stopped and looked curiously at Dorothy. They hesitated for a moment, then walked on, but halted again by a lamp-post five yards away. Dorothy saw them looking back at her and talking among themselves. One of the youths was about twenty, narrow-chested, black-haired, ruddy-cheeked, good-looking in a nosy cockney way, and dressed in the wreck of a raffishly smart blue suit and a check cap. The other was about twenty-six, squat, nimble, and powerful, with a snub nose, a clear pink skin and huge lips as coarse as sausages, exposing strong yellow teeth. He was frankly ragged, and he had a mat of orange-coloured hair cropped short and growing low on his head, which gave him a startling resemblance to an orang-outang. The girl was a silly-looking, plump creature, dressed in clothes very like Dorothy's own. Dorothy could hear some of what they were saying:

'That tart looks ill,' said the girl.

The orange-headed one, who was singing 'Sonny Boy' in a good baritone voice, stopped singing to answer. 'She ain't ill,' he said. 'She's on the beach all right, though. Same as us.'

'She'd do jest nicely for Nobby, wouldn't she?' said the dark-haired one.

'Oh, YOU!' exclaimed the girl with a shocked-amorous air, pretending to smack the dark one over the head.

The youths had lowered their bundles and leaned them against the lamp-post. All three of them now came rather hesitantly towards Dorothy, the orange-headed one, whose name seemed to be Nobby, leading the way as their ambassador. He moved with a gambolling, apelike gait, and his grin was so frank and wide that it was impossible not to smile back at him. He addressed Dorothy in a friendly way.

'Hullo, kid!'

'Hullo!'

'You on the beach, kid?'

'On the beach?'

'Well, on the bum?'

'On the bum?'

'Christ! she's batty,' murmured the girl, twitching at the black- haired one's arm as though to pull him away.

'Well, what I mean to say, kid—have you got any money?'

'I don't know.'

At this all three looked at one another in stupefaction. For a moment they probably thought that Dorothy really WAS batty. But simultaneously Dorothy, who had earlier discovered a small pocket in the side of her dress, put her hand into it and felt the outline of a large coin.

'I believe I've got a penny,' she said.

'A penny!' said the dark youth disgustedly, '—lot of good that is to us!'

Dorothy drew it out. It was a half-crown. An astonishing change came over the faces of the three others. Nobby's mouth split open with delight, he gambolled several steps to and fro like some great jubilant ape, and then, halting, took Dorothy confidentially by the arm.

'That's the mulligatawny!' he said. 'We've struck it lucky—and so've you, kid, believe me. You're going to bless the day you set eyes on us lot. We're going to make your fortune for you, we are. Now, see here, kid—are you on to go into cahoots with us three?'

'What?' said Dorothy.

'What I mean to say—how about you chumming in with Flo and Charlie and me? Partners, see? Comrades all, shoulder to shoulder. United we stand, divided we fall. We put up the brains, you put up the money. How about it, kid? Are you on, or are you off?'

'Shut up, Nobby!' interrupted the girl. 'She don't understand a word of what you're saying. Talk to her proper, can't you?'

'That'll do, Flo,' said Nobby equably. 'You keep it shut and leave the talking to me. I got a way with the tarts, I have. Now, you listen to me, kid—what might your name happen to be, kid?'

Dorothy was within an ace of saying 'I don't know,' but she was sufficiently on the alert to stop herself in time. Choosing a feminine name from the half-dozen that sprang immediately into her mind, she answered, 'Ellen.'

'Ellen. That's the mulligatawny. No surnames when you're on the bum. Well now, Ellen dear, you listen to me. Us three are going down hopping, see—'

'Hopping?'

''Opping!' put in the dark youth impatiently, as though disgusted by Dorothy's ignorance. His voice and manner were rather sullen, and his accent much baser than Nobby's. 'Pickin' 'ops—dahn in Kent! C'n understand that, can't yer?'

'Oh, HOPS! For beer?'

'That's the mulligatawny! Coming on fine, she is. Well, kid, 'z I was saying, here's us three going down hopping, and got a job promised us and all—Blessington's farm, Lower Molesworth. Only we're just a bit in the mulligatawny, see? Because we ain't got a brown between us, and we got to do it on the toby—thirty-five miles it is—and got to tap for our tommy and skipper at night as well. And that's a bit of a mulligatawny, with ladies in the party. But now s'pose f'rinstance you was to come along with us, see? We c'd take the twopenny tram far as Bromley, and that's fifteen miles done, and we won't need skipper more'n one night on the way. And you can chum in at our bin—four to a bin's the best picking—and if Blessington's paying twopence a bushel you'll turn your ten bob a week easy. What do you say to it, kid? Your two and a tanner won't do you much good here in Smoke. But you go into partnership with us, and you'll get your kip for a month and something over—and WE'LL get a lift to Bromley and a bit of scran as well.'

About a quarter of his speech was intelligible to Dorothy. She asked rather at random:

'What is SCRAN?'

'Scran? Tommy—food. I can see YOU ain't been long on the beach, kid.'

'Oh.... Well, you want me to come down hop-picking with you, is that it?'

'That's it, Ellen my dear. Are you on, or are you off?'

'All right,' said Dorothy promptly. 'I'll come.'

She made this decision without any misgiving whatever. It is true that if she had had time to think over her position, she would probably have acted differently; in all probability she would have gone to a police station and asked for assistance. That would have been the sensible course to take. But Nobby and the others had appeared just at the critical moment, and, helpless as she was, it seemed quite natural to throw in her lot with the first human being who presented himself. Moreover, for some reason which she did not understand, it reassured her to hear that they were making for Kent. Kent, it seemed to her, was the very place to which she wanted to go. The others showed no further curiosity, and asked no uncomfortable questions. Nobby simply said, 'O.K. That's the mulligatawny!' and then gently took Dorothy's half-crown out of her hand and slid it into his pocket—in case she should lose it, he explained. The dark youth—apparently his name was Charlie—said in his surly, disagreeable way:

'Come on, less get movin'! It's 'ar-parse two already. We don't want to miss that there —— tram. Where d'they start from, Nobby?'

'The Elephant,' said Nobby: 'and we got to catch it before four o'clock, because they don't give no free rides after four.'

'Come on, then, don't less waste no more time. Nice job we'll 'ave of it if we got to 'ike it down to Bromley AND look for a place to skipper in the —— dark. C'm on, Flo.'

'Quick march!' said Nobby, swinging his bundle on to his shoulder.

They set out, without more words said, Dorothy, still bewildered but feeling much better than she had felt half an hour ago, walked beside Flo and Charlie, who talked to one another and took no further notice of her. From the very first they seemed to hold themselves a little aloof from Dorothy—willing enough to share her half-crown, but with no friendly feelings towards her. Nobby marched in front, stepping out briskly in spite of his burden, and singing, with spirited imitations of military music, the well-known military song of which the only recorded words seem to be:

> '"——!" was all the band could play;
> "——! ——!" And the same to you!'

2

This was the twenty-ninth of August. It was on the night of the twenty-first that Dorothy had fallen asleep in the conservatory; so that there had been an interregnum in her life of not quite eight days.

The thing that had happened to her was commonplace enough—almost every week one reads in the newspapers of a similar case. A man disappears from home, is lost sight of for days or weeks, and presently fetches up at a police station or in a hospital, with no notion of who he is or where he has come from. As a rule it is impossible to tell how he has spent the intervening time; he has been wandering, presumably, in some hypnotic or somnambulistic state in which he has nevertheless been able to pass for normal. In Dorothy's case only one thing is certain, and that is that she had been robbed at some time during her travels; for the clothes she was wearing were not her own, and her gold cross was missing.

At the moment when Nobby accosted her, she was already on the road to recovery; and if she had been properly cared for, her memory might have come back to her within a few days or even hours. A very small thing would have been enough to accomplish it; a chance meeting with a friend, a photograph of her home, a few questions skilfully put. But as it was, the slight mental stimulus that she needed was never given. She was left in the peculiar state in which she had first found herself—a state in which her mind was potentially normal, but not quite strung up to the effort of puzzling out her own identity.

For of course, once she had thrown in her lot with Nobby and the others, all chance of reflection was gone. There was no time to sit down and think the matter over—no time to come to grips with her difficulty and reason her way to its solution. In the strange, dirty sub-world into which she was instantly plunged, even five minutes of consecutive thought would have been impossible. The days passed in ceaseless nightmarish activity. Indeed, it was very like a nightmare; a nightmare not of urgent terrors, but of hunger, squalor, and fatigue, and of alternating heat and cold. Afterwards, when she looked back upon that time, days and nights merged themselves together so that she could never remember with perfect certainty how many of them there had been. She only knew that for some indefinite period she had been perpetually footsore and almost perpetually hungry. Hunger and the soreness of her feet were her clearest memories of that time; and also the cold of the nights, and a peculiar, blowsy, witless feeling that came of sleeplessness and constant exposure to the air.

After getting to Bromley they had 'drummed up' on a horrible, paper-littered rubbish dump, reeking with the refuse of several slaughter-houses, and then passed a shuddering night, with only sacks for cover, in long wet grass on the edge of a recreation ground. In the morning they had started out, on foot, for the hopfields. Even at this early date Dorothy had discovered that the tale Nobby had told her, about the promise of a job, was totally untrue. He had invented it—he confessed this quite light-heartedly—to induce her to come with them. Their only chance of getting a job was to march down into the hop country and apply at every farm till they found one where pickers were still needed.

They had perhaps thirty-five miles to go, as the crow flies, and yet at the end of three days they had barely reached the fringe of the hopfields. The need of getting food, of course, was what slowed their progress. They could have marched the whole distance in two days or even in a day if they had not been obliged to feed themselves. As it was, they had hardly even time to think of whether they were going in the direction of the hopfields or not; it was food that dictated all their movements. Dorothy's half-crown had melted within a few hours, and after that there was nothing for it except to beg. But there came the difficulty. One person can beg his food easily enough on the road, and even two can manage it, but it is a very different matter when there are four people together. In such circumstances one can only keep alive if one hunts for food as persistently and single-mindedly as a wild beast. Food—that was their sole preoccupation during those three days—just food, and the endless difficulty of getting it.

From morning to night they were begging. They wandered enormous distances, zigzagging right across the country, trailing from village to village and from house to house, 'tapping' at every butcher's and every baker's and every likely looking cottage, and hanging hopefully round picnic parties, and waving—always vainly— at passing cars, and accosting old gentlemen with the right kind of face and pitching hard-up stories. Often they went five miles out of their way to get a crust of bread or a handful of scraps of bacon. All of them begged, Dorothy with the others; she had no remembered past, no standards of comparison to make her ashamed of it. And yet with all their efforts they would have gone empty- bellied half the time if they had not stolen as well as begged. At dusk and in the early mornings they pillaged the orchards and the fields, stealing apples, damsons, pears, cobnuts, autumn raspberries, and, above all, potatoes; Nobby counted it a sin to pass a potato field without getting at least a pocketful. It was Nobby who did most of the stealing, while the others kept guard. He was a bold thief; it was his peculiar boast that he would steal anything that was not tied down, and he would have landed them all in prison if they had not restrained him sometimes. Once he even laid hands on a goose, but the goose set up a fearful clamour, and Charlie and Dorothy dragged Nobby off just as the owner came out of doors to see what was the matter.

Each of those first days they walked between twenty and twenty-five miles. They trailed across commons and through buried villages with incredible names, and lost themselves in lanes that led nowhere, and sprawled exhausted in dry ditches smelling of fennel and tansies, and sneaked into private woods and 'drummed up' in thickets where firewood and water were handy, and cooked strange, squalid meals in the two two-pound snuff-tins that were their only cooking pots. Sometimes, when their luck was in, they had excellent stews of cadged bacon and stolen cauliflowers, sometimes great insipid gorges of potatoes roasted in the ashes, sometimes jam made of stolen autumn raspberries which they boiled in one of the snuff-tins and devoured while it was still scalding hot. Tea was the one thing they never ran short of. Even when there was no food at all there was always tea, stewed, dark brown and reviving. It is a thing that can be begged more easily than most. 'Please, ma'am, could you spare me a pinch of tea?' is a plea that seldom fails, even with the case-hardened Kentish housewives.

The days were burning hot, the white roads glared and the passing cars sent stinging dust into their faces. Often families of hop- pickers drove past, cheering, in lorries piled sky-high with furniture, children, dogs, and birdcages. The nights were always cold. There is hardly such a thing as a night in England when it is really warm after midnight. Two large sacks were all the bedding they had between them. Flo and Charlie had one sack, Dorothy had the other, and Nobby slept on the bare ground. The discomfort was almost as bad as the cold. If you lay on your back, your head, with no pillow, lolled backwards so that your neck seemed to be breaking; if you lay on your side, your hip-bone pressing against the earth caused you torments. Even when, towards the small hours, you managed to fall asleep by fits and starts, the cold penetrated into your deepest dreams. Nobby was the only one who could really stand it. He could sleep as peacefully in a nest of sodden grass as in a bed, and his coarse, simian face, with barely a dozen red-gold hairs glittering on the chin like snippings of copper wire, never lost its warm, pink colour. He was one of those red-haired people who seem to glow with an inner radiance that warms not only themselves but the surrounding air.

All this strange, comfortless life Dorothy took utterly for granted—only dimly aware, if at all, that the other, unremembered life that lay behind her had been in some way different from this. After only a couple of days she had ceased to wonder any longer about her queer predicament. She accepted everything—accepted the dirt and hunger and fatigue, the endless trailing to and fro, the hot, dusty days and the sleepless, shivering nights. She was, in any case, far too tired to think. By the afternoon of the second day they were all desperately, overwhelmingly tired, except Nobby, whom nothing could tire. Even the fact that soon after they set out a nail began to work its way through the sole of his boot hardly seemed to trouble him. There were periods of an hour at a time when Dorothy seemed almost to be sleeping as she walked. She had a burden to carry now, for as the two men were already loaded and Flo steadfastly refused to carry anything, Dorothy had volunteered to carry the sack that held the stolen potatoes. They generally had ten pounds or so of potatoes in reserve. Dorothy slung the sack over her shoulder as Nobby and Charlie did with their bundles, but the string cut into her like a saw and the sack bumped against her hip and chafed it so that finally it began to bleed. Her wretched, flimsy shoes had begun to go to pieces from the very beginning. On the second day the heel of her right shoe came off and left her hobbling; but Nobby, expert in such matters, advised her to tear the heel off the other shoe and walk flatfooted. The result was a fiery pain down her shins when she walked uphill, and a feeling as though the soles of her feet had been hammered with an iron bar.

But Flo and Charlie were in a much worse case than she. They were not so much exhausted as amazed and scandalized by the distances they were expected to walk. Walking twenty miles in a day was a thing they had never heard of till now. They were cockneys born and bred, and though they had had several months of destitution in London, neither of them had ever been on the road before. Charlie, till fairly recently, had been in good employment, and Flo, too, had had a good home until she had been seduced and turned out of doors to live on the streets. They had fallen in with Nobby in Trafalgar Square and agreed to come hop-picking with him, imagining that it would be a bit of a lark. Of course, having been 'on the beach' a comparatively short time, they looked down on Nobby and Dorothy. They valued Nobby's knowledge of the road and his boldness in thieving, but he was their social inferior—that was their attitude. And as for Dorothy, they scarcely even deigned to look at her after her half-crown came to an end.

Even on the second day their courage was failing. They lagged behind, grumbled incessantly, and demanded more than their fair share of food. By the third day it was almost impossible to keep them on the road at all. They were pining to be back in London, and had long ceased to care whether they ever got to the hopfields or not; all they wanted to do was to sprawl in any comfortable halting place they could find, and, when there was any food left, devour endless snacks. After every halt there was a tedious argument before they could be got to their feet again.

'Come on, blokes!' Nobby would say. 'Pack your peter up, Charlie. Time we was getting off.'

'Oh, —— getting off!' Charlie would answer morosely.

'Well, we can't skipper here, can we? We said we was going to hike as far as Sevenoaks tonight, didn't we?'

'Oh, —— Sevenoaks! Sevenoaks or any other bleeding place—it don't make any bleeding difference to me.'

'But —— it! We want to get a job tomorrow, don't we? And we got to get down among the farms 'fore we can start looking for one.'

'Oh, —— the farms! I wish I'd never 'eard of a —— 'op! I wasn't brought up to this —— 'iking and skippering like you was. I'm fed up; that's what I am —— fed up.'

'If this is bloody 'opping,' Flo would chime in, 'I've 'ad my bloody bellyful of it already.'

Nobby gave Dorothy his private opinion that Flo and Charlie would probably 'jack off' if they got the chance of a lift back to London. But as for Nobby, nothing disheartened him or ruffled his good temper, not even when the nail in his boot was at its worst and his filthy remnant of a sock was dark with blood. By the third day the nail had worn a permanent hole in his foot, and Nobby had to halt once in a mile to hammer it down.

''Scuse me, kid,' he would say; 'got to attend to my bloody hoof again. This nail's a mulligatawny.'

He would search for a round stone, squat in the ditch and carefully hammer the nail down.

'There!' he would say optimistically, feeling the place with his thumb. 'THAT b—'s in his grave!'

The epitaph should have been Resurgam, however. The nail invariably worked its way up again within a quarter of an hour.

Nobby had tried to make love to Dorothy, of course, and, when she repulsed him, bore her no grudge. He had that happy temperament that is incapable of taking its own reverses very seriously. He was always debonair, always singing in a lusty baritone voice—his three favourite songs were: 'Sonny Boy', "Twas Christmas Day in the Workhouse' (to the tune of 'The Church's One Foundation'), and '"——!" was all the band could play', given with lively renderings of military music. He was twenty-six years old and was a widower, and had been successively a seller of newspapers, a petty thief, a Borstal boy, a soldier, a burglar, and a tramp. These facts, however, you had to piece together for yourself, for he was not equal to giving a consecutive account of his life. His conversation was studded with casual picturesque memories—the six months he had served in a line regiment before he was invalided out with a damaged eye, the loathsomeness of the skilly in Holloway, his childhood in the Deptford gutters, the death of his wife, aged eighteen, in childbirth, when he was twenty, the horrible suppleness of the Borstal canes, the dull boom of the nitro- glycerine, blowing in the safe door at Woodward's boot and shoe factory, where Nobby had cleared a hundred and twenty-five pounds and spent it in three weeks.

On the afternoon of the third day they reached the fringe of the hop country, and began to meet discouraged people, mostly tramps, trailing back to London with the news that there was nothing doing— hops were bad and the price was low, and the gypsies and 'home pickers' had collared all the jobs. At this Flo and Charlie gave up hope altogether, but by an adroit mixture of bullying and persuasion Nobby managed to drive them a few miles farther. In a little village called Wale they fell in with an old Irishwoman— Mrs McElligot was her name—who had just been given a job at a neighbouring hopfield, and they swapped some of their stolen apples for a piece of meat she had 'bummed' earlier in the day. She gave them some useful hints about hop-picking and about what farms to try. They were all sprawling on the village green, tired out, opposite a little general shop with some newspaper posters outside.

'You'd best go down'n have a try at Chalmers's,' Mrs McElligot advised them in her base Dublin accent. 'Dat's a bit above five mile from here. I've heard tell as Chalmers wants a dozen pickers still. I daresay he'd give y'a job if you gets dere early enough.'

'Five miles! Cripes! Ain't there none nearer'n that?' grumbled Charlie.

'Well, dere's Norman's. I got a job at Norman's meself—I'm startin' tomorrow mornin'. But 'twouldn't be no use for you to try at Norman's. He ain't takin' on none but home pickers, an' dey say as he's goin' to let half his hops blow.'

'What's home pickers?' said Nobby.

'Why, dem as has got homes o' deir own. Eider you got to live in de neighbourhood, or else de farmer's got to give y'a hut to sleep in. Dat's de law nowadays. In de ole days when you come down hoppin', you kipped in a stable an' dere was no questions asked. But dem bloody interferin' gets of a Labour Government brought in a law to say as no pickers was to be taken on widout de farmer had proper accommodation for 'em. So Norman only takes on folks as has got homes o' deir own.'

'Well, you ain't got a home of your own, have you?'

'No bloody fear! But Norman t'inks I have. I kidded'm I was stayin' in a cottage near by. Between you an' me, I'm skipperin' in a cow byre. 'Tain't so bad except for de stink o' de muck, but you got to be out be five in de mornin', else de cowmen 'ud catch you.'

'We ain't got no experience of hopping,' Nobby said. 'I wouldn't know a bloody hop if I saw one. Best to let on you're an old hand when you go up for a job, eh?'

'Hell! Hops don't need no experience. Tear 'em off an' fling 'em into de bin. Dat's all der is to it, wid hops.'

Dorothy was nearly asleep. She heard the others talking desultorily, first about hop-picking, then about some story in the newspapers of a girl who had disappeared from home. Flo and Charlie had been reading the posters on the shop-front opposite; and this had revived them somewhat, because the posters reminded them of London and its joys. The missing girl, in whose fate they seemed to be rather interested, was spoken of as 'The Rector's Daughter'.

'J'a see that one, Flo?' said Charlie, reading a poster aloud with intense relish: '"Secret Love Life of Rector's Daughter. Startling Revelations." Coo! Wish I 'ad a penny to 'ave a read of that!'

'Oh? What's 't all about, then?'

'What? Didn't j'a read about it? Papers 'as bin full of it. Rector's Daughter this and Rector's Daughter that—wasn't 'alf smutty, some of it, too.'

'She's bit of hot stuff, the ole Rector's Daughter,' said Nobby reflectively, lying on his back. 'Wish she was here now! I'd know what to do with her, all right, I would.'

''Twas a kid run away from home,' put in Mrs McElligot. 'She was carryin' on wid a man twenty year older'n herself, an' now she's disappeared an' dey're searchin' for her high an' low.'

'Jacked off in the middle of the night in a motor-car with no clo'es on 'cep' 'er nightdress,' said Charlie appreciatively. 'The 'ole village sore 'em go.'

'Dere's some t'ink as he's took her abroad an' sold her to one o' dem flash cat-houses in Parrus,' added Mrs McElligot.

'No clo'es on 'cep' 'er nightdress? Dirty tart she must 'a been!'

The conversation might have proceeded to further details, but at this moment Dorothy interrupted it. What they were saying had roused a faint curiosity in her. She realized that she did not know the meaning of the word 'Rector'. She sat up and asked Nobby:

'What is a Rector?'

'Rector? Why, a sky-pilot—parson bloke. Bloke that preaches and gives out the hymns and that in church. We passed one of 'em yesterday—riding a green bicycle and had his collar on back to front. A priest—clergyman. YOU know.'

'Oh.... Yes, I think so.'

'Priests! Bloody ole getsies dey are too, some o' dem,' said Mrs McElligot reminiscently.

Dorothy was left not much the wiser. What Nobby had said did enlighten her a little, but only a very little. The whole train of thought connected with 'church' and 'clergyman' was strangely vague and blurred in her mind. It was one of the gaps—there was a number of such gaps—in the mysterious knowledge that she had brought with her out of the past.

That was their third night on the road. When it was dark they slipped into a spinney as usual to 'skipper', and a little after midnight it began to pelt with rain. They spent a miserable hour stumbling to and fro in the darkness, trying to find a place to shelter, and finally found a hay-stack, where they huddled themselves on the lee side till it was light enough to see. Flo blubbered throughout the night in the most intolerable manner, and by the morning she was in a state of semi-collapse. Her silly fat face, washed clean by rain and tears, looked like a bladder of lard, if one can imagine a bladder of lard contorted with self- pity. Nobby rooted about under the hedge until he had collected an armful of partially dry sticks, and then managed to get a fire going and boil some tea as usual. There was no weather so bad that Nobby could not produce a can of tea. He carried, among other things, some pieces of old motor tyre that would make a flare when the wood was wet, and he even possessed the art, known only to a few cognoscenti among tramps, of getting water to boil over a candle.

Everyone's limbs had stiffened after the horrible night, and Flo declared herself unable to walk a step farther. Charlie backed her up. So, as the other two refused to move, Dorothy and Nobby went on to Chalmers's farm, arranging a rendezvous where they should meet when they had tried their luck. They got to Chalmers's, five miles away, found their way through vast orchards to the hop- fields, and were told that the overseer 'would be along presently'. So they waited four hours on the edge of the plantation, with the sun drying their clothes on their backs, watching the hop-pickers at work. It was a scene somehow peaceful and alluring. The hop bines, tall climbing plants like runner beans enormously magnified, grew in green leafy lanes, with the hops dangling from them in pale green bunches like gigantic grapes. When the wind stirred them they shook forth a fresh, bitter scent of sulphur and cool beer. In each lane of bines a family of sunburnt people were shredding the hops into sacking bins, and singing as they worked; and presently a hooter sounded and they knocked off to boil cans of tea over crackling fires of hop bines. Dorothy envied them greatly. How happy they looked, sitting round the fires with their cans of tea and their hunks of bread and bacon, in the smell of hops and wood smoke! She pined for such a job—however, for the present there was nothing doing. At about one o'clock the overseer arrived and told them that he had no jobs for them, so they trailed back to the road, only avenging themselves on Chalmers's farm by stealing a dozen apples as they went.

When they reached their rendezvous, Flo and Charlie had vanished. Of course they searched for them, but, equally of course, they knew very well what had happened. Indeed, it was perfectly obvious. Flo had made eyes at some passing lorry driver, who had given the two of them a lift back to London for the chance of a good cuddle on the way. Worse yet, they had stolen both bundles. Dorothy and Nobby had not a scrap of food left, not a crust of bread nor a potato nor a pinch of tea, no bedding, and not even a snuff-tin in which to cook anything they could cadge or steal—nothing, in fact, except the clothes they stood up in.

The next thirty-six hours were a bad time—a very bad time. How they pined for a job, in their hunger and exhaustion! But the chances of getting one seemed to grow smaller and smaller as they got farther into the hop country. They made interminable marches from farm to farm, getting the same answer everywhere—no pickers needed—and they were so busy marching to and fro that they had not even time to beg, so that they had nothing to eat except stolen apples and damsons that tormented their stomachs with their acid juice and yet left them ravenously hungry. It did not rain that night, but it was much colder than before. Dorothy did not even attempt to sleep, but spent the night in crouching over the fire and keeping it alight. They were hiding in a beech wood, under a squat, ancient tree that kept the wind away but also wetted them periodically with sprinklings of chilly dew. Nobby, stretched on his back, mouth open, one broad cheek faintly illumined by the feeble rays of the fire, slept as peacefully as a child. All night long a vague wonder, born of sleeplessness and intolerable discomfort, kept stirring in Dorothy's mind. Was this the life to which she had been bred—this life of wandering empty-bellied all day and shivering at night under dripping trees? Had it been like this even in the blank past? Where had she come from? Who was she? No answer came, and they were on the road at dawn. By the evening they had tried at eleven farms in all, and Dorothy's legs were giving out, and she was so dizzy with fatigue that she found difficulty in walking straight.

But late in the evening, quite unexpectedly, their luck turned. They tried at a farm named Cairns's, in the village of Clintock, and were taken on immediately, with no questions asked. The overseer merely looked them up and down, said briefly, 'Right you are—you'll do. Start in the morning; bin number 7, set 19,' and did not even bother to ask their names. Hop-picking, it seemed, needed neither character nor experience.

They found their way to the meadow where the pickers' camp was situated. In a dreamlike state, between exhaustion and the joy of having got a job at last, Dorothy found herself walking through a maze of tin-roofed huts and gypsies' caravans with many-coloured washing hanging from the windows. Hordes of children swarmed in the narrow grass alleys between the huts, and ragged, agreeable- looking people were cooking meals over innumerable faggot fires. At the bottom of the field there were some round tin huts, much inferior to the others, set apart for unmarried people. An old man who was toasting cheese at a fire directed Dorothy to one of the women's huts.

Dorothy pushed open the door of the hut. It was about twelve feet across, with unglazed windows which had been boarded up, and it had no furniture whatever. There seemed to be nothing in it but an enormous pile of straw reaching to the roof—in fact, the hut was almost entirely filled with straw. To Dorothy's eyes, already sticky with sleep, the straw looked paradisically comfortable. She began to push her way into it, and was checked by a sharp yelp from beneath her.

"Ere! What yer doin' of? Get off of it! 'Oo asked YOU to walk about on my belly, stoopid?'

Seemingly there were women down among the straw. Dorothy burrowed forward more circumspectly, tripped over something, sank into the straw and in the same instant began to fall asleep. A rough- looking woman, partially undressed, popped up like a mermaid from the strawy sea.

''Ullo, mate!' she said. 'Jest about all in, ain't you, mate?'

'Yes, I'm tired—very tired.'

'Well, you'll bloody freeze in this straw with no bed-clo'es on you. Ain't you got a blanket?'

'No.'

''Alf a mo, then. I got a poke 'ere.'

She dived down into the straw and re-emerged with a hop-poke seven feet long. Dorothy was asleep already. She allowed herself to be woken up, and inserted herself somehow into the sack, which was so long that she could get into it head and all; and then she was half wriggling, half sinking down, deep down, into a nest of straw warmer and drier than she had conceived possible. The straw tickled her nostrils and got into her hair and pricked her even through the sack, but at that moment no imaginable sleeping place— not Cleopatra's couch of swan's-down nor the floating bed of Haroun al Raschid—could have caressed her more voluptuously.

3

It was remarkable how easily, once you had got a job, you settled down to the routine of hop-picking. After only a week of it you ranked as an expert picker, and felt as though you had been picking hops all your life.

It was exceedingly easy work. Physically, no doubt, it was exhausting—it kept you on your feet ten or twelve hours a day, and you were dropping with sleep by six in the evening—but it needed no kind of skill. Quite a third of the pickers in the camp were as new to the job as Dorothy herself. Some of them had come down from London with not the dimmest idea of what hops were like, or how you picked them, or why. One man, it was said, on his first morning on the way to the fields, had asked, 'Where are the spades?' He imagined that hops were dug up out of the ground.

Except for Sundays, one day at the hop camp was very like another. At half past five, at a tap on the wall of your hut, you crawled out of your sleeping nest and began searching for your shoes, amid sleepy curses from the women (there were six or seven or possibly even eight of them) who were buried here and there in the straw. In that vast pile of straw any clothes that you were so unwise as to take off always lost themselves immediately. You grabbed an armful of straw and another of dried hop bines, and a faggot from the pile outside, and got the fire going for breakfast. Dorothy always cooked Nobby's breakfast as well as her own, and tapped on the wall of his hut when it was ready, she being better at waking up in the morning than he. It was very cold on those September mornings, the eastern sky was fading slowly from black to cobalt, and the grass was silvery white with dew. Your breakfast was always the same—bacon, tea, and bread fried in the grease of the bacon. While you ate it you cooked another exactly similar meal, to serve for dinner, and then, carrying your dinner-pail, you set out for the fields, a mile-and-a-half walk through the blue, windy dawn, with your nose running so in the cold that you had to stop occasionally and wipe it on your sacking apron.

The hops were divided up into plantations of about an acre, and each set—forty pickers or thereabouts, under a foreman who was often a gypsy—picked one plantation at a time. The bines grew twelve feet high or more, and they were trained up strings and slung over horizontal wires, in rows a yard or two apart; in each row there was a sacking bin like a very deep hammock slung on a heavy wooden frame. As soon as you arrived you swung your bin into position, slit the strings from the next two bines, and tore them down—huge, tapering strands of foliage, like the plaits of Rapunzel's hair, that came tumbling down on top of you, showering you with dew. You dragged them into place over the bin, and then, starting at the thick end of the bine, began tearing off the heavy bunches of hops. At that hour of the morning you could only pick slowly and awkwardly. Your hands were still stiff and the coldness of the dew numbed them, and the hops were wet and slippery. The great difficulty was to pick the hops without picking the leaves and stalks as well; for the measurer was liable to refuse your hops if they had too many leaves among them.

The stems of the bines were covered with minute thorns which within two or three days had torn the skin of your hands to pieces. In the morning it was a torment to begin picking when your fingers were almost too stiff to bend and bleeding in a dozen places; but the pain wore off when the cuts had reopened and the blood was flowing freely. If the hops were good and you picked well, you could strip a bine in ten minutes, and the best bines yielded half a bushel of hops. But the hops varied greatly from one plantation to another. In some they were as large as walnuts, and hung in great leafless bunches which you could rip off with a single twist; in others they were miserable things no bigger than peas, and grew so thinly that you had to pick them one at a time. Some hops were so bad that you could not pick a bushel of them in an hour.

It was slow work in the early morning, before the hops were dry enough to handle. But presently the sun came out, and the lovely, bitter odour began to stream from the warming hops, and people's early-morning surliness wore off, and the work got into its stride. From eight till midday you were picking, picking, picking, in a sort of passion of work—a passionate eagerness, which grew stronger and stronger as the morning advanced, to get each bine done and shift your bin a little farther along the row. At the beginning of each plantation all the bins started abreast, but by degrees the better pickers forged ahead, and some of them had finished their lane of hops when the others were barely halfway along; whereupon, if you were far behind, they were allowed to turn back and finish your row for you, which was called 'stealing your hops'. Dorothy and Nobby were always among the last, there being only two of them—there were four people at most of the bins. And Nobby was a clumsy picker, with his great coarse hands; on the whole, the women picked better than the men.

It was always a neck and neck race between the two bins on either side of Dorothy and Nobby, bin number 6 and bin number 8. Bin number 6 was a family of gypsies—a curly-headed, ear-ringed father, an old dried-up leather-coloured mother, and two strapping sons—and bin number 8 was an old East End costerwoman who wore a broad hat and long black cloak and took snuff out of a papiermache box with a steamer painted on the lid. She was always helped by relays of daughters and granddaughters who came down from London for two days at a time. There was quite a troop of children working with the set, following the bins with baskets and gathering up the fallen hops while the adults picked. And the old costerwoman's tiny, pale granddaughter Rose, and a little gypsy girl, dark as an Indian, were perpetually slipping off to steal autumn raspberries and make swings out of hop bines; and the constant singing round the bins was pierced by shrill cries from the costerwoman of, 'Go on, Rose, you lazy little cat! Pick them 'ops up! I'll warm your a— for you!' etc., etc.

Quite half the pickers in the set were gypsies—there were not less than two hundred of them in the camp. Diddykies, the other pickers called them. They were not a bad sort of people, friendly enough, and they flattered you grossly when they wanted to get anything out of you; yet they were sly, with the impenetrable slyness of savages. In their oafish, Oriental faces there was a look as of some wild but sluggish animal—a look of dense stupidity existing side by side with untameable cunning. Their talk consisted of about half a dozen remarks which they repeated over and over again without ever growing tired of them. The two young gypsies at bin number 6 would ask Nobby and Dorothy as many as a dozen times a day the same conundrum:

'What is it the cleverest man in England couldn't do?'

'I don't know. What?'

'Tickle a gnat's a— with a telegraph pole.'

At this, never-failing bellows of laughter. They were all abysmally ignorant; they informed you with pride that not one of them could read a single word. The old curly-headed father, who had conceived some dim notion that Dorothy was a 'scholard', once seriously asked her whether he could drive his caravan to New York.

At twelve o'clock a hooter down at the farm signalled to the pickers to knock off work for an hour, and it was generally a little before this that the measurer came round to collect the hops. At a warning shout from the foreman of ''Ops ready, number nineteen!' everyone would hasten to pick up the fallen hops, finish off the tendrils that had been left unpicked here and there, and clear the leaves out of the bin. There was an art in that. It did not pay to pick too 'clean', for leaves and hops alike all went to swell the tally. The old hands, such as the gypsies, were adepts at knowing just how 'dirty' it was safe to pick.

The measurer would come round, carrying a wicker basket which held a bushel, and accompanied by the 'bookie,' who entered the pickings of each bin in a ledger. The 'bookies' were young men, clerks and chartered accountants and the like, who took this job as a paying holiday. The measurer would scoop the hops out of the bin a bushel at a time, intoning as he did so, 'One! Two! Three! Four!' and the pickers would enter the number in their tally books. Each bushel they picked earned them twopence, and naturally there were endless quarrels and accusations of unfairness over the measuring. Hops are spongy things—you can crush a bushel of them into a quart pot if you choose; so after each scoop one of the pickers would lean over into the bin and stir the hops up to make them lie looser, and then the measurer would hoist the end of the bin and shake the hops together again. Some mornings he had orders to 'take them heavy', and would shovel them in so that he got a couple of bushels at each scoop, whereat there were angry yells of, 'Look how the b—'s ramming them down! Why don't you bloody well stamp on them?' etc.; and the old hands would say darkly that they had known measurers to be ducked in cowponds on the last day of picking. From the bins the hops were put into pokes which theoretically held a hundredweight; but it took two men to hoist a full poke when the measurer had been 'taking them heavy'. You had an hour for dinner, and you made a fire of hop bines—this was forbidden, but everyone did it—and heated up your tea and ate your bacon sandwiches. After dinner you were picking again till five or six in the evening, when the measurer came once more to take your hops, after which you were free to go back to the camp.

Looking back, afterwards, upon her interlude of hop-picking, it was always the afternoons that Dorothy remembered. Those long, laborious hours in the strong sunlight, in the sound of forty voices singing, in the smell of hops and wood smoke, had a quality peculiar and unforgettable. As the afternoon wore on you grew almost too tired to stand, and the small green hop lice got into your hair and into your ears and worried you, and your hands, from the sulphurous juice, were as black as a Negro's except where they were bleeding. Yet you were happy, with an unreasonable happiness. The work took hold of you and absorbed you. It was stupid work, mechanical, exhausting, and every day more painful to the hands, and yet you never wearied of it; when the weather was fine and the hops were good you had the feeling that you could go on picking for ever and for ever. It gave you a physical joy, a warm satisfied feeling inside you, to stand there hour after hour, tearing off the heavy clusters and watching the pale green pile grow higher and higher in your bin, every bushel another twopence in your pocket. The sun burned down upon you, baking you brown, and the bitter, never-palling scent, like a wind from oceans of cool beer, flowed into your nostrils and refreshed you. When the sun was shining everybody sang as they worked; the plantations rang with singing. For some reason all the songs were sad that autumn—songs about rejected love and fidelity unrewarded, like gutter versions of Carmen and Manon Lescaut. There was:

> THERE they GO—IN their joy—
> 'APPY girl—LUCKY boy—
> But 'ere am _I-I-I_—
> Broken—'A-A-Arted!

And there was:

> But I'm dan—cing with tears—in my eyes—
> 'Cos the girl—in my arms—isn't you-o-ou!

And:

> The bells—are ringing—for Sally—
> But no-o-ot—for Sally—and me!

The little gypsy girl used to sing over and over again:

> We're so misable, all so misable,
> Down on Misable Farm!

And though everyone told her that the name of it was Misery Farm, she persisted in calling it Misable Farm. The old costerwoman and her granddaughter Rose had a hop-picking song which went:

> 'Our lousy 'ops!
> Our lousy 'ops!
> When the measurer 'e comes round,

Pick 'em up, pick 'em up off the ground!
When 'e comes to measure,
'E never knows where to stop;
Ay, ay, get in the bin
And take the bloody lot!'

'There they go in their joy', and 'The bells are ringing for Sally', were the especial favourites. The pickers never grew tired of singing them; they must have sung both of them several hundred times over before the season came to an end. As much a part of the atmosphere of the hopfields as the bitter scent and the blowsy sunlight were the tunes of those two songs, ringing through the leafy lanes of the bines.

When you got back to the camp, at half past six or thereabouts, you squatted down by the stream that ran past the huts, and washed your face, probably for the first time that day. It took you twenty minutes or so to get the coal-black filth off your hands. Water and even soap made no impression on it; only two things would remove it—one of them was mud, and the other, curiously enough, was hop juice. Then you cooked your supper, which was usually bread and tea and bacon again, unless Nobby had been along to the village and bought two pennyworth of pieces from the butcher. It was always Nobby who did the shopping. He was the sort of man who knows how to get four pennyworth of meat from the butcher for twopence, and, besides, he was expert in tiny economies. For instance, he always bought a cottage loaf in preference to any of the other shapes, because, as he used to point out, a cottage loaf seems like two loaves when you tear it in half.

Even before you had eaten your supper you were dropping with sleep, but the huge fires that people used to build between the huts were too agreeable to leave. The farm allowed two faggots a day for each hut, but the pickers plundered as many more as they wanted, and also great lumps of elm root which kept smouldering till morning. On some nights the fires were so enormous that twenty people could sit round them in comfort, and there was singing far into the night, and telling of stories and roasting of stolen apples. Youths and girls slipped off to the dark lanes together, and a few bold spirits like Nobby set out with sacks and robbed the neighbouring orchards, and the children played hide-and-seek in the dusk and harried the nightjars which haunted the camp and which, in their cockney ignorance, they imagined to be pheasants. On Saturday nights fifty or sixty of the pickers used to get drunk in the pub and then march down the village street roaring bawdy songs, to the scandal of the inhabitants, who looked on the hopping season as decent provincials in Roman Gaul might have looked on the yearly incursion of the Goths.

When finally you managed to drag yourself away to your nest in the straw, it was none too warm or comfortable. After that first blissful night, Dorothy discovered that straw is wretched stuff to sleep in. It is not only prickly, but, unlike hay, it lets in the draught from every possible direction. However, you had the chance to steal an almost unlimited number of hop-pokes from the fields, and by making herself a sort of cocoon of four hop-pokes, one on top of the other, she managed to keep warm enough to sleep at any rate five hours a night.

4

As to what you earned by hop-picking, it was just enough to keep body and soul together, and no more.

The rate of pay at Cairns's was twopence a bushel, and given good hops a practised picker can average three bushels an hour. In theory, therefore, it would have been possible to earn thirty shillings by a sixty-hour week. Actually, no one in the camp came anywhere near this figure. The best pickers of all earned thirteen or fourteen shillings a week, and the worst hardly as much as six shillings. Nobby and Dorothy, pooling their hops and dividing the proceeds, made round about ten shillings a week each.

There were various reasons for this. To begin with, there was the badness of the hops in some of the fields. Again, there were the delays which wasted an hour or two of every day. When one plantation was finished you had to carry your bin to the next, which might be a mile distant; and then perhaps it would turn out that there was some mistake, and the set, struggling under their bins (they weighed a hundredweight), would have to waste another half-hour in traipsing elsewhere. Worst of all, there was the rain. It was a bad September that year, raining one day in three. Sometimes for a whole morning or afternoon you shivered miserably in the shelter of the unstripped bines, with a dripping hop-poke round your shoulders, waiting for the rain to stop. It was impossible to pick when it was raining. The hops were too slippery to handle, and if you did pick them it was worse than useless, for when sodden with water they shrank all to nothing in the bin. Sometimes you were in the fields all day to earn a shilling or less.

This did not matter to the majority of the pickers, for quite half of them were gypsies and accustomed to starvation wages, and most of the others were respectable East Enders, costermongers and small shopkeepers and the like, who came hop-picking for a holiday and were satisfied if they earned enough for their fare both ways and a bit of fun on Saturday nights. The farmers knew this and traded on it. Indeed, were it not that hop-picking is regarded as a holiday, the industry would collapse forthwith, for the price of hops is now so low that no farmer could afford to pay his pickers a living wage.

Twice a week you could 'sub' up to the amount of half your earnings. If you left before the picking was finished (an inconvenient thing for the farmers) they had the right to pay you off at the rate of a penny a bushel instead of twopence—that is, to pocket half of what they owed you. It was also common knowledge that towards the end of the season, when all the pickers had a fair sum owing to them and would not want to sacrifice it by throwing up their jobs, the farmer would reduce the rate of payment from twopence a bushel to a penny halfpenny. Strikes were practically impossible. The pickers had no union, and the foremen of the sets, instead of being paid twopence a bushel like the others, were paid a weekly wage which stopped automatically if there was a strike; so naturally they would raise Heaven and earth to prevent one. Altogether, the farmers had the pickers in a cleft stick; but it was not the farmers who were to blame—the low price of hops was the root of the trouble. Also as Dorothy observed later, very few of the pickers had more than a dim idea of the amount they earned. The system of piecework disguised the low rate of payment.

For the first few days, before they could 'sub', Dorothy and Nobby very nearly starved, and would have starved altogether if the other pickers had not fed them. But everyone was extraordinarily kind. There was a party of people who shared one of the larger huts a little farther up the row, a flower-seller named Jim Burrows and a man named Jim Turle who was vermin man at a large London restaurant, who had married sisters and were close friends, and these people had taken a liking to Dorothy. They saw to it that she and Nobby should not starve. Every evening during the first few days May Turle, aged fifteen, would arrive with a saucepan full of stew, which was presented with studied casualness, lest there should be any hint of charity about it. The formula was always the same:

'Please, Ellen, mother says as she was just going to throw this stew away, and then she thought as p'raps you might like it. She ain't got no use for it, she says, and so you'd be doing her a kindness if you was to take it.'

It was extraordinary what a lot of things the Turles and the Burrowses were 'just going to throw away' during those first few days. On one occasion they even gave Nobby and Dorothy half a pig's head ready stewed; and besides food they gave them several cooking pots and a tin plate which could be used as a frying-pan. Best of all, they asked no uncomfortable questions. They knew well enough that there was some mystery in Dorothy's life—'You could see,' they said, 'as Ellen had COME DOWN IN THE WORLD'—but they made it a point of honour not to embarrass her by asking questions about it. It was not until she had been more than a fortnight at the camp that Dorothy was even obliged to put herself to the trouble of inventing a surname.

As soon as Dorothy and Nobby could 'sub', their money troubles were at an end. They lived with surprising ease at the rate of one and sixpence a day for the two of them. Fourpence of this went on tobacco for Nobby, and fourpence-halfpenny on a loaf of bread; and they spent about sevenpence a day on tea, sugar, milk (you could get milk at the farm at a halfpenny a half-pint), and margarine and 'pieces' of bacon. But, of course, you never got through the day without squandering another penny or two. You were everlastingly hungry, everlastingly doing sums in farthings to see whether you could afford a kipper or a doughnut or a pennyworth of potato chips, and, wretched as the pickers' earnings were, half the population of Kent seemed to be in conspiracy to tickle their money out of their pockets. The local shopkeepers, with four hundred hop-pickers quartered upon them, made more during the hop season than all the rest of the year put together, which did not prevent them from looking down on the pickers as cockney dirt. In the afternoon the farm hands would come round the bins selling apples and pears at seven a penny, and London hawkers would come with baskets of doughnuts or water ices or 'halfpenny lollies'. At night the camp was thronged by hawkers who drove down from London with vans of horrifyingly cheap groceries, fish and chips, jellied eels, shrimps, shop-soiled cakes, and gaunt, glassy-eyed rabbits which had lain two years on the ice and were being sold off at ninepence a time.

For the most part it was a filthy diet upon which the hop-pickers lived—inevitably so, for even if you had the money to buy proper food, there was no time to cook it except on Sundays. Probably it was only the abundance of stolen apples that prevented the camp from being ravaged by scurvy. There was constant, systematic thieving of apples; practically everyone in the camp either stole them or shared them. There were even parties of young men (employed, so it was said, by London fruit-costers) who bicycled down from London every week-end for the purpose of raiding the orchards. As for Nobby, he had reduced fruit-stealing to a science. Within a week he had collected a gang of youths who looked up to him as a hero because he was a real burglar and had been in jail four times, and every night they would set out at dusk with sacks and come back with as much as two hundredweight of fruit. There were vast orchards near the hopfields, and the apples, especially the beautiful little Golden Russets, were lying in piles under the trees, rotting, because the farmers could not sell them. It was a sin not to rake them, Nobby said. On two occasions he and his gang even stole a chicken. How they managed to do it without waking the neighbourhood was a mystery; but it appeared that Nobby knew some dodge of slipping a sack over a chicken's head, so that it 'ceas'd upon the midnight with no pain'—or at any rate, with no noise.

In this manner a week and then a fortnight went by, and Dorothy was no nearer to solving the problem of her own identity. Indeed, she was further from it than ever, for except at odd moments the subject had almost vanished from her mind. More and more she had come to take her curious situation for granted, to abandon all thoughts of either yesterday or tomorrow. That was the natural effect of life in the hopfields; it narrowed the range of your consciousness to the passing minute. You could not struggle with nebulous mental problems when you were everlastingly sleepy and everlastingly occupied—for when you were not at work in the fields you were either cooking, or fetching things from the village, or coaxing a fire out of wet sticks, or trudging to and fro with cans of water. (There was only one water tap in the camp, and that was two hundred yards from Dorothy's hut, and the unspeakable earth latrine was at the same distance.) It was a life that wore you out, used up every ounce of your energy, and kept you profoundly, unquestionably happy. In the literal sense of the word, it stupefied you. The long days in the fields, the coarse food and insufficient sleep, the smell of hops and wood smoke, lulled you into an almost beastlike heaviness. Your wits seemed to thicken, just as your skin did, in the rain and sunshine and perpetual fresh air.

On Sundays, of course, there was no work in the fields; but Sunday morning was a busy time, for it was then that people cooked their principal meal of the week, and did their laundering and mending. All over the camp, while the jangle of bells from the village church came down the wind, mingling with the thin strains of 'O God our Help' from the ill-attended open-air service held by St Somebody's Mission to Hop-pickers, huge faggot fires were blazing, and water boiling in buckets and tin cans and saucepans and anything else that people could lay their hands on, and ragged washing fluttering from the roofs of all the huts. On the first Sunday Dorothy borrowed a basin from the Turles and washed first her hair, then her underclothes and Nobby's shirt. Her underclothes were in a shocking state. How long she had worn them she did not know, but certainly not less than ten days, and they had been slept in all that while. Her stockings had hardly any feet left to them, and as for her shoes, they only held together because of the mud that caked them.

After she had set the washing to dry she cooked the dinner, and they dined opulently off half a stewed chicken (stolen), boiled potatoes (stolen), stewed apples (stolen), and tea out of real tea- cups with handles on them, borrowed from Mrs Burrows. And after dinner, the whole afternoon, Dorothy sat against the sunny side of the hut, with a dry hop-poke across her knees to hold her dress down, alternately dozing and reawakening. Two-thirds of the people in the camp were doing exactly the same thing; just dozing in the sun, and waking to gaze at nothing, like cows. It was all you felt equal to, after a week of heavy work.

About three o'clock, as she sat there on the verge of sleep, Nobby sauntered by, bare to the waist—his shirt was drying—with a copy of a Sunday newspaper that he had succeeded in borrowing. It was Pippin's Weekly, the dirtiest of the five dirty Sunday newspapers. He dropped it in Dorothy's lap as he passed.

'Have a read of that, kid,' he said generously.

Dorothy took Pippin's Weekly and laid it across her knees, feeling herself far too sleepy to read. A huge headline stared her in the face: 'PASSION DRAMA IN COUNTRY RECTORY.' And then there were some more headlines, and something in leaded type, and an inset photograph of a girl's face. For the space of five seconds or thereabouts Dorothy was actually gazing at a blackish, smudgy, but quite recognizable portrait of herself.

There was a column or so of print beneath the photograph. As a matter of fact, most of the newspapers had dropped the 'Rector's Daughter' mystery by this time, for it was more than a fortnight old and stale news. But Pippin's Weekly cared little whether its news was new so long as it was spicy, and that week's crop of rapes and murders had been a poor one. They were giving the 'Rector's Daughter' one final boost—giving her, in fact, the place of honour at the top left-hand corner of the front page.

Dorothy gazed inertly at the photograph. A girl's face, looking out at her from beds of black unappetizing print—it conveyed absolutely nothing to her mind. She re-read mechanically the words, 'PASSION DRAMA IN COUNTRY RECTORY', without either understanding them or feeling the slightest interest in them. She was, she discovered, totally unequal to the effort of reading; even the effort of looking at the photographs was too much for her. Heavy sleep was weighing down her head. Her eyes, in the act of closing, flitted across the page to a photograph that was either of Lord Snowden or of the man who wouldn't wear a truss, and then, in the same instant, she fell asleep, with Pippin's Weekly across her knees.

It was not uncomfortable against the corrugated iron wall of the hut, and she hardly stirred till six o'clock, when Nobby woke her up to tell her that he had got tea ready; whereat Dorothy put Pippin's Weekly thriftily away (it would come in for lighting the fire), without looking at it again. So for the moment the chance of solving her problem passed by. And the problem might have remained unsolved even for months longer, had not a disagreeable accident, a week later, frightened her out of the contented and unreflecting state in which she was living.

5

The following Sunday night two policemen suddenly descended upon the camp and arrested Nobby and two others for theft.

It happened all in a moment, and Nobby could not have escaped even if he had been warned beforehand, for the countryside was pullulating with special constables. There are vast numbers of special constables in Kent. They are sworn in every autumn—a sort of militia to deal with the marauding tribes of hop-pickers. The farmers had been growing tired of the orchard-robbing, and had decided to make an example, in terrorem.

Of course there was a tremendous uproar in the camp. Dorothy came out of her hut to discover what was the matter, and saw a firelit ring of people towards which everyone was running. She ran after them, and a horrid chill went through her, because it seemed to her that she knew already what it was that had happened. She managed to wriggle her way to the front of the crowd, and saw the very thing that she had been fearing.

There stood Nobby, in the grip of an enormous policeman, and another policeman was holding two frightened youths by the arms. One of them, a wretched child hardly sixteen years old, was crying bitterly. Mr Cairns, a stiff-built man with grey whiskers, and two farm hands, were keeping guard over the stolen property that had been dug out of the straw of Nobby's hut. Exhibit A, a pile of apples; Exhibit B, some blood-stained chicken feathers. Nobby caught sight of Dorothy among the crowd, grinned at her with a flash of large teeth, and winked. There was a confused din of shouting:

'Look at the pore little b— crying! Let 'im go! Bloody shame, pore little kid like that! Serve the young bastard right, getting us all into trouble! Let 'im go! Always got to put the blame on us bloody hop-pickers! Can't lose a bloody apple without it's us that's took it. Let 'im go! Shut up, can't you? S'pose they was YOUR bloody apples? Wouldn't YOU bloodiwell—' etc., etc., etc. And then: 'Stand back mate! 'Ere comes the kid's mother.'

A huge Toby jug of a woman, with monstrous breasts and her hair coming down her back, forced her way through the ring of people and began roaring first at the policeman and Mr Cairns, then at Nobby, who had led her son astray. Finally the farm hands managed to drag her away. Through the woman's yells Dorothy could hear Mr Cairns gruffly interrogating Nobby:

'Now then, young man, just you own up and tell us who you shared them apples with! We're going to put a stop to this thieving game, once and for all. You own up, and I dessay we'll take it into consideration.'

Nobby answered, as blithely as ever, 'Consideration, your a—!'

'Don't you get giving me any of your lip, young man! Or else you'll catch it all the hotter when you go up before the magistrate.'

'Catch it hotter, your a—!'

Nobby grinned. His own wit filled him with delight. He caught Dorothy's eye and winked at her once again before being led away. And that was the last she ever saw of him.

There was further shouting, and when the prisoners were removed a few dozen men followed them, booing at the policemen and Mr Cairns, but nobody dared to interfere. Dorothy meanwhile had crept away; she did not even stop to find out whether there would be an opportunity of saying goodbye to Nobby—she was too frightened, too anxious to escape. Her knees were trembling uncontrollably. When she got back to the hut, the other women were sitting up, talking excitedly about Nobby's arrest. She burrowed deep into the straw and hid herself, to be out of the sound of their voices. They continued talking half the night, and of course, because Dorothy had supposedly been Nobby's 'tart', they kept condoling with her and plying her with questions. She did not answer them—pretended to be asleep. But there would be, she knew well enough, no sleep for her that night.

The whole thing had frightened and upset her—but it had frightened her more than was reasonable or understandable. For she was in no kind of danger. The farm hands did not know that she had shared the stolen apples—for that matter, nearly everyone in the camp had shared them—and Nobby would never betray her. It was not even that she was greatly concerned for Nobby, who was frankly not troubled by the prospect of a month in jail. It was something that was happening inside her—some change that was taking place in the atmosphere of her mind.

It seemed to her that she was no longer the same person that she had been an hour ago. Within her and without, everything was changed. It was as though a bubble in her brain had burst, setting free thoughts, feelings, fears of which she had forgotten the existence. All the dreamlike apathy of the past three weeks was shattered. For it was precisely as in a dream that she had been living—it is the especial condition of a dream that one accepts everything, questions nothing. Dirt, rags, vagabondage, begging, stealing—all had seemed natural to her. Even the loss of her memory had seemed natural; at least, she had hardly given it a thought till this moment. The question 'WHO AM I?' had faded out of her mind till sometimes she had forgotten it for hours together. It was only now that it returned with any real urgency.

For nearly the whole of a miserable night that question went to and fro in her brain. But it was not so much the question itself that troubled her as the knowledge that it was about to be answered. Her memory was coming back to her, that was certain, and some ugly shock was coming with it. She actually feared the moment when she should discover her own identity. Something that she did not want to face was waiting just below the surface of her consciousness.

At half past five she got up and groped for her shoes as usual. She went outside, got the fire going, and stuck the can of water among the hot embers to boil. Just as she did so a memory, seeming irrelevant, flashed across her mind. It was of that halt on the village green at Wale, a fortnight ago—the time when they had met the old Irishwoman, Mrs McElligot. Very vividly she remembered the scene. Herself lying exhausted on the grass, with her arm over her face; and Nobby and Mrs McElligot talking across her supine body; and Charlie, with succulent relish, reading out the poster, 'Secret Love Life of Rector's Daughter'; and herself, mystified but not deeply interested, sitting up and asking, 'What is a Rector?'

At that a deadly chill, like a hand of ice, fastened about her heart. She got up and hurried, almost ran back to the hut, then burrowed down to the place where her sacks lay and felt in the straw beneath them. In that vast mound of straw all your loose possessions got lost and gradually worked their way to the bottom. But after searching for some minutes, and getting herself well cursed by several women who were still half asleep, Dorothy found what she was looking for. It was the copy of Pippin's Weekly which Nobby had given her a week ago. She took it outside, knelt down, and spread it out in the light of the fire.

It was on the front page—a photograph, and three big headlines. Yes! There it was!

PASSION DRAMA IN COUNTRY RECTORY

PARSON'S DAUGHTER AND ELDERLY SEDUCER

WHITE-HAIRED FATHER PROSTRATE WITH GRIEF

(Pippin's Weekly Special)

'I would sooner have seen her in her grave!' was the heartbroken cry of the Rev. Charles Hare, Rector of Knype Hill, Suffolk, on learning of his twenty-eight-year-old daughter's elopement with an elderly bachelor named Warburton, described as an artist.

Miss Hare, who left the town on the night of the twenty-first of August, is still missing, and all attempts to trace her have failed. [In leaded type] Rumour, as yet unconfirmed, states that she was recently seen with a male companion in a hotel of evil repute in Vienna.

Readers of Pippin's Weekly will recall that the elopement took place in dramatic circumstances. A little before midnight on the twenty-first of August, Mrs Evelina Semprill, a widowed lady who inhabits the house next door to Mr Warburton's, happened by chance to look out of her bedroom window and saw Mr Warburton standing at his front gate in conversation with a young woman. As it was a clear moonlight night, Mrs Semprill was able to distinguish this young woman as Miss Hare, the Rector's daughter. The pair remained at the gate for several minutes, and before going indoors they exchanged embraces which Mrs Semprill describes as being of a passionate nature. About half an hour later they reappeared in Mr Warburton's car, which was backed out of the front gate, and drove off in the direction of the Ipswich road. Miss Hare was dressed in scanty attire, and appeared to be under the influence of alcohol.

It is now learned that for some time past Miss Hare had been in the habit of making clandestine visits to Mr Warburton's house. Mrs Semprill, who could only with great difficulty be persuaded to speak upon so painful a subject, has further revealed—

Dorothy crumpled Pippin's Weekly violently between her hands and thrust it into the fire, upsetting the can of water. There was a cloud of ashes and sulphurous smoke, and almost in the same instant Dorothy pulled the paper out of the fire unburnt. No use funking it—better to learn the worst. She read on, with a horrible fascination. It was not a nice kind of story to read about yourself. For it was strange, but she had no longer any shadow of doubt that this girl of whom she was reading was herself. She examined the photograph. It was a blurred, nebulous thing, but quite unmistakable. Besides, she had no need of the photograph to remind her. She could remember everything—every circumstance of her life, up to that evening when she had come home tired out from Mr Warburton's house, and, presumably, fallen asleep in the conservatory. It was all so clear in her mind that it was almost incredible that she had ever forgotten it.

She ate no breakfast that day, and did not think to prepare anything for the midday meal; but when the time came, from force of habit, she set out for the hopfields with the other pickers. With difficulty, being alone, she dragged the heavy bin into position, pulled the next bine down and began picking. But after a few minutes she found that it was quite impossible; even the mechanical labour of picking was beyond her. That horrible, lying story in Pippin's Weekly had so unstrung her that it was impossible even for an instant to focus her mind upon anything else. Its lickerish phrases were going over and over in her head. 'Embraces of a passionate nature'—'in scanty attire'—'under the influence of alcohol'—as each one came back into her memory it brought with it such a pang that she wanted to cry out as though in physical pain.

After a while she stopped even pretending to pick, let the bine fall across her bin, and sat down against one of the posts that supported the wires. The other pickers observed her plight, and were sympathetic. Ellen was a bit cut up, they said. What else could you expect, after her bloke had been knocked off? (Everyone in the camp, of course, had taken it for granted that Nobby was Dorothy's lover.) They advised her to go down to the farm and report sick. And towards twelve o'clock, when the measurer was due, everyone in the set came across with a hatful of hops and dropped it into her bin.

When the measurer arrived he found Dorothy still sitting on the ground. Beneath her dirt and sunburn she was very pale; her face looked haggard, and much older than before. Her bin was twenty yards behind the rest of the set, and there were less than three bushels of hops in it.

'What's the game?' he demanded. 'You ill?'

'No.'

'Well, why ain't you bin pickin', then? What you think this is— toff's picnic? You don't come up 'ere to sit about on the ground, you know.'

'You cheese it and don't get nagging of 'er!' shouted the old cockney costerwoman suddenly. 'Can't the pore girl 'ave a bit of rest and peace if she wants it? Ain't 'er bloke in the clink thanks to you and your bloody nosing pals of coppers? She's got enough to worry 'er 'thout being —— about by every bloody copper's nark in Kent!'

'That'll be enough from you, Ma!' said the measurer gruffly, but he looked more sympathetic on hearing that it was Dorothy's lover who had been arrested on the previous night. When the costerwoman had got her kettle boiling she called Dorothy to her bin and gave her a cup of strong tea and a hunk of bread and cheese; and after the dinner interval another picker who had no partner was sent up to share Dorothy's bin. He was a small, weazened old tramp named Deafie. Dorothy felt somewhat better after the tea. Encouraged by Deafie's example—for he was an excellent picker—she managed to do her fair share of work during the afternoon.

She had thought things over, and was less distracted than before. The phrases in Pippin's Weekly still made her wince with shame, but she was equal now to facing the situation. She understood well enough what had happened to her, and what had led to Mrs Semprill's libel. Mrs Semprill had seen them together at the gate and had seen Mr Warburton kissing her; and after that, when they were both missing from Knype Hill, it was only too natural—natural for Mrs Semprill, that is—to infer that they had eloped together. As for the picturesque details, she had invented them later. Or HAD she invented them? That was the one thing you could never be certain of with Mrs Semprill—whether she told her lies consciously and deliberately AS lies, or whether, in her strange and disgusting mind, she somehow succeeded in believing them.

Well, anyway, the harm was done—no use worrying about it any longer. Meanwhile, there was the question of getting back to Knype Hill. She would have to send for some clothes, and she would need two pounds for her train fare home. Home! The word sent a pang through her heart. Home, after weeks of dirt and hunger! How she longed for it, now that she remembered it!

But—!

A chilly little doubt raised its head. There was one aspect of the matter that she had not thought of till this moment. COULD she, after all, go home? Dared she?

Could she face Knype Hill after everything that had happened? That was the question. When you have figured on the front page of Pippin's Weekly—'in scanty attire'—'under the influence of alcohol'—ah, don't let's think of it again! But when you have been plastered all over with horrible, dishonouring libels, can you go back to a town of two thousand inhabitants where everybody knows everybody else's private history and talks about it all day long?

She did not know—could not decide. At one moment it seemed to her that the story of her elopement was so palpably absurd that no one could possibly have believed it. Mr Warburton, for instance, could contradict it—most certainly would contradict it, for every possible reason. But the next moment she remembered that Mr Warburton had gone abroad, and unless this affair had got into the continental newspapers, he might not even have heard of it; and then she quailed again. She knew what it means to have to live down a scandal in a small country town. The glances and furtive nudges when you passed! The prying eyes following you down the street from behind curtained windows! The knots of youths on the corners round Blifil-Gordon's factory, lewdly discussing you!

'George! Say, George! J'a see that bit of stuff over there? With fair 'air?'

'What, the skinny one? Yes. 'Oo's she?'

'Rector's daughter, she is. Miss 'Are. But, say! What you think she done two years ago? Done a bunk with a bloke old enough to bin 'er father. Regular properly went on the razzle with 'im in Paris! Never think it to look at 'er, would you?'

'GO on!'

'She did! Straight, she did. It was in the papers and all. Only 'e give 'er the chuck three weeks afterwards, and she come back 'ome again as bold as brass. Nerve, eh?'

Yes, it would take some living down. For years, for a decade it might be, they would be talking about her like that. And the worst of it was that the story in Pippin's Weekly was probably a mere bowdlerized vestige of what Mrs Semprill had been saying in the town. Naturally, Pippin's Weekly had not wanted to commit itself too far. But was there anything that would ever restrain Mrs Semprill? Only the limits of her imagination—and they were almost as wide as the sky.

One thing, however, reassured Dorothy, and that was the thought that her father, at any rate, would do his best to shield her. Of course, there would be others as well. It was not as though she were friendless. The church congregation, at least, knew her and trusted her, and the Mothers' Union and the Girl Guides and the women on her visiting list would never believe such stories about her. But it was her father who mattered most. Almost any situation is bearable if you have a home to go back to and a family who will stand by you. With courage, and her father's support, she might face things out. By the evening she had decided that it would be perfectly all right to go back to Knype Hill, though no doubt it would be disagreeable at first, and when work was over for the day she 'subbed' a shilling, and went down to the general shop in the village and bought a penny packet of notepaper. Back in the camp, sitting on the grass by the fire—no tables or chairs in the camp, of course—she began to write with a stump of pencil:

Dearest Father,—I can't tell you how glad I am, after everything that has happened, to be able to write to you again. And I do hope you have not been too anxious about me or too worried by those horrible stories in the newspapers. I don't know what you must have thought when I suddenly disappeared like that and you didn't hear from me for nearly a month. But you see—'

How strange the pencil felt in her torn and stiffened fingers! She could only write a large, sprawling hand like that of a child. But she wrote a long letter, explaining everything, and asking him to send her some clothes and two pounds for her fare home. Also, she asked him to write to her under an assumed name she gave him—Ellen Millborough, after Millborough in Suffolk. It seemed a queer thing to have to do, to use a false name; dishonest—criminal, almost. But she dared not risk its being known in the village, and perhaps in the camp as well, that she was Dorothy Hare, the notorious 'Rector's Daughter'.

6

Once her mind was made up, Dorothy was pining to escape from the hop camp. On the following day she could hardly bring herself to go on with the stupid work of picking, and the discomforts and bad food were intolerable now that she had memories to compare them with. She would have taken to flight immediately if only she had had enough money to get her home. The instant her father's letter with the two pounds arrived, she would say good-bye to the Turles and take the train for home, and breathe a sigh of relief to get there, in spite of the ugly scandals that had got to be faced.

On the third day after writing she went down the village post office and asked for her letter. The postmistress, a woman with the face of a dachshund and a bitter contempt for all hop-pickers, told her frostily that no letter had come. Dorothy was disappointed. A pity—it must have been held up in the post. However, it didn't matter; tomorrow would be soon enough—only another day to wait.

The next evening she went again, quite certain that it would have arrived this time. Still no letter. This time a misgiving assailed her; and on the fifth evening, when there was yet again no letter, the misgiving changed into a horrible panic. She bought another packet of notepaper and wrote an enormous letter, using up the whole four sheets, explaining over and over again what had happened and imploring her father not to leave her in such suspense. Having posted it, she made up her mind that she would let a whole week go by before calling at the post office again.

This was Saturday. By Wednesday her resolve had broken down. When the hooter sounded for the midday interval she left her bin and hurried down to the post office—it was a mile and a half away, and it meant missing her dinner. Having got there she went shame- facedly up to the counter, almost afraid to speak. The dog-faced postmistress was sitting in her brass-barred cage at the end of the counter, ticking figures in a long shaped account book. She gave Dorothy a brief nosy glance and went on with her work, taking no notice of her.

Something painful was happening in Dorothy's diaphragm. She was finding it difficult to breathe, 'Are there any letters for me?' she managed to say at last.

'Name?' said the postmistress, ticking away.

'Ellen Millborough.'

The postmistress turned her long dachshund nose over her shoulder for an instant and glanced at the M partition of the Poste Restante letter-box.

'No,' she said, turning back to her account book.

In some manner Dorothy got herself outside and began to walk back towards the hopfields, then halted. A deadly feeling of emptiness at the pit of her stomach, caused partly by hunger, made her too weak to walk.

Her father's silence could mean only one thing. He believed Mrs Semprill's story—believed that she, Dorothy, had run away from home in disgraceful circumstances and then told lies to excuse herself. He was too angry and too disgusted to write to her. All he wanted was to get rid of her, drop all communication with her; get her out of sight and out of mind, as a mere scandal to be covered up and forgotten.

She could not go home after this. She dared not. Now that she had seen what her father's attitude was, it had opened her eyes to the rashness of the thing she had been contemplating. Of COURSE she could not go home! To slink back in disgrace, to bring shame on her father's house by coming there—ah, impossible, utterly impossible! How could she even have thought of it?

What then? There was nothing for it but to go right away—right away to some place that was big enough to hide in. London, perhaps. Somewhere where nobody knew her and the mere sight of her face or mention of her name would not drag into the light a string of dirty memories.

As she stood there the sound of bells floated towards her, from the village church round the bend of the road, where the ringers were amusing themselves by ringing 'Abide with Me', as one picks out a tune with one finger on the piano. But presently 'Abide with Me' gave way to the familiar Sunday-morning jangle. 'Oh do leave my wife alone! She is so drunk she can't get home!'—the same peal that the bells of St Athelstan's had been used to ring three years ago before they were unswung. The sound planted a spear of homesickness in Dorothy's heart, bringing back to her with momentary vividness a medley of remembered things—the smell of the glue-pot in the conservatory when she was making costumes for the school play, and the chatter of starlings outside her bedroom window, interrupting her prayers before Holy Communion, and Mrs Pither's doleful voice chronicling the pains in the backs of her legs, and the worries of the collapsing belfry and the shop-debts and the bindweed in the peas—all the multitudinous, urgent details of a life that had alternated between work and prayer.

Prayer! For a very short time, a minute perhaps, the thought arrested her. Prayer—in those days it had been the very source and centre of her life. In trouble or in happiness, it was to prayer that she had turned. And she realized—the first time that it had crossed her mind—that she had not uttered a prayer since leaving home, not even since her memory had come back to her. Moreover, she was aware that she had no longer the smallest impulse to pray. Mechanically, she began a whispered prayer, and stopped almost instantly; the words were empty and futile. Prayer, which had been the mainstay of her life, had no meaning for her any longer. She recorded this fact as she walked slowly up the road, and she recorded it briefly, almost casually, as though it had been something seen in passing—a flower in the ditch or a bird crossing the road—something noticed and then dismissed. She had not even the time to reflect upon what it might mean. It was shouldered out of her mind by more momentous things.

It was of the future that she had got to be thinking now. She was already fairly clear in her mind as to what she must do. When the hop-picking was at an end she must go up to London, write to her father for money and her clothes—for however angry he might be, she could not believe that he intended to leave her utterly in the lurch—and then start looking for a job. It was the measure of her ignorance that those dreaded words 'looking for a job' sounded hardly at all dreadful in her ears. She knew herself strong and willing—knew that there were plenty of jobs that she was capable of doing. She could be a nursery governess, for instance—no, better, a housemaid or a parlourmaid. There were not many things in a house that she could not do better than most servants; besides, the more menial her job, the easier it would be to keep her past history secret.

At any rate, her father's house was closed to her, that was certain. From now on she had got to fend for herself. On this decision, with only a very dim idea of what it meant, she quickened her pace and got back to the fields in time for the afternoon shift.

The hop-picking season had not much longer to run. In a week or thereabouts Cairns's would be closing down, and the cockneys would take the hoppers' train to London, and the gypsies would catch their horses, pack their caravans, and march northward to Lincolnshire, to scramble for jobs in the potato fields. As for the cockneys, they had had their bellyful of hop-picking by this time. They were pining to be back in dear old London, with Woolworths and the fried-fish shop round the corner, and no more sleeping in straw and frying bacon in tin lids with your eyes weeping from wood smoke. Hopping was a holiday, but the kind of holiday that you were glad to see the last of. You came down cheering, but you went home cheering louder still and swearing that you would never go hopping again—until next August, when you had forgotten the cold nights and the bad pay and the damage to your hands, and remembered only the blowsy afternoons in the sun and the boozing of stone pots of beer round the red camp fires at night.

The mornings were growing bleak and Novemberish; grey skies, the first leaves falling, and finches and starlings already flocking for the winter. Dorothy had written yet again to her father, asking for money and some clothes; he had left her letter unanswered, nor had anybody else written to her. Indeed, there was no one except her father who knew her present address; but somehow she had hoped that Mr Warburton might write. Her courage almost failed her now, especially at nights in the wretched straw, when she lay awake thinking of the vague and menacing future. She picked her hops with a sort of desperation, a sort of frenzy of energy, more aware each day that every handful of hops meant another fraction of a farthing between herself and starvation. Deafie, her bin-mate, like herself, was picking against time, for it was the last money he would earn till next year's hopping season came round. The figure they aimed at was five shillings a day— thirty bushels—between the two of them, but there was no day when they quite attained it.

Deafie was a queer old man and a poor companion after Nobby, but not a bad sort. He was a ship's steward by profession, but a tramp of many years' standing, as deaf as a post and therefore something of a Mr F.'s aunt in conversation. He was also an exhibitionist, but quite harmless. For hours together he used to sing a little song that went 'With my willy willy—WITH my willy willy', and though he could not hear what he was singing it seemed to cause him some kind of pleasure. He had the hairiest ears Dorothy had ever seen. There were tufts like miniature Dundreary whiskers growing out of each of his ears. Every year Deafie came hop-picking at Cairns's farm, saved up a pound, and then spent a paradisiac week in a lodging-house in Newington Butts before going back to the road. This was the only week in the year when he slept in what could be called, except by courtesy, a bed.

The picking came to an end on 28 September. There were several fields still unpicked, but they were poor hops and at the last moment Mr Cairns decided to 'let them blow'. Set number 19 finished their last field at two in the afternoon, and the little gypsy foreman swarmed up the poles and retrieved the derelict bunches, and the measurer carted the last hops away. As he disappeared there was a sudden shout of 'Put 'em in the bins!' and Dorothy saw six men bearing down upon her with a fiendish expression on their faces, and all the women in the set scattering and running. Before she could collect her wits to escape the men had seized her, laid her at full length in a bin and swung her violently from side to side. Then she was dragged out and kissed by a young gypsy smelling of onions. She struggled at first, but she saw the same thing being done to the other women in the set, so she submitted. It appeared that putting the women in the bins was an invariable custom on the last day of picking. There were great doings in the camp that night, and not much sleep for anybody. Long after midnight Dorothy found herself moving with a ring of people about a mighty fire, one hand clasped by a rosy butcher-boy and the other by a very drunk old woman in a Scotch bonnet out of a cracker, to the tune of 'Auld Lang Syne'.

In the morning they went up to the farm to draw their money, and Dorothy drew one pound and fourpence, and earned another fivepence by adding up their tally books for people who could not read or write. The cockney pickers paid you a penny for this job; the gypsies paid you only in flattery. Then Dorothy set out for West Ackworth station, four miles away, together with the Turles, Mr Turle carrying the tin trunk, Mrs Turle carrying the baby, the other children carrying various odds and ends, and Dorothy wheeling the perambulator which held the Turles' entire stock of crockery, and which had two circular wheels and two elliptical.

They got to the station about midday, the hoppers' train was due to start at one, and it arrived at two and started at a quarter past three. After a journey of incredible slowness, zigzagging all over Kent to pick up a dozen hop-pickers here and half a dozen there, going back on its tracks over and over again and backing into sidings to let other trains pass—taking, in fact, six hours to do thirty-five miles—it landed them in London a little after nine at night.

7

Dorothy slept that night with the Turles. They had grown so fond of her that they would have given her shelter for a week or a fortnight if she had been willing to impose on their hospitality.

Their two rooms (they lived in a tenement house not far from Tower Bridge Road) were a tight fit for seven people including children, but they made her a bed of sorts on the floor out of two rag mats, an old cushion and an overcoat.

In the morning she said good-bye to the Turles and thanked them for all their kindness towards her, and then went straight to Bermondsey public baths and washed off the accumulated dirt of five weeks. After that she set out to look for a lodging, having in her possession sixteen and eightpence in cash, and the clothes she stood up in. She had darned and cleaned her clothes as best she could, and being black they did not show the dirt quite as badly as they might have done. From the knees down she was now passably respectable. On the last day of picking a 'home picker' in the next set, named Mrs Killfrew, had presented her with a good pair of shoes that had been her daughter's, and a pair of woollen stockings.

It was not until the evening that Dorothy managed to find herself a room. For something like ten hours she was wandering up and down, from Bermondsey into Southwark, from Southwark into Lambeth, through labyrinthine streets where snotty-nosed children played at hop-scotch on pavements horrible with banana skins and decaying cabbage leaves. At every house she tried it was the same story— the landlady refused point-blank to take her in. One after another a succession of hostile women, standing in their doorways as defensively as though she had been a motor bandit or a government inspector, looked her up and down, said briefly, 'We don't TAKE single girls,' and shut the door in her face. She did not know it, of course, but the very look of her was enough to rouse any respectable landlady's suspicions. Her stained and ragged clothes they might possibly have put up with; but the fact that she had no luggage damned her from the start. A single girl with no luggage is invariably a bad lot—this is the first and greatest of the apophthegms of the London landlady.

At about seven o'clock, too tired to stand on her feet any longer, she ventured into a filthy, flyblown little cafe near the Old Vic theatre and asked for a cup of tea. The proprietress, getting into conversation with her and learning that she wanted a room, advised her to 'try at Mary's, in Wellings Court, jest orff the Cut'. 'Mary', it appeared, was not particular and would let a room to anybody who could pay. Her proper name was Mrs Sawyer, but the boys all called her Mary.

Dorothy found Wellings Court with some difficulty. You went along Lambeth Cut till you got to a Jew clothes-shop called Knockout Trousers Ltd, then you turned up a narrow alley, and then turned to your left again up another alley so narrow that its grimy plaster walls almost brushed you as you went. In the plaster, persevering boys had cut the word —— innumerable times and too deeply to be erased. At the far end of the alley you found yourself in a small court where four tall narrow houses with iron staircases stood facing one another.

Dorothy made inquiries and found 'Mary' in a subterranean den beneath one of the houses. She was a drabby old creature with remarkably thin hair and face so emaciated that it looked like a rouged and powdered skull. Her voice was cracked, shrewish, and nevertheless ineffably dreary. She asked Dorothy no questions, and indeed scarcely even looked at her, but simply demanded ten shillings and then said in her ugly voice:

'Twenty-nine. Third floor. Go up be the back stairs.'

Apparently the back stairs were those inside the house. Dorothy went up the dark, spiral staircase, between sweating walls, in a smell of old overcoats, dishwater and slops. As she reached the second floor there was a loud squeal of laughter, and two rowdy- looking girls came out of one of the rooms and stared at her for a moment. They looked young, their faces being quite hidden under rouge and pink powder, and their lips painted scarlet as geranium petals. But amid the pink powder their china-blue eyes were tired and old; and that was somehow horrible, because it reminded you of a girl's mask with an old woman's face behind it. The taller of the two greeted Dorothy.

''Ullo, dearie!'

'Hullo!'

'You new 'ere? Which room you kipping in?'

'Number twenty-nine.'

'God, ain't that a bloody dungeon to put you in! You going out tonight?'

'No, I don't think so,' said Dorothy, privately a little astonished at the question. 'I'm too tired.'

'Thought you wasn't, when I saw you 'adn't dolled up. But, say! dearie, you ain't on the beach, are you? Not spoiling the ship for a 'aporth of tar? Because f'rinstance if you want the lend of a lipstick, you only got to say the word. We're all chums 'ere, you know.'

'Oh.... No, thank you,' said Dorothy, taken aback.

'Oh, well! Time Doris and me was moving. Got a 'portant business engagement in Leicester Square.' Here she nudged the other girl with her hip, and both of them sniggered in a silly mirthless manner. 'But, say!' added the taller girl confidentially, 'ain't it a bloody treat to 'ave a good night's kip all alone once in a way? Wish _I_ could. All on your Jack Jones with no bloody great man's feet shoving you about. 'S all right when you can afford it, eh?'

'Yes,' said Dorothy, feeling that this answer was expected of her, and with only a very vague notion of what the other was talking about.

'Well, ta ta, dearie! Sleep tight. And jes' look out for the smash and grab raiders 'bout 'ar-parse one!'

When the two girls had skipped downstairs with another of their meaningless squeals of laughter, Dorothy found her way to room number 29 and opened the door. A cold, evil smell met her. The room measured about eight feet each way, and was very dark. The furniture was simple. In the middle of the room, a narrow iron bedstead with a ragged coverlet and greyish sheets; against the wall, a packing case with a tin basin and an empty whisky bottle intended for water; tacked over the bed, a photograph of Bebe Daniels torn out of Film Fun.

The sheets were not only dirty, but damp. Dorothy got into the bed, but she had only undressed to her chemise, or what was left of her chemise, her underclothes by this time being almost entirely in ruins; she could not bring herself to lay her bare body between those nauseous sheets. And once in bed, though she was aching from head to foot with fatigue, she could not sleep. She was unnerved and full of forebodings. The atmosphere of this vile place brought home to her more vividly than before the fact that she was helpless and friendless and had only six shillings between herself and the streets. Moreover, as the night wore on the house grew noisier and noisier. The walls were so thin that you could hear everything that was happening. There were bursts of shrill idiotic laughter, hoarse male voices singing, a gramophone drawling out limericks, noisy kisses, strange deathlike groans, and once or twice the violent rattling of an iron bed. Towards midnight the noises began to form themselves into a rhythm in Dorothy's brain, and she fell lightly and unrestfully asleep. She was woken about a minute later, as it seemed, by her door being flung open, and two dimly seen female shapes rushed in, tore every scrap of clothing from her bed except the sheets, and rushed out again. There was a chronic shortage of blankets at 'Mary's', and the only way of getting enough of them was to rob somebody else's bed. Hence the term 'smash and grab raiders'.

In the morning, half an hour before opening time, Dorothy went to the nearest public library to look at the advertisements in the newspapers. Already a score of vaguely mangy-looking people were prowling up and down, and the number swelled by ones and twos till there were no less than sixty. Presently the doors of the library opened, and in they all surged, racing for a board at the other end of the reading-room where the 'Situations Vacant' columns from various newspapers had been cut out and pinned up. And in the wake of the job-hunters came poor old bundles of rags, men and women both, who had spent the night in the streets and came to the library to sleep. They came shambling in behind the others, flopped down with grunts of relief at the nearest table, and pulled the nearest periodical towards them; it might be the Free Church Messenger, it might be the Vegetarian Sentinel—it didn't matter what it was, but you couldn't stay in the library unless you pretended to be reading. They opened their papers, and in the same instant fell asleep, with their chins on their breasts. And the attendant walked round prodding them in turn like a stoker poking a succession of fires, and they grunted and woke up as he prodded them, and then fell asleep again the instant he had passed.

Meanwhile a battle was raging round the advertisement board, everybody struggling to get to the front. Two young men in blue overalls came running up behind the others, and one of them put his head down and fought his way through the crowd as though it had been a football scrum. In a moment he was at the board. He turned to his companion: ''Ere we are, Joe—I got it! "Mechanics wanted— Locke's Garage, Camden Town." C'm on out of it!' He fought his way out again, and both of them scooted for the door. They were going to Camden Town as fast as their legs would carry them. And at this moment, in every public library in London, mechanics out of work were reading that identical notice and starting on the race for the job, which in all probability had already been given to someone who could afford to buy a paper for himself and had seen the notice at six in the morning.

Dorothy managed to get to the board at last, and made a note of some of the addresses where 'cook generals' were wanted.

There were plenty to choose from—indeed, half the ladies in London seemed to be crying out for strong capable general servants. With a list of twenty addresses in her pocket, and having had a breakfast of bread and margarine and tea which cost her threepence, Dorothy set out to look for a job, not unhopefully.

She was too ignorant as yet to know that her chances of finding work unaided were practically nil; but the next four days gradually enlightened her. During those four days she applied for eighteen jobs, and sent written applications for four others. She trudged enormous distances all through the southern suburbs: Clapham, Brixton, Dulwich, Penge, Sydenham, Beckenham, Norwood—even as far as Croydon on one occasion. She was haled into neat suburban drawing-rooms and interviewed by women of every conceivable type— large, chubby, bullying women, thin, acid, catty women, alert frigid women in gold pince-nez, vague rambling women who looked as though they practised vegetarianism or attended spiritualist seances. And one and all, fat or thin, chilly or motherly, they reacted to her in precisely the same way. They simply looked her over, heard her speak, stared inquisitively, asked her a dozen embarrassing and impertinent questions, and then turned her down.

Any experienced person could have told her how it would be. In her circumstances it was not to be expected that anyone would take the risk of employing her. Her ragged clothes and her lack of references were against her, and her educated accent, which she did not know how to disguise, wrecked whatever chances she might have had. The tramps and cockney hop-pickers had not noticed her accent, but the suburban housewives noticed it quickly enough, and it scared them in just the same way as the fact that she had no luggage had scared the landladies. The moment they had heard her speak, and spotted her for a gentlewoman, the game was up. She grew quite used to the startled, mystified look that came over their faces as soon as she opened her mouth—the prying, feminine glance from her face to her damaged hands, and from those to the darns in her skirt. Some of the women asked her outright what a girl of her class was doing seeking work as a servant. They sniffed, no doubt, that she had 'been in trouble'—that is, had an illegitimate baby—and after probing her with their questions they got rid of her as quickly as possible.

As soon as she had an address to give Dorothy had written to her father, and when on the third day no answer came, she wrote again, despairingly this time—it was her fifth letter, and four had gone unanswered—telling him that she must starve if he did not send her money at once. There was just time for her to get an answer before her week at 'Mary's' was up and she was thrown out for not paying her rent.

Meanwhile, she continued the useless search for work, while her money dwindled at the rate of a shilling a day—a sum just sufficient to keep her alive while leaving her chronically hungry. She had almost given up the hope that her father would do anything to help her. And strangely enough her first panic had died down, as she grew hungrier and the chances of getting a job grew remoter, into a species of miserable apathy. She suffered, but she was not greatly afraid. The sub-world into which she was descending seemed less terrible now that it was nearer.

The autumn weather, though fine, was growing colder. Each day the sun, fighting his losing battle against the winter, struggled a little later through the mist to dye the house-fronts with pale aquarelle colours. Dorothy was in the streets all day, or in the public library, only going back to 'Mary's' to sleep, and then taking the precaution of dragging her bed across the door. She had grasped by this time that 'Mary's' was—not actually a brothel, for there is hardly such a thing in London, but a well-known refuge of prostitutes. It was for that reason that you paid ten shillings a week for a kennel not worth five. Old 'Mary' (she was not the proprietress of the house, merely the manageress) had been a prostitute herself in her day, and looked it. Living in such a place damned you even in the eyes of Lambeth Cut. Women sniffed when you passed them, men took an offensive interest in you. The Jew on the corner, the owner of Knockout Trousers Ltd, was the worst of all. He was a solid young man of about thirty, with bulging red cheeks and curly black hair like astrakhan. For twelve hours a day he stood on the pavement roaring with brazen lungs that you couldn't get a cheaper pair of trousers in London, and obstructing the passers-by. You had only to halt for a fraction of a second, and he seized you by the arm and bundled you inside the shop by main force. Once he got you there his manner became positively threatening. If you said anything disparaging about his trousers he offered to fight, and weak-minded people bought pairs of trousers in sheer physical terror. But busy though he was, he kept a sharp eye open for the 'birds', as he called them; and Dorothy appeared to fascinate him beyond all other 'birds'. He had grasped that she was not a prostitute, but living at 'Mary's', she must—so he reasoned—be on the very verge of becoming one. The thought made his mouth water. When he saw her coming down the alley he would post himself at the corner, with his massive chest well displayed and one black lecherous eye turned inquiringly upon her ('Are you ready to begin yet?' his eye seemed to be saying), and, as she passed, give her a discreet pinch on the backside.

On the last morning of her week at 'Mary's', Dorothy went downstairs and looked, with only a faint flicker of hope, at the slate in the hallway where the names of people for whom there were letters were chalked up. There was no letter for 'Ellen Millborough'. That settled it; there was nothing left to do except to walk out into the street. It did not occur to her to do as every other woman in the house would have done—that is, pitch a hard-up tale and try to cadge another night's lodging rent free.

She simply walked out of the house, and had not even the nerve to tell 'Mary' that she was going.

She had no plan, absolutely no plan whatever. Except for half an hour at noon when she went out to spend threepence out of her last fourpence on bread and margarine and tea, she passed the entire day in the public library, reading weekly papers. In the morning she read the Barber's Record, and in the afternoon Cage Birds. They were the only papers she could get hold of, for there were always so many idlers in the library that you had to scramble to get hold of a paper at all. She read them from cover to cover, even the advertisements. She pored for hours together over such technicalities as How to strop French Razors, Why the Electric Hairbrush is Unhygienic, Do Budgies thrive on Rapeseed? It was the only occupation that she felt equal to. She was in a strange lethargic state in which it was easier to interest herself in How to strop French Razors than in her own desperate plight. All fear had left her. Of the future she was utterly unable to think; even so far ahead as tonight she could barely see. There was a night in the streets ahead of her, that was all she knew, and even about that she only vaguely cared. Meanwhile there were Cage Birds and the Barber's Record; and they were, strangely, absorbingly interesting.

At nine o'clock the attendant came round with a long hooked pole and turned out the gaslights, the library was closed. Dorothy turned to the left, up the Waterloo Road, towards the river. On the iron footbridge she halted for a moment. The night wind was blowing. Deep banks of mist, like dunes, were rising from the river, and, as the wind caught them, swirling north-eastward across the town. A swirl of mist enveloped Dorothy, penetrating her thin clothes and making her shudder with a sudden foretaste of the night's cold. She walked on and arrived, by the process of gravitation that draws all roofless people to the same spot, at Trafalgar Square.

CHAPTER 3

1

[SCENE: Trafalgar Square. Dimly visible through the mist, a dozen people, Dorothy among them, are grouped about one of the benches near the north parapet.]

CHARLIE [singing]: 'Ail Mary, 'ail Mary, 'a-il Ma-ary—[Big Ben strikes ten.]

SNOUTER [mimicking the noise]: Ding dong, ding dong! Shut your —— noise, can't you? Seven more hours of it on this —— square before we get the chance of a setdown and a bit of sleep! Cripes!

MR TALLBOYS [to himself]: Non sum qualis eram boni sub regno Edwardi! In the days of my innocence, before the Devil carried me up into a high place and dropped me into the Sunday newspapers— that is to say when I was Rector of Little Fawley-cum-Dewsbury....

DEAFIE [singing]: With my willy willy, WITH my willy willy—

MRS WAYNE: Ah, dearie, as soon as I set eyes on you I knew as you was a lady born and bred. You and me've known what it is to come down in the world, haven't we, dearie? It ain't the same for us as what it is for some of these others here.

CHARLIE [singing]: 'Ail Mary, 'ail Mary, 'a-il Ma-ary, full of grace!

MRS BENDIGO: Calls himself a bloody husband, does he?

Four pound a week in Covent Garden and 'is wife doing a starry in the bloody Square! Husband!

MR TALLBOYS [to himself]: Happy days, happy days! My ivied church under the sheltering hillside—my red-tiled Rectory slumbering among Elizabethan yews! My library, my vinery, my cook, house- parlourmaid and groom-gardener! My cash in the bank, my name in Crockford! My black suit of irreproachable cut, my collar back to front, my watered silk cassock in the church precincts....

MRS WAYNE: Of course the one thing I DO thank God for, dearie, is that my poor dear mother never lived to see this day. Because if she ever HAD of lived to see the day when her eldest daughter—as was brought up, mind you, with no expense spared and milk straight from the cow....

MRS BENDIGO: HUSBAND!

GINGER: Come on, less 'ave a drum of tea while we got the chance. Last we'll get tonight—coffee shop shuts at 'ar-parse ten.

THE KIKE: Oh Jesus! This bloody cold's gonna kill me! I ain't got nothing on under my trousers. Oh Je-e-e-EEZE!

CHARLIE [singing]: 'Ail Mary, 'ail Mary—

SNOUTER: Fourpence! Fourpence for six —— hours on the bum! And that there nosing sod with the wooden leg queering our pitch at every boozer between Aldgate and the Mile End Road. With 'is —— wooden leg and 'is war medals as 'e bought in Lambeth Cut! Bastard!

DEAFIE [singing]: With my willy willy, WITH my willy willy—

MRS BENDIGO: Well, I told the bastard what I thought of 'im, anyway. 'Call yourself a man?' I says. 'I've seen things like you kep' in a bottle at the 'orspital,' I says....

MR TALLBOYS [to himself]: Happy days, happy days! Roast beef and bobbing villagers, and the peace of God that passeth all understanding! Sunday mornings in my oaken stall, cool flower scent and frou-frou of surplices mingling in the sweet corpse-laden air! Summer evenings when the late sun slanted through my study window—I pensive, boozed with tea, in fragrant wreaths of Cavendish, thumbing drowsily some half-calf volume—Poetical Works of William Shenstone, Esq., Percy's Reliques of Ancient English Poetry, J. Lempriere, D.D., professor of immoral theology...

GINGER: Come on, 'oo's for that drum of riddleme-ree? We got the milk and we got the tea. Question is, 'oo's got any bleeding sugar?

DOROTHY: This cold, this cold! It seems to go right through you! Surely it won't be like this all night?

MRS BENDIGO: Oh, cheese it! I 'ate these snivelling tarts.

CHARLIE: Ain't it going to be a proper perisher, too? Look at the perishing river mist creeping up that there column. Freeze the fish-hooks off of ole Nelson before morning.

MRS WAYNE: Of course, at the time that I'm speaking of we still had our little tobacco and sweetstuff business on the corner, you'll understand....

THE KIKE: Oh Je-e-e-EEZE! Lend's that overcoat of yours, Ginger. I'm bloody freezing!

SNOUTER: —— double-crossing bastard! P'raps I won't bash 'is navel in when I get a 'old of 'im!

CHARLIE: Fortunes o' war, boy, fortunes o' war. Perishing Square tonight—rumpsteak and kip on feathers tomorrow. What else d'you expect on perishing Thursday?

MRS BENDIGO: Shove up, Daddy, shove up! Think I want your lousy old 'ed on my shoulder—me a married woman?

MR TALLBOYS [to himself]: For preaching, chanting, and intoning I was unrivalled. My Lift up your Hearts' was renowned throughout the diocese. All styles I could do you, High Church, Low Church, Broad Church and No Church. Throaty

Anglo-Cat Warblings, straight from the shoulder muscular Anglican, or the adenoidal Low Church whine in which still lurk the Houyhnhnm-notes of neighing chapel elders....

DEAFIE [singing]: WITH my willy willy—

GINGER: Take your 'ands off that bleeding overcoat, Kikie. You don't get no clo'es of mine while you got the chats on you.

CHARLIE [singing]:

As pants the 'art for cooling streams, When 'eated in the chase—

MRS MCELLIGOT [in her sleep]: Was 'at you, Michael dear?

MRS BENDIGO: It's my belief as the sneaking bastard 'ad another wife living when 'e married me.

MR TALLBOYS [from the roof of his mouth, stage curate-wise, reminiscently]: If any of you know cause of just impediment why these two persons should not be joined together in holy matrimony...

THE KIKE: A pal! A bloody pal! And won't lend his bloody overcoat!

MRS WAYNE: Well, now as you've mentioned it, I must admit as I never WAS one to refuse a nice cup of tea. I know that when our poor dear mother was alive, pot after pot we used to...

NOSY WATSON [to himself, angrily]: Sod!... Gee'd into it and then a stretch all round.... Never even done the bloody job.... Sod!

DEAFIE [singing]: WITH my willy willy—

MRS MCELLIGOT [half asleep]: DEAR Michael.... He was real loving, Michael was. Tender an' true.... Never looked at another man since dat evenin' when I met'm outside Kronk's slaughter-house an' he gimme de two pound o' sausage as he'd bummed off de International Stores for his own supper....

MRS BENDIGO: Well, I suppose we'll get that bloody tea this time tomorrow.

MR TALLBOYS [chanting, reminiscently]: By the waters of Babylon we sat down and wept, when we remembered thee, O Zion!…

DOROTHY: Oh, this cold, this cold!

SNOUTER: Well, I don't do no more —— starries this side of Christmas. I'll 'ave my kip tomorrow if I 'ave to cut it out of their bowels.

NOSY WATSON: Detective, is he? Smith of the Flying Squad! Flying Judas more likely! All they can bloody do—copping the old offenders what no beak won't give a fair chance.

GINGER: Well, I'm off for the fiddlede-dee. 'Oo's got a couple of clods for the water?

MRS MCELLIGOT [waking]: Oh dear, oh dear! If my back ain't fair broke! Oh holy Jesus, if dis bench don't catch you across de kidneys! An' dere was me dreamin' I was warm in kip wid a nice cup a' tea an' two o' buttered toast waitin' by me bedside. Well, dere goes me last wink o' sleep till I gets into Lambeth public lib'ry tomorrow.

DADDY [his head emerging from within his overcoat like a tortoise's from within its shell]: Wassat you said, boy? Paying money for water! How long've you bin on the road, you ignorant young scut? Money for bloody water? Bum it, boy, bum it! Don't buy what you can bum and don't bum what you can steal. That's my word—fifty year on the road, man and boy. [Retires within his coat.]

MR TALLBOYS [chanting]: O all ye works of the Lord—

DEAFIE [singing]: WITH my willy willy—

CHARLIE: 'Oo was it copped you, Nosy?

THE KIKE: Oh Je-e-e-EEZE!

MRS BENDIGO: Shove up, shove up! Seems to me some folks think they've took a mortgage on this bloody seat.

MR TALLBOYS [chanting]: O all ye works of the Lord, curse ye the Lord, curse Him and vilify Him for ever!

MRS MCELLIGOT: What I always says is, it's always us poor bloody Catholics dat's down in de bloody dumps.

NOSY WATSON: Smithy. Flying Squad—flying sod! Give us the plans of the house and everything, and then had a van full of coppers waiting and nipped the lot of us. I wrote it up in the Black Maria:

'Detective Smith knows how to gee; Tell him he's a —— from me.'

SNOUTER: 'Ere, what about our —— tea? Go on, Kikie, you're a young 'un; shut that —— noise and take the drums. Don't you pay nothing. Worm it out of the old tart. Snivel. Do the doleful.

MR TALLBOYS [chanting]: O all ye children of men, curse ye the Lord, curse Him and vilify Him for ever!

CHARLIE: What, is Smithy crooked too?

MRS BENDIGO: I tell you what, girls, I tell you what gets ME down, and that's to think of my bloody husband snoring under four blankets and me freezing in this bloody Square. That's what _I_ can't stomach. The unnatural sod!

GINGER [singing]: THERE they go—IN their joy—Don't take that there drum with the cold sausage in it, Kikie.

NOSY WATSON: Crooked? CROOKED? Why, a corkscrew 'ud look like a bloody bradawl beside of him! There isn't one of them double —— sons of whores in the Flying Squad but 'ud sell his grandmother to the knackers for two pound ten and then sit on her gravestone eating potato crisps. The geeing, narking toe rag!

CHARLIE: Perishing tough. 'Ow many convictions you got?

GINGER [singing]:

THERE they go—IN their joy— 'APpy girl—LUcky boy—

NOSY WATSON: Fourteen. You don't stand no chance with that lot against you.

MRS WAYNE: What, don't he keep you, then?

MRS BENDIGO: No, I'm married to this one, sod 'im!

CHARLIE: I got perishing nine myself.

MR TALLBOYS [chanting]: O Ananias, Azarias and Misael, curse ye the Lord, curse Him and vilify Him for ever!

GINGER [singing]:

THERE they go—IN their joy— 'APpy girl—LUcky boy— But 'ere am _I-I-I_— Broken—'A-A-AARted!

God, I ain't 'ad a dig in the grave for three days. 'Ow long since you washed your face, Snouter?

MRS MCELLIGOT: Oh dear, oh dear! If dat boy don't come soon wid de tea me insides'll dry up like a bloody kippered herring.

CHARLIE: YOU can't sing, none of you. Ought to 'ear Snouter and me 'long towards Christmas time when we pipe up 'Good King Wenceslas' outside the boozers. 'Ymns, too. Blokes in the bar weep their perishing eyes out to 'ear us. 'Member when we tapped twice at the same 'ouse by mistake, Snouter? Old tart fair tore the innards out of us.

MR TALLBOYS [marching up and down behind an imaginary drum and singing]:

All things vile and damnable, All creatures great and small—

[Big Ben strikes half past ten.]

SNOUTER [mimicking the clock]: Ding dong, ding dong! Six and a —— half hours of it! Cripes!

GINGER: Kikie and me knocked off four of them safety-razor blades in Woolworth's 's afternoon. I'll 'ave a dig in the bleeding fountains tomorrow if I can bum a bit of soap.

DEAFIE: When I was a stooard in the P. & O., we used to meet them black Indians two days out at sea, in them there great canoes as they call catamarans, catching sea-turtles the size of dinner tables.

MRS WAYNE: Did yoo used to be a clergyman, then, sir?

MR TALLBOYS [halting]: After the order of Melchizedec. There is no question of 'used to be', Madam. Once a priest always a priest. Hoc est corpus hocus-pocus. Even though unfrocked—un-Crocked, we call it—and dog-collar publicly torn off by the bishop of the diocese.

GINGER [singing]: THERE they go—IN their joy—Thank Christ! 'Ere comes Kikie. Now for the consultation-free!

MRS BENDIGO: Not before it's bloody needed.

CHARLIE: 'Ow come they give you the sack, mate? Usual story? Choirgirls in the family way?

MRS MCELLIGOT: You've took your time, ain't you, young man? But come on, let's have a sup of it before me tongue falls out o' me bloody mouth.

MRS BENDIGO: Shove up, Daddy! You're sitting on my packet of bloody sugar.

MR TALLBOYS: Girls is a euphemism. Only the usual flannel- bloomered hunters of the unmarried clergy. Church hens—altar- dressers and brass-polishers—spinsters growing bony and desperate. There is a demon that enters into them at thirty-five.

THE KIKE: The old bitch wouldn't give me the hot water. Had to tap a toff in the street and pay a penny for it.

SNOUTER: —— likely story! Bin swigging it on the way more likely.

DADDY [emerging from his overcoat]: Drum o' tea, eh? I could sup a drum o' tea. [Belches slightly.]

CHARLIE: When their bubs get like perishing razor stops? _I_ know.

NOSY WATSON: Tea—bloody catlap. Better'n that cocoa in the stir, though. Lend's your cup, matie.

GINGER: Jest wait'll I knock a 'ole in this tin of milk. Shy us a money or your life, someone.

MRS BENDIGO: Easy with that bloody sugar! 'Oo paid for it, I sh'd like to know?

MR TALLBOYS: When their bubs get like razor stops. I thank thee for that humour. Pippin's Weekly made quite a feature of the case. 'Missing Canon's Sub Rosa Romance. Intimate Revelations.' And also an Open Letter in John Bull: 'To a Skunk in Shepherd's Clothing'. A pity—I was marked out for preferment. [To Dorothy] Gaiters in the family, if you understand me. You would not think, would you, that the time has been when this unworthy backside dented the plush cushions of a cathedral stall?

CHARLIE: 'Ere comes Florry. Thought she'd be along soon as we got the tea going. Got a nose like a perishing vulture for tea, that girl 'as.

SNOUTER: Ay, always on the tap. [Singing]

Tap, tap, tappety tap, I'm a perfec' devil at that—

MRS MCELLIGOT: De poor kid, she ain't got no sense. Why don't she go up to Piccadilly Circus where she'd get her five bob reg'lar? She won't do herself no good bummin' round de Square wid a set of miserable ole Tobies.

DOROTHY: Is that milk all right?

GINGER: All right? [Applies his mouth to one of the holes in the tin and blows. A sticky greyish stream dribbles from the other.]

CHARLIE: What luck, Florry? 'Ow 'bout that perishing toff as I see you get off with just now?

DOROTHY: It's got 'Not fit for babies' on it.

MRS BENDIGO: Well, you ain't a bloody baby, are you? You can drop your Buckingham Palace manners, 'ere, dearie.

FLORRY: Stood me a coffee and a fag—mingy bastard! That tea you got there, Ginger? You always WAS my favourite, Ginger dear.

MRS WAYNE: There's jest thirteen of us.

MR TALLBOYS: As we are not going to have any dinner you need not disturb yourself.

GINGER: What-o, ladies and gents! Tea is served. Cups forward, please!

THE KIKE: Oh Jeez! You ain't filled my bloody cup half full!

MRS MCELLIGOT: Well, here's luck to us all, an' a better bloody kip tomorrow. I'd ha' took shelter in one o' dem dere churches meself, only de b—s won't let you in if so be as dey t'ink you got de chats on you. [Drinks.]

MRS WAYNE: Well, I can't say as this is exactly the way as I've been ACCUSTOMED to drinking a cup of tea—but still—[Drinks.]

CHARLIE: Perishing good cup of tea. [Drinks.]

DEAFIE: And there was flocks of them there green parakeets in the coco-nut palms, too. [Drinks.]

MR TALLBOYS:

What potions have I drunk of siren tears, Distilled from limbecs foul as Hell within!

[Drinks.]

SNOUTER: Last we'll get till five in the —— morning. [Drinks.]

[Florry produces a broken shop-made cigarette from her stocking, and cadges a match. The men, except Daddy, Deafie, and Mr Tallboys, roll cigarettes from picked-up fag-ends. The red ends glow through the misty twilight, like a crooked constellation, as the smokers sprawl on the bench, the ground, or the slope of the parapet.]

MRS WAYNE: Well, there now! A nice cup of tea do seem to warm you up, don't it, now? Not but what I don't feel it a bit different, as you might say, not having no nice clean table-cloth like I've been accustomed to, and the beautiful china tea service as our mother used to have; and always, of course, the very best tea as money could buy—real Pekoe Points at two and nine a pound....

GINGER [singing]:

THERE they go—IN their joy— 'APPY girl—LUCKY boy—

MR TALLBOYS [singing, to the tune of 'Deutschland, Deutschland uber alles']: Keep the aspidistra flying—

CHARLIE: 'Ow long you two kids been in Smoke?

SNOUTER: I'm going to give them boozers such a doing tomorrow as they won't know if theyr'e on their 'eads or their —— 'eels. I'll 'ave my 'alf dollar if I 'ave to 'old them upside down and —— shake 'em.

GINGER: Three days. We come down from York—skippering 'alf the way. God, wasn't it jest about bleeding nine carat gold, too!

FLORRY: Got any more tea there, Ginger dear? Well, so long, folks. See you all at Wilkins's tomorrow morning.

MRS BENDIGO: Thieving little tart! Swallers 'er tea and then jacks off without so much as a thank you. Can't waste a bloody moment.

MRS MCELLIGOT: Cold? Ay, I b'lieve you. Skipperin' in de long grass wid no blanket an' de bloody dew fit to drown you, an' den can't get your bloody fire going' in de mornin', an' got to tap de milkman 'fore you can make yourself a drum o' tea. I've had some'v it when me and Michael was on de toby.

MRS BENDIGO: Even go with blackies and Chinamen she will, the dirty little cow.

DOROTHY: How much does she get each time?

SNOUTER: Tanner.

DOROTHY: SIXPENCE?

CHARLIE: Bet your life. Do it for a perishing fag along towards morning.

MRS MCELLIGOT: I never took less'n a shilling, never.

GINGER: Kikie and me skippered in a boneyard one night. Woke up in the morning and found I was lying on a bleeding gravestone.

THE KIKE: She ain't half got the crabs on her, too.

MRS MCELLIGOT: Michael an' me skippered in a pigsty once. We was just a-creepin' in, when, 'Holy Mary!' says Michael, 'dere's a pig in here!' 'Pig be ——!' I says, 'he'll keep us warm anyway.' So in we goes, an' dere was an old sow lay on her side snorin' like a traction engine. I creeps up agen her an' puts me arms round her, an' begod she kept me warm all night. I've skippered worse.

DEAFIE [singing]: WITH my willy willy—

CHARLIE: Don't ole Deafie keep it up? Sets up a kind of a 'umming inside of 'im, 'e says.

DADDY: When I was a boy we didn't live on this 'ere bread and marg and tea and suchlike trash. Good solid tommy we 'ad in them days. Beef stoo. Black pudden. Bacon dumpling. Pig's 'ead. Fed like a fighting-cock on a tanner a day. And now fifty year I've 'ad of it on the toby. Spud-grabbing, pea-picking, lambing, turnip-topping— everythink. And sleeping in wet straw and not once in a year you don't fill your guts right full. Well—! [Retires within his coat.]

MRS MCELLIGOT: But he was real bold, Michael was. He'd go in anywhere. Many's de time we've broke into an empty house an kipped in de best bed. 'Other people got homes,' he'd say. 'Why shouln't we have'm too!'

GINGER [singing]: But I'm dan—cing with tears—in my eyes—

MR TALLBOYS [to himself]: Absumet haeres Caecuba dignior! To think that there were twenty-one bottles of Clos St Jacques 1911 in my cellar still, that night when the baby was born and I left for London on the milk train!...

MRS WAYNE: And as for the WREATHS we 'as sent us when our mother died—well, you wouldn't believe! 'Uge, they was....

MRS BENDIGO: If I 'ad my time over again I'd marry for bloody money.

GINGER [singing]:

But I'm dan—cing with tears—in my eyes— 'Cos the girl— in my arms—isn't you-o-ou!

NOSY WATSON: Some of you lot think you got a bloody lot to howl about, don't you? What about a poor sod like me? You wasn't narked into the stir when you was eighteen year old, was you?

THE KIKE: Oh Je-e-eEEZE!

CHARLIE: Ginger, you can't sing no more'n a perishing tomcat with the guts-ache. Just you listen to me. I'll give y'a treat. [Singing]: Jesu, lover OF my soul—

MR TALLBOYS [to himself]: Et ego in Crockford.... With Bishops and Archbishops and with all the Company of Heaven....

NOSY WATSON: D'you know how I got in the stir the first time? Narked by my own sister—yes, my own bloody sister! My sister's a cow if ever there was one. She got married to a religious maniac— he's so bloody religious that she's got fifteen kids now—well, it was him put her up to narking me. But I got back on 'em, _I_ can tell you. First thing, I done when I come out of the stir, I buys a hammer and goes round to my sister's house, and smashed her piano to bloody matchwood. 'There!' I says, 'that's what you get for narking ME! You nosing mare!' I says.

DOROTHY: This cold, this cold! I don't know whether my feet are there or not.

MRS MCELLIGOT: Bloody tea don't warm you for long, do it? I'm fair froze myself.

MR TALLBOYS [to himself]: My curate days, my curate days! My fancywork bazaars and morris-dancers in aid of on the village green, my lectures to the Mothers' Union-missionary work in Western China with fourteen magic lantern slides! My Boys' Cricket Club, teetotallers only, my Confirmation classes—purity lecture once monthly in the Parish Hall—my Boy Scout orgies! The Wolf Cubs will deliver the Grand Howl. Household Hints for the Parish Magazine, 'Discarded fountain-pen fillers can be used as enemas for canaries....'

CHARLIE [singing]: Jesu, lover OF my soul—

GINGER: 'Ere comes the bleeding flattie! Get up off the ground, all of you. [Daddy emerges from his overcoat.]

THE POLICEMAN [shaking the sleepers on the next bench]: Now then, wake up, wake up! Rouse up, you! Got to go home if you want to sleep. This isn't a common lodging house. Get up, there! [etc., etc.]

MRS BENDIGO: It's that nosy young sod as wants promotion. Wouldn't let you bloody breathe if 'e 'ad 'is way.

CHARLIE [singing]:

Jesu, lover of my soul, Let me TO Thy bosom fly—

THE POLICEMAN: Now then, YOU! What you think THIS is? Baptist prayer meeting? [To the Kike] Up you get, and look sharp about it!

CHARLIE: I can't 'elp it, sergeant. It's my toonful nature. It comes out of me natural-like.

THE POLICEMAN [shaking Mrs Bendigo]: Wake up, mother, wake up!

MRS BENDIGO: Mother? MOTHER, is it? Well, if I am a mother, thank God I ain't got a bloody son like you! And I'll tell you another little secret, constable. Next time I want a man's fat 'ands feeling round the back of my neck, I won't ask YOU to do it. I'll 'ave someone with a bit more sex-appeal.

THE POLICEMAN: Now then, now then! No call to get abusive, you know. We got our orders to carry out. [Exit majestically.]

SNOUTER [sotto voce]: —— off, you —— son of a ——!

CHARLIE [singing]:

While the gathering waters roll, While the tempest still is 'igh!

Sung bass in the choir my last two years in Dartmoor, I did.

MRS BENDIGO: I'll bloody mother 'im! [Shouting after the policeman] 'I! Why don't you get after them bloody cat burglars 'stead of coming nosing round a respectable married woman?

GINGER: Kip down, blokes. 'E's jacked. [Daddy retires within his coat.]

NOSY WATSON: Wassit like in Dartmoor now? D'they give you jam now?

MRS WAYNE: Of course, you can see as they couldn't reely allow people to sleep in the streets—I mean, it wouldn't be quite nice— and then you've got to remember as it'd be encouraging of all the people as haven't got homes of their own—the kind of riff-raff, if you take my meaning....

MR TALLBOYS [to himself]: Happy days, happy days! Outings with the Girl Guides in Epping Forest—hired brake and sleek roan horses, and I on the box in my grey flannel suit, speckled straw hat, and discreet layman's necktie. Buns and ginger pop under the green elms. Twenty Girl Guides pious yet susceptible frisking in the breast-high bracken, and I a happy curate sporting among them, in loco parentis pinching the girls' backsides....

MRS MCELLIGOT: Well, you may talk about kippin' down, but begod dere won't be much sleep for my poor ole bloody bones tonight. I can't skipper it now de way me and Michael used to.

CHARLIE: Not jam. Gets cheese, though, twice a week.

THE KIKE: Oh Jeez! I can't stand it no longer. I going down to the M.A.B.

[Dorothy stands up, and then, her knees having stiffened with the cold, almost falls.]

GINGER: Only send you to the bleeding Labour Home. What you say we all go up to Covent Garden tomorrow morning? Bum a few pears if we get there early enough.

CHARLIE: I've 'ad my perishing bellyful of Dartmoor, b'lieve me. Forty on us went through 'ell for getting off with the ole women down on the allotments. Ole trots seventy years old they was— spud-grabbers. Didn't we cop it just! Bread and water, chained to the wall—perishing near murdered us.

MRS BENDIGO: No fear! Not while my bloody husband's there. One black eye in a week's enough for me, thank you.

MR TALLBOYS [chanting, reminiscently]: As for our harps, we hanged them up, upon the willow trees of Babylon!...

MRS MCELLIGOT: Hold up, kiddie! Stamp your feet an' get de blood back into 'm. I'll take y'a walk up to Paul's in a coupla minutes.

DEAFIE [singing]: WITH my willy willy—

[Big Ben strikes eleven.]

SNOUTER: Six more—hours! Cripes!

[An hour passes. Big Ben stops striking. The mist thins and the cold increases. A grubby-faced moon is seen sneaking among the clouds of the southern sky. A dozen hardened old men remain on the benches, and still contrive to sleep, doubled up and hidden in their greatcoats. Occasionally they groan in their sleep. The others set out in all directions, intending to walk all night and so keep their blood flowing, but nearly all of them have drifted back to the Square by midnight. A new policeman comes on duty. He strolls through the Square at intervals of half an hour, scrutinizing the faces of the sleepers but letting them alone when he has made sure that they are only asleep and not dead. Round each bench revolves a knot of people who take it in turns to sit down and are driven to their feet by the cold after a few minutes. Ginger and Charlie fill two drums at the fountains and set out in the desperate hope of boiling some tea over the navvies' clinker fire in Chandos Street; but a policeman is warming himself at the fire, and orders them away. The Kike suddenly vanishes, probably to beg a bed at the M.A.B. Towards one o'clock a rumour goes round that a lady is distributing hot coffee, ham sandwiches, and packets of cigarettes under Charing Cross Bridge; there is a rush to the spot, but the rumour turns out to be unfounded. As the Square fills again the ceaseless changing of places upon the benches quickens until it is a game of musical chairs. Sitting down, with one's hands under one's armpits, it is possible to get into a kind of sleep, or doze, for two or three minutes on end. In this state, enormous ages seem to pass. One sinks into a complex, troubling dreams which leave one conscious of one's surroundings and of the bitter cold. The night is growing clearer and colder every minute. There is a chorus of varying sound—groans, curses, bursts of laughter, and singing, and through them all the uncontrollable chattering of teeth.]

MR TALLBOYS [chanting]: I am poured out like water, and all my bones are out of joint!...

MRS MCELLIGOT: Ellen an' me bin wanderin' round de City dis two hours. Begod it's like a bloody tomb wid dem great lamps glarin' down on you an' not a soul stirren' excep' de flatties strollin' two an' two.

SNOUTER: Five past —— one and I ain't 'ad a bite since dinner! Course it 'ad to 'appen to us on a —— night like this!

MR TALLBOYS: A drinking night I should have called it. But every man to his taste. [Chanting] 'My strength is dried like a potsherd, and my tongue cleaveth to my gums!'...

CHARLIE: Say, what you think? Nosy and me done a smash jest now. Nosy sees a tobacconist's show-case full of them fancy boxes of Gold Flake, and 'e says, 'By cripes I'm going to 'ave some of them fags if they give me a perishing stretch for it!' 'e says. So 'e wraps 'is scarf round 'is 'and, and we waits till there's a perishing great van passing as'll drown the noise, and then Nosy lets fly—biff! We nipped a dozen packets of fags, and then I bet you didn't see our a—s for dust. And when we gets round the corner and opens them, there wasn't no perishing fags inside! Perishing dummy boxes. I 'ad to laugh.

DOROTHY: My knees are giving way. I can't stand up much longer.

MRS BENDIGO: Oh, the sod, the sod! To turn a woman out of doors on a night like bloody this! You wait'll I get 'im drunk o'

Saturday night and 'e can't 'it back. I'll mash 'im to bloody shin of beef, I will. 'E'll look like two pennorth of pieces after I've swiped 'im with the bloody flat-iron.

MRS MCELLIGOT: Here, make room'n let de kid sit down. Press up agen ole Daddy, dear. Put his arm round you. He's chatty, but he'll keep you warm.

GINGER [double marking time]: Stamp your feet on the ground—only bleeding thing to do. Strike up a song, someone, and less all stamp our bleeding feet in time to it.

DADDY [waking and emerging]: Wassat? [Still half asleep, he lets his head fall back, with mouth open and Adam's apple protruding from his withered throat like the blade of a tomahawk.]

MRS BENDIGO: There's women what if they'd stood what I'VE stood, they'd ave put spirits of salts in 'is cup of bloody tea.

MR TALLBOYS [beating an imaginary drum and singing]: Onward, heathen so-oldiers—

MRS WAYNE: Well, reely now! If any of us'd ever of thought, in the dear old days when we used to sit round our own Silkstone coal fire, with the kettle on the hob and a nice dish of toasted crumpets from the baker's over the way....

[The chattering of her teeth silences her.]

CHARLIE: No perishing church trap now, matie. I'll give y'a bit of smut—something as we can perishing dance to. You listen t'me.

MRS MCELLIGOT: Don't you get talkin' about crumpets, Missis. Me bloody belly's rubbin' agen me backbone already.

[Charlie draws himself up, clears his throat, and in an enormous voice roars out a song entitled 'Rollicking Bill the Sailor'. A laugh that is partly a shudder bursts from the people on the bench. They sing the song through again, with increasing volume of noise, stamping and clapping in time. Those sitting down, packed elbow to elbow, sway grotesquely from side to side, working their feet as though stamping on the pedals of a harmonium.

Even Mrs Wayne joins in after a moment, laughing in spite of herself. They are all laughing, though with chattering teeth. Mr Tallboys marches up and down behind his vast swag belly, pretending to carry a banner or crozier in front of him. The night is now quite clear, and an icy wind comes shuddering at intervals through the Square. The stamping and clapping rise to a kind of frenzy as the people feel the deadly cold penetrate to their bones. Then the policeman is seen wandering into the Square from the eastern end, and the singing ceases abruptly.]

CHARLIE: There! You can't say as a bit of music don't warm you up.

MRS BENDIGO: This bloody wind! And I ain't even got any drawers on, the bastard kicked me out in such a 'urry.

MRS MCELLIGOT: Well, glory be to Jesus, 'twon't be long before dat dere church in de Gray's Inn Road opens up for de winter. Dey gives you a roof over your head of a night, 't any rate.

THE POLICEMAN: Now then, now THEN! D'you think this is the time of night to begin singing like a blooming bear garden? I shall have to send you back to your homes if you can't keep quiet.

SNOUTER [sotto voce]: You —— son of a ——!

GINGER: Yes—they lets you kip on the bleeding stone floor with three newspaper posters 'stead of blankets. Might as well be in the Square and 'ave done with it. God, I wish I was in the bleeding spike.

MRS MCELLIGOT: Still, you gets a cup of Horlicks an' two slices. I bin glad to kip dere often enough.

MR TALLBOYS [chanting]: I was glad when they said unto me, We will go into the house of the Lord!…

DOROTHY [starting up]: Oh, this cold, this cold! I don't know whether it's worse when you're sitting down or when you're standing up. Oh, how can you all stand it? Surely you don't have to do this every night of your lives?

MRS WAYNE: You mustn't think, dearie, as there isn't SOME of us wasn't brought up respectable.

CHARLIE [singing]: Cheer up, cully, you'll soon be dead! Brrh! Perishing Jesus! Ain't my fish-hooks blue! [Double marks time and beats his arms against his sides.]

DOROTHY: Oh, but how can you stand it? How can you go on like this, night after night, year after year? It's not possible that people can live so! It's so absurd that one wouldn't believe it if one didn't know it was true. It's impossible!

SNOUTER: —— possible if you ask me.

MR TALLBOYS [stage curate-wise]: With God, all things are possible.

[Dorothy sinks back on to the bench, her knees still being unsteady.]

CHARLIE: Well, it's jest on 'ar-parse one. Either we got to get moving, or else make a pyramid on that perishing bench. Unless we want to perishing turn up our toes. 'Oo's for a little constitootional up to the Tower of London?

MRS MCELLIGOT: 'Twon't be me dat'll walk another step tonight. Me bloody legs've given out on me.

GINGER: What-o for the pyramid! This is a bit too bleeding nine- day-old for me. Less scrum into that bench—beg pardon, Ma!

DADDY [sleepily]: Wassa game? Can't a man get a bit of kip but what you must come worriting 'in and shaking of 'im?

CHARLIE: That's the stuff! Shove in! Shift yourself, Daddy, and make room for my little sit-me-down. Get one atop of each other. That's right. Never mind the chats. Jam all together like pilchards in a perishing tin.

MRS WAYNE: Here! I didn't ask you to sit on my lap, young man!

GINGER: Sir on mine, then, mother—'sall the same. What-o! First bit of stuff I've 'ad my arm round since Easter.

[They pile themselves in a monstrous shapeless clot, men and women clinging indiscriminately together, like a bunch of toads at spawning time. There is a writhing movement as the heap settles down, and a sour stench of clothes diffuses itself. Only Mr Tallboys remains marching up and down.]

MR TALLBOYS [declaiming]: O ye nights and days, ye light and darkness, ye lightnings and clouds, curse ye the Lord!

[Deafie, someone having sat on his diaphragm, utters a strange, unreproducible sound.]

MRS BENDIGO: Get off my bad leg, can't you? What you think I am? Bloody drawing-room sofa?

CHARLIE: Don't ole Daddy stink when you get up agen 'im?

GINGER: Bleeding Bank 'oliday for the chats this'll be.

DOROTHY: Oh, God, God!

MR TALLBOYS [halting]: Why call on God, you puling deathbed penitent? Stick to your guns and call on the Devil as I do. Hail to thee, Lucifer, Prince of the Air! [Singing to the tune of 'Holy, holy holy']: Incubi and Succubi, falling down before Thee!...

MRS BENDIGO: Oh, shut up, you blarsphemous old sod! 'E's too bloody fat to feel the cold, that's what's wrong with 'im.

CHARLIE: Nice soft be'ind you got, Ma. Keep an eye out for the perishing flattie, Ginger.

MR TALLBOYS: Malecidite, omnia opera! The Black Mass! Why not? Once a priest always a priest. Hand me a chunk of toke and I will work the miracle. Sulphur candles, Lord's Prayer backwards, crucifix upside down. [To Dorothy] If we had a black he-goat you would come in useful.

[The animal heat of the piled bodies had already made itself felt. A drowsiness is descending upon everyone.]

MRS WAYNE: You mustn't think as I'm ACCUSTOMED to sitting on a gentleman's knee, you know...

MRS MCELLIGOT [drowsily]: It took my sacraments

reg'lar till de bloody priest wouldn't give me absolution along o' my Michael. De ole get, de ole getsie!...

MR TALLBOYS [striking an attitude]: Per aquam sacratam quam nunc spargo, signumque crucis quod nunc facio....

GINGER: 'Oo's got a fill of 'ard-up? I've smoked by last bleeding fag-end.

MR TALLBOYS [as at the altar]: Dearly beloved brethren we are gathered together in the sight of God for the solemnization of unholy blasphemy. He has afflicted us with dirt and cold, with hunger and solitude, with the pox and the itch, with the headlouse and the crablouse. Our food is damp crusts and slimy meat-scraps handed out in packets from hotel doorways. Our pleasure is stewed tea and sawdust cakes bolted in reeking cellars, bar-rinsing sand spittle of common ale, the embrace of toothless hags. Our destiny is the pauper's grave, twenty-feet deep in deal coffins, the kip- house of underground. It is very meet, right and our bounden duty at all times and in all places to curse Him and revile Him. Therefore with Demons and Archdemons [etc., etc., etc.].

MRS MCELLIGOT [drowsily]: By holy Jesus, I'm half asleep right now, only some b—'s lyin' across my legs and crushin' 'em.

MR TALLBOYS: Amen. Evil from us deliver, but temptation into not us lead [etc., etc., etc.].

[As he reaches the first word of the prayer he tears the consecrated bread across. The blood runs out of it. There is a rolling sound, as of thunder, and the landscape changes. Dorothy's feet are very cold. Monstrous winged shapes of Demons and Archdemons are dimly visible, moving to and fro. Something, beak or claw, closes upon Dorothy's shoulder, reminding her that her feet and hands are aching with cold.]

THE POLICEMAN [shaking Dorothy by the shoulder]: Wake up, now, wake up, wake up! Haven't you got an overcoat?

You're as white as death. Don't you know better than to let yourself sprawl about in the cold like that?

[Dorothy finds that she is stiff with cold. The sky is now quite clear, with gritty little stars twinkling like electric lamps enormously remote. The pyramid has unrolled itself.]

MRS MCELLIGOT: De poor kid, she ain't used to roughin' it de way us others are.

GINGER [beating his arms]: Brr! Woo! 'Taters in the bleeding mould!

MRS WAYNE: She's a lady born and bred.

THE POLICEMAN: Is that so?—See here, Miss, you best come down to the M.A.B. with me. They'll give you a bed all right. Anyone can see with half an eye as you're a cut above these others here.

MRS BENDIGO: Thank you, constable, THANK you! 'Ear that, girls? 'A cut above us,' 'e says. Nice, ain't it? [To the policeman] Proper bloody Ascot swell yourself, ain't you?

DOROTHY: No, no! Leave me, I'd rather stay here.

THE POLICEMAN: Well, please yourself. You looked real bad just now. I'll be along later and take a look at you. [Moves off doubtfully.]

CHARLIE: Wait'll the perisher's round the corner and then pile up agen. Only perishing way we'll keep warm.

MRS MCELLIGOT: Come on, kid. Get underneath an' let'm warm you.

SNOUTER: Ten minutes to —— two. Can't last for ever, I s'pose.

MR TALLBOYS [chanting]: I am poured out like water, and all my bones are out of joint. My heart also in the midst of my body is like unto melting wax!...

[Once more the people pile themselves on the bench. But the temperature is now not many degrees above freezing-point, and the wind is blowing more cuttingly. The people wriggle their wind- nipped faces into the heap like sucking pigs struggling for their mother's teats. One's interludes of sleep shrink to a few seconds, and one's dreams grow more monstrous, troubling, and undreamlike. There are times when the nine people are talking almost normally, times when they can even laugh at their situation, and times when they press themselves together in a kind of frenzy, with deep groans of pain. Mr Tallboys suddenly becomes exhausted and his monologue degenerates into a stream of nonsense. He drops his vast bulk on top of the others, almost suffocating them. The heap rolls apart. Some remain on the bench, some slide to the ground and collapse against the parapet or against the others' knees. The policeman enters the Square and orders those on the ground to their feet. They get up, and collapse again the moment he is gone. There is no sound from the ten people save of snores that are partly groans. Their heads nod like those of joined porcelain Chinamen as they fall asleep and reawake as rhythmically as the ticking of a clock. Three strikes somewhere. A voice yells like a trumpet from the eastern end of the Square: 'Boys! Up you get! The noospapers is come!']

CHARLIE [starting from his sleep]: The perishing papers! C'm on, Ginger! Run like Hell!

[They run, or shamble, as fast as they can to the corner of the Square, where three youths are distributing surplus posters given away in charity by the morning newspapers. Charlie and Ginger come back with a thick wad of posters. The five largest men now jam themselves together on the bench, Deafie and the four women sitting across their knees; then, with infinite difficulty (as it has to be done from the inside), they wrap themselves in a monstrous cocoon of paper, several sheets thick, tucking the loose ends into their necks or breasts or between their shoulders and the back of the bench. Finally nothing is uncovered save their heads and the lower part of their legs. For their heads they fashion hoods of paper. The paper constantly comes loose and lets in cold shafts of wind, but it is now possible to sleep for as much as five minutes consecutively. At this time—between three and five in the morning—it is customary with the police not to disturb the Square sleepers. A measure of warmth steals through everyone and extends even to their feet. There is some furtive fondling of the women under cover of the paper. Dorothy is too far gone to care.

By a quarter past four the paper is all crumpled and torn to nothing, and it is far too cold to remain sitting down. The people get up, swear, find their legs somewhat rested, and begin to slouch to and fro in couples, frequently halting from mere lassitude. Every belly is now contorted with hunger. Ginger's tin of condensed milk is torn open and the contents devoured, everyone dipping their fingers into it and licking them. Those who have no money at all leave the Square for the Green Park, where they will be undisturbed till seven. Those who can command even a halfpenny make for Wilkins's cafe not far from the Charing Cross Road. It is known that the cafe will not open till five o'clock; nevertheless, a crowd is waiting outside the door by twenty to five.]

MRS MCELLIGOT: Got your halfpenny, dearie? Dey won't let more'n four of us in on one cup o'tea, de stingy ole gets!

MR TALLBOYS [singing]: The roseate hu-ues of early da-awn—

GINGER: God, that bit of sleep we 'ad under the newspapers done me some good. [Singing] But I'm dan-cing with tears—in my eyes—

CHARLIE: Oh, boys, boys! Look through that perishing window, will you? Look at the 'eat steaming down the window pane! Look at the tea-urns jest on the boil, and them great piles of 'ot toast and 'am sandwiches, and them there sausages sizzling in the pan! Don't it make your belly turn perishing summersaults to see 'em?

DOROTHY: I've got a penny. I can't get a cup of tea for that, can I?

SNOUTER: —— lot of sausages we'll get this morning with fourpence between us. 'Alf a cup of tea and a —— doughnut more likely. There's a breakfus' for you!

MRS MCELLIGOT: You don't need buy a cup o' tea all to yourself. I got a halfpenny an' so's Daddy, an' we'll put'm to your penny an' have a cup between de t'ree of us. He's got sores on his lip, but Hell! who cares? Drink near de handle an' dere's no harm done.

[A quarter to five strikes.]

MRS BENDIGO: I'd bet a dollar my ole man's got a bit of 'addock to 'is breakfast. I 'ope it bloody chokes 'im.

GINGER [singing]: But I'm dan-cing with tears—in my eyes—

MR TALLBOYS [singing]: Early in the morning my song shall rise to Thee!

MRS MCELLIGOT: You gets a bit o' kip in dis place, dat's one comfort. Dey lets you sleep wid your head on de table till seven o'clock. It's a bloody godsend to us Square Tobies.

CHARLIE [slavering like a dog]: Sausages! Perishing sausages! Welsh rabbit! 'Ot dripping toast! And a rump-steak two inches thick with chips and a pint of Ole Burton! Oh, perishing Jesus!

[He bounds forward, pushes his way through the crowd and rattles the handle of the glass door. The whole crowd of people, about forty strong, surge forward and attempt to storm the door, which is stoutly held within by Mr Wilkins, the proprietor of the cafe. He menaces them through the glass. Some press their breasts and faces against the window as though warming themselves. With a whoop and a rush Florry and four other girls, comparatively fresh from having spent part of the night in bed, debouch from a neighbouring alley, accompanied by a gang of youths in blue suits. They hurl themselves upon the rear of the crowd with such momentum that the door is almost broken. Mr Wilkins pulls it furiously open and shoves the leaders back. A fume of sausages, kippers, coffee, and hot bread streams into the outer cold.]

YOUTHS VOICES FROM THE REAR: Why can't he —— open before five? We're starving for our —— tea! Ram the —— door in! [etc., etc.]

MR WILKINS: Get out! Get out, the lot of you! Or by God not one of you comes in this morning!

GIRLS' VOICES FROM THE REAR: Mis-ter Wil-kins! Mis-ter Wil-kins! BE a sport and let us in! I'll give y'a kiss all free for nothing. BE a sport now! [etc., etc.]

MR WILKINS: Get on out of it! We don't open before five, and you know it. [Slams the door.]

MRS MCELLIGOT: Oh, holy Jesus, if dis ain't de longest ten minutes o' de whole bloody night! Well, I'll give me poor ole legs a rest, anyway. [Squats on her heels coal-miner-fashion. Many others do the same.]

GINGER: 'Oo's got a 'alfpenny? I'm ripe to go fifty-fifty on a doughnut.

YOUTHS' VOICES [imitating military music, then singing]:

'——!' was all the band could play; '——! ——' And the same to you!

DOROTHY [to Mrs McElligot]: Look at us all! Just look at us! What clothes! What faces!

MRS BENDIGO: You're no Greta Garbo yourself, if you don't mind my mentioning it.

MRS WAYNE: Well, now, the time DO seem to pass slowly when you're waiting for a nice cup of tea, don't it now?

MR TALLBOYS [chanting]: For our soul is brought low, even unto the dust: our belly cleaveth unto the ground!

CHARLIE: Kippers! Perishing piles of 'em! I can smell 'em through the perishing glass.

GINGER [singing]:

But I'm dan-cing with tears—in my eyes— 'Cos the girl—in my arms—isn't you-o-ou!

[Much time passes. Five strikes. Intolerable ages seem to pass. Then the door is suddenly wrenched open and the people stampede in to fight for the corner seats. Almost swooning in the hot air, they fling themselves down and sprawl across the tables, drinking in the heat and the smell of food through all their pores.]

MR WILKINS: Now then, all! You know the rules, I s'pose. No hokey-pokey this morning! Sleep till seven if you like, but if I see any man asleep after that, out he goes on his neck. Get busy with that tea, girls!

A DEAFENING CHORUS Of YELLS: Two teas 'ere! Large tea and a doughnut between us four! Kippers! Mis-ter Wil-kins! 'Ow much them sausages? Two slices! Mis-ter Wil-kins! Got any fag papers? Kipp-ers! [etc., etc.]

MR WILKINS: Shut up, shut up! Stop that hollering or I don't serve any of you.

MRS MCELLIGOT: D'you feel de blood runnin' back into your toes, dearie?

MRS WAYNE: He do speak rough to you, don't he? Not what I'd call a reely gentlemanly kind of man.

SNOUTER: This is —— starvation Corner, this is. Cripes! Couldn't I do a couple of them sausages!

THE TARTS [in chorus]: Kippers 'ere! 'Urry up with them kippers! Mis-ter Wilkins! Kippers all round! AND a doughnut!

CHARLIE: Not 'alf! Got to fill up on the smell of 'em this morning. Sooner be 'ere than on the perishing Square, ALL the same.

GINGER: 'Ere, Deafie! You've 'ad your 'alf! Gimme me that bleeding cup.

MR TALLBOYS [chanting]: Then was our mouth filled with laughter, and our tongue with joy!...

MRS MCELLIGOT: Begod I'm half asleep already. It's de heat o' de room as does it.

MR WILKINS: Stop that singing there! You know the rules.

THE TARTS [in chorus]: Kipp-ers!

SNOUTER: —— doughnuts! Cold prog! It turns my belly sick.

DADDY: Even the tea they give you ain't no more than water with a bit of dust in it. [Belches.]

CHARLIE: Bes' thing—'ave a bit of shut-eye and forget about it. Dream about perishing cut off the joint and two veg. Less get our 'eads on the table and pack up comfortable.

MRS MCELLIGOT: Lean up agen me shoulder, dearie. I've got more flesh on me bones'n what you have.

GINGER: I'd give a tanner for a bleeding fag, if I 'ad a bleeding tanner.

CHARLIE: Pack up. Get your 'ead agenst mine, Snouter. That's right. Jesus, won't I perishing sleep!

[A dish of smoking kippers is borne past to the tarts' table.]

SNOUTER [drowsily]: More —— kippers. Wonder 'ow many times she's bin on 'er back to pay for that lot.

MRS MCELLIGOT [half-asleep]: 'Twas a pity, 'twas a real pity, when Michael went off on his jack an' left me wid de bloody baby an' all....

MRS BENDIGO [furiously, following the dish of kippers with accusing finger]: Look at that, girls! Look at that! Kippers! Don't it make you bloody wild? We don't get kippers for breakfast, do we, girls? Bloody tarts swallering down kippers as fast as they can turn 'em out of the pan, and us 'ere with a cup of tea between four of us and lucky to get that! Kippers!

MR TALLBOYS [stage curate-wise]: The wages of sin is kippers.

GINGER: Don't breathe in my face, Deafie. I can't bleeding stand it.

CHARLIE [in his sleep]: Charles-Wisdom-drunk-and-incapable-drunk?- yes-six-shillings-move-on-NEXT!

DOROTHY [on Mrs McElligot's bosom]: Oh, joy, joy!

[They are asleep.]

2

And so it goes on.

Dorothy endured this life for ten days—to be exact, nine days and ten nights. It was hard to see what else she could do. Her father, seemingly, had abandoned her altogether, and though she had friends in London who would readily have helped her, she did not feel that she could face them after what had happened, or what was supposed to have happened. And she dared not apply to organized charity because it would almost certainly lead to the discovery of her name, and hence, perhaps, to a fresh hullabaloo about the 'Rector's Daughter'.

So she stayed in London, and became one of that curious tribe, rare but never quite extinct—the tribe of women who are penniless and homeless, but who make such desperate efforts to hide it that they very nearly succeed; women who wash their faces at drinking fountains in the cold of the dawn, and carefully uncrumple their clothes after sleepless nights, and carry themselves with an air of reserve and decency, so that only their faces, pale beneath sunburn, tell you for certain that they are destitute. It was not in her to become a hardened beggar like most of the people about her. Her first twenty-four hours on the Square she spent without any food whatever, except for the cup of tea that she had had overnight and a third of a cup more that she had had at Wilkins's cafe in the morning. But in the evening, made desperate by hunger and the others' example, she walked up to a strange woman, mastered her voice with an effort, and said:

'Please, Madam, could you give me twopence? I have had nothing to eat since yesterday.' The woman stared, but she opened her purse and gave Dorothy threepence. Dorothy did not know it, but her educated accent, which had made it impossible to get work as a servant, was an invaluable asset to her as a beggar.

After that she found that it was really very easy to beg the daily shilling or so that was needed to keep her alive. And yet she never begged—it seemed to her that actually she could not do it— except when hunger was past bearing or when she had got to lay in the precious penny that was the passport to Wilkins's cafe in the morning. With Nobby, on the way to the hopfields, she had begged without fear or scruple. But it had been different then; she had not known what she was doing. Now, it was only under the spur of actual hunger that she could screw her courage to the point, and ask for a few coppers from some woman whose face looked friendly. It was always women that she begged from, of course. She did once try begging from a man—but only once.

For the rest, she grew used to the life that she was leading—used to the enormous sleepless nights, the cold, the dirt, the boredom, and the horrible communism of the Square. After a day or two she had ceased to feel even a flicker of surprise at her situation. She had come, like everyone about her, to accept this monstrous existence almost as though it were normal. The dazed, witless feeling that she had known on the way to the hopfields had come back upon her more strongly than before. It is the common effect of sleeplessness and still more of exposure. To live continuously in the open air, never going under a roof for more than an hour or two, blurs your perceptions like a strong light glaring in your eyes or a noise drumming in your ears. You act and plan and suffer, and yet all the while it is as though everything were a little out of focus, a little unreal. The world, inner and outer, grows dimmer till it reaches almost the vagueness of a dream.

Meanwhile, the police were getting to know her by sight. On the Square people are perpetually coming and going, more or less unnoticed. They arrive from nowhere with their drums and their bundles, camp for a few days and nights, and then disappear as mysteriously as they come. If you stay for more than a week or thereabouts, the police will mark you down as an habitual beggar, and they will arrest you sooner or later. It is impossible for them to enforce the begging laws at all regularly, but from time to time they make a sudden raid and capture two or three of the people they have had their eye on. And so it happened in Dorothy's case.

One evening she was 'knocked off', in company with Mrs McElligot and another woman whose name she did not know. They had been careless and begged off a nasty old lady with a face like a horse, who had promptly walked up to the nearest policeman and given them in charge.

Dorothy did not mind very much. Everything was dreamlike now—the face of the nasty old lady, eagerly accusing them, and the walk to the station with a young policeman's gentle, almost deferential hand on her arm; and then the white-tiled cell, with the fatherly sergeant handing her a cup of tea through the grille and telling her that the magistrate wouldn't be too hard on her if she pleaded guilty. In the cell next door Mrs McElligot stormed at the sergeant, called him a bloody get, and then spent half the night in bewailing her fate. But Dorothy had no feeling save vague relief at being in so clean and warm a place. She crept immediately on to the plank bed that was fixed like a shelf to the wall, too tired even to pull the blankets about her, and slept for ten hours without stirring. It was only on the following morning that she began to grasp the reality of her situation, as the Black Maria rolled briskly up to Old Street Police Court, to the tune of 'Adeste fideles' shouted by five drunks inside.

CHAPTER 4

1

Dorothy had wronged her father in supposing that he was willing to let her starve to death in the street. He had, as a matter of fact, made efforts to get in touch with her, though in a roundabout and not very helpful way.

His first emotion on learning of Dorothy's disappearance had been rage pure and simple. At about eight in the morning, when he was beginning to wonder what had become of his shaving water, Ellen had come into his bedroom and announced in a vaguely panic-stricken tone:

'Please, Sir, Miss Dorothy ain't in the house, Sir. I can't find her nowhere!'

'What?' said the Rector.

'She ain't in the house, Sir! And her bed don't look as if it hadn't been slept in, neither. It's my belief as she's GORN, Sir!'

'Gone!' exclaimed the Rector, partly sitting up in bed. 'What do you mean—GONE?'

'Well, Sir, I believe she's run away from 'ome, Sir!'

'Run away from home! At THIS hour of the morning? And what about my breakfast, pray?'

By the time the Rector got downstairs—unshaven, no hot water having appeared—Ellen had gone down into the town to make fruitless inquiries for Dorothy. An hour passed, and she did not return. Whereupon there occurred a frightful, unprecedented thing— a thing never to be forgotten this side of the grave; the Rector was obliged to prepare his own breakfast—yes, actually to mess about with a vulgar black kettle and rashers of Danish bacon—with his own sacerdotal hands.

After that, of course, his heart was hardened against Dorothy for ever. For the rest of the day he was far too busy raging over unpunctual meals to ask himself WHY she had disappeared and whether any harm had befallen her. The point was that the confounded girl (he said several times 'confounded girl', and came near to saying something stronger) HAD disappeared, and had upset the whole household by doing so. Next day, however, the question became more urgent, because Mrs Semprill was now publishing the story of the elopement far and wide. Of course, the Rector denied it violently, but in his heart he had a sneaking suspicion that it might be true. It was the kind of thing, he now decided, that Dorothy WOULD do. A girl who would suddenly walk out of the house without even taking thought for her father's breakfast was capable of anything.

Two days later the newspapers got hold of the story, and a nosy young reporter came down to Knype Hill and began asking questions. The Rector made matters worse by angrily refusing to interview the reporter, so that Mrs Semprill's version was the only one that got into print. For about a week, until the papers got tired of Dorothy's case and dropped her in favour of a plesiosaurus that had been seen at the mouth of the Thames, the Rector enjoyed a horrible notoriety. He could hardly open a newspaper without seeing some flaming headline about 'Rector's Daughter. Further Revelations', or 'Rector's Daughter. Is she in Vienna? Reported seen in Low- class Cabaret'. Finally there came an article in the Sunday Spyhole, which began, 'Down in a Suffolk Rectory a broken old man sits staring at the wall', and which was so absolutely unbearable that the Rector consulted his solicitor about an action for libel. However, the solicitor was against it; it might lead to a verdict, he said, but it would certainly lead to further publicity. So the Rector did nothing, and his anger against Dorothy, who had brought this disgrace upon him, hardened beyond possibility of forgiveness.

After this there came three letters from Dorothy, explaining what had happened. Of course the Rector never really believed that Dorothy had lost her memory. It was too thin a story altogether. He believed that she either HAD eloped with Mr Warburton, or had gone off on some similar escapade and had landed herself penniless in Kent; at any rate—this he had settled once and for all, and no argument would ever move him from it—whatever had happened to her was entirely her own fault. The first letter he wrote was not to Dorothy herself but to his cousin Tom, the baronet. For a man of the Rector's upbringing it was second nature, in any serious trouble, to turn to a rich relative for help. He had not exchanged a word with his cousin for the last fifteen years, since they had quarrelled over a little matter of a borrowed fifty pounds; still, he wrote fairly confidently, asking Sir Thomas to get in touch with Dorothy if it could be done, and to find her some kind of job in London. For of course, after what had happened, there could be no question of letting her come back to Knype Hill.

Shortly after this there came two despairing letters from Dorothy, telling him that she was in danger of starvation and imploring him to send her some money. The Rector was disturbed. It occurred to him—it was the first time in his life that he had seriously considered such a thing—that it IS possible to starve if you have no money. So, after thinking it over for the best part of a week, he sold out ten pounds' worth of shares and sent a cheque for ten pounds to his cousin, to be kept for Dorothy till she appeared. At the same time he sent a cold letter to Dorothy herself, telling her that she had better apply to Sir Thomas Hare. But several more days passed before this letter was posted, because the Rector had qualms about addressing a letter to 'Ellen Millborough'—he dimly imagined that it was against the law to use false names—and, of course, he had delayed far too long. Dorothy was already in the streets when the letter reached 'Mary's'.

Sir Thomas Hare was a widower, a good-hearted, chuckle-headed man of about sixty-five, with an obtuse rosy face and curling moustaches. He dressed by preference in checked overcoats and curly brimmed bowler hats that were at once dashingly smart and four decades out of date. At a first glance he gave the impression of having carefully disguised himself as a cavalry major of the 'nineties, so that you could hardly look at him without thinking of devilled bones with a b and s, and the tinkle of hansom bells, and the Pink 'Un in its great 'Pitcher' days, and Lottie Collins and 'Tarara-BOOM-deay'. But his chief characteristic was an abysmal mental vagueness. He was one of those people who say 'Don't you know?' and 'What! What!' and lose themselves in the middle of their sentences. When he was puzzled or in difficulties, his moustaches seemed to bristle forward, giving him the appearance of a well- meaning but exceptionally brainless prawn.

So far as his own inclinations went Sir Thomas was not in the least anxious to help his cousins, for Dorothy herself he had never seen, and the Rector he looked on as a cadging poor relation of the worst possible type. But the fact was that he had had just about as much of this 'Rector's Daughter' business as he could stand. The accursed chance that Dorothy's surname was the same as his own had made his life a misery for the past fortnight, and he foresaw further and worse scandals if she were left at large any longer. So, just before leaving London for the pheasant shooting, he sent for his butler, who was also his confidant and intellectual guide, and held a council of war.

'Look here, Blyth, dammit,' said Sir Thomas prawnishly (Blyth was the butler's name), 'I suppose you've seen all this damn' stuff in the newspapers, hey? This "Rector's Daughter" stuff? About this damned niece of mine.'

Blyth was a small sharp-featured man with a voice that never rose above a whisper. It was as nearly silent as a voice can be while still remaining a voice. Only by watching his lips as well as listening closely could you catch the whole of what he said. In this case his lips signalled something to the effect that Dorothy was Sir Thomas's cousin, not his niece.

'What, my cousin, is she?' said Sir Thomas. 'So she is, by Jove! Well, look here, Blyth, what I mean to say—it's about time we got hold of the damn' girl and locked her up somewhere. See what I mean? Get hold of her before there's any MORE trouble. She's knocking about somewhere in London, I believe. What's the best way of getting on her track? Police? Private detectives and all that? D'you think we could manage it?'

Blyth's lips registered disapproval. It would, he seemed to be saying, be possible to trace Dorothy without calling in the police and having a lot of disagreeable publicity.

'Good man!' said Sir Thomas. 'Get to it, then. Never mind what it costs. I'd give fifty quid not to have that "Rector's Daughter" business over again. And for God's sake, Blyth,' he added confidentially, 'once you've got hold of the damn' girl, don't let her out of your sight. Bring her back to the house and damn' well keep her here. See what I mean? Keep her under lock and key till I get back. Or else God knows what she'll be up to next.'

Sir Thomas, of course, had never seen Dorothy, and it was therefore excusable that he should have formed his conception of her from the newspaper reports.

It took Blyth about a week to track Dorothy down. On the morning after she came out of the police-court cells (they had fined her six shillings, and, in default of payment, detained her for twelve hours: Mrs McElligot, as an old offender, got seven days), Blyth came up to her, lifted his bowler hat a quarter of an inch from his head, and inquired noiselessly whether she were not Miss Dorothy Hare. At the second attempt Dorothy understood what he was saying, and admitted that she WAS Miss Dorothy Hare; whereupon Blyth explained that he was sent by her cousin, who was anxious to help her, and that she was to come home with him immediately.

Dorothy followed him without more words said. It seemed queer that her cousin should take this sudden interest in her, but it was no queerer than the other things that had been happening lately. They took the bus to Hyde Park Corner, Blyth paying the fares, and then walked to a large, expensive-looking house with shuttered windows, on the borderland between Knightsbridge and Mayfair. They went down some steps, and Blyth produced a key and they went in. So, after an absence of something over six weeks, Dorothy returned to respectable society, by the area door.

She spent three days in the empty house before her cousin came home. It was a queer, lonely time. There were several servants in the house, but she saw nobody except Blyth, who brought her her meals and talked to her, noiselessly, with a mixture of deference and disapproval. He could not quite make up his mind whether she was a young lady of family or a rescued Magdalen, and so treated her as something between the two. The house had that hushed, corpselike air peculiar to houses whose master is away, so that you instinctively went about on tiptoe and kept the blinds over the windows. Dorothy did not even dare to enter any of the main rooms. She spent all the daytime lurking in a dusty, forlorn room at the top of the house which was a sort of museum of bric-a-brac dating from 1880 onwards. Lady Hare, dead these five years, had been an industrious collector of rubbish, and most of it had been stowed away in this room when she died. It was a doubtful point whether the queerest object in the room was a yellowed photograph of Dorothy's father, aged eighteen but with respectable side-whiskers, standing self-consciously beside an 'ordinary' bicycle—this was in 1888; or whether it was a little sandalwood box labelled 'Piece of Bread touched by Cecil Rhodes at the City and South Africa Banquet, June 1897'. The sole books in the room were some grisly school prizes that had been won by Sir Thomas's children—he had three, the youngest being the same age as Dorothy.

It was obvious that the servants had orders not to let her go out of doors. However, her father's cheque for ten pounds had arrived, and with some difficulty she induced Blyth to get it cashed, and, on the third day, went out and bought herself some clothes. She bought herself a ready-made tweed coat and skirt and a jersey to go with them, a hat, and a very cheap frock of artificial printed silk; also a pair of passable brown shoes, three pairs of lisle stockings, a nasty, cheap little handbag, and a pair of grey cotton gloves that would pass for suede at a little distance. That came to eight pounds ten, and she dared not spend more. As for underclothes, nightdresses, and handkerchiefs, they would have to wait. After all, it is the clothes that show that matter.

Sir Thomas arrived on the following day, and never really got over the surprise that Dorothy's appearance gave him. He had been expecting to see some rouged and powdered siren who would plague him with temptations to which alas! he was no longer capable of succumbing; and this countrified, spinsterish girl upset all his calculations. Certain vague ideas that had been floating about his mind, of finding her a job as a manicurist or perhaps as a private secretary to a bookie, floated out of it again. From time to time Dorothy caught him studying her with a puzzled, prawnish eye, obviously wondering how on earth such a girl could ever have figured in an elopement. It was very little use, of course, telling him that she had NOT eloped. She had given him her version of the story, and he had accepted it with a chivalrous 'Of course, m'dear, of course!' and thereafter, in every other sentence, betrayed the fact that he disbelieved her.

So for a couple of days nothing definite was done. Dorothy continued her solitary life in the room upstairs, and Sir Thomas went to his club for most of his meals, and in the evening there were discussions of the most unutterable vagueness. Sir Thomas was genuinely anxious to find Dorothy a job, but he had great difficulty in remembering what he was talking about for more than a few minutes at a time. 'Well, m'dear,' he would start off, 'you'll understand, of course, that I'm very keen to do what I can for you. Naturally, being your uncle and all that—what? What's that? Not your uncle? No, I suppose I'm not, by Jove! Cousin—that's it; cousin. Well, now, m'dear, being your cousin—now, what was I saying?' Then, when Dorothy had guided him back to the subject, he would throw out some such suggestion as, 'Well, now, for instance, m'dear, how would you like to be companion to an old lady? Some dear old girl, don't you know—black mittens and rheumatoid arthritis. Die and leave you ten thousand quid and care of the parrot. What, what?' which did not get them very much further. Dorothy repeated a number of times that she would rather be a housemaid or a parlourmaid, but Sir Thomas would not hear of it. The very idea awakened in him a class-instinct which he was usually too vague-minded to remember. 'What!' he would say. 'A dashed skivvy? Girl of your upbringing? No, m'dear—no, no! Can't do THAT kind of thing, dash it!'

But in the end everything was arranged, and with surprising ease; not by Sir Thomas, who was incapable of arranging anything, but by his solicitor, whom he had suddenly thought of consulting. And the solicitor, without even seeing Dorothy, was able to suggest a job for her. She could, he said, almost certainly find a job as a schoolmistress. Of all jobs, that was the easiest to get.

Sir Thomas came home very pleased with this suggestion, which struck him as highly suitable. (Privately, he thought that

Dorothy had just the kind of face that a schoolmistress ought to have.) But Dorothy was momentarily aghast when she heard of it.

'A schoolmistress!' she said. 'But I couldn't possibly! I'm sure no school would give me a job. There isn't a single subject I can teach.'

'What? What's that? Can't teach? Oh, dash it! Of course you can! Where's the difficulty?'

'But I don't know enough! I've never taught anybody anything, except cooking to the Girl Guides. You have to be properly qualified to be a teacher.'

'Oh, nonsense! Teaching's the easiest job in the world. Good thick ruler—rap 'em over the knuckles. They'll be glad enough to get hold of a decently brought up young woman to teach the youngsters their ABC. That's the line for you, m'dear— schoolmistress. You're just cut out for it.'

And sure enough, a schoolmistress Dorothy became. The invisible solicitor had made all the arrangements in less than three days. It appeared that a certain Mrs Creevy, who kept a girls' day school in the suburb of Southbridge, was in need of an assistant, and was quite willing to give Dorothy the job. How it had all been settled so quickly, and what kind of school it could be that would take on a total stranger, and unqualified at that, in the middle of the term, Dorothy could hardly imagine. She did not know, of course, that a bribe of five pounds, miscalled a premium, had changed hands.

So, just ten days after her arrest for begging, Dorothy set out for Ringwood House Academy, Brough Road, Southbridge, with a small trunk decently full of clothes and four pounds ten in her purse— for Sir Thomas had made her a present of ten pounds. When she thought of the ease with which this job had been found for her, and then of the miserable struggles of three weeks ago, the contrast amazed her. It brought home to her, as never before, the mysterious power of money. In fact, it reminded her of a favourite saying of Mr Warburton's, that if you took 1 Corinthians, chapter thirteen, and in every verse wrote 'money' instead of 'charity', the chapter had ten times as much meaning as before.

2

Southbridge was a repellent suburb ten or a dozen miles from London. Brough Road lay somewhere at the heart of it, amid labyrinths of meanly decent streets, all so indistinguishably alike, with their ranks of semi-detached houses, their privet and laurel hedges and plots of ailing shrubs at the crossroads, that you could lose yourself there almost as easily as in a Brazilian forest. Not only the houses themselves, but even their names were the same over and over again. Reading the names on the gates as you came up Brough Road, you were conscious of being haunted by some half-remembered passage of poetry; and when you paused to identify it, you realized that it was the first two lines of Lycidas.

Ringwood House was a dark-looking, semi-detached house of yellow brick, three storeys high, and its lower windows were hidden from the road by ragged and dusty laurels. Above the laurels, on the front of the house, was a board inscribed in faded gold letters:

RINGWOOD HOUSE ACADEMY FOR GIRLS
Ages 5 to 18
Music and Dancing Taught
Apply within for Prospectus

Edge to edge with this board, on the other half of the house, was another board which read:

RUSHINGTON GRANGE HIGH SCHOOL FOR BOYS
Ages 6 to 16
Book-keeping and Commercial Arithmetic a Speciality
Apply within for Prospectus

The district pullulated with small private schools; there were four of them in Brough Road alone. Mrs Creevy, the Principal of Ringwood House, and Mr Boulger, the Principal of Rushington Grange, were in a state of warfare, though their interests in no way clashed with one another. Nobody knew what the feud was about, not even Mrs Creevy or Mr Boulger themselves; it was a feud that they had inherited from earlier proprietors of the two schools. In the mornings after breakfast they would stalk up and down their respective back gardens, beside the very low wall that separated them, pretending not to see one another and grinning with hatred.

Dorothy's heart sank at the sight of Ringwood House. She had not been expecting anything very magnificent or attractive, but she had expected something a little better than this mean, gloomy house, not one of whose windows was lighted, though it was after 8 o'clock in the evening. She knocked at the door, and it was opened by a woman, tall and gaunt-looking in the dark hallway, whom Dorothy took for a servant, but who was actually Mrs Creevy herself. Without a word, except to inquire Dorothy's name, the woman led the way up some dark stairs to a twilit, fireless drawing-room, where she turned up a pinpoint of gas, revealing a black piano, stuffed horsehair chairs, and a few yellowed, ghostly photos on the walls.

Mrs Creevy was a woman somewhere in her forties, lean, hard, and angular, with abrupt decided movements that indicated a strong will and probably a vicious temper. Though she was not in the least dirty or untidy there was something discoloured about her whole appearance, as though she lived all her life in a bad light; and the expression of her mouth, sullen and ill-shaped with the lower lip turned down, recalled that of a toad. She spoke in a sharp, commanding voice, with a bad accent and occasional vulgar turns of speech. You could tell her at a glance for a person who knew exactly what she wanted, and would grasp it as ruthlessly as any machine; not a bully exactly—you could somehow infer from her appearance that she would not take enough interest in you to want to bully you—but a person who would make use of you and then throw you aside with no more compunction than if you had been a worn-out scrubbing-brush.

Mrs Creevy did not waste any words on greetings. She motioned Dorothy to a chair, with the air rather of commanding than of inviting her to sir down, and then sat down herself, with her hands clasped on her skinny forearms.

'I hope you and me are going to get on well together, Miss Millborough,' she began in her penetrating, subhectoring voice. (On the advice of Sir Thomas's everwise solicitor, Dorothy had stuck to the name of Ellen Millborough.) 'And I hope I'm not going to have the same nasty business with you as I had with my last two assistants. You say you haven't had an experience of teaching before this?'

'Not in a school,' said Dorothy—there had been a tarradiddle in her letter of introduction, to the effect that she had had experience of 'private teaching'.

Mrs Creevy looked Dorothy over as though wondering whether to induct her into the inner secrets of school-teaching, and then appeared to decide against it.

'Well, we shall see,' she said. 'I must say,' she added complainingly, 'it's not easy to get hold of good hardworking assistants nowadays. You give them good wages and good treatment, and you get no thanks for it. The last one I had—the one I've just had to get rid of—Miss Strong, wasn't so bad so far as the teaching part went; in fact, she was a B.A., and I don't know what you could have better than a B.A., unless it's an M.A. You don't happen to be a B.A. or an M.A., do you, Miss Millborough?'

'No, I'm afraid not,' said Dorothy.

'Well, that's a pity. It looks so much better on the prospectus if you've got a few letters after your name. Well! Perhaps it doesn't matter. I don't suppose many of OUR parents'd know what B.A. stands for; and they aren't so keen on showing their ignorance. I suppose you can talk French, of course?'

'Well—I've learnt French.'

'Oh, that's all right, then. Just so as we can put it on the prospectus. Well, now, to come back to what I was saying, Miss Strong was all right as a teacher, but she didn't come up to my ideas on what I call the MORAL SIDE. We're very strong on the moral side at Ringwood House. It's what counts most with the parents, you'll find. And the one before Miss Strong, Miss Brewer— well, she had what I call a weak nature. You don't get on with girls if you've got a weak nature. The end of it all was that one morning one little girl crept up to the desk with a box of matches and set fire to Miss Brewer's skirt. Of course I wasn't going to keep her after that. In fact I had her out of the house the same afternoon—and I didn't give her any refs either, I can tell you!'

'You mean you expelled the girl who did it?' said Dorothy, mystified.

'What? The GIRL? Not likely! You don't suppose I'd go and turn fees away from my door, do you? I mean I got rid of Miss Brewer, not the GIRL. It's no good having teachers who let the girls get saucy with them. We've got twenty-one in the class just at present, and you'll find they need a strong hand to keep them down.'

'You don't teach yourself?' said Dorothy.

'Oh dear, no!' said Mrs Creevy almost contemptuously. 'I've got a lot too much on my hands to waste my time TEACHING. There's the house to look after, and seven of the children stay to dinner—I've only a daily woman at present. Besides, it takes me all my time getting the fees out of the parents. After all, the fees ARE what matter, aren't they?'

'Yes. I suppose so,' said Dorothy.

'Well, we'd better settle about your wages,' continued Mrs Creevy. 'In term time I'll give you your board and lodging and ten shillings a week; in the holidays it'll just be your board and lodging. You can have the use of the copper in the kitchen for your laundering, and I light the geyser for hot baths every Saturday night; or at least MOST Saturday nights. You can't have the use of this room we're in now, because it's my reception-room, and I don't want you to go wasting the gas in your bedroom. But you can have the use of the morning-room whenever you want it.'

'Thank you,' said Dorothy.

'Well, I should think that'll be about all. I expect you're feeling ready for bed. You'll have had your supper long ago, of course?'

This was clearly intended to mean that Dorothy was not going to get any food tonight, so she answered Yes, untruthfully, and the conversation was at an end. That was always Mrs Creevy's way—she never kept you talking an instant longer than was necessary. Her conversation was so very definite, so exactly to the point, that it was not really conversation at all. Rather, it was the skeleton of conversation; like the dialogue in a badly written novel where everyone talks a little too much in character. But indeed, in the proper sense of the word she did not TALK; she merely said, in her brief shrewish way, whatever it was necessary to say, and then got rid of you as promptly as possible. She now showed Dorothy along the passage to her bedroom, and lighted a gas-jet no bigger than an acorn, revealing a gaunt bedroom with a narrow white-quilted bed, a rickety wardrobe, one chair and a wash-hand-stand with a frigid white china basin and ewer. It was very like the bedrooms in seaside lodging houses, but it lacked the one thing that gives such rooms their air of homeliness and decency—the text over the bed.

'This is your room,' Mrs Creevy said; 'and I just hope you'll keep it a bit tidier than what Miss Strong used to. And don't go burning the gas half the night, please, because I can tell what time you turn it off by the crack under the door.'

With this parting salutation she left Dorothy to herself. The room was dismally cold; indeed, the whole house had a damp, chilly feeling, as though fires were rarely lighted in it. Dorothy got into bed as quickly as possible, feeling bed to be the warmest place. On top of the wardrobe, when she was putting her clothes away, she found a cardboard box containing no less than nine empty whisky bottles—relics, presumably, of Miss Strong's weakness on the MORAL SIDE.

At eight in the morning Dorothy went downstairs and found Mrs Creevy already at breakfast in what she called the 'morning-room'. This was a smallish room adjoining the kitchen, and it had started life as the scullery; but Mrs Creevy had converted it into the 'morning-room' by the simple process of removing the sink and copper into the kitchen. The breakfast table, covered with a cloth of harsh texture, was very large and forbiddingly bare. Up at Mrs Creevy's end were a tray with a very small teapot and two cups, a plate on which were two leathery fried eggs, and a dish of marmalade; in the middle, just within Dorothy's reach if she stretched, was a plate of bread and butter; and beside her plate— as though it were the only thing she could be trusted with—a cruet stand with some dried-up, clotted stuff inside the bottles.

'Good morning, Miss Millborough,' said Mrs Creevy. 'It doesn't matter this morning, as this is the first day, but just remember another time that I want you down here in time to help me get breakfast ready.'

'I'm so sorry,' said Dorothy.

'I hope you're fond of fried eggs for your breakfast?' went on Mrs Creevy.

Dorothy hastened to assure her that she was very fond of fried eggs.

'Well, that's a good thing, because you'll always have to have the same as what I have. So I hope you're not going to be what I call DAINTY about your food. I always think,' she added, picking up her knife and fork, 'that a fried egg tastes a lot better if you cut it well up before you eat it.'

She sliced the two eggs into thin strips, and then served them in such a way that Dorothy received about two-thirds of an egg. With some difficulty Dorothy spun out her fraction of egg so as to make half a dozen mouthfuls of it, and then, when she had taken a slice of bread and butter, she could not help glancing hopefully in the direction of the dish of marmalade. But Mrs Creevy was sitting with her lean left arm—not exactly ROUND the marmalade, but in a protective position on its left flank, as though she suspected that Dorothy was going to make an attack upon it. Dorothy's nerve failed her, and she had no marmalade that morning—nor, indeed, for many mornings to come.

Mrs Creevy did not speak again during breakfast, but presently the sound of feet on the gravel outside, and of squeaky voices in the schoolroom, announced that the girls were beginning to arrive. They came in by a side-door that was left open for them. Mrs Creevy got up from the table and banged the breakfast things together on the tray. She was one of those women who can never move anything without banging it about; she was as full of thumps and raps as a poltergeist. Dorothy carried the tray into the kitchen, and when she returned Mrs Creevy produced a penny notebook from a drawer in the dresser and laid it open on the table.

'Just take a look at this,' she said. 'Here's a list of the girls' names that I've got ready for you. I shall want you to know the whole lot of them by this evening.' She wetted her thumb and turned over three pages: 'Now, do you see these three lists here?'

'Yes,' said Dorothy.

'Well, you'll just have to learn those three lists by heart, and make sure you know what girls are on which. Because I don't want you to go thinking that all the girls are to be treated alike. They aren't—not by a long way, they aren't. Different girls, different treatment—that's my system. Now, do you see this lot on the first page?'

'Yes,' said Dorothy again.

'Well, the parents of that lot are what I call the good payers. You know what I mean by that? They're the ones that pay cash on the nail and no jibbing at an extra half-guinea or so now and again. You're not to smack any of that lot, not on ANY account. This lot over here are the MEDIUM payers. Their parents do pay up sooner or later, but you don't get the money out of them without you worry them for it night and day. You can smack that lot if they get saucy, but don't go and leave a mark their parents can see. If you'll take MY advice, the best thing with children is to twist their ears. Have you ever tried that?'

'No,' said Dorothy.

'Well, I find it answers better than anything. It doesn't leave a mark, and the children can't bear it. Now these three over here are the BAD payers. Their fathers are two terms behind already, and I'm thinking of a solicitor's letter. I don't care WHAT you do to that lot—well, short of a police-court case, naturally. Now, shall I take you in and start you with the girls? You'd better bring that book along with you, and just keep your eye on it all the time so as there'll be no mistakes.'

They went into the schoolroom. It was a largish room, with grey- papered walls that were made yet greyer by the dullness of the light, for the heavy laurel bushes outside choked the windows, and no direct ray of the sun ever penetrated into the room. There was a teacher's desk by the empty fireplace, and there were a dozen small double desks, a light blackboard, and, on the mantelpiece, a black clock that looked like a miniature mausoleum; but there were no maps, no pictures, nor even, as far as Dorothy could see, any books. The sole objects in the room that could be called ornamental were two sheets of black paper pinned to the walls, with writing on them in chalk in beautiful copperplate. On one was 'Speech is Silver. Silence is Golden', and on the other 'Punctuality is the Politeness of Princes'.

The girls, twenty-one of them, were already sitting at their desks. They had grown very silent when they heard footsteps approaching, and as Mrs Creevy came in they seemed to shrink down in their places like partridge chicks when a hawk is soaring. For the most part they were dull-looking, lethargic children with bad complexions, and adenoids seemed to be remarkably common among them. The eldest of them might have been fifteen years old, the youngest was hardly more than a baby. The school had no uniform, and one or two of the children were verging on raggedness.

'Stand up, girls,' said Mrs Creevy as she reached the teacher's desk. 'We'll start off with the morning prayer.'

The girls stood up, clasped their hands in front of them, and shut their eyes. They repeated the prayer in unison, in weak piping voices, Mrs Creevy leading them, her sharp eyes darting over them all the while to see that they were attending.

'Almighty and everlasting Father,' they piped, 'we beseech Thee that our studies this day may be graced by Thy divine guidance. Make us to conduct ourselves quietly and obediently; look down upon our school and make it to prosper, so that it may grow in numbers and be a good example to the neighbourhood and not a disgrace like some schools of which Thou knowest, O Lord. Make us, we beseech Thee, O Lord, industrious, punctual, and ladylike, and worthy in all possible respects to walk in Thy ways: for Jesus Christ's sake, our Lord, Amen.'

This prayer was of Mrs Creevy's own composition. When they had finished it, the girls repeated the Lord's Prayer, and then sat down.

'Now, girls,' said Mrs Creevy, 'this is your new teacher, Miss Millborough. As you know, Miss Strong had to leave us all of a sudden after she was taken so bad in the middle of the arithmetic lesson; and I can tell you I've had a hard week of it looking for a new teacher. I had seventy-three applications before I took on Miss Millborough, and I had to refuse them all because their qualifications weren't high enough. Just you remember and tell your parents that, all of you—seventy-three applications! Well, Miss Millborough is going to take you in Latin, French, history, geography, mathematics, English literature and composition, spelling, grammar, handwriting, and freehand drawing; and Mr Booth will take you in chemistry as usual on Thursday afternoons. Now, what's the first lesson on your time-table this morning?'

'History, Ma'am,' piped one or two voices.

'Very well. I expect Miss Millborough'll start off by asking you a few questions about the history you've been learning. So just you do your best, all of you, and let her see that all the trouble we've taken over you hasn't been wasted. You'll find they can be quite a sharp lot of girls when they try, Miss Millborough.'

'I'm sure they are,' said Dorothy.

'Well, I'll be leaving you, then. And just you behave yourselves, girls! Don't you get trying it on with Miss Millborough like you did with Miss Brewer, because I warn you she won't stand it. If I hear any noise coming from this room, there'll be trouble for somebody.'

She gave a glance round which included Dorothy and indeed suggested that Dorothy would probably be the 'somebody' referred to, and departed.

Dorothy faced the class. She was not afraid of them—she was too used to dealing with children ever to be afraid of them—but she did feel a momentary qualm. The sense of being an impostor (what teacher has not felt it at times?) was heavy upon her. It suddenly occurred to her, what she had only been dimly aware of before, that she had taken this teaching job under flagrantly false pretences, without having any kind of qualification for it. The subject she was now supposed to be teaching was history, and, like most 'educated' people, she knew virtually no history. How awful, she thought, if it turned out that these girls knew more history than she did! She said tentatively:

'What period exactly were you doing with Miss Strong?'

Nobody answered. Dorothy saw the older girls exchanging glances, as though asking one another whether it was safe to say anything, and finally deciding not to commit themselves.

'Well, whereabouts had you got to?' she said, wondering whether perhaps the word 'period' was too much for them.

Again no answer.

'Well, now, surely you remember SOMETHING about it? Tell me the names of some of the people you were learning about in your last history lesson.'

More glances were exchanged, and a very plain little girl in the front row, in a brown jumper and skirt, with her hair screwed into two tight pigtails, remarked cloudily, 'It was about the Ancient Britons.' At this two other girls took courage, and answered simultaneously. One of them said, 'Columbus', and the other 'Napoleon'.

Somehow, after that, Dorothy seemed to see her way more clearly. It was obvious that instead of being uncomfortably knowledgeable as she had feared, the class knew as nearly as possible no history at all. With this discovery her stage-fright vanished. She grasped that before she could do anything else with them it was necessary to find out what, if anything, these children knew.

So, instead of following the time-table, she spent the rest of the morning in questioning the entire class on each subject in turn; when she had finished with history (and it took about five minutes to get to the bottom of their historical knowledge) she tried them with geography, with English grammar, with French, with arithmetic—with everything, in fact, that they were supposed to have learned. By twelve o'clock she had plumbed, though not actually explored, the frightful abysses of their ignorance.

For they knew nothing, absolutely nothing—nothing, nothing, nothing, like the Dadaists. It was appalling that even children could be so ignorant. There were only two girls in the class who knew whether the earth went round the sun or the sun round the earth, and not a single one of them could tell Dorothy who was the last king before George V, or who wrote Hamlet, or what was meant by a vulgar fraction, or which ocean you crossed to get to America, the Atlantic or the Pacific. And the big girls of fifteen were not much better than the tiny infants of eight, except that the former could at least read consecutively and write neat copperplate. That was the one thing that nearly all of the older girls could do—they could write neatly. Mrs Creevy had seen to that. And of course, here and there in the midst of their ignorance, there were small, disconnected islets of knowledge; for example, some odd stanzas from 'pieces of poetry' that they had learned by heart, and a few Ollendorffian French sentences such as 'Passez-moi le beurre, s'il vous plait' and 'Le fils du jardinier a perdu son chapeau', which they appeared to have learned as a parrot learns 'Pretty Poll'. As for their arithmetic, it was a little better than the other subjects. Most of them knew how to add and subtract, about half of them had some notion of how to multiply, and there were even three or four who had struggled as far as long division. But that was the utmost limit of their knowledge; and beyond, in every direction, lay utter, impenetrable night.

Moreover, not only did they know nothing, but they were so unused to being questioned that it was often difficult to get answers out of them at all. It was obvious that whatever they knew they had learned in an entirely mechanical manner, and they could only gape in a sort of dull bewilderment when asked to think for themselves. However, they did not seem unwilling, and evidently they had made up their minds to be 'good'—children are always 'good' with a new teacher; and Dorothy persisted, and by degrees the children grew, or seemed to grow, a shade less lumpish. She began to pick up, from the answers they gave her, a fairly accurate notion of what Miss Strong's regime had been like.

It appeared that, though theoretically they had learned all the usual school subjects, the only ones that had been at all seriously taught were handwriting and arithmetic. Mrs Creevy was particularly keen on handwriting. And besides this they had spent great quantities of time—an hour or two out of every day, it seemed—in drudging through a dreadful routine called 'copies.' 'Copies' meant copying things out of textbooks or off the blackboard. Miss Strong would write up, for example, some sententious little 'essay' (there was an essay entitled 'Spring' which recurred in all the older girls' books, and which began, 'Now, when girlish April is tripping through the land, when the birds are chanting gaily on the boughs and the dainty flowerets bursting from their buds', etc., etc.), and the girls would make fair copies of it in their copybooks; and the parents, to whom the copybooks were shown from time to time, were no doubt suitably impressed. Dorothy began to grasp that everything that the girls had been taught was in reality aimed at the parents. Hence the 'copies', the insistence on handwriting, and the parroting of ready-made French phrases; they were cheap and easy ways of creating an impression. Meanwhile, the little girls at the bottom of the class seemed barely able to read and write, and one of them— her name was Mavis Williams, and she was a rather sinister-looking child of eleven, with eyes too far apart—could not even count. This child seemed to have done nothing at all during the past term and a half except to write pothooks. She had quite a pile of books filled with pothooks—page after page of pothooks, looping on and on like the mangrove roots in some tropical swamp.

Dorothy tried not to hurt the children's feelings by exclaiming at their ignorance, but in her heart she was amazed and horrified. She had not known that schools of this description still existed in the civilized world. The whole atmosphere of the place was so curiously antiquated—so reminiscent of those dreary little private schools that you read about in Victorian novels. As for the few textbooks that the class possessed, you could hardly look at them without feeling as though you had stepped back into the mid nineteenth century. There were only three textbooks of which each child had a copy. One was a shilling arithmetic, pre Great War but fairly serviceable, and another was a horrid little book called The Hundred Page History of Britain—a nasty little duodecimo book with a gritty brown cover, and, for frontispiece, a portrait of Boadicea with a Union Jack draped over the front of her chariot. Dorothy opened this book at random, came to page 91, and read:

> After the French Revolution was over, the self-styled Emperor Napoleon Buonaparte attempted to set up his sway, but though he won a few victories against continental troops, he soon found that in the 'thin red line' he had more than met his match. Conclusions were tried upon the field of Waterloo, where 50,000 Britons put to flight 70,000 Frenchmen—for the Prussians, our allies, arrived too late for the battle. With a ringing British cheer our men charged down the slope and the enemy broke and fled. We now come on to the great Reform Bill of 1832, the first of those beneficent reforms

which have made British liberty what it is and marked us off from the less fortunate nations [etc., etc.]....

The date of the book was 1888. Dorothy, who had never seen a history book of this description before, examined it with a feeling approaching horror. There was also an extraordinary little 'reader', dated 1863. It consisted mostly of bits out of Fenimore Cooper, Dr Watts, and Lord Tennyson, and at the end there were the queerest little 'Nature Notes' with woodcut illustrations. There would be a woodcut of an elephant, and underneath in small print: 'The elephant is a sagacious beast. He rejoices in the shade of the Palm Trees, and though stronger than six horses he will allow a little child to lead him. His food is Bananas.' And so on to the Whale, the Zebra, and Porcupine, and the Spotted Camelopard. There were also, in the teacher's desk, a copy of Beautiful Joe, a forlorn book called Peeps at Distant Lands, and a French phrase- book dated 1891. It was called All you will need on your Parisian Trip, and the first phrase given was 'Lace my stays, but not too tightly'. In the whole room there was not such a thing as an atlas or a set of geometrical instruments.

At eleven there was a break of ten minutes, and some of the girls played dull little games at noughts and crosses or quarrelled over pencil-cases, and a few who had got over their first shyness clustered round Dorothy's desk and talked to her. They told her some more about Miss Strong and her methods of teaching, and how she used to twist their ears when they made blots on their copybooks. It appeared that Miss Strong had been a very strict teacher except when she was 'taken bad', which happened about twice a week. And when she was taken bad she used to drink some medicine out of a little brown bottle, and after drinking it she would grow quite jolly for a while and talk to them about her brother in Canada. But on her last day—the time when she was taken so bad during the arithmetic lesson—the medicine seemed to make her worse than ever, because she had no sooner drunk it than she began sinking and fell across a desk, and Mrs Creevy had to carry her out of the room.

After the break there was another period of three quarters of an hour, and then school ended for the morning. Dorothy felt stiff and tired after three hours in the chilly but stuffy room, and she would have liked to go out of doors for a breath of fresh air, but Mrs Creevy had told her beforehand that she must come and help get dinner ready. The girls who lived near the school mostly went home for dinner, but there were seven who had dinner in the 'morning- room' at tenpence a time. It was an uncomfortable meal, and passed in almost complete silence, for the girls were frightened to talk under Mrs Creevy's eye. The dinner was stewed scrag end of mutton, and Mrs Creevy showed extraordinary dexterity in serving the pieces of lean to the 'good payers' and the pieces of fat to the 'medium payers'. As for the three 'bad payers', they ate a shamefaced lunch out of paper bags in the school-room.

School began again at two o'clock. Already, after only one morning's teaching, Dorothy went back to her work with secret shrinking and dread. She was beginning to realize what her life would be like, day after day and week after week, in that sunless room, trying to drive the rudiments of knowledge into unwilling brats. But when she had assembled the girls and called their names over, one of them, a little peaky child with mouse-coloured hair, called Laura Firth, came up to her desk and presented her with a pathetic bunch of browny-yellow chrysanthemums, 'from all of us'. The girls had taken a liking to Dorothy, and had subscribed fourpence among themselves, to buy her a bunch of flowers.

Something stirred in Dorothy's heart as she took the ugly flowers. She looked with more seeing eyes than before at the anaemic faces and shabby clothes of the children, and was all of a sudden horribly ashamed to think that in the morning she had looked at them with indifference, almost with dislike. Now, a profound pity took possession of her. The poor children, the poor children! How they had been stunted and maltreated! And with it all they had retained the childish gentleness that could make them squander their few pennies on flowers for their teacher.

She felt quite differently towards her job from that moment onwards. A feeling of loyalty and affection had sprung up in her heart. This school was HER school; she would work for it and be proud of it, and make every effort to turn it from a place of bondage into a place human and decent. Probably it was very little that she could do. She was so inexperienced and unfitted for her job that she must educate herself before she could even begin to educate anybody else. Still, she would do her best; she would do whatever willingness and energy could do to rescue these children from the horrible darkness in which they had been kept.

3

During the next few weeks there were two things that occupied Dorothy to the exclusion of all others. One, getting her class into some kind of order; the other, establishing a concordat with Mrs Creevy.

The second of the two was by a great deal the more difficult. Mrs Creevy's house was as vile a house to live in as one could possibly imagine. It was always more or less cold, there was not a comfortable chair in it from top to bottom, and the food was disgusting. Teaching is harder work than it looks, and a teacher needs good food to keep him going. It was horribly dispiriting to have to work on a diet of tasteless mutton stews, damp boiled potatoes full of little black eyeholes, watery rice puddings, bread and scrape, and weak tea—and never enough even of these. Mrs Creevy, who was mean enough to take a pleasure in skimping even her own food, ate much the same meals as Dorothy, but she always had the lion's share of them. Every morning at breakfast the two fried eggs were sliced up and unequally partitioned, and the dish of marmalade remained for ever sacrosanct. Dorothy grew hungrier and hungrier as the term went on. On the two evenings a week when she managed to get out of doors she dipped into her dwindling store of money and bought slabs of plain chocolate, which she ate in the deepest secrecy—for Mrs Creevy, though she starved Dorothy more or less intentionally, would have been mortally offended if she had known that she bought food for herself.

The worst thing about Dorothy's position was that she had no privacy and very little time that she could call her own. Once school was over for the day her only refuge was the 'morning-room', where she was under Mrs Creevy's eye, and Mrs Creevy's leading idea was that Dorothy must never be left in peace for ten minutes together. She had taken it into her head, or pretended to do so, that Dorothy was an idle person who needed keeping up to the mark. And so it was always, 'Well, Miss Millborough, you don't seem to have very much to do this evening, do you? Aren't there some exercise books that want correcting? Or why don't you get your needle and do a bit of sewing? I'm sure _I_ couldn't bear to just sit in my chair doing nothing like you do!' She was for ever finding household jobs for Dorothy to do, even making her scrub the schoolroom floor on Saturday mornings when the girls did not come to school; but this was done out of pure ill nature, for she did not trust Dorothy to do the work properly, and generally did it again after her. One evening Dorothy was unwise enough to bring back a novel from the public library. Mrs Creevy flared up at the very sight of it. 'Well, really, Miss Millborough! I shouldn't have thought you'd have had time to READ!' she said bitterly. She herself had never read a book right through in her life, and was proud of it.

Moreover, even when Dorothy was not actually under her eye, Mrs Creevy had ways of making her presence felt. She was for ever prowling in the neighbourhood of the schoolroom, so that Dorothy never felt quite safe from her intrusion; and when she thought there was too much noise she would suddenly rap on the wall with her broom-handle in a way that made the children jump and put them off their work. At all hours of the day she was restlessly, noisily active. When she was not cooking meals she was banging about with broom and dustpan, or harrying the charwoman, or pouncing down upon the schoolroom to 'have a look round' in hopes of catching Dorothy or the children up to mischief, or 'doing a bit of gardening'—that is, mutilating with a pair of shears the unhappy little shrubs that grew amid wastes of gravel in the back garden. On only two evenings a week was Dorothy free of her, and that was when Mrs Creevy sallied forth on forays which she called 'going after the girls'; that is to say, canvassing likely parents. These evenings Dorothy usually spent in the public library, for when Mrs Creevy was not at home she expected Dorothy to keep out of the house, to save fire and gas-light. On other evenings Mrs Creevy was busy writing dunning letters to the parents, or letters to the editor of the local paper, haggling over the price of a dozen advertisements, or poking about the girls' desks to see that their exercise books had been properly corrected, or 'doing a bit of sewing'. Whenever occupation failed her for even five minutes she got out her workbox and 'did a bit of sewing'—generally restitching some bloomers of harsh white linen of which she had pairs beyond number. They were the most chilly looking garments that one could possibly imagine; they seemed to carry upon them, as no nun's coif or anchorite's hair shirt could ever have done, the impress of a frozen and awful chastity. The sight of them set you wondering about the late Mr Creevy, even to the point of wondering whether he had ever existed.

Looking with an outsider's eye at Mrs Creevy's manner of life, you would have said that she had no PLEASURES whatever. She never did any of the things that ordinary people do to amuse themselves— never went to the pictures, never looked at a book, never ate sweets, never cooked a special dish for dinner or dressed herself in any kind of finery. Social life meant absolutely nothing to her. She had no friends, was probably incapable of imagining such a thing as friendship, and hardly ever exchanged a word with a fellow being except on business. Of religious belief she had not the smallest vestige. Her attitude towards religion, though she went to the Baptist Chapel every Sunday to impress the parents with her piety, was a mean anti-clericalism founded on the notion that the clergy are 'only after your money'. She seemed a creature utterly joyless, utterly submerged by the dullness of her existence. But in reality it was not so. There were several things from which she derived acute and inexhaustible pleasure.

For instance, there was her avarice over money. It was the leading interest of her life. There are two kinds of avaricious person— the bold, grasping type who will ruin you if he can, but who never looks twice at twopence, and the petty miser who has not the enterprise actually to MAKE money, but who will always, as the saying goes, take a farthing from a dunghill with his teeth. Mrs Creevy belonged to the second type. By ceaseless canvassing and impudent bluff she had worked her school up to twenty-one pupils, but she would never get it much further, because she was too mean to spend money on the necessary equipment and to pay proper wages to her assistant. The fees the girls paid, or didn't pay, were five guineas a term with certain extras, so that, starve and sweat her assistant as she might, she could hardly hope to make more than a hundred and fifty pounds a year clear profit.

But she was fairly satisfied with that. It meant more to her to save sixpence than to earn a pound. So long as she could think of a way of docking Dorothy's dinner of another potato, or getting her exercise books a halfpenny a dozen cheaper, or shoving an unauthorized half guinea on to one of the 'good payers" bills, she was happy after her fashion.

And again, in pure, purposeless malignity—in petty acts of spite, even when there was nothing to be gained by them—she had a hobby of which she never wearied. She was one of those people who experience a kind of spiritual orgasm when they manage to do somebody else a bad turn. Her feud with Mr Boulger next door—a one-sided affair, really, for poor Mr Boulger was not up to Mrs Creevy's fighting weight—was conducted ruthlessly, with no quarter given or expected. So keen was Mrs Creevy's pleasure in scoring off Mr Boulger that she was even willing to spend money on it occasionally. A year ago Mr Boulger had written to the landlord (each of them was for ever writing to the landlord, complaining about the other's behaviour), to say that Mrs Creevy's kitchen chimney smoked into his back windows, and would she please have it heightened two feet. The very day the landlord's letter reached her, Mrs Creevy called in the bricklayers and had the chimney lowered two feet. It cost her thirty shillings, but it was worth it. After that there had been the long guerrilla campaign of throwing things over the garden wall during the night, and Mrs Creevy had finally won with a dustbinful of wet ashes thrown on to Mr Boulger's bed of tulips. As it happened, Mrs Creevy won a neat and bloodless victory soon after Dorothy's arrival. Discovering by chance that the roots of Mr Boulger's plum tree had grown under the wall into her own garden, she promptly injected a whole tin of weed-killer into them and killed the tree. This was remarkable as being the only occasion when Dorothy ever heard Mrs Creevy laugh.

But Dorothy was too busy, at first, to pay much attention to Mrs Creevy and her nasty characteristics. She saw quite clearly that Mrs Creevy was an odious woman and that her own position was virtually that of a slave; but it did not greatly worry her. Her work was too absorbing, too all-important. In comparison with it, her own comfort and even her future hardly seemed to matter.

It did not take her more than a couple of days to get her class into running order. It was curious, but though she had no experience of teaching and no preconceived theories about it, yet from the very first day she found herself, as though by instinct, rearranging, scheming, innovating. There was so much that was crying out to be done. The first thing, obviously, was to get rid of the grisly routine of 'copies', and after Dorothy's second day no more 'copies' were done in the class, in spite of a sniff or two from Mrs Creevy. The handwriting lessons, also, were cut down. Dorothy would have liked to do away with handwriting lessons altogether so far as the older girls were concerned—it seemed to her ridiculous that girls of fifteen should waste time in practising copperplate—but Mrs Creevy would not hear of it. She seemed to attach an almost superstitious value to handwriting lessons. And the next thing, of course, was to scrap the repulsive Hundred Page History and the preposterous little 'readers'. It would have been worse than useless to ask Mrs Creevy to buy new books for the children, but on her first Saturday afternoon Dorothy begged leave to go up to London, was grudgingly given it, and spent two pounds three shillings out of her precious four pounds ten on a dozen secondhand copies of a cheap school edition of Shakespeare, a big second-hand atlas, some volumes of Hans Andersen's stories for the younger children, a set of geometrical instruments, and two pounds of plasticine. With these, and history books out of the public library, she felt that she could make a start.

She had seen at a glance that what the children most needed, and what they had never had, was individual attention. So she began by dividing them up into three separate classes, and so arranging things that two lots could be working by themselves while she 'went through' something with the third. It was difficult at first, especially with the younger girls, whose attention wandered as soon as they were left to themselves, so that you could never really take your eyes off them. And yet how wonderfully, how unexpectedly, nearly all of them improved during those first few weeks! For the most part they were not really stupid, only dazed by a dull, mechanical rigmarole. For a week, perhaps, they continued unteachable; and then, quite suddenly, their warped little minds seemed to spring up and expand like daisies when you move the garden roller off them.

Quite quickly and easily Dorothy broke them in to the habit of thinking for themselves. She got them to make up essays out of their own heads instead of copying out drivel about the birds chanting on the boughs and the flowerets bursting from their buds. She attacked their arithmetic at the foundations and started the little girls on multiplication and piloted the older ones through long division to fractions; she even got three of them to the point where there was talk of starting on decimals. She taught them the first rudiments of French grammar in place of 'Passez-moi le beurre, s'il vous plait' and 'Le fils du jardinier a perdu son chapeau'. Finding that not a girl in the class knew what any of the countries of the world looked like (though several of them knew that Quito was the capital of Ecuador), she set them to making a large contour-map of Europe in plasticine, on a piece of three-ply wood, copying it in scale from the atlas. The children adored making the map; they were always clamouring to be allowed to go on with it. And she started the whole class, except the six youngest girls and Mavis Williams, the pothook specialist, on reading Macbeth. Not a child among them had ever voluntarily read anything in her life before, except perhaps the Girl's Own Paper; but they took readily to Shakespeare, as all children do when he is not made horrible with parsing and analysing.

History was the hardest thing to teach them. Dorothy had not realized till now how hard it is for children who come from poor homes to have even a conception of what history means. Every upper-class person, however ill-informed, grows up with some notion of history; he can visualize a Roman centurion, a medieval knight, an eighteenth-century nobleman; the terms Antiquity, Middle Ages, Renaissance, Industrial Revolution evoke some meaning, even if a confused one, in his mind. But these children came from bookless homes and from parents who would have laughed at the notion that the past has any meaning for the present. They had never heard of Robin Hood, never played at being Cavaliers and Roundheads, never wondered who built the English churches or what Fid. Def. on a penny stands for. There were just two historical characters of whom all of them, almost without exception, had heard, and those were Columbus and Napoleon. Heaven knows why—perhaps Columbus and Napoleon get into the newspapers a little oftener than most historical characters. They seemed to have swelled up in the children's minds, like Tweedledum and Tweedledee, till they blocked out the whole landscape of the past. Asked when motor-cars were invented, one child, aged ten, vaguely hazarded, 'About a thousand years ago, by Columbus.'

Some of the older girls, Dorothy discovered, had been through the Hundred Page History as many as four times, from Boadicea to the first Jubilee, and forgotten practically every word of it. Not that that mattered greatly, for most of it was lies. She started the whole class over again at Julius Caesar's invasion, and at first she tried taking history books out of the public library and reading them aloud to the children; but that method failed, because they could understand nothing that was not explained to them in words of one or two syllables. So she did what she could in her own words and with her own inadequate knowledge, making a sort of paraphrase of what she read and delivering it to the children; striving all the while to drive into their dull little minds some picture of the past, and what was always more difficult, some interest in it. But one day a brilliant idea struck her. She bought a roll of cheap plain wallpaper at an upholsterer's shop, and set the children to making an historical chart. They marked the roll of paper into centuries and years, and stuck scraps that they cut out of illustrated papers—pictures of knights in armour and Spanish galleons and printing-presses and railway trains—at the appropriate places. Pinned round the walls of the room, the chart presented, as the scraps grew in number, a sort of panorama of English history. The children were even fonder of the chart than of the contour map. They always, Dorothy found, showed more intelligence when it was a question of MAKING something instead of merely learning. There was even talk of making a contour map of the world, four feet by four, in papiermache, if Dorothy could 'get round' Mrs Creevy to allow the preparation of the papiermache—a messy process needing buckets of water.

Mrs Creevy watched Dorothy's innovations with a jealous eye, but she did not interfere actively at first. She was not going to show it, of course, but she was secretly amazed and delighted to find that she had got hold of an assistant who was actually willing to work. When she saw Dorothy spending her own money on textbooks for the children, it gave her the same delicious sensation that she would have had in bringing off a successful swindle. She did, however, sniff and grumble at everything that Dorothy did, and she wasted a great deal of time by insisting on what she called 'thorough correction' of the girls' exercise books. But her system of correction, like everything else in the school curriculum, was arranged with one eye on the parents.

Periodically the children took their books home for their parents' inspection, and Mrs Creevy would never allow anything disparaging to be written in them. Nothing was to be marked 'bad' or crossed out or too heavily underlined; instead, in the evenings, Dorothy decorated the books, under Mrs Creevy's dictation, with more or less applauding comments in red ink. 'A very creditable performance', and 'Excellent! You are making great strides. Keep it up!' were Mrs Creevy's favourites. All the children in the school, apparently, were for ever 'making great strides'; in what direction they were striding was not stated. The parents, however, seemed willing to swallow an almost unlimited amount of this kind of thing.

There were times, of course, when Dorothy had trouble with the girls themselves. The fact that they were all of different ages made them difficult to deal with, and though they were fond of her and were very 'good' with her at first, they would not have been children at all if they had been invariably 'good'. Sometimes they were lazy and sometimes they succumbed to that most damnable vice of schoolgirls—giggling. For the first few days Dorothy was greatly exercised over little Mavis Williams, who was stupider than one would have believed it possible for any child of eleven to be. Dorothy could do nothing with her at all. At the first attempt to get her to do anything beyond pothooks a look of almost subhuman blankness would come into her wide-set eyes. Sometimes, however, she had talkative fits in which she would ask the most amazing and unanswerable questions. For instance, she would open her 'reader', find one of the illustrations—the sagacious Elephant, perhaps—and ask Dorothy:

'Please, Miss, wass 'at thing there?' (She mispronounced her words in a curious manner.)

'That's an elephant, Mavis.'

'Wass a elephant?'

'An elephant's a kind of wild animal.'

'Wass a animal?'

'Well—a dog's an animal.'

'Wass a dog?'

And so on, more or less indefinitely. About half-way through the fourth morning Mavis held up her hand and said with a sly politeness that ought to have put Dorothy on her guard:

'Please, Miss, may I be 'scused?'

'Yes,' said Dorothy.

One of the bigger girls put up her hand, blushed, and put her hand down again as though too bashful to speak. On being prompted by Dorothy, she said shamefacedly:

'Please, Miss, Miss Strong didn't used to let Mavis go to the lavatory alone. She locks herself in and won't come out, and then Mrs Creevy gets angry, Miss.'

Dorothy dispatched a messenger, but it was too late. Mavis remained in latebra pudenda till twelve o'clock. Afterwards, Mrs Creevy explained privately to Dorothy that Mavis was a congenital idiot—or, as she put it, 'not right in the head'. It was totally impossible to teach her anything. Of course, Mrs Creevy didn't 'let on' to Mavis's parents, who believed that their child was only 'backward' and paid their fees regularly. Mavis was quite easy to deal with. You just had to give her a book and a pencil and tell her to draw pictures and be quiet. But Mavis, a child of habit, drew nothing but pothooks—remaining quiet and apparently happy for hours together, with her tongue hanging out, amid festoons of pothooks.

But in spite of these minor difficulties, how well everything went during those first few weeks! How ominously well, indeed! About the tenth of November, after much grumbling about the price of coal, Mrs Creevy started to allow a fire in the schoolroom. The children's wits brightened noticeably when the room was decently warm. And there were happy hours, sometimes, when the fire crackled in the grate, and Mrs Creevy was out of the house, and the children were working quietly and absorbedly at one of the lessons that were their favourites. Best of all was when the two top classes were reading Macbeth, the girls squeaking breathlessly through the scenes, and Dorothy pulling them up to make them pronounce the words properly and to tell them who Bellona's bridegroom was and how witches rode on broomsticks; and the girls wanting to know, almost as excitedly as though it had been a detective story, how Birnam Wood could possible come to Dunsinane and Macbeth be killed by a man who was not of woman born. Those are the times that make teaching worth while—the times when the children's enthusiasm leaps up, like an answering flame, to meet your own, and sudden unlooked-for gleams of intelligence reward your earlier drudgery. No job is more fascinating than teaching if you have a free hand at it. Nor did Dorothy know, as yet, that that 'if' is one of the biggest 'ifs' in the world.

Her job suited her, and she was happy in it. She knew the minds of the children intimately by this time, knew their individual peculiarities and the special stimulants that were needed before you could get them to think. She was more fond of them, more interested in their development, more anxious to do her best for them, than she would have conceived possible a short while ago. The complex, never-ended labour of teaching filled her life just as the round of parish jobs had filled it at home. She thought and dreamed of teaching; she took books out of the public library and studied theories of education. She felt that quite willingly she would go on teaching all her life, even at ten shillings a week and her keep, if it could always be like this. It was her vocation, she thought.

Almost any job that fully occupied her would have been a relief after the horrible futility of the time of her destitution. But this was more than a mere job; it was—so it seemed to her—a mission, a life-purpose. Trying to awaken the dulled minds of these children, trying to undo the swindle that had been worked upon them in the name of education—that, surely, was something to which she could give herself heart and soul? So for the time being, in the interest of her work, she disregarded the beastliness of living in Mrs Creevy's house, and quite forgot her strange, anomalous position and the uncertainty of her future.

4

But of course, it could not last.

Not many weeks had gone by before the parents began interfering with Dorothy's programme of work. That—trouble with the parents— is part of the regular routine of life in a private school. All parents are tiresome from a teacher's point of view, and the parents of children at fourth-rate private schools are utterly impossible. On the one hand, they have only the dimmest idea of what is meant by education; on the other hand, they look on 'schooling' exactly as they look on a butcher's bill or a grocer's bill, and are perpetually suspicious that they are being cheated. They bombard the teacher with ill-written notes making impossible demands, which they send by hand and which the child reads on the way to school. At the end of the first fortnight Mabel Briggs, one of the most promising girls in the class, brought Dorothy the following note:

> Dear Miss,—Would you please give Mabel a bit more ARITHMETIC? I feel that what your giving her is not practacle enough. All these maps and that. She wants practacle work, not all this fancy stuff. So more ARITHMETIC, please. And remain,
>
> Yours Faithfully,
> Geo. Briggs

> P.S. Mabel says your talking of starting her on something called decimals. I don't want her taught decimals, I want her taught ARITHMETIC.

So Dorothy stopped Mabel's geography and gave her extra arithmetic instead, whereat Mabel wept. More letters followed. One lady was disturbed to hear that her child was being given Shakespeare to read. 'She had heard', she wrote, 'that this Mr Shakespeare was a writer of stage-plays, and was Miss Millborough quite certain that he wasn't a very IMMORAL writer? For her own part she had never so much as been to the pictures in her life, let alone to a stage- play, and she felt that even in READING stage-plays there was a very grave danger,' etc., etc. She gave way, however, on being informed that Mr Shakespeare was dead. This seemed to reassure her. Another parent wanted more attention to his child's handwriting, and another thought French was a waste of time; and so it went on, until Dorothy's carefully arranged time-table was almost in ruins. Mrs Creevy gave her clearly to understand that whatever the parents demanded she must do, or pretend to do. In many cases it was next door to impossible, for it disorganized everything to have one child studying, for instance, arithmetic while the rest of the class were doing history or geography. But in private schools the parents' word is law. Such schools exist, like shops, by flattering their customers, and if a parent wanted his child taught nothing but cat's-cradle and the cuneiform alphabet, the teacher would have to agree rather than lose a pupil.

The fact was that the parents were growing perturbed by the tales their children brought home about Dorothy's methods. They saw no sense whatever in these new-fangled ideas of making plasticine maps and reading poetry, and the old mechanical routine which had so horrified Dorothy struck them as eminently sensible. They became more and more restive, and their letters were peppered with the word 'practical', meaning in effect more handwriting lessons and more arithmetic. And even their notion of arithmetic was limited to addition, subtraction, multiplication and 'practice', with long division thrown in as a spectacular tour de force of no real value. Very few of them could have worked out a sum in decimals themselves, and they were not particularly anxious for their children to be able to do so either.

However, if this had been all, there would probably never have been any serious trouble. The parents would have nagged at Dorothy, as all parents do; but Dorothy would finally have learned—as, again, all teachers finally learn—that if one showed a certain amount of tact one could safely ignore them. But there was one fact that was absolutely certain to lead to trouble, and that was the fact that the parents of all except three children were Nonconformists, whereas Dorothy was an Anglican. It was true that Dorothy had lost her faith—indeed, for two months past, in the press of varying adventures, had hardly thought either of her faith or of its loss. But that made very little difference; Roman or Anglican, Dissenter, Jew, Turk or infidel, you retain the habits of thought that you have been brought up with. Dorothy, born and bred in the precincts of the Church, had no understanding of the Nonconformist mind. With the best will in the world, she could not help doing things that would cause offence to some of the parents.

Almost at the beginning there was a skirmish over the Scripture lessons—twice a week the children used to read a couple of chapters from the Bible. Old Testament and New Testament alternately—several of the parents writing to say, would Miss Millborough please NOT answer the children when they asked questions about the Virgin Mary; texts about the Virgin Mary were to be passed over in silence, or, if possible, missed out altogether. But it was Shakespeare, that immoral writer, who brought things to a head. The girls had worked their way through Macbeth, pining to know how the witches' prophecy was to be fulfilled. They reached the closing scenes. Birnam Wood had come to Dunsinane—that part was settled, anyway; now what about the man who was not of woman born? They came to the fatal passage:

> MACBETH: Thou losest labour; As easy may'st thou the intrenchant air With thy keen sword impress, as make me bleed: Let fall thy blade on vulnerable crests, I bear a charmed life, which must not yield To one of woman born.
>
> MACDUFF: Despair thy charm, And let the Angel whom thou still hast served Tell thee, Macduff was from his mother's womb Untimely ripp'd.

The girls looked puzzled. There was a momentary silence, and then a chorus of voices round the room:

'Please, Miss, what does that mean?'

Dorothy explained. She explained haltingly and incompletely, with a sudden horrid misgiving—a premonition that this was going to lead to trouble—but still, she did explain. And after that, of course, the fun began.

About half the children in the class went home and asked their parents the meaning of the word 'womb'. There was a sudden commotion, a flying to and fro of messages, an electric thrill of horror through fifteen decent Nonconformist homes. That night the parents must have held some kind of conclave, for the following evening, about the time when school ended, a deputation called upon Mrs Creevy. Dorothy heard them arriving by ones and twos, and guessed what was going to happen. As soon as she had dismissed the children, she heard Mrs Creevy call sharply down the stairs:

'Come up here a minute, Miss Millborough!'

Dorothy went up, trying to control the trembling of her knees. In the gaunt drawing-room Mrs Creevy was standing grimly beside the piano, and six parents were sitting round on horsehair chairs like a circle of inquisitors. There was the Mr Geo. Briggs who had written the letter about Mabel's arithmetic—he was an alert- looking greengrocer with a dried-up, shrewish wife—and there was a large, buffalo-like man with drooping moustaches and a colourless, peculiarly FLAT wife who looked as though she had been flattened out by the pressure of some heavy object—her husband, perhaps. The names of these two Dorothy did not catch. There was also Mrs Williams, the mother of the congenital idiot, a small, dark, very obtuse woman who always agreed with the last speaker, and there was a Mr Poynder, a commercial traveller. He was a youngish to middle- aged man with a grey face, mobile lips, and a bald scalp across which some strips of rather nasty-looking damp hair were carefully plastered. In honour of the parents' visit, a fire composed of three large coals was sulking in the grate.

'Sit down there, Miss Millborough,' said Mrs Creevy, pointing to a hard chair which stood like a stool of repentance in the middle of the ring of parents.

Dorothy sat down.

'And now,' said Mrs Creevy, 'just you listen to what Mr Poynder's got to say to you.'

Mr Poynder had a great deal to say. The other parents had evidently chosen him as their spokesman, and he talked till flecks of yellowish foam appeared at the corners of his mouth. And what was remarkable, he managed to do it all—so nice was his regard for the decencies—without ever once repeating the word that had caused all the trouble.

'I feel that I'm voicing the opinion of all of us,' he said with his facile bagman's eloquence, 'in saying that if Miss

Millborough knew that this play—Macduff, or whatever its name is—contained such words as—well, such words as we're speaking about, she never ought to have given it to the children to read at all. To my mind it's a disgrace that schoolbooks can be printed with such words in them. I'm sure if any of us had ever known that Shakespeare was that kind of stuff, we'd have put our foot down at the start. It surprises me, I must say. Only the other morning I was reading a piece in my News Chronicle about Shakespeare being the father of English Literature; well, if that's Literature, let's have a bit LESS Literature, say I! I think everyone'll agree with me there. And on the other hand, if Miss Millborough didn't know that the word—well, the word I'm referring to—was coming, she just ought to have gone straight on and taken no notice when it did come. There wasn't the slightest need to go explaining it to them. Just tell them to keep quiet and not get asking questions—that's the proper way with children.'

'But the children wouldn't have understood the play if I hadn't explained!' protested Dorothy for the third or fourth time.

'Of course they wouldn't! You don't seem to get my point, Miss Millborough! We don't want them to understand. Do you think we want them to go picking up dirty ideas out of books? Quite enough of that already with all these dirty films and these twopenny girls' papers that they get hold of—all these filthy, dirty love- stories with pictures of—well, I won't go into it. We don't send our children to school to have ideas put into their heads. I'm speaking for all the parents in saying this. We're all of decent God-fearing folk—some of us are Baptists and some of us are Methodists, and there's even one or two Church of England among us; but we can sink our differences when it comes to a case like this— and we try to bring our children up decent and save them from knowing anything about the Facts of Life. If I had my way, no child—at any rate, no girl—would know anything about the Facts of Life till she was twenty-one.'

There was a general nod from the parents, and the buffalo-like man added, 'Yer, yer! I'm with you there, Mr Poynder. Yer, yer!' deep down in his inside.

After dealing with the subject of Shakespeare, Mr Poynder added some remarks about Dorothy's new-fangled methods of teaching, which gave Mr Geo. Briggs the opportunity to rap out from time to time, 'That's it! Practical work—that's what we want—practical work! Not all this messy stuff like po'try and making maps and sticking scraps of paper and such like. Give 'em a good bit of figuring and handwriting and bother the rest. Practical work! You've said it!'

This went on for about twenty minutes. At first Dorothy attempted to argue, but she saw Mrs Creevy angrily shaking her head at her over the buffalo-like man's shoulder, which she rightly took as a signal to be quiet. By the time the parents had finished they had reduced Dorothy very nearly to tears, and after this they made ready to go. But Mrs Creevy stopped them.

'JUST a minute, ladies and gentlemen,' she said. 'Now that you've all had your say—and I'm sure I'm most glad to give you the opportunity—I'd just like to say a little something on my own account. Just to make things clear, in case any of you might think _I_ was to blame for this nasty business that's happened. And YOU stay here too, Miss Millborough!' she added.

She turned on Dorothy, and, in front of the parents, gave her a venomous 'talking to' which lasted upwards of ten minutes. The burden of it all was that Dorothy had brought these dirty books into the house behind her back; that it was monstrous treachery and ingratitude; and that if anything like it happened again, out Dorothy would go with a week's wages in her pocket. She rubbed it in and in and in. Phrases like 'girl that I've taken into my house', 'eating my bread', and even 'living on my charity', recurred over and over again. The parents sat round watching, and in their crass faces—faces not harsh or evil, only blunted by ignorance and mean virtues—you could see a solemn approval, a solemn pleasure in the spectacle of sin rebuked. Dorothy understood this; she understood that it was necessary that Mrs Creevy should give her her 'talking to' in front of the parents, so that they might feel that they were getting their money's worth and be satisfied. But still, as the stream of mean, cruel reprimand went on and on, such anger rose in her heart that she could with pleasure have stood up and struck Mrs Creevy across the face. Again and again she thought, 'I won't stand it, I won't stand it any longer! I'll tell her what I think of her and then walk straight out of the house!' But she did nothing of the kind. She saw with dreadful clarity the helplessness of her position. Whatever happened, whatever insults it meant swallowing, she had got to keep her job. So she sat still, with pink humiliated face, amid the circle of parents, and presently her anger turned to misery, and she realized that she was going to begin crying if she did not struggle to prevent it. But she realized, too, that if she began crying it would be the last straw and the parents would demand her dismissal. To stop herself, she dug her nails so hard into the palms that afterwards she found that she had drawn a few drops of blood.

Presently the 'talking to' wore itself out in assurances from Mrs Creevy that this should never happen again and that the offending Shakespeares should be burnt immediately. The parents were now satisfied. Dorothy had had her lesson and would doubtless profit by it; they did not bear her any malice and were not conscious of having humiliated her. They said good-bye to Mrs Creevy, said good-bye rather more coldly to Dorothy, and departed. Dorothy also rose to go, but Mrs Creevy signed to her to stay where she was.

'Just you wait a minute,' she said ominously as the parents left the room. 'I haven't finished yet, not by a long way I haven't.'

Dorothy sat down again. She felt very weak at the knees, and nearer to tears than ever. Mrs Creevy, having shown the parents out by the front door, came back with a bowl of water and threw it over the fire—for where was the sense of burning good coals after the parents had gone? Dorothy supposed that the 'talking to' was going to begin afresh. However, Mrs Creevy's wrath seemed to have cooled—at any rate, she had laid aside the air of outraged virtue that it had been necessary to put on in front of the parents.

'I just want to have a bit of a talk with you, Miss Millborough,' she said. 'It's about time we got it settled once and for all how this school's going to be run and how it's not going to be run.'

'Yes,' said Dorothy.

'Well, I'll be straight with you. When you came here I could see with half an eye that you didn't know the first thing about school- teaching; but I wouldn't have minded that if you'd just had a bit of common sense like any other girl would have had. Only it seems you hadn't. I let you have your own way for a week or two, and the first thing you do is to go and get all the parents' backs up. Well, I'm not going to have THAT over again. From now on I'm going to have things done MY way, not YOUR way. Do you understand that?'

'Yes,' said Dorothy again.

'You're not to think as I can't do without you, mind,' proceeded Mrs Creevy. 'I can pick up teachers at two a penny any day of the week, M.A.s and B.A.s and all. Only the M.A.s and B.A.s mostly take to drink, or else they—well, no matter what—and I will say for you you don't seem to be given to the drink or anything of that kind. I dare say you and me can get on all right if you'll drop these new-fangled ideas of yours and understand what's meant by practical school-teaching. So just you listen to me.'

Dorothy listened. With admirable clarity, and with a cynicism that was all the more disgusting because it was utterly unconscious, Mrs Creevy explained the technique of the dirty swindle that she called practical school-teaching.

'What you've got to get hold of once and for all,' she began, 'is that there's only one thing that matters in a school, and that's the fees. As for all this stuff about "developing the children's minds", as you call it, it's neither here nor there. It's the fees I'm after, not DEVELOPING THE CHILDREN'S MINDS. After all, it's no more than common sense. It's not to be supposed as anyone'd go to all the trouble of keeping school and having the house turned upside down by a pack of brats, if it wasn't that there's a bit of money to be made out of it. The fees come first, and everything else comes afterwards. Didn't I tell you that the very first day you came here?'

'Yes,' admitted Dorothy humbly.

'Well, then, it's the parents that pay the fees, and it's the parents you've got to think about. Do what the parents want— that's our rule here. I dare say all this messing about with plasticine and paper-scraps that you go in for doesn't do the children any particular harm; but the parents don't want it, and there's an end of it. Well, there's just two subjects that they DO want their children taught, and that's handwriting and arithmetic. Especially handwriting. That's something they CAN see the sense of. And so handwriting's the thing you've got to keep on and on at. Plenty of nice neat copies that the girls can take home, and that the parents'll show off to the neighbours and give us a bit of a free advert. I want you to give the children two hours a day just at handwriting and nothing else.'

'Two hours a day just at handwriting,' repeated Dorothy obediently.

'Yes. And plenty of arithmetic as well. The parents are very keen on arithmetic: especially money-sums. Keep your eye on the parents all the time. If you meet one of them in the street, get hold of them and start talking to them about their own girl.

Make out that she's the best girl in the class and that if she stays just three terms longer she'll be working wonders. You see what I mean? Don't go and tell them there's no room for improvement; because if you tell them THAT, they generally take their girls away. Just three terms longer—that's the thing to tell them. And when you make out the end of term reports, just you bring them to me and let me have a good look at them. I like to do the marking myself.'

Mrs Creevy's eye met Dorothy's. She had perhaps been about to say that she always arranged the marks so that every girl came out somewhere near the top of the class; but she refrained. Dorothy could not answer for a moment. Outwardly she was subdued, and very pale, but in her heart were anger and deadly repulsion against which she had to struggle before she could speak. She had no thought, however, of contradicting Mrs Creevy. The 'talking to' had quite broken her spirit. She mastered her voice, and said:

'I'm to teach nothing but handwriting and arithmetic—is that it?'

'Well, I didn't say that exactly. There's plenty of other subjects that look well on the prospectus. French, for instance—French looks VERY well on the prospectus. But it's not a subject you want to waste much time over. Don't go filling them up with a lot of grammar and syntax and verbs and all that. That kind of stuff doesn't get them anywhere so far as _I_ can see. Give them a bit of "Parley vous Francey", and "Passey moi le beurre", and so forth; that's a lot more use than grammar. And then there's Latin—I always put Latin on the prospectus. But I don't suppose you're very great on Latin, are you?'

'No,' admitted Dorothy.

'Well, it doesn't matter. You won't have to teach it. None of OUR parents'd want their children to waste time over Latin. But they like to see it on the prospectus. It looks classy. Of course there's a whole lot of subjects that we can't actually teach, but we have to advertise them all the same. Book-keeping and typing and shorthand, for instance; besides music and dancing. It all looks well on the prospectus.'

'Arithmetic, handwriting, French—is there anything else?' Dorothy said.

'Oh, well, history and geography and English Literature, of course. But just drop that map-making business at once—it's nothing but waste of time. The best geography to teach is lists of capitals. Get them so that they can rattle off the capitals of all the English counties as if it was the multiplication table. Then they've got something to show for what they've learnt, anyway. And as for history, keep on with the Hundred Page History of Britain. I won't have them taught out of those big history books you keep bringing home from the library. I opened one of those books the other day, and the first thing I saw was a piece where it said the English had been beaten in some battle or other. There's a nice thing to go teaching children! The parents won't stand for THAT kind of thing, I can tell you!'

'And Literature?' said Dorothy.

'Well, of course they've got to do a bit of reading, and I can't think why you wanted to turn up your nose at those nice little readers of ours. Keep on with the readers. They're a bit old, but they're quite good enough for a pack of children, I should have thought. And I suppose they might as well learn a few pieces of poetry by heart. Some of the parents like to hear their children say a piece of poetry. "The Boy stood on the Burning Deck"—that's a very good piece—and then there's "The Wreck of the Steamer"— now, what was that ship called? "The Wreck of the Steamer Hesperus". A little poetry doesn't hurt now and again. But don't let's have any more SHAKESPEARE, please!'

Dorothy got no tea that day. It was now long past tea-time, but when Mrs Creevy had finished her harangue she sent

Dorothy away without saying anything about tea. Perhaps this was a little extra punishment for l'affaire Macbeth.

Dorothy had not asked permission to go out, but she did not feel that she could stay in the house any longer. She got her hat and coat and set out down the ill-lit road, for the public library. It was late into November. Though the day had been damp the night wind blew sharply, like a threat, through the almost naked trees, making the gas-lamps flicker in spite of their glass chimneys, and stirring the sodden plane leaves that littered the pavement. Dorothy shivered slightly. The raw wind sent through her a bone- deep memory of the cold of Trafalgar Square. And though she did not actually think that if she lost her job it would mean going back to the sub-world from which she had come—indeed, it was not so desperate as that; at the worst her cousin or somebody else would help her—still, Mrs Creevy's 'talking to' had made Trafalgar Square seem suddenly very much nearer. It had driven into her a far deeper understanding than she had had before of the great modern commandment—the eleventh commandment which has wiped out all the others: 'Thou shalt not lose thy job.'

But as to what Mrs Creevy had said about 'practical school-teaching', it had been no more than a realistic facing of the facts. She had merely said aloud what most people in her position think but never say. Her oft-repeated phrase, 'It's the fees I'm after', was a motto that might be—indeed, ought to be—written over the doors of every private school in England.

There are, by the way, vast numbers of private schools in England. Second-rate, third-rate, and fourth-rate (Ringwood House was a specimen of the fourth-rate school), they exist by the dozen and the score in every London suburb and every provincial town. At any given moment there are somewhere in the neighbourhood of ten thousand of them, of which less than a thousand are subject to Government inspection. And though some of them are better than others, and a certain number, probably, are better than the council schools with which they compete, there is the same fundamental evil in all of them; that is, that they have ultimately no purpose except to make money. Often, except that there is nothing illegal about them, they are started in exactly the same spirit as one would start a brothel or a bucket shop. Some snuffy little man of business (it is quite usual for these schools to be owned by people who don't teach themselves) says one morning to his wife:

'Emma, I got a notion! What you say to us two keeping school, eh? There's plenty of cash in a school, you know, and there ain't the same work in it as what there is in a shop or a pub. Besides, you don't risk nothing; no over'ead to worry about, 'cept jest your rent and few desks and a blackboard. But we'll do it in style. Get in one of these Oxford and Cambridge chaps as is out of a job and'll come cheap, and dress 'im up in a gown and—what do they call them little square 'ats with tassels on top? That 'ud fetch the parents, eh? You jest keep your eyes open and see if you can't pick on a good district where there's not too many on the same game already.'

He chooses a situation in one of those middle-class districts where the people are too poor to afford the fees of a decent school and too proud to send their children to the council schools, and 'sets up'. By degrees he works up a connexion in very much the same manner as a milkman or a greengrocer, and if he is astute and tactful and has not too many competitors, he makes his few hundreds a year out of it.

Of course, these schools are not all alike. Not every principal is a grasping low-minded shrew like Mrs Creevy, and there are plenty of schools where the atmosphere is kindly and decent and the teaching is as good as one could reasonably expect for fees of five pounds a term. On the other hand, some of them are crying scandals. Later on, when Dorothy got to know one of the teachers at another private school in Southbridge, she heard tales of schools that were worse by far than Ringwood House. She heard of a cheap boarding-school where travelling actors dumped their children as one dumps luggage in a railway cloakroom, and where the children simply vegetated, doing absolutely nothing, reaching the age of sixteen without learning to read; and another school where the days passed in a perpetual riot, with a broken-down old hack of a master chasing the boys up and down and slashing at them with a cane, and then suddenly collapsing and weeping with his head on a desk, while the boys laughed at him. So long as schools are run primarily for money, things like this will happen. The expensive private schools to which the rich send their children are not, on the surface, so bad as the others, because they can afford a proper staff, and the Public School examination system keeps them up to the mark; but they have the same essential taint.

It was only later, and by degrees, that Dorothy discovered these facts about private schools. At first, she used to suffer from an absurd fear that one day the school inspectors would descend upon Ringwood House, find out what a sham and a swindle it all was, and raise the dust accordingly. Later on, however, she learned that this could never happen. Ringwood House was not 'recognized', and therefore was not liable to be inspected. One day a Government inspector did, indeed, visit the school, but beyond measuring the dimensions of the schoolroom to see whether each girl had her right number of cubic feet of air, he did nothing; he had no power to do more. Only the tiny minority of 'recognized' schools—less than one in ten—are officially tested to decide whether they keep up a reasonable educational standard. As for the others, they are free to teach or not teach exactly as they choose. No one controls or inspects them except the children's parents—the blind leading the blind.

5

Next day Dorothy began altering her programme in accordance with Mrs Creevy's orders. The first lesson of the day was handwriting, and the second was geography.

'That'll do, girls,' said Dorothy as the funereal clock struck ten. 'We'll start our geography lesson now.'

The girls flung their desks open and put their hated copybooks away with audible sighs of relief. There were murmurs of 'Oo, jography! Good!' It was one of their favourite lessons. The two girls who were 'monitors' for the week, and whose job it was to clean the blackboard, collect exercise books and so forth (children will fight for the privilege of doing jobs of that kind), leapt from their places to fetch the half-finished contour map that stood against the wall. But Dorothy stopped them.

'Wait a moment. Sit down, you two. We aren't going to go on with the map this morning.'

There was a cry of dismay. 'Oh, Miss! Why can't we, Miss? PLEASE let's go on with it!'

'No. I'm afraid we've been wasting a little too much time over the map lately. We're going to start learning some of the capitals of the English counties. I want every girl in the class to know the whole lot of them by the end of the term.'

The children's faces fell. Dorothy saw it, and added with an attempt at brightness—that hollow, undeceiving brightness of a teacher trying to palm off a boring subject as an interesting one:

'Just think how pleased your parents will be when they can ask you the capital of any county in England and you can tell it them!'

The children were not in the least taken in. They writhed at the nauseous prospect.

'Oh, CAPITALS! Learning CAPITALS! That's just what we used to do with Miss Strong. Please, Miss, WHY can't we go on with the map?'

'Now don't argue. Get your notebooks out and take them down as I give them to you. And afterwards we'll say them all together.'

Reluctantly, the children fished out their notebooks, still groaning. 'Please, Miss, can we go on with the map NEXT time?'

'I don't know. We'll see.'

That afternoon the map was removed from the schoolroom, and Mrs Creevy scraped the plasticine off the board and threw it away. It was the same with all the other subjects, one after another. All the changes that Dorothy had made were undone. They went back to the routine of interminable 'copies' and interminable 'practice' sums, to the learning parrot-fashion of 'Passez-moi le beurre' and 'Le fils du jardinier a perdu son chapeau', to the Hundred Page History and the insufferable little 'reader'. (Mrs Creevy had impounded the Shakespeares, ostensibly to burn them. The probability was that she had sold them.) Two hours a day were set apart for handwriting lessons. The two depressing pieces of black paper, which Dorothy had taken down from the wall, were replaced, and their proverbs written upon them afresh in neat copperplate. As for the historical chart, Mrs Creevy took it away and burnt it.

When the children saw the hated lessons, from which they had thought to have escaped for ever, coming back upon them one by one, they were first astonished, then miserable, then sulky. But it was far worse for Dorothy than for the children. After only a couple of days the rigmarole through which she was obliged to drive them so nauseated her that she began to doubt whether she could go on with it any longer. Again and again she toyed with the idea of disobeying Mrs Creevy. Why not, she would think, as the children whined and groaned and sweated under their miserable bondage—why not stop it and go back to proper lessons, even if it was only for an hour or two a day? Why not drop the whole pretence of lessons and simply let the children play? It would be so much better for them than this. Let them draw pictures or make something out of plasticine or begin making up a fairy tale—anything REAL, anything that would interest them, instead of this dreadful nonsense. But she dared not. At any moment Mrs Creevy was liable to come in, and if she found the children 'messing about' instead of getting on with their routine work, there would be fearful trouble. So Dorothy hardened her heart, and obeyed Mrs Creevy's instructions to the letter, and things were very much as they had been before Miss Strong was 'taken bad'.

The lessons reached such a pitch of boredom that the brightest spot in the week was Mr Booth's so-called chemistry lecture on Thursday afternoons. Mr Booth was a seedy, tremulous man of about fifty, with long, wet, cowdung-coloured moustaches. He had been a Public School master once upon a time, but nowadays he made just enough for a life of chronic sub-drunkenness by delivering lectures at two and sixpence a time. The lectures were unrelieved drivel. Even in his palmiest days Mr Booth had not been a particularly brilliant lecturer, and now, when he had had his first go of delirium tremens and lived in a daily dread of his second, what chemical knowledge he had ever had was fast deserting him. He would stand dithering in front of the class, saying the same thing over and over again and trying vainly to remember what he was talking about. 'Remember, girls,' he would say in his husky, would-be fatherly voice, 'the number of the elements is ninety-three—ninety-three elements, girls—you all of you know what an element is, don't you?—there are just ninety-three of them—remember that number, girls—ninety-three,' until Dorothy (she had to stay in the schoolroom during the chemistry lectures, because Mrs Creevy considered that it DIDN'T DO to leave the girls alone with a man) was miserable with vicarious shame. All the lectures started with the ninety-three elements, and never got very much further. There was also talk of 'a very interesting little experiment that I'm going to perform for you next week, girls—very interesting you'll find it—we'll have it next week without fail—a very interesting little experiment', which, needless to say, was never performed. Mr Booth possessed no chemical apparatus, and his hands were far too shaky to have used it even if he had had any. The girls sat through his lectures in a suety stupor of boredom, but even he was a welcome change from handwriting lessons.

The children were never quite the same with Dorothy after the parents' visit. They did not change all in a day, of course. They had grown to be fond of 'old Millie', and they expected that after a day or two of tormenting them with handwriting and 'commercial arithmetic' she would go back to something interesting. But the handwriting and arithmetic went on, and the popularity Dorothy had enjoyed, as a teacher whose lessons weren't boring and who didn't slap you, pinch you, or twist your ears, gradually vanished. Moreover, the story of the row there had been over Macbeth was not long in leaking out. The children grasped that old Millie had done something wrong—they didn't exactly know what—and had been given a 'talking to'. It lowered her in their eyes. There is no dealing with children, even with children who are fond of you, unless you can keep your prestige as an adult; let that prestige be once damaged, and even the best-hearted children will despise you.

So they began to be naughty in the normal, traditional way. Before, Dorothy had only had to deal with occasional laziness, outbursts of noise and silly giggling fits; now there were spite and deceitfulness as well. The children revolted ceaselessly against the horrible routine. They forgot the short weeks when old Millie had seemed quite a good sort and school itself had seemed rather fun. Now, school was simply what it had always been, and what indeed you expected it to be—a place where you slacked and yawned and whiled the time away by pinching your neighbour and trying to make the teacher lose her temper, and from which you burst with a yell of relief the instant the last lesson was over. Sometimes they sulked and had fits of crying, sometimes they argued in the maddening persistent way that children have, 'WHY should we do this? WHY does anyone have to learn to read and write?' over and over again, until Dorothy had to stand over them and silence them with threats of blows. She was growing almost habitually irritable nowadays; it surprised and shocked her, but she could not stop it. Every morning she vowed to herself, 'Today I will NOT lose my temper', and every morning, with depressing regularity, she DID lose her temper, especially at about half past eleven when the children were at their worst. Nothing in the world is quite so irritating as dealing with mutinous children. Sooner or later, Dorothy knew, she would lose control of herself and begin hitting them. It seemed to her an unforgivable thing to do, to hit a child; but nearly all teachers come to it in the end. It was impossible now to get any child to work except when your eye was upon it. You had only to turn your back for an instant and blotting-paper pellets were flying to and fro. Nevertheless, with ceaseless slave-driving the children's handwriting and 'commercial arithmetic' did certainly show some improvement, and no doubt the parents were satisfied.

The last few weeks of the term were a very bad time. For over a fortnight Dorothy was quite penniless, for Mrs Creevy had told her that she couldn't pay her her term's wages 'till some of the fees came in'. So she was deprived of the secret slabs of chocolate that had kept her going, and she suffered from a perpetual slight hunger that made her languid and spiritless. There were leaden mornings when the minutes dragged like hours, when she struggled with herself to keep her eyes away from the clock, and her heart sickened to think that beyond this lesson there loomed another just like it, and more of them and more, stretching on into what seemed like a dreary eternity. Worse yet were the times when the children were in their noisy mood and it needed a constant exhausting effort of the will to keep them under control at all; and beyond the wall, of course, lurked Mrs Creevy, always listening, always ready to descend upon the schoolroom, wrench the door open, and glare round the room with 'Now then! What's all this noise about, please?' and the sack in her eye.

Dorothy was fully awake, now, to the beastliness of living in Mrs Creevy's house. The filthy food, the cold, and the lack of baths seemed much more important than they had seemed a little while ago. Moreover, she was beginning to appreciate, as she had not done when the joy of her work was fresh upon her, the utter loneliness of her position. Neither her father nor Mr Warburton had written to her, and in two months she had made not a single friend in Southbridge. For anyone so situated, and particularly for a woman, it is all but impossible to make friends. She had no money and no home of her own, and outside the school her sole places of refuge were the public library, on the few evenings when she could get there, and church on Sunday mornings. She went to church regularly, of course—Mrs Creevy had insisted on that. She had settled the question of Dorothy's religious observances at breakfast on her first Sunday morning.

'I've just been wondering what Place of Worship you ought to go to,' she said. 'I suppose you were brought up C. of E., weren't you?'

'Yes,' said Dorothy.

'Hm, well. I can't quite make up my mind where to send you. There's St George's—that's the C. of E.—and there's the Baptist Chapel where I go myself. Most of our parents are Nonconformists, and I don't know as they'd quite approve of a C. of E. teacher. You can't be too careful with the parents. They had a bit of a scare two years ago when it turned out that the teacher I had then was actually a Roman Catholic, if you please! Of course she kept it dark as long as she could, but it came out in the end, and three of the parents took their children away. I got rid of her the same day as I found it out, naturally.'

Dorothy was silent.

'Still,' went on Mrs Creevy, 'we HAVE got three C. of E. pupils, and I don't know as the Church connexion mightn't be worked up a bit. So perhaps you'd better risk it and go to St George's. But you want to be a bit careful, you know. I'm told St George's is one of these churches where they go in for a lot of bowing and scraping and crossing yourself and all that. We've got two parents that are Plymouth Brothers, and they'd throw a fit if they heard you'd been seen crossing yourself. So don't go and do THAT, whatever you do.'

'Very well,' said Dorothy.

'And just you keep your eyes well open during the sermon. Have a good look round and see if there's any young girls in the congregation that we could get hold of. If you see any likely looking ones, get on to the parson afterwards and try and find out their names and addresses.'

So Dorothy went to St George's. It was a shade 'Higher' than St Athelstan's had been; chairs, not pews, but no incense, and the vicar (his name was Mr Gore-Williams) wore a plain cassock and surplice except on festival days. As for the services, they were so like those at home that Dorothy could go through them, and utter all the responses at the right moment, in a state of the completest abstraction.

There was never a moment when the power of worship returned to her. Indeed, the whole concept of worship was meaningless to her now; her faith had vanished, utterly and irrevocably. It is a mysterious thing, the loss of faith—as mysterious as faith itself. Like faith, it is ultimately not rooted in logic; it is a change in the climate of the mind. But however little the church services might mean to her, she did not regret the hours she spent in church. On the contrary, she looked forward to her

Sunday mornings as blessed interludes of peace; and that not only because Sunday morning meant a respite from Mrs Creevy's prying eye and nagging voice. In another and deeper sense the atmosphere of the church was soothing and reassuring to her. For she perceived that in all that happens in church, however absurd and cowardly its supposed purpose may be, there is something—it is hard to define, but something of decency, of spiritual comeliness—that is not easily found in the world outside. It seemed to her that even though you no longer believe, it is better to go to church than not; better to follow in the ancient ways, than to drift in rootless freedom. She knew very well that she would never again be able to utter a prayer and mean it; but she knew also that for the rest of her life she must continue with the observances to which she had been bred. Just this much remained to her of the faith that had once, like the bones in a living frame, held all her life together.

But as yet she did not think very deeply about the loss of her faith and what it might mean to her in the future. She was too busy merely existing, merely struggling to make her nerves hold out for the rest of that miserable term. For as the term drew to an end, the job of keeping the class in order grew more and more exhausting. The girls behaved atrociously, and they were all the bitterer against Dorothy because they had once been fond of her. She had deceived them, they felt. She had started off by being decent, and now she had turned out to be just a beastly old teacher like the rest of them—a nasty old beast who kept on and on with those awful handwriting lessons and snapped your head off if you so much as made a blot on your book. Dorothy caught them eyeing her face, sometimes, with the aloof, cruel scrutiny of children. They had thought her pretty once, and now they thought her ugly, old, and scraggy. She had grown, indeed, much thinner since she had been at Ringwood House. They hated her now, as they had hated all their previous teachers.

Sometimes they baited her quite deliberately. The older and more intelligent girls understood the situation well enough—understood that Millie was under old Creevy's thumb and that she got dropped on afterwards when they had been making too much noise; sometimes they made all the noise they dared, just so as to bring old Creevy in and have the pleasure of watching Millie's face while old Creevy told her off. There were times when Dorothy could keep her temper and forgive them all they did, because she realized that it was only a healthy instinct that made them rebel against the loathsome monotony of their work. But there were other times when her nerves were more on edge than usual, and when she looked round at the score of silly little faces, grinning or mutinous, and found it possible to hate them. Children are so blind, so selfish, so merciless. They do not know when they are tormenting you past bearing, and if they did know they would not care. You may do your very best for them, you may keep your temper in situations that would try a saint, and yet if you are forced to bore them and oppress them, they will hate you for it without ever asking themselves whether it is you who are to blame. How true—when you happen not to be a school-teacher yourself—how true those often- quoted lines sound—

> Under a cruel eye outworn The little ones spend the day In sighing and dismay!

But when you yourself are the cruel eye outworn, you realize that there is another side to the picture.

The last week came, and the dirty farce of 'exams', was carried through. The system, as explained by Mrs Creevy, was quite simple. You coached the children in, for example, a series of sums until you were quite certain that they could get them right, and then set them the same sums as an arithmetic paper before they had time to forget the answers; and so with each subject in turn. The children's papers were, of course, sent home for their parents' inspection. And Dorothy wrote the reports under Mrs Creevy's dictation, and she had to write 'excellent' so many times that—as sometimes happens when you write a word over and over again—she forgot how to spell it and began writing in 'excelent', 'exsellent', 'ecsellent', 'eccelent'.

The last day passed in fearful tumults. Not even Mrs Creevy herself could keep the children in order. By midday Dorothy's nerves were in rags, and Mrs Creevy gave her a 'talking to' in front of the seven children who stayed to dinner. In the afternoon the noise was worse than ever, and at last Dorothy, overcome, appealed to the girls almost tearfully to stop.

'Girls!' she called out, raising her voice to make herself heard through the din. 'PLEASE stop it, PLEASE! You're behaving horribly to me. Do you think it's kind to go on like this?'

That was fatal, of course. Never, never, never throw yourself on the mercy of a child! There was an instant's hush, and then one child cried out, loudly and derisively, 'Mill-iee!' The next moment the whole class had taken it up, even the imbecile Mavis, chanting all together 'Mill-iee! Mill-iee! Mill-iee!' At that, something within Dorothy seemed to snap. She paused for an instant, picked out the girl who was making the most noise, walked up to her, and gave her a smack across the ear almost as hard as she could hit. Happily it was only one of the 'medium payers'.

6

On the first day of the holidays Dorothy received a letter from Mr Warburton.

My Dear Dorothy [he wrote],—Or should I call you Ellen, as I understand that is your new name? You must, I am afraid, have thought it very heartless of me not to have written sooner, but I assure you that it was not until ten days ago that I even heard anything about our supposed escapade. I have been abroad, first in various parts of France, then in Austria and then in Rome, and, as you know, I avoid my fellow countrymen most strenuously on these trips. They are disgusting enough even at home, but in foreign parts their behaviour makes me so ashamed of them that I generally try to pass myself off as an American.

When I got to Knype Hill your father refused to see me, but I managed to get hold of Victor Stone, who gave me your address and the name you are using. He seemed rather reluctant to do so, and I gathered that even he, like everyone else in this poisonous town, still believes that you have misbehaved yourself in some way. I think the theory that you and I eloped together has been dropped, but you must, they feel, have done SOMETHING scandalous. A young woman has left home suddenly, therefore there must be a man in the case; that is how the provincial mind works, you see. I need not tell you that I have been contradicting the whole story with the utmost vigour. You will be glad to hear that I managed to corner that disgusting hag, Mrs Semprill, and give her a piece of my mind; and I assure you that a piece of MY mind is distinctly formidable. But the woman is simply sub-human. I could get nothing out of her except hypocritical snivellings about 'poor, POOR Dorothy'.

I hear that your father misses you very much, and would gladly have you home again if it were not for the scandal. His meals are never punctual nowadays, it seems. He gives it out that you 'went away to recuperate from a slight illness and have now got an excellent post at a girls' school'. You will be surprised to hear of one thing that has happened to him. He has been obliged to pay off all his debts! I am told that the tradesmen rose in a body and held what was practically a creditors' meeting in the Rectory. Not the kind of thing that could have happened at

Plumstead Episcopi—but these are democratic days, alas! You, evidently, were the only person who could keep the tradesmen permanently at bay.

And now I must tell you some of my own news, etc., etc., etc.

At this point Dorothy tore the letter up in disappointment and even in annoyance. He might have shown a little more sympathy! she thought. It was just like Mr Warburton after getting her into serious trouble—for after all, he was principally to blame for what had happened—to be so flippant and unconcerned about it. But when she had thought it over she acquitted him of heartlessness. He had done what little was possible to help her, and he could not be expected to pity her for troubles of which he had not heard. Besides, his own life had been a series of resounding scandals; probably he could not understand that to a woman a scandal is a serious matter.

At Christmas Dorothy's father also wrote, and what was more, sent her a Christmas present of two pounds. It was evident from the tone of his letter that he had forgiven Dorothy by this time. WHAT exactly he had forgiven her was not certain, because it was not certain what exactly she had done; but still, he had forgiven her. The letter started with some perfunctory but quite friendly inquiries. He hoped her new job suited her, he wrote. And were her rooms at the school comfortable and the rest of the staff congenial? He had heard that they did one very well at schools nowadays—very different from what it had been forty years ago. Now, in his day, etc., etc., etc. He had, Dorothy perceived, not the dimmest idea of her present circumstances. At the mention of schools his mind flew to Winchester, his old school; such a place as Ringwood House was beyond his imagining.

The rest of the letter was taken up with grumblings about the way things were going in the parish. The Rector complained of being worried and overworked. The wretched churchwardens kept bothering him with this and that, and he was growing very tired of Proggett's reports about the collapsing belfry, and the daily woman whom he had engaged to help Ellen was a great nuisance and had put her broom-handle through the face of the grandfather clock in his study—and so on, and so forth, for a number of pages. He said several times in a mumbling roundabout way that he wished Dorothy were there to help him; but he did not actually suggest that she should come home. Evidently it was still necessary that she should remain out of sight and out of mind—a skeleton in a distant and well-locked cupboard.

The letter filled Dorothy with sudden painful homesickness. She found herself pining to be back at her parish visiting and her Girl Guides' cooking class, and wondering unhappily how her father had got on without her all this while and whether those two women were looking after him properly. She was fond of her father, in a way that she had never dared to show; for he was not a person to whom you could make any display of affection. It surprised and rather shocked her to realize how little he had been in her thoughts during the past four months. There had been periods of weeks at a time when she had forgotten his existence. But the truth was that the mere business of keeping body and soul together had left her with no leisure for other emotions.

Now, however, school work was over, and she had leisure and to spare, for though Mrs Creevy did her best she could not invent enough household jobs to keep Dorothy busy for more than part of the day. She made it quite plain to Dorothy that during the holidays she was nothing but a useless expense, and she watched her at her meals (obviously feeling it an outrage that she should eat when she wasn't working) in a way that finally became unbearable. So Dorothy kept out of the house as much as possible, and, feeling fairly rich with her wages (four pounds ten, for nine weeks) and her father's two pounds, she took to buying sandwiches at the ham and beef shop in the town and eating her dinner out of doors. Mrs Creevy acquiesced, half sulkily because she liked to have Dorothy in the house to nag at her, and half pleased at the chance of skimping a few more meals.

Dorothy went for long solitary walks, exploring Southbridge and its yet more desolate neighbours, Dorley, Wembridge, and West Holton. Winter had descended, dank and windless, and more gloomy in those colourless labyrinthine suburbs than in the bleakest wilderness. On two or three occasions, though such extravagance would probably mean hungry days later on, Dorothy took a cheap return ticket to Iver Heath or Burnham Beeches. The woods were sodden and wintry, with great beds of drifted beech leaves that glowed like copper in the still, wet air, and the days were so mild that you could sit out of doors and read if you kept your gloves on. On Christmas Eve Mrs Creevy produced some sprigs of holly that she had saved from last year, dusted them, and nailed them up; but she did not, she said, intend to have a Christmas dinner. She didn't hold with all this Christmas nonsense, she said—it was just a lot of humbug got up by the shopkeepers, and such an unnecessary expense; and she hated turkey and Christmas pudding anyway. Dorothy was relieved; a Christmas dinner in that joyless 'morning-room' (she had an awful momentary vision of Mrs Creevy in a paper hat out of a cracker) was something that didn't bear thinking about. She ate her Christmas dinner—a hard-boiled egg, two cheese sandwiches, and a bottle of lemonade—in the woods near Burnham, against a great gnarled beech tree, over a copy of George Gissing's The Odd Women.

On days when it was too wet to go for walks she spent most of her time in the public library—becoming, indeed, one of the regular habituees of the library, along with the out-of-work men who sat drearily musing over illustrated papers which they did not read, and the elderly discoloured bachelor who lived in 'rooms' on two pounds a week and came to the library to study books on yachting by the hour together. It had been a great relief to her when the term ended, but this feeling soon wore off; indeed, with never a soul to talk to, the days dragged even more heavily than before. There is perhaps no quarter of the inhabited world where one can be quite so completely alone as in the London suburbs. In a big town the throng and bustle give one at least the illusion of companionship, and in the country everyone is interested in everyone else—too much so, indeed. But in places like Southbridge, if you have no family and no home to call your own, you could spend half a lifetime without managing to make a friend. There are women in such places, and especially derelict gentlewomen in ill-paid jobs, who go for years upon end in almost utter solitude. It was not long before Dorothy found herself in a perpetually low-spirited, jaded state in which, try as she would, nothing seemed able to interest her. And it was in the hateful ennui of this time—the corrupting ennui that lies in wait for every modern soul—that she first came to a full understanding of what it meant to have lost her faith.

She tried drugging herself with books, and it succeeded for a week or so. But after a while very nearly all books seemed wearisome and unintelligible; for the mind will not work to any purpose when it is quite alone. In the end she found that she could not cope with anything more difficult than a detective story. She took walks of ten and fifteen miles, trying to tire herself into a better mood; but the mean suburban roads, and the damp, miry paths through the woods, the naked trees, the sodden moss and great spongy fungi, afflicted her with a deadly melancholy. It was human companionship that she needed, and there seemed no way of getting it. At nights' when she walked back to the school and looked at the warm-lit windows of the houses, and heard voices laughing and gramophones playing within, her heart swelled with envy. Ah, to be like those people in there—to have at least a home, a family, a few friends who were interested in you! There were days when she pined for the courage to speak to strangers in the street. Days, too, when she contemplated shamming piety in order to scrape acquaintance with the Vicar of St George's and his family, and perhaps get the chance of occupying herself with a little parish work; days, even, when she was so desperate that she thought of joining the Y.W.C.A.

But almost at the end of the holidays, through a chance encounter at the library, she made friends with a little woman named Miss Beaver, who was geography mistress at Toot's Commercial College, another of the private schools in Southbridge. Toot's Commerical College was a much larger and more pretentious school than Ringwood House—it had about a hundred and fifty day-pupils of both sexes and even rose to the dignity of having a dozen boarders—and its curriculum was a somewhat less blatant swindle. It was one of those schools that are aimed at the type of parent who blathers about 'up-to-date business training', and its watch-word was Efficiency; meaning a tremendous parade of hustling, and the banishment of all humane studies. One of its features was a kind of catechism called the Efficiency Ritual, which all the children were required to learn by heart as soon as they joined the school. It had questions and answers such as:

> Q. What is the secret of success?
> A. The secret of success is efficiency.
> Q. What is the test of efficiency?
> A. The test of efficiency is success.

And so on and so on. It was said that the spectacle of the whole school, boys and girls together, reciting the Efficiency Ritual under the leadership of the Headmaster—they had this ceremony two mornings a week instead of prayers—was most impressive.

Miss Beaver was a prim little woman with a round body, a thin face, a reddish nose, and the gait of a guinea-hen. After twenty years of slave-driving she had attained to an income of four pounds a week and the privilege of 'living out' instead of having to put the boarders to bed at nights. She lived in 'rooms'—that is, in a bed-sitting room—to which she was sometimes able to invite Dorothy when both of them had a free evening. How Dorothy looked forward to those visits! They were only possible at rare intervals, because Miss Beaver's landlady 'didn't approve of visitors', and even when you got there there was nothing much to do except to help solve the crossword puzzle out of the Daily Telegraph and look at the photographs Miss Beaver had taken on her trip (this trip had been the summit and glory of her life) to the Austrian Tyrol in 1913. But still, how much it meant to sit talking to somebody in a friendly way and to drink a cup of tea less wishy-washy than Mrs Creevy's! Miss Beaver had a spirit lamp in a japanned travelling case (it had been with her to the Tyrol in 1913) on which she brewed herself pots of tea as black as coal-tar, swallowing about a bucketful of this stuff during the day. She confided to Dorothy that she always took a Thermos flask to school and had a nice hot cup of tea during the break and another after dinner. Dorothy perceived that by one of two well-beaten roads every third-rate schoolmistress must travel: Miss Strong's road, via whisky to the workhouse; or Miss Beaver's road, via strong tea to a decent death in the Home for Decayed Gentlewomen.

Miss Beaver was in truth a dull little woman. She was a memento mori, or rather memento senescere, to Dorothy. Her soul seemed to have withered until it was as forlorn as a dried-up cake of soap in a forgotten soap dish. She had come to a point where life in a bed-sitting room under a tyrannous landlady and the 'efficient' thrusting of Commercial Geography down children's retching throats, were almost the only destiny she could imagine. Yet Dorothy grew to be very fond of Miss Beaver, and those occasional hours that they spent together in the bed-sitting room, doing the Daily Telegraph crossword over a nice hot cup of tea, were like oases in her life.

She was glad when the Easter term began, for even the daily round of slave-driving was better than the empty solitude of the holidays. Moreover, the girls were much better in hand this term; she never again found it necessary to smack their heads. For she had grasped now that it is easy enough to keep children in order if you are ruthless with them from the start. Last term the girls had behaved badly, because she had started by treating them as human beings, and later on, when the lessons that interested them were discontinued, they had rebelled like human beings. But if you are obliged to teach children rubbish, you mustn't treat them as human beings. You must treat them like animals—driving, not persuading. Before all else, you must teach them that it is more painful to rebel than to obey. Possibly this kind of treatment is not very good for children, but there is no doubt they understand it and respond to it.

She learned the dismal arts of the school-teacher. She learned to glaze her mind against the interminable boring hours, to economize her nervous energy, to be merciless and ever-vigilant, to take a kind of pride and pleasure in seeing a futile rigmarole well done. She had grown, quite suddenly it seemed, much tougher and maturer. Her eyes had lost the half-childish look that they had once had, and her face had grown thinner, making her nose seem longer. At times it was quite definitely a schoolmarm's face; you could imagine pince-nez upon it. But she had not become cynical as yet. She still knew that these children were the victims of a dreary swindle, still longed, if it had been possible, to do something better for them. If she harried them and stuffed their heads with rubbish, it was for one reason alone: because whatever happened she had got to keep her job.

There was very little noise in the schoolroom this term. Mrs Creevy, anxious as she always was for a chance of finding fault, seldom had reason to rap on the wall with her broom-handle. One morning at breakfast she looked rather hard at Dorothy, as though weighing a decision, and then pushed the dish of marmalade across the table.

'Have some marmalade if you like, Miss Millborough,' she said, quite graciously for her.

It was the first time that marmalade had crossed Dorothy's lips since she had come to Ringwood House. She flushed slightly. 'So the woman realizes that I have done my best for her,' she could not help thinking.

Thereafter she had marmalade for breakfast every morning. And in other ways Mrs Creevy's manner became—not indeed, genial, for it could never be that, but less brutally offensive. There were even times when she produced a grimace that was intended for a smile; her face, it seemed to Dorothy, CREASED with the effort. About this time her conversation became peppered with references to 'next term'. It was always 'Next term we'll do this', and 'Next term I shall want you to do that', until Dorothy began to feel that she had won Mrs Creevy's confidence and was being treated more like a colleague than a slave. At that a small, unreasonable but very exciting hope took root in her heart. Perhaps Mrs Creevy was going to raise her wages! It was profoundly unlikely, and she tried to break herself of hoping for it, but could not quite succeed. If her wages were raised even half a crown a week, what a difference it would make!

The last day came. With any luck Mrs Creevy might pay her wages tomorrow, Dorothy thought. She wanted the money very badly indeed; she had been penniless for weeks past, and was not only unbearably hungry, but also in need of some new stockings, for she had not a pair that were not darned almost out of existence. The following morning she did the household jobs allotted to her, and then, instead of going out, waited in the 'morning-room' while Mrs Creevy banged about with her broom and pan upstairs. Presently Mrs Creevy came down.

'Ah, so THERE you are, Miss Millborough!' she said in a peculiar meaning tone. 'I had a sort of an idea you wouldn't be in such a hurry to get out of doors this morning. Well, as you ARE here, I suppose I may as well pay you your wages.'

'Thank you,' said Dorothy.

'And after that,' added Mrs Creevy, 'I've got a little something as I want to say to you.'

Dorothy's heart stirred. Did that 'little something' mean the longed-for rise in wages? It was just conceivable. Mrs Creevy produced a worn, bulgy leather purse from a locked drawer in the dresser, opened it and licked her thumb.

'Twelve weeks and five days,' she said. 'Twelve weeks is near enough. No need to be particular to a day. That makes six pounds.'

She counted out five dingy pound notes and two ten-shilling notes; then, examining one of the notes and apparently finding it too clean, she put it back into her purse and fished out another that had been torn in half. She went to the dresser, got a piece of transparent sticky paper and carefully stuck the two halves together. Then she handed it, together with the other six, to Dorothy.

'There you are, Miss Millborough,' she said. 'And now, will you just leave the house AT once, please? I shan't be wanting you any longer.'

'You won't be—'

Dorothy's entrails seemed to have turned to ice. All the blood drained out of her face. But even now, in her terror and despair, she was not absolutely sure of the meaning of what had been said to her. She still half thought that Mrs Creevy merely meant that she was to stay out of the house for the rest of the day.

'You won't be wanting me any longer?' she repeated faintly.

'No. I'm getting in another teacher at the beginning of next term. And it isn't to be expected as I'd keep you through the holidays all free for nothing, is it?'

'But you don't mean that you want me to LEAVE—that you're dismissing me?'

'Of course I do. What else did you think I meant?'

'But you've given me no notice!' said Dorothy.

'Notice!' said Mrs Creevy, getting angry immediately. 'What's it got to do with YOU whether I give you notice or not? You haven't got a written contract, have you?'

'No... I suppose not.'

'Well, then! You'd better go upstairs and start packing your box. It's no good your staying any longer, because I haven't got anything in for your dinner.'

Dorothy went upstairs and sat down on the side of the bed. She was trembling uncontrollably, and it was some minutes before she could collect her wits and begin packing. She felt dazed. The disaster that had fallen upon her was so sudden, so apparently causeless, that she had difficulty in believing that it had actually happened. But in truth the reason why Mrs Creevy had sacked her was quite simple and adequate.

Not far from Ringwood House there was a poor, moribund little school called The Gables, with only seven pupils. The teacher was an incompetent old hack called Miss Allcock, who had been at thirty-eight different schools in her life and was not fit to have charge of a tame canary. But Miss Allcock had one outstanding talent; she was very good at double-crossing her employers. In these third-rate and fourth-rate private schools a sort of piracy is constantly going on. Parents are 'got round' and pupils stolen from one school to another. Very often the treachery of the teacher is at the bottom of it. The teacher secretly approaches the parents one by one ('Send your child to me and I'll take her at ten shillings a term cheaper'), and when she has corrupted a sufficient number she suddenly deserts and 'sets up' on her own, or carries the children off to another school. Miss Allcock had succeeded in stealing three out of her employer's seven pupils, and had come to Mrs Creevy with the offer of them. In return, she was to have Dorothy's place and a fifteen-per-cent commission on the pupils she brought.

There were weeks of furtive chaffering before the bargain was clinched, Miss Allcock being finally beaten down from fifteen per cent to twelve and a half. Mrs Creevy privately resolved to sack old Allcock the instant she was certain that the three children she brought with her would stay. Simultaneously, Miss Allcock was planning to begin stealing old Creevy's pupils as soon as she had got a footing in the school.

Having decided to sack Dorothy, it was obviously most important to prevent her from finding it out. For, of course, if she knew what was going to happen, she would begin stealing pupils on her own account, or at any rate wouldn't do a stroke of work for the rest of the term. (Mrs Creevy prided herself on knowing human nature.) Hence the marmalade, the creaky smiles, and the other ruses to allay Dorothy's suspicions. Anyone who knew the ropes would have begun thinking of another job the very moment when the dish of marmalade was pushed across the table.

Just half an hour after her sentence of dismissal, Dorothy, carrying her handbag, opened the front gate. It was the fourth of April, a bright blowy day, too cold to stand about in, with a sky as blue as a hedgesparrow's egg, and one of those spiteful spring winds that come tearing along the pavement in sudden gusts and blow dry, stinging dust into your face. Dorothy shut the gate behind her and began to walk very slowly in the direction of the main-line station.

She had told Mrs Creevy that she would give her an address to which her box could be sent, and Mrs Creevy had instantly exacted five shillings for the carriage. So Dorothy had five pounds fifteen in hand, which might keep her for three weeks with careful economy. What she was going to do, except that she must start by going to London and finding a suitable lodging, she had very little idea. But her first panic had worn off, and she realized that the situation was not altogether desperate. No doubt her father would help her, at any rate for a while, and at the worst, though she hated even the thought of doing it, she could ask her cousin's help a second time. Besides, her chances of finding a job were probably fairly good. She was young, she spoke with a genteel accent, and she was willing to drudge for a servant's wages—qualities that are much sought after by the proprietors of fourth-rate schools. Very likely all would be well. But that there was an evil time ahead of her, a time of job-hunting, of uncertainty and possibly of hunger— that, at any rate, was certain.

CHAPTER 5

1

However, it turned out quite otherwise. For Dorothy had not gone five yards from the gate when a telegraph boy came riding up the street in the opposite direction, whistling and looking at the names of the houses. He saw the name Ringwood House, wheeled his bicycle round, propped it against the kerb, and accosted Dorothy.

'Miss Mill-BURROW live 'ere?' he said, jerking his head in the direction of Ringwood House.

'Yes. I am Miss Millborough.'

'Gotter wait case there's a answer,' said the boy, taking an orange-coloured envelope from his belt.

Dorothy put down her bag. She had once more begun trembling violently. And whether this was from joy or fear she was not certain, for two conflicting thoughts had sprung almost simultaneously into her brain. One, 'This is some kind of good news!' The other, 'Father is seriously ill!' She managed to tear the envelope open, and found a telegram which occupied two pages, and which she had the greatest difficulty in understanding. It ran:

Rejoice in the lord o ye righteous note of exclamation great news note of exclamation your reputation absolutely reestablished stop mrs semprill fallen into the pit that she hath digged stop action for libel stop no one believes her any longer stop your father wishes you return home immediately stop am coming up to town myself comma will pick you up if you like stop arriving shortly after this stop wait for me stop praise him with the loud cymbals note of exclamation much love stop.

No need to look at the signature. It was from Mr Warburton, of course. Dorothy felt weaker and more tremulous than ever. She was dimly aware the telegraph boy was asking her something.

'Any answer?' he said for the third or fourth time.

'Not today, thank you,' said Dorothy vaguely.

The boy remounted his bicycle and rode off, whistling with extra loudness to show Dorothy how much he despised her for not tipping him. But Dorothy was unaware of the telegraph's boy's scorn. The only phrase of the telegram that she had fully understood was 'your father wishes you return home immediately', and the surprise of it had left her in a semi-dazed condition. For some indefinite time she stood on the pavement, until presently a taxi rolled up the street, with Mr Warburton inside it. He saw Dorothy, stopped the taxi, jumped out and came across to meet her, beaming. He seized her both hands.

'Hullo!' he cried, and at once threw his arm pseudo-paternally about her and drew her against him, heedless of who might be looking. 'How are you? But by Jove, how thin you've got! I can feel all your ribs. Where is this school of yours?'

Dorothy, who had not yet managed to get free of his arm, turned partly round and cast a glance towards the dark windows of Ringwood House.

'What! That place? Good God, what a hole! What have you done with your luggage?'

'It's inside. I've left them the money to send it on. I think it'll be all right.'

'Oh, nonsense! Why pay? We'll take it with us. It can go on top of the taxi.'

'No, no! Let them send it. I daren't go back. Mrs Creevy would be horribly angry.'

'Mrs Creevy? Who's Mrs Creevy?'

'The headmistress—at least, she owns the school.'

'What, a dragon, is she? Leave her to me—I'll deal with her. Perseus and the Gorgon, what? You are Andromeda. Hi!' he called to the taxi-driver.

The two of them went up to the front door and Mr Warburton knocked. Somehow, Dorothy never believed that they would succeed in getting her box from Mrs Creevy. In fact, she half expected to see them come out flying for their lives, and Mrs Creevy after them with her broom. However, in a couple of minutes they reappeared, the taxi- driver carrying the box on his shoulder. Mr Warburton handed Dorothy into the taxi and, as they sat down, dropped half a crown into her hand.

'What a woman! What a woman!' he said comprehensively as the taxi bore them away. 'How the devil have you put up with it all this time?'

'What is this?' said Dorothy, looking at the coin.

'Your half-crown that you left to pay for the luggage. Rather a feat getting it out of the old girl, wasn't it?'

'But I left five shillings!' said Dorothy.

'What! The woman told me you only left half a crown. By God, what impudence! We'll go back and have the half-crown out of her. Just to spite her!' He tapped on the glass.

'No, no!' said Dorothy, laying her hand on his arm. 'It doesn't matter in the least. Let's get away from here—right away. I couldn't bear to go back to that place again—EVER!'

It was quite true. She felt that she would sacrifice not merely half a crown, but all the money in her possession, sooner than set eyes on Ringwood House again. So they drove on, leaving Mrs Creevy victorious. It would be interesting to know whether this was another of the occasions when Mrs Creevy laughed.

Mr Warburton insisted on taking the taxi the whole way into London, and talked so voluminously in the quieter patches of the traffic that Dorothy could hardly get a word in edgeways.

It was not till they had reached the inner suburbs that she got from him an explanation of the sudden change in her fortunes.

'Tell me,' she said, 'what is it that's happened? I don't understand. Why is it all right for me to go home all of a sudden? Why don't people believe Mrs Semprill any longer? Surely she hasn't confessed?'

'Confessed? Not she! But her sins have found her out, all the same. It was the kind of thing that you pious people would ascribe to the finger of Providence. Cast thy bread upon the waters, and all that. She got herself into a nasty mess—an action for libel. We've talked of nothing else in Knype Hill for the last fortnight. I though you would have seen something about it in the newspapers.'

'I've hardly looked at a paper for ages. Who brought an action for libel? Not my father, surely?'

'Good gracious, no! Clergymen can't bring actions for libel. It was the bank manager. Do you remember her favourite story about him—how he was keeping a woman on the bank's money, and so forth?'

'Yes, I think so.'

'A few months ago she was foolish enough to put some of it in writing. Some kind friend—some female friend, I presume—took the letter round to the bank manager. He brought an action—Mrs Semprill was ordered to pay a hundred and fifty pounds damages. I don't suppose she paid a halfpenny, but still, that's the end of her career as a scandalmonger. You can go on blackening people's reputations for years, and everyone will believe you, more or less, even when it's perfectly obvious that you're lying. But once you've been proved a liar in open court, you're disqualified, so to speak. Mrs Semprill's done for, so far as Knype Hill goes. She left the town between days—practically did a moonlight flit, in fact. I believe she's inflicting herself on Bury St Edmunds at present.'

'But what has all that got to do with the things she said about you and me?'

'Nothing—nothing whatever. But why worry? The point is that you're reinstated; and all the hags who've been smacking their chops over you for months past are saying, "Poor, poor Dorothy, how SHOCKINGLY that dreadful woman has treated her!"'

'You mean they think that because Mrs Semprill was telling lies in one case she must have been telling lies in another?'

'No doubt that's what they'd say if they were capable of reasoning it out. At any rate, Mrs Semprill's in disgrace, and so all the people she's slandered must be martyrs. Even MY reputation is practically spotless for the time being.'

'And do you think that's really the end of it? Do you think they honestly believe that it was all an accident—that I only lost my memory and didn't elope with anybody?'

'Oh, well, I wouldn't go as far as that. In these country places there's always a certain amount of suspicion knocking about. Not suspicion of anything in particular, you know; just generalized suspicion. A sort of instinctive rustic dirty-mindedness. I can imagine its being vaguely rumoured in the bar parlour of the Dog and Bottle in ten years' time that you've got some nasty secret in your past, only nobody can remember what. Still, your troubles are over. If I were you I wouldn't give any explanations till you're asked for them. The official theory is that you had a bad attack of flu and went away to recuperate. I should stick to that. You'll find they'll accept it all right. Officially, there's nothing against you.

Presently they got to London, and Mr Warburton took Dorothy to lunch at a restaurant in Coventry Street, where they had a young chicken, roasted, with asparagus and tiny, pearly-white potatoes that had been ripped untimely from their mother earth, and also treacle tart and a nice warm bottle of Burgundy; but what gave Dorothy the most pleasure of all, after Mrs Creevy's lukewarm water tea, was the black coffee they had afterwards. After lunch they took another taxi to Liverpool Street Station and caught the 2.45. It was a four-hour journey to Knype Hill.

Mr Warburton insisted on travelling first-class, and would not hear of Dorothy paying her own fare; he also, when Dorothy was not looking, tipped the guard to let them have a carriage to themselves. It was one of those bright cold days which are spring or winter according as you are indoors or out. From behind the shut windows of the carriage the too-blue sky looked warm and kind, and all the slummy wilderness through which the train was rattling—the labyrinths of little dingy-coloured houses, the great chaotic factories, the miry canals, and derelict building lots littered with rusty boilers and overgrown by smoke-blackened weeds—all were redeemed and gilded by the sun. Dorothy hardly spoke for the first half-hour of the journey. For the moment she was too happy to talk. She did not even think of anything in particular, but merely sat there luxuriating in the glass-filtered sunlight, in the comfort of the padded seat and the feeling of having escaped from Mrs Creevy's clutches. But she was aware that this mood could not last very much longer. Her contentment, like the warmth of the wine that she had drunk at lunch, was ebbing away, and thoughts either painful or difficult to express were taking shape in her mind. Mr Warburton had been watching her face, more observantly than was usual for him, as though trying to gauge the changes that the past eight months had worked in her.

'You look older,' he said finally.

'I am older,' said Dorothy.

'Yes; but you look—well, more completely grown up. Tougher. Something has changed in your face. You look—if you'll forgive the expression—as though the Girl Guide had been exorcized from you for good and all. I hope seven devils haven't entered into you instead?' Dorothy did not answer, and he added:

'I suppose, as a matter of fact, you must have had the very devil of a time?'

'Oh, beastly! Sometimes too beastly for words. Do you know that sometimes—'

She paused. She had been about to tell him how she had had to beg for her food; how she had slept in the streets; how she had been arrested for begging and spent a night in the police cells; how Mrs Creevy had nagged at her and starved her. But she stopped, because she had suddenly realized that these were not the things that she wanted to talk about. Such things as these, she perceived, are of no real importance; they are mere irrelevant accidents, not essentially different from catching a cold in the head or having to wait two hours at a railway junction. They are disagreeable, but they do not matter. The truism that all real happenings are in the mind struck her more forcibly than ever before, and she said:

'Those things don't really matter. I mean, things like having no money and not having enough to eat. Even when you're practically starving—it doesn't CHANGE anything inside you.'

'Doesn't it? I'll take your word for it. I should be very sorry to try.'

'Oh, well, it's beastly while it's happening, of course; but it doesn't make any real difference; it's the things that happen inside you that matter.'

'Meaning?' said Mr Warburton.

'Oh—things change in your mind. And then the whole world changes, because you look at it differently.'

She was still looking out of the window. The train had drawn clear of the eastern slums and was running at gathering speed past willow-bordered streams and low-lying meadows upon whose hedges the first buds made a faint soft greenness, like a cloud. In a field near the line a month-old calf, flat as a Noah's Ark animal, was bounding stiff-legged after its mother, and in a cottage garden an old labourer, with slow, rheumatic movements, was turning over the soil beneath a pear tree covered with ghostly bloom. His spade flashed in the sun as the train passed. The depressing hymn-line 'Change and decay in all around I see' moved through Dorothy's mind. It was true what she had said just now. Something had happened in her heart, and the world was a little emptier, a little poorer from that minute. On such a day as this, last spring or any earlier spring, how joyfully, and how unthinkingly, she would have thanked God for the first blue skies and the first flowers of the reviving year! And now, seemingly, there was no God to thank, and nothing—not a flower or a stone or a blade of grass—nothing in the universe would ever be the same again.

'Things change in your mind,' she repeated. 'I've lost my faith,' she added, somewhat abruptly, because she found herself half ashamed to utter the words.

'You've lost your WHAT?' said Mr Warburton, less accustomed than she to this kind of phraseology.

'My faith. Oh, you know what I mean! A few months ago, all of a sudden, it seemed as if my whole mind had changed. Everything that I'd believed in till then—everything—seemed suddenly meaningless and almost silly. God—what I'd meant by God—immortal life, Heaven and Hell—everything. It had all gone. And it wasn't that I'd reasoned it out; it just happened to me. It was like when you're a child, and one day, for no particular reason, you stop believing in fairies. I just couldn't go on believing in it any longer.'

'You never did believe in it,' said Mr Warburton unconcernedly.

'But I did, really I did! I know you always thought I didn't—you thought I was just pretending because I was ashamed to own up. But it wasn't that at all. I believed it just as I believe that I'm sitting in this carriage.'

'Of course you didn't, my poor child! How could you, at your age? You were far too intelligent for that. But you'd been brought up in these absurd beliefs, and you'd allowed yourself to go on thinking, in a sort of way, that you could still swallow them. You'd built yourself a life-pattern—if you'll excuse a bit of psychological jargon—that was only possible for a believer, and naturally it was beginning to be a strain on you. In fact, it was obvious all the time what was the matter with you. I should say that in all probability that was why you lost your memory.'

'What do you mean?' she said, rather puzzled by this remark.

He saw that she did not understand, and explained to her that loss of memory is only a device, unconsciously used, to escape from an impossible situation. The mind, he said, will play curious tricks when it is in a tight corner. Dorothy had never heard of anything of this kind before, and she could not at first accept his explanation. Nevertheless she considered it for a moment, and perceived that, even if it were true, it did not alter the fundamental fact.

'I don't see that it makes any difference,' she said finally.

'Doesn't it? I should have said it made a considerable difference.'

'But don't you see, if my faith is gone, what does it matter whether I've only lost it now or whether I'd really lost it years ago? All that matters is that it's gone, and I've got to begin my life all over again.'

'Surely I don't take you to mean,' said Mr Warburton, 'that you actually REGRET losing your faith, as you call it? One might as well regret losing a goitre. Mind you, I'm speaking, as it were, without the book—as a man who never had very much faith to lose. The little I had passed away quite painlessly at the age of nine. But it's hardly the kind of thing I should have thought anyone would REGRET losing. Used you not, if I remember rightly, to do horrible things like getting up at five in the morning to go to

Holy Communion on an empty belly? Surely you're not homesick for that kind of thing?'

'I don't believe in it any longer, if that's what you mean. And I see now that a lot of it was rather silly. But that doesn't help. The point is that all the beliefs I had are gone, and I've nothing to put in their place.'

'But good God! why do you want to put anything in their place? You've got rid of a load of superstitious rubbish, and you ought to be glad of it. Surely it doesn't make you any happier to go about quaking in fear of Hell fire?'

'But don't you see—you must see—how different everything is when all of a sudden the whole world is empty?'

'Empty?' exclaimed Mr Warburton. 'What do you mean by saying it's empty? I call that perfectly scandalous in a girl of your age. It's not empty at all, it's a deuced sight too full, that's the trouble with it. We're here today and gone tomorrow, and we've no time to enjoy what we've got.'

'But how CAN one enjoy anything when all the meaning's been taken out of it?'

'Good gracious! What do you want with a meaning? When I eat my dinner I don't do it to the greater glory of God; I do it because I enjoy it. The world's full of amusing things—books, pictures, wine, travel, friends—everything. I've never seen any meaning in it all, and I don't want to see one. Why not take life as you find it?'

'But—'

She broke off, for she saw already that she was wasting words in trying to make herself clear to him. He was quite incapable of understanding her difficulty—incapable of realizing how a mind naturally pious must recoil from a world discovered to be meaningless. Even the loathsome platitudes of the pantheists would be beyond his understanding. Probably the idea that life was essentially futile, if he thought of it at all, struck him as rather amusing than otherwise. And yet with all this he was sufficiently acute. He could see the difficulty of her own particular position, and he adverted to it a moment later.

'Of course,' he said, 'I can see that things are going to be a little awkward for you when you get home. You're going to be, so to speak, a wolf in sheep's clothing. Parish work—Mothers' Meetings, prayers with the dying, and all that—I suppose it might be a little distasteful at times. Are you afraid you won't be able to keep it up—is that the trouble?'

'Oh, no. I wasn't thinking of that. I shall go on with it, just the same as before. It's what I'm most used to. Besides, Father needs my help. He can't afford a curate, and the work's got to be done.'

'Then what's the matter? Is it the hypocrisy that's worrying you? Afraid that the consecrated bread might stick in your throat, and so forth? I shouldn't trouble. Half the parsons' daughters in England are probably in the same difficulty. And quite nine-tenths of the parsons, I should say.'

'It's partly that. I shall have to be always pretending—oh, you can't imagine in what ways! But that's not the worst. Perhaps that part of it doesn't matter, really. Perhaps it's better to be a hypocrite—THAT kind of hypocrite—than some things.'

'Why do you say THAT kind of hypocrite? I hope you don't mean that pretending to believe is the next best thing to believing?'

'Yes... I suppose that's what I do mean. Perhaps it's better—less selfish—to pretend one believes even when one doesn't, than to say openly that one's an unbeliever and perhaps help turn other people into unbelievers too.'

'My dear Dorothy,' said Mr Warburton, 'your mind, if you'll excuse my saying so, is in a morbid condition. No, dash it! it's worse than morbid; it's downright septic. You've a sort of mental gangrene hanging over from your Christian upbringing. You tell me that you've got rid of these ridiculous beliefs that were stuffed into you from your cradle upwards, and yet you're taking an attitude to life which is simply meaningless without those beliefs. Do you call that reasonable?'

'I don't know. No perhaps it's not. But I suppose it's what comes naturally to me.'

'What you're trying to do, apparently,' pursued Mr Warburton, 'is to make the worst of both worlds. You stick to the Christian scheme of things, but you leave Paradise out of it. And I suppose, if the truth were known, there are quite a lot of your kind wandering about among the ruins of C. of E. You're practically a sect in yourselves,' he added reflectively: 'the Anglican Atheists. Not a sect I should care to belong to, I must say.'

They talked for a little while longer, but not to much purpose. In reality the whole subject of religious belief and religious doubt was boring and incomprehensible to Mr Warburton. Its only appeal to him was as a pretext for blasphemy. Presently he changed the subject, as though giving up the attempt to understand Dorothy's outlook.

'This is nonsense that we're talking,' he said. 'You've got hold of some very depressing ideas, but you'll grow out of them later on, you know. Christianity isn't really an incurable disease. However, there was something quite different that I was going to say to you. I want you to listen to me for a moment. You're coming home, after being away eight months, to what I expect you realize is a rather uncomfortable situation. You had a hard enough life before—at least, what I should call a hard life—and now that you aren't quite such a good Girl Guide as you used to be, it's going to be a great deal harder. Now, do you think it's absolutely necessary to go back to it?'

'But I don't see what else I can do, unless I could get another job. I've really no alternative.'

Mr Warburton, with his head cocked a little on one side, gave Dorothy a rather curious look.

'As a matter of fact,' he said, in a more serious tone than usual, 'there's at least one other alternative that I could suggest to you.'

'You mean that I could go on being a schoolmistress? Perhaps that's what I ought to do, really. I shall come back to it in the end, in any case.'

'No. I don't think that's what I should advise.'

All this time Mr Warburton, unwilling as ever to expose his baldness, had been wearing his rakish, rather broad-brimmed grey felt hat. Now, however, he took it off and laid it carefully on the empty seat beside him. His naked cranium, with only a wisp or two of golden hair lingering in the neighbourhood of the ears, looked like some monstrous pink pearl. Dorothy watched him with a slight surprise.

'I am taking my hat off,' he said, 'in order to let you see me at my very worst. You will understand why in a moment. Now, let me offer you another alternative besides going back to your Girl Guides and your Mothers' Union, or imprisoning yourself in some dungeon of a girls' school.'

'What do you mean?' said Dorothy.

'I mean, will you—think well before you answer; I admit there are some very obvious objections, but—will you marry me?'

Dorothy's lips parted with surprise. Perhaps she turned a little paler. With a hasty, almost unconscious recoil she moved as far away from him as the back of the seat would allow. But he had made no movement towards her. He said with complete equanimity:

'You know, of course, that Dolores [Dolores was Mr Warburton's ex- mistress] left me a year ago?'

'But I can't, I can't!' exclaimed Dorothy. 'You know I can't! I'm not—like that. I thought you always knew. I shan't ever marry.'

Mr Warburton ignored this remark.

'I grant you,' he said, still with exemplary calmness, 'that I don't exactly come under the heading of eligible young men. I am somewhat older than you. We both seem to be putting our cards on the table today, so I'll let you into a great secret and tell you that my age is forty-nine. And then I've three children and a bad reputation. It's a marriage that your father would—well, regard with disfavour. And my income is only seven hundred a year. But still, don't you think it's worth considering!'

'I can't, you know why I can't!' repeated Dorothy.

She took it for granted that he 'knew why she couldn't', though she had never explained to him, or to anyone else, why it was impossible for her to marry. Very probably, even if she had explained, he would not have understood her. He went on speaking, not appearing to notice what she had said.

'Let me put it to you', he said, 'in the form of a bargain. Of course, I needn't tell you that it's a great deal more than that. I'm not a marrying kind of man, as the saying goes, and I shouldn't ask you to marry me if you hadn't a rather special attraction for me. But let me put the business side of it first. You need a home and a livelihood; I need a wife to keep me in order. I'm sick of these disgusting women I've spent my life with, if you'll forgive my mentioning them, and I'm rather anxious to settle down. A bit late in the day, perhaps, but better late than never. Besides, I need somebody to look after the children; the BASTARDS, you know. I don't expect you to find me overwhelmingly attractive,' he added, running a hand reflectively over his bald crown, 'but on the other hand I am very easy to get on with. Immoral people usually are, as a matter of fact. And from your own point of view the scheme would have certain advantages. Why should you spend your life delivering parish magazines and rubbing nasty old women's legs with Elliman's embrocation? You would be happier married, even to a husband with a bald head and a clouded past. You've had a hard, dull life for a girl of your age, and your future isn't exactly rosy. Have you really considered what your future will be like if you don't marry?'

'I don't know. I have to some extent,' she said.

As he had not attempted to lay hands on her or to offer any endearments, she answered his question without repeating her previous refusal. He looked out of the window, and went on in a musing voice, much quieter than his normal tone, so that at first she could barely hear him above the rattle of the train; but presently his voice rose, and took on a note of seriousness that she had never heard in it before, or even imagined that it could hold.

'Consider what your future would be like,' he repeated. 'It's the same future that lies before any woman of your class with no husband and no money. Let us say your father will live another ten years. By the end of that time the last penny of his money will have gone down the sink. The desire to squander it will keep him alive just as long as it lasts, and probably no longer. All that time he will be growing more senile, more tiresome, more impossible to live with; he will tyrannize over you more and more, keep you shorter and shorter of money, make more and more trouble for you with the neighbours and the tradesmen. And you will go on with that slavish, worrying life that you have lived, struggling to make both ends meet, drilling the Girl Guides, reading novels to the Mothers' Union, polishing the altar brasses, cadging money for the organ fund, making brown paper jackboots for the schoolchildren's plays, keeping your end up in the vile little feuds and scandals of the church hen-coop. Year after year, winter and summer, you will bicycle from one reeking cottage to another, to dole out pennies from the poor box and repeat prayers that you don't even believe in any longer. You will sit through interminable church services which in the end will make you physically sick with their sameness and futility. Every year your life will be a little bleaker, a little fuller of those deadly little jobs that are shoved off on to lonely women. And remember that you won't always be twenty-eight. All the while you will be fading, withering, until one morning you will look in the glass and realize that you aren't a girl any longer, only a skinny old maid. You'll fight against it, of course. You'll keep your physical energy and your girlish mannerisms—you'll keep them just a little bit too long. Do you know that type of bright—too bright—spinster who says "topping" and "ripping" and "right-ho", and prides herself on being such a good sport, and she's such a good sport that she makes everyone feel a little unwell? And she's so splendidly hearty at tennis and so handy at amateur theatricals, and she throws herself with a kind of desperation into her Girl Guide work and her parish visiting, and she's the life and soul of Church socials, and always, year after year, she thinks of herself as a young girl still and never realizes that behind her back everyone laughs at her for a poor, disappointed old maid? That's what you'll become, what you must become, however much you foresee it and try to avoid it. There's no other future possible to you unless you marry. Women who don't marry wither up—they wither up like aspidistras in back-parlour windows; and the devilish thing is that they don't even know that they're withering.'

Dorothy sat silent and listening with intent and horrified fascination. She did not even notice that he had stood up, with one hand on the door to steady him against the swaying of the train. She was as though hypnotized, not so much by his voice as by the visions that his words had evoked in her. He had described her life, as it must inevitably be, with such dreadful fidelity that he seemed actually to have carried her ten years onward into the menacing future, and she felt herself no longer a girl full of youth and energy, but a desperate, worn virgin of thirty-eight. As he went on he took her hand, which was lying idle on the arm of the seat; and even that she scarcely noticed.

'After ten years,' he continued, 'your father will die, and he will leave you with not a penny, only debts. You will be nearly forty, with no money, no profession, no chance of marrying; just a derelict parson's daughter like the ten thousand others in England. And after that, what do you suppose will become of you? You will have to find yourself a job—the sort of job that parsons' daughters get. A nursery governess, for instance, or companion to some diseased hag who will occupy herself in thinking of ways to humiliate you. Or you will go back to school-teaching; English mistress in some grisly girls' school, seventy-five pounds a year and your keep, and a fortnight in a seaside boarding-house every August. And all the time withering, drying up, growing more sour and more angular and more friendless. And therefore—'

As he said 'therefore' he pulled Dorothy to her feet. She made no resistance. His voice had put her under a spell. As her mind took in the prospect of that forbidding future, whose emptiness she was far more able to appreciate than he, such a despair had grown in her that if she had spoken at all it would have been to say, 'Yes, I will marry you.' He put his arm very gently about her and drew her a little towards him, and even now she did not attempt to resist. Her eyes, half hypnotized, were fixed upon his. When he put his arm about her it was as though he were protecting her, sheltering her, drawing her away from the brink of grey, deadly poverty and back to the world of friendly and desirable things—to security and ease, to comely houses and good clothes, to books and friends and flowers, to summer days and distant lands. So for nearly a minute the fat, debauched bachelor and the thin, spinsterish girl stood face to face, their eyes meeting, their bodies all but touching, while the train swayed them in its motion, and clouds and telegraph poles and bud-misted hedges and fields green with young wheat raced past unseen.

Mr Warburton tightened his grip and pulled her against him. It broke the spell. The visions that had held her helpless—visions of poverty and of escape from poverty—suddenly vanished and left only a shocked realization of what was happening to her. She was in the arms of a man—a fattish, oldish man! A wave of disgust and deadly fear went through her, and her entrails seemed to shrink and freeze. His thick male body was pressing her backwards and downwards, his large, pink face, smooth, but to her eyes old, was bearing down upon her own. The harsh odour of maleness forced itself into her nostrils. She recoiled. Furry thighs of satyrs! She began to struggle furiously, though indeed he made hardly any effort to retain her, and in a moment she had wrenched herself free and fallen back into her seat, white and trembling. She looked up at him with eyes which, from fear and aversion, were for a moment those of a stranger.

Mr Warburton remained on his feet, regarding her with an expression of resigned, almost amused disappointment. He did not seem in the least distressed. As her calmness returned to her she perceived that all he had said had been no more than a trick to play upon her feelings and cajole her into saying that she would marry him; and what was stranger yet, that he had said it without seriously caring whether she married him or not. He had, in fact, merely been amusing himself. Very probably the whole thing was only another of his periodical attempts to seduce her.

He sat down, but more deliberately than she, taking care of the creases of his trousers as he did so.

'If you want to pull the communication cord,' he said mildly, 'you had better let me make sure that I have five pounds in my pocket- book.'

After that he was quite himself again, or as nearly himself as anyone could possibly be after such a scene, and he went on talking without the smallest symptom of embarrassment. His sense of shame, if he had ever possessed one, had perished many years ago. Perhaps it had been killed by overwork in a lifetime of squalid affairs with women.

For an hour, perhaps, Dorothy was ill at ease, but after that the train reached Ipswich, where it stopped for a quarter of an hour, and there was the diversion of going to the refreshment room for a cup of tea. For the last twenty miles of the journey they talked quite amicably. Mr Warburton did not refer again to his proposal of marriage, but as the train neared Knype Hill he returned, less seriously than before, to the question of Dorothy's future.

'So you really propose', he said 'to go back to your parish work? "The trivial round, the common task?" Mrs Pither's rheumatism and Mrs Lewin's corn-plaster and all the rest of it? The prospect doesn't dismay you?'

'I don't know—sometimes it does. But I expect it'll be all right once I'm back at work. I've got the habit, you see.'

'And you really feel equal to years of calculated hypocrisy? For that's what it amounts to, you know. Not afraid of the cat getting out of the bag? Quite sure you won't find yourself teaching the Sunday School kids to say the Lord's Prayer backwards, or reading Gibbon's fifteenth chapter to the Mothers' Union instead of Gene Stratton Porter?'

'I don't think so. Because, you see, I do feel that that kind of work, even if it means saying prayers that one doesn't believe in, and even if it means teaching children things that one doesn't always think are true—I do feel that in a way it's useful.'

'Useful?' said Mr Warburton distastefully. 'You're a little too fond of that depressing word "useful". Hypertrophy of the sense of duty—that's what's the matter with you. Now, to me, it seems the merest common sense to have a bit of fun while the going's good.'

'That's just hedonism,' Dorothy objected.

'My dear child, can you show me a philosophy of life that isn't hedonism? Your verminous Christian saints are the biggest hedonists of all. They're out for an eternity of bliss, whereas we poor sinners don't hope for more than a few years of it. Ultimately we're all trying for a bit of fun; but some people take it in such perverted forms. Your notion of fun seems to be massaging Mrs Pither's legs.'

'It's not that exactly, but—oh! somehow I can't explain!'

What she would have said was that though her faith had left her, she had not changed, could not change, did not want to change, the spiritual background of her mind; that her cosmos, though now it seemed to her empty and meaningless, was still in a sense the Christian cosmos; that the Christian way of life was still the way that must come naturally to her. But she could not put this into words, and felt that if she tried to do so he would probably begin making fun of her. So she concluded lamely:

'Somehow I feel that it's better for me to go on as I was before.'

'EXACTLY the same as before? The whole bill of fare? The Girl Guides, the Mothers' Union, the Band of Hope, the Companionship of Marriage, parish visiting and Sunday School teaching, Holy Communion twice a week and here we go round the doxology-bush, chanting Gregorian plain-song? You're quite certain you can manage it?'

Dorothy smiled in spite of herself. 'Not plain-song. Father doesn't like it.'

'And you think that, except for your inner thoughts, your life will be precisely what it was before you lost your faith? There will be NO change in your habits?'

Dorothy thought. Yes, there WOULD be changes in her habits; but most of them would be secret ones. The memory of the disciplinary pin crossed her mind. It had always been a secret from everyone except herself and she decided not to mention it.

'Well,' she said finally, 'perhaps at Holy Communion I shall kneel down on Miss Mayfill's right instead of on her left.'

2

A week had gone by.

Dorothy rode up the hill from the town and wheeled her bicycle in at the Rectory gate. It was a fine evening, clear and cold, and the sun, unclouded, was sinking in remote, greenish skies. Dorothy noticed that the ash tree by the gate was in bloom, with clotted dark red blossoms that looked like festerings from a wound.

She was rather tired. She had had a busy week of it, what with visiting all the women on her list in turn and trying to get the parish affairs into some kind of order again. Everything was in a fearful mess after her absence. The church was dirty beyond all belief—in fact, Dorothy had had to spend the best part of a day cleaning up with scrubbing-brushes, broom and dustpan, and the beds of 'mouse dirts' that she had found behind the organ made her wince when she thought of them. (The reason why the mice came there was because Georgie Frew, the organ-blower, WOULD bring penny packets of biscuits into church and eat them during the sermon.) All the Church associations had been neglected, with the result that the Band of Hope and the Companionship of Marriage had now given up the ghost, Sunday School attendance had dropped by half, and there was internecine warfare going on in the Mothers' Union because of some tactless remark that Miss Foote had made. The belfry was in a worse state than ever. The parish magazine had not been delivered regularly and the money for it had not been collected. None of the accounts of the Church Funds had been properly kept up, and there was nineteen shillings unaccounted for in all, and even the parish registers were in a muddle—and so on and so on, ad infinitum. The Rector had let everything slide.

Dorothy had been up to her eyes in work from the moment of reaching home. Indeed, things had slipped back into their old routine with astonishing swiftness. It was as though it had been only yesterday that she had gone away. Now that the scandal had blown over, her return to Knype Hill had aroused very little curiosity. Some of the women on her visiting list, particularly Mrs Pither, were genuinely glad to see her back, and Victor Stone, perhaps, seemed just a little ashamed of having temporarily believed Mrs Semprill's libel; but he soon forgot it in recounting to Dorothy his latest triumph in the Church Times. Various of the coffee-ladies, of course, had stopped Dorothy in the street with 'My dear, how VERY nice to see you back again! You HAVE been away a long time! And you know, dear, we all thought it such a SHAME when that horrible woman was going round telling those stories about you. But I do hope you'll understand, dear, that whatever anyone else may have thought, I never believed a word of them', etc., etc., etc. But nobody had asked her the uncomfortable questions that she had been fearing. 'I've been teaching in a school near London' had satisfied everyone; they had not even asked her the name of the school. Never, she saw, would she have to confess that she had slept in Trafalgar Square and been arrested for begging. The fact is that people who live in small country towns have only a very dim conception of anything that happens more than ten miles from their own front door. The world outside is a terra incognita, inhabited, no doubt, by dragons and anthropophagi, but not particularly interesting.

Even Dorothy's father had greeted her as though she had only been away for the week-end. He was in his study when she arrived, musingly smoking his pipe in front of the grandfather clock, whose glass, smashed by the charwoman's broom-handle four months ago, was still unmended. As Dorothy came into the room he took his pipe out of his mouth and put it away in his pocket with an absent-minded, old-mannish movement. He looked a great deal older, Dorothy thought.

'So here you are at last,' he said. 'Did you have a good journey?'

Dorothy put her arms round his neck and touched his silver-pale cheek with her lips. As she disengaged herself he patted her shoulder with a just perceptible trace more affection than usual.

'What made you take it into your head to run away like that?' he said.

'I told you, Father—I lost my memory.'

'Hm,' said the Rector; and Dorothy saw that he did not believe her, never would believe her, and that on many and many a future occasion, when he was in a less agreeable mood than at present, that escapade would be brought up against her. 'Well,' he added, 'when you've taken your bag upstairs, just bring your typewriter down here, would you? I want you to type out my sermon.'

Not much that was of interest had happened in the town. Ye Olde Tea Shoppe was enlarging its premises, to the further disfigurement of the High Street. Mrs Pither's rheumatism was better (thanks to the angelica tea, no doubt), but Mr Pither had 'been under the doctor' and they were afraid he had stone in the bladder. Mr Blifil-Gordon was now in Parliament, a docile deadhead on the back benches of the Conservative Party. Old Mr Tombs had died just after Christmas, and Miss Foote had taken over seven of his cats and made heroic efforts to find homes for the others. Eva Twiss, the niece of Mr Twiss the ironmonger, had had an illegitimate baby, which had died. Proggett had dug the kitchen garden and sowed a few seeds, and the broad beans and the first peas were just showing. The shop-debts had begun to mount up again after the creditors' meeting, and there was six pounds owing to Cargill. Victor Stone had had a controversy with Professor Coulton in the Church Times, about the Holy Inquisition, and utterly routed him. Ellen's eczema had been very bad all the winter. Walph Blifil- Gordon had had two poems accepted by the London Mercury.

Dorothy went into the conservatory. She had got a big job on hand— costumes for a pageant that the schoolchildren were going to have on St George's Day, in aid of the organ fund. Not a penny had been paid towards the organ during the past eight months, and it was perhaps as well that the Rector always threw the organ-people's bills away unopened, for their tone was growing more and more sulphurous. Dorothy had racked her brains for a way of raising some money, and finally decided on a historical pageant, beginning with Julius Caesar and ending with the Duke of Wellington. They might raise two pounds by a pageant, she thought—with luck and a fine day, they might even raise three pounds!

She looked round the conservatory. She had hardly been in here since coming home, and evidently nothing had been touched during her absence. Her things were lying just as she had left them; but the dust was thick on everything. Her sewing-machine was on the table amid the old familiar litter of scraps of cloth, sheets of brown paper, cotton-reels and pots of paint, and though the needle had rusted, the thread was still in it. And, yes! there were the jackboots that she had been making the night she went away. She picked one of them up and looked at it. Something stirred in her heart. Yes, say what you like, they WERE good jackboots! What a pity they had never been used! However, they would come in useful for the pageant. For Charles II, perhaps—or, no, better not have Charles II; have Oliver Cromwell instead; because if you had Oliver Cromwell you wouldn't have to make him a wig.

Dorothy lighted the oilstove, found her scissors and two sheets of brown paper, and sat down. There was a mountain of clothes to be made. Better start off with Julius Caesar's breastplate, she thought. It was always that wretched armour that made all the trouble! What did a Roman soldier's armour look like? Dorothy made an effort, and called to mind the statue of some idealized curly-bearded emperor in the Roman Room at the British Museum. You might make a sort of rough breastplate out of glue and brown paper, and glue narrow strips of paper across it to represent the plates of the armour, and then silver them over. No helmet to make, thank goodness! Julius

Caesar always wore a laurel wreath—ashamed of his baldness, no doubt, like Mr Warburton. But what about greaves? Did they wear greaves in Julius Caesar's time? And boots? Was a caligum a boot or a sandal?

After a few moments she stopped with the shears resting on her knee. A thought which had been haunting her like some inexorcizable ghost at every unoccupied moment during the past week had returned once more to distract her. It was the thought of what Mr Warburton had said to her in the train—of what her life was going to be like hereafter, unmarried and without money.

It was not that she was in any doubt about the external facts of her future. She could see it all quite clearly before her. Ten years, perhaps, as unsalaried curate, and then back to school- teaching. Not necessarily in quite such a school as Mrs Creevy's— no doubt she could do something rather better for herself than that—but at least in some more or less shabby, more or less prison-like school; or perhaps in some even bleaker, even less human kind of drudgery. Whatever happened, at the very best, she had got to face the destiny that is common to all lonely and penniless women. 'The Old Maids of Old England', as somebody called them. She was twenty-eight—just old enough to enter their ranks.

But it didn't matter, it didn't matter! That was the thing that you could never drive into the heads of the Mr Warburtons of this world, not if you talked to them for a thousand years; that mere outward things like poverty and drudgery, and even loneliness, don't matter in themselves. It is the things that happen in your heart that matter. For just a moment—an evil moment—while Mr Warburton was talking to her in the train, she had known the fear of poverty. But she had mastered it; it was not a thing worth worrying about. It was not because of THAT that she had got to stiffen her courage and remake the whole structure of her mind.

No, it was something far more fundamental; it was the deadly emptiness that she had discovered at the heart of things. She thought of how a year ago she had sat in this chair, with these scissors in her hand, doing precisely what she was doing now; and yet it was as though then and now she had been two different beings. Where had she gone, that well-meaning, ridiculous girl who had prayed ecstatically in summer-scented fields and pricked her arm as a punishment for sacrilegious thoughts? And where is any of ourselves of even a year ago? And yet after all—and here lay the trouble—she WAS the same girl. Beliefs change, thoughts change, but there is some inner part of the soul that does not change. Faith vanishes, but the need for faith remains the same as before.

And given only faith, how can anything else matter? How can anything dismay you if only there is some purpose in the world which you can serve, and which, while serving it, you can understand? Your whole life is illumined by the sense of purpose. There is no weariness in your heart, no doubts, no feeling of futility, no Baudelairean ennui waiting for unguarded hours. Every act is significant, every moment sanctified, woven by faith as into a pattern, a fabric of never-ending joy.

She began to meditate upon the nature of life. You emerged from the womb, you lived sixty or seventy years, and then you died and rotted. And in every detail of your life, if no ultimate purpose redeemed it, there was a quality of greyness, of desolation, that could never be described, but which you could feel like a physical pang at your heart. Life, if the grave really ends it, is monstrous and dreadful. No use trying to argue it away. Think of life as it really is, think of the DETAILS of life; and then think that there is no meaning in it, no purpose, no goal except the grave. Surely only fools or self-deceivers, or those whose lives are exceptionally fortunate, can face that thought without flinching?

She shifted her position in her chair. But after all there must be SOME meaning, SOME purpose in it all! The world cannot be an accident. Everything that happens must have a cause—ultimately, therefore, a purpose. Since you exist, God must have created you, and since He created you a conscious being, He must be conscious. The greater doesn't come out of the less. He created you, and He will kill you, for His own purpose. But that purpose is inscrutable. It is in the nature of things that you can never discover it, and perhaps even if you did discover it you would be averse to it. Your life and death, it may be, are a single note in the eternal orchestra that plays for His diversion. And suppose you don't like the tune? She thought of that dreadful unfrocked clergyman in Trafalgar Square. Had she dreamed the things he said, or had he really said them? 'Therefore with Demons and Archdemons and with all the company of Hell'. But that was silly, really. For your not liking the tune was also part of the tune.

Her mind struggled with the problem, while perceiving that there was no solution. There was, she saw clearly, no possible substitute for faith; no pagan acceptance of life as sufficient to itself, no pantheistic cheer-up stuff, no pseudo-religion of 'progress' with visions of glittering Utopias and ant-heaps of steel and concrete. It is all or nothing. Either life on earth is a preparation for something greater and more lasting, or it is meaningless, dark, and dreadful.

Dorothy started. A frizzling sound was coming from the glue-pot. She had forgotten to put any water in the saucepan, and the glue was beginning to burn. She took the saucepan, hastened to the scullery sink to replenish it, then brought it back and put it on the oilstove again. I simply MUST get that breastplate done before supper! she thought. After Julius Caesar there was William the Conqueror to be thought of. More armour! And presently she must go along to the kitchen and remind Ellen to boil some potatoes to go with the minced beef for supper; also there was her 'memo list' to be written out for tomorrow. She shaped the two halves of the breastplate, cut out the armholes and neckholes, and then stopped again.

Where had she got to? She had been saying that if death ends all, then there is no hope and no meaning in anything. Well, what then?

The action of going to the scullery and refilling the saucepan had changed the tenor of her thoughts. She perceived, for a moment at least, that she had allowed herself to fall into exaggeration and self-pity. What a fuss about nothing, after all! As though in reality there were not people beyond number in the same case as herself! All over the world, thousands, millions of them; people who had lost their faith without losing their need of faith. 'Half the parsons' daughters in England,' Mr Warburton had said. He was probably right. And not only parsons' daughters; people of every description—people in illness and loneliness and failure, people leading thwarted, discouraging lives—people who needed faith to support them, and who hadn't got it. Perhaps even nuns in convents, scrubbing floors and singing Ave Marias, secretly unbelieving.

And how cowardly, after all, to regret a superstition that you had got rid of—to want to believe something that you knew in your bones to be untrue!

And yet—!

Dorothy had put down her scissors. Almost from force of habit, as though her return home, which had not restored her faith, had restored the outward habits of piety, she knelt down beside her chair. She buried her face in her hands. She began to pray.

'Lord, I believe, help Thou my unbelief. Lord, I believe, I believe; help Thou my unbelief.'

It was useless, absolutely useless. Even as she spoke the words she was aware of their uselessness, and was half ashamed of her action. She raised her head. And at that moment there stole into her nostrils a warm, evil smell, forgotten these eight months but unutterably familiar—the smell of glue. The water in the saucepan was bubbling noisily. Dorothy jumped to her feet and felt the handle of the glue-brush. The glue was softening—would be liquid in another five minutes.

The grandfather clock in her father's study struck six. Dorothy started. She realized that she had wasted twenty minutes, and her conscience stabbed her so hard that all the questions that had been worrying her fled out of her mind. What on earth have I been doing all this time? she thought; and at that moment it really seemed to her that she did not know what she had been doing. She admonished herself. Come on, Dorothy! No slacking, please! You've got to get that breastplate done before supper. She sat down, filled her mouth with pins and began pinning the two halves of the breastplate together, to get it into shape before the glue should be ready.

The smell of glue was the answer to her prayer. She did not know this. She did not reflect, consciously, that the solution to her difficulty lay in accepting the fact that there was no solution; that if one gets on with the job that lies to hand, the ultimate purpose of the job fades into insignificance; that faith and no faith are very much the same provided that one is doing what is customary, useful, and acceptable. She could not formulate these thoughts as yet, she could only live them. Much later, perhaps, she would formulate them and draw comfort from them.

There was still a minute or two before the glue would be ready to use. Dorothy finished pinning the breastplate together, and in the same instant began mentally sketching the innumerable costumes that were yet to be made. After William the Conqueror—was it chain mail in William the Conqueror's day?—there were Robin Hood— Lincoln Green and a bow and arrow—and Thomas a Becket in his cope and mitre, and Queen

Elizabeth's ruff, and a cocked hat for the Duke of Wellington. And I must go and see about those potatoes at half past six, she thought. And there was her 'memo list' to be written out for tomorrow. Tomorrow was Wednesday—mustn't forget to set the alarm clock for half past five. She took a slip of paper and began writing out the 'memo list':

> 7 oc. H.C.
> Mrs J. baby next month go and see her.
> BREAKFAST. Bacon.

She paused to think of fresh items. Mrs J. was Mrs Jowett, the blacksmith's wife; she came sometimes to be churched after her babies were born, but only if you coaxed her tactfully beforehand. And I must take old Mrs Frew some paregoric lozenges, Dorothy thought, and then perhaps she'll speak to Georgie and stop him eating those biscuits during the sermon. She added Mrs Frew to her list. And then what about tomorrow's dinner—luncheon? We simply MUST pay Cargill something! she thought. And tomorrow was the day of the Mothers' Union tea, and they had finished the novel that Miss Foote had been reading to them. The question was, what to get for them next? There didn't seem to be any more books by Gene Stratton Porter, their favourite. What about Warwick Deeping? Too highbrow, perhaps? And I must ask Proggett to get us some young cauliflowers to plant out, she thought finally.

The glue had liquefied. Dorothy took two fresh sheets of brown paper, sliced them into narrow strips, and—rather awkwardly, because of the difficulty of keeping the breastplate convex—pasted the strips horizontally across it, back and front. By degrees it stiffened under her hands. When she had reinforced it all over she set it on end to look at it. It really wasn't half bad! One more coating of paper and it would be almost like real armour. We MUST make that pageant a success! she thought. What a pity we can't borrow a horse from somebody and have Boadicea in her chariot! We might make five pounds if we had a really good chariot, with scythes on the wheels. And what about Hengist and Horsa? Cross- gartering and winged helmets. Dorothy sliced two more sheets of brown paper into strips, and took up the breastplate to give it its final coating. The problem of faith and no faith had vanished utterly from her mind. It was beginning to get dark, but, too busy to stop and light the lamp, she worked on, pasting strip after strip of paper into place, with absorbed, with pious concentration, in the penetrating smell of the glue-pot.

The End